THE SISTER OF MARY DYER: THE HIGH PRICE OF FREEDOM

A Biographical Novel

THE SISTER OF MARY DYER:
THE HIGH PRICE OF FREEDOM

A Biographical Novel

By

Ann Bell

Katy Crossing Press

The Sister of Mary Dyer: The High Price of Freedom
Published by Katy Crossing Press
300 Katy Crossing
Georgetown, TX 78626
www.katycrossingpress.com
annamaebell@yahoo.com

ISBN-10: 0984968482
ISBN-13: 978-0-9849684-8-0

Copyright @ 2013 by Ann Bell

Mary Dyer
Quaker
Witness for Religious Freedom
Hanged on Boston Common 1660
"My life not availeth me
in comparison to the
liberty of the truth."

Major New England Settlements in the Mid-1600's

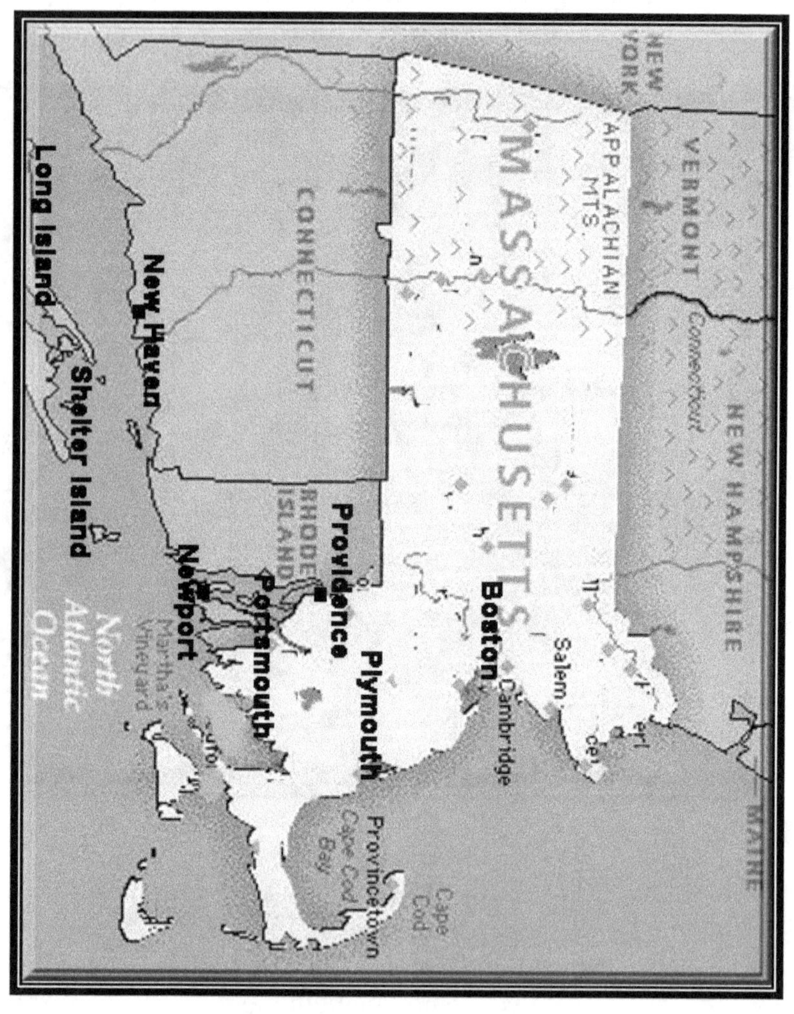

List of Characters

Aspinwall, William - Historical character - Notary, court recorder, and surveyor in Boston. Signer of the Wheelwright petition.

Austin, Ann - Historical Character - (? - 1665) One of the first female Quaker travelling preachers.

Bartholomew, William - Historical Character - Boston Magistrate.

Burden, Anne - Historical Character - Quaker woman who returns from England to claim husband's debts only to be thrown into the Boston jail with Mary Dyer.

Clarke, Reverend John - Historical Character - (1609-1676) Co-founder of Rhode Island Colony.

Clarke, Martha - *Fictional Character* - Sister of Mary Dyer

Clarke, Randall - *Fictional Character* - Husband of Martha Clarke, Brother-in-Law of Mary Dyer

Coddington, William - Historical Character - (c. 1601 – 1678) Early magistrate of the Massachusetts Bay Colony, and later of the Colony of Rhode Island and Providence Plantations. Served as the Judge of Portsmouth and Newport. Governor of Portsmouth and Newport. Deputy Governor and Governor of Rhode Island.

Coggeshall, John - Historical Character - (1601 – 1647) One of the founders of Rhode Island and the first President of all four towns in the Colony of Rhode Island.

Coggeshall, Nicholas - Historical Character - Son of John Coggeshall.

Cooley, Captain - Historical Character - Captain of ship taking the Bodie Politick advance party to Aquidneck Island.

Copeland, John - Historical Character - Quaker man who was persecuted by the Puritans. Arrived on the ship *Woodhouse.*

Cotton, Reverend John - Historical Character - (1585 – 1652) Clergyman in England and the American colonies, and the preeminent minister and theologian of the Massachusetts Bay Colony.

Dudley, Deputy Governor Thomas - Historical Character - (1576 – July 1653) Colonial magistrate who served several terms as governor of the Massachusetts Bay Colony.

Dyer, Mary - Historical Character - (c. 1611 — June 1, 1660) An English Puritan turned Quaker hanged in Boston, for repeatedly defying a Puritan law banning Quakers from the colony.

> **Dyer Children**
> Samuel, (1635 - 1679) - Married about 1660, Anne Hutchinson, granddaughter
> Stillborn daughter, (October 17, 1637)
> William, (1640 - 1688)
> Mahershallahasbaz, (1643 - before 1670)
> Henry, (1647 - 1690)
> Mary, (1647 - 1679)
> Charles, (1650 - 1727)

Dyer, William - Historical Character (1609 – by 1677) - Husband of Mary Dyer - A founding settler of both Portsmouth and Newport. Secretary, General Recorder, Attorney General, Commissioner, and Deputy of Rhode Island.

Easton, Elizabeth - Historical Character - Wife of Nicholas Easton

Easton, Nicholas - Historical Character - (1609 - by 1677) A founding settler of both Portsmouth and Newport. Governor of Rhode Island.

Endicott, Governor John - Historical Character - (before 1601 – 1665) English colonial magistrate, soldier and governor of the Massachusetts Bay Colony.

Fisher, Mary - Historical Character - (c.1623 – 1698) One of first female travelling Quaker ministers.

Fox, George - Historical Character - (1624 – 1691) English Dissenter and a founder of the Religious Society of Friends, commonly known as the Quakers or Friends.

Hawkins, Jane (Goody) - Historical Character - Midwife in Boston and Rhode Island.

Holder, Christopher - Historical Character - (c. 1631—post-1676) English Quaker minister who immigrated to the Massachusetts Bay Colony, where he was persecuted for his beliefs. Arrived on the ship *Woodhouse.*

Hooker, Peter - *Fictional Character* - Quaker traveler.

Hutchinson, Anne - Historical Character - (1591–1643), Puritan spiritual adviser, mother of fifteen children. Leader of the so-called Antinomians.

> **Children of Anne and William Hutchinson:** Edward, Susanna, Richard, Faith, Bridget, Francis, Elizabeth, William, Samuel, Anne, Mary, Katherine, William, Susanna, Zuriel   .

Hutchinson, William (Will) - Historical Character - (1586–1641) Husband of Anne Hutchinson. Judge (chief magistrate) of Portsmouth.

Leonard, Sarah - *Fictional Character* - Quaker woman in London.

Lott, Henry - *Fictional Character* - Meets Mary Dyer in prison and delivers letter to William Dyer in Newport.

Norton, Humphrey - Historical Character - Persecuted Quaker - Arrived on ship *Woodhouse.*

Norton, Reverend John - Historical Character - Puritan minister in Boston.

Oliver, Captain James - Historical Character - Officer in Boston Court during Quaker persecutions.

Oliver, Sergeant John - Historical Character - Deputy who signed the Wheelwright petition.

Robinson, William - Historical Character - (? - Oct. 27, 1659) Quaker martyr executed by public hanging. Arrived on the ship *Woodhouse*.

Savage, Thomas - Historical Character - (1608 - 1682) Anne Hutchinson's son-in-law.

Scott, Catherine - Historical Character - Sister of Mary Dyer.
Children: Mary, Patience

Southwick, Cassandra - Historical Character - (c. 1600-1660) Devout Quaker persecuted for her beliefs. Wife of Lawrence Southwick. Died at Shelter Island.

Southwick, Lawrence - Historical Character - (c. 1600-1660) Devout Quaker persecuted for his beliefs. Husband of Cassandra Southwick. Died at Shelter Island.

Stevenson, Marmaduke - Historical Character - (? - Oct. 27, 1659) Quaker martyr executed by public hanging for his religious beliefs.

Sylvester, Gissel - Historical Character - Owner of Shelter Island. Wife of Nathaniel Sylvester.

Sylvester, Nathaniel - Historical Character - (1610-1680) An Anglo-Dutch sugar merchant. Owner of Shelter Island. Husband of Gissel Sylvester.

Symmes, Reverend Zechariah - Historical Character - Puritan Clergy prominent ship *Griffin,* when Anne Hutchinson made the voyage from England to New England with her husband and 10 of her 11 living children.

Vane, Sir Henry - Historical Character - (1613 – 1662) Son of Henry Vane the Elder (often referred to as Harry Vane to distinguish him from his father) Served one term as the Governor of the Massachusetts Bay Colony before returning to England in 1637. Supported the creation of Roger Williams' Rhode Island Colony.

Wanton, Edward - Historical Character - (1629-1716)
Administered public floggings and executions of Quakers.
Converted to the Quaker faith and became an ardent preacher and
activist.

Webb, Captain John - Historical Character - (aka Captain John
Evered) (ca.1611–1668) Involved in the hanging of Mary Dyer.

Weld, Joseph - Historical Character - Owner of house in Roxbury
where Anne was under house arrest.

Wheelwright, Reverend John - Historical Character - (c.1592–
1679) Puritan clergyman in England and America. Banished from
the Massachusetts Bay Colony during the Antinomian
Controversy. Brother-in-law of Anne Hutchinson.

Williams, Reverend Roger - Historical Character - (c. 1603 –
1683) English Protestant theologian who was an early proponent of
religious freedom and the separation of church and state. In 1636,
he began the colony of Providence Plantation, which provided a
refuge for religious minorities.

Wilson, Reverend John - Historical Character - (c.1591–1667)
Puritan clergyman of First Church of Boston from its beginning in
1630 until his death in 1667. He is most noted for being a minister
at odds with Anne Hutchinson during the Antinomian Controversy
from 1636 to 1638, and for being an attending minister during the
execution of Mary Dyer in 1660.

Winslow, Governor Josiah - Historical Character (1628 - 1680)
Governor of the Plymouth Colony.

Winthrop, Governor John - Historical Character - (1587 - 1649)
Leading figure in the founding of Massachusetts Bay Colony.
Governor of Massachusetts.

Winthrop, Governor John Jr. - Historical Character - (1606 -
1676) Governor of Connecticut.

Chapter One
Disillusionment

Boston in Lincolnshire, England, 1633

Martha Clarke lifted her skirts from the mud and trudged toward the city market. The unfamiliar streets confused her, but she did her best to cope with her new environment. *One advantage of living here is that I will never get lost. The church spire can be seen for miles throughout the countryside; I can always get my sense of direction by locating the spire. Randall claims the church has control over whoever lives within the view of it, but I do not understand how that can be.*

Suddenly, the pounding of horses' hoofs and the creaking of wheels behind her interrupted her thoughts. She glanced over her shoulder and much to her surprise a passing horse and carriage were heading straight toward her with little regard for her presence. She jumped aside while mud splattered her skirt and sleeves. *Are people going to be as rude here as in London? At least in London I had my family and friends. I do not know a soul here. Randall has no idea how lonely this move has been for me.*

The number of women and children on the street increased, and the stench of rotting meat indicated the marketplace was nearby. Trying to avoid the jostling of the crowd, Martha went from booth to booth examining the vegetables and inquiring about the prices. *I try to cook the best meals possible for Randall, but with limited money, market day is extremely difficult. With any luck, I will find a good, inexpensive chicken and cauliflower for supper tonight that will please him. He is working too hard trying to set up his woodworking shop, but I am afraid he is also getting discouraged. Good food always seems to lift his spirits.*

Still having mud on her skirt from the last horse and wagon, she heard the thundering of hooves and creaking wheels approaching her once again. Martha whirled toward the sound. Horror gripped her. Her muscles tightened and a gasp escaped her lips. A curly-haired child had followed a calico cat into the street and had fallen facedown into a puddle in front of a team of draft horses and wagon that had rounded a corner a few feet away.

Martha threw her wicker-shopping basket onto the ground and raced toward the little girl. She grabbed the child's arm and jerked her aside only seconds before the horses raced by them, casting mud onto their faces and clothing. Picking up the child, Martha hugged her tightly against her chest and patted her on the back to comfort her while the little girl continued to scream with terror. Mud from the sobbing child's clothing smeared Martha's dress and apron.

"The Lord be praised," a woman behind her shouted. "You saved my child."

Martha turned as a plain woman in a grey dress and bonnet rushed toward her carrying an infant. The woman's white apron could not hide her expanding waistline.

With her free hand, the mother stroked her older child's hair and wiped the tears from her eyes while she cradled the infant in her other arm. The little girl reached for her mother, but pulled back and cried louder when she realized her mother could not take her.

"Please, let me hold your baby." Martha reached for the infant. "I think your daughter needs assurance from her mother and not a stranger."

Carefully, the two women exchanged children. The frightened toddler clung to her mother and sobbed while her mother rubbed her back and stroked her hair. Gradually, the child relaxed and the sobs became further and further apart until they stopped completely. Martha cradled the infant in one arm while she stooped to retrieve her wicker basket.

"How can I ever thank you for saving my child's life?" the mother asked. "Let me at least buy you a chicken for supper."

Without waiting for Martha's response, the mother stopped at the next booth, handed a coin to the vendor, and placed a freshly plucked hen in her basket. She then motioned for Martha to follow her to a bench in front of the Ox Haven Inn.

Martha sank onto the bench and breathed deeply as the fresh, crisp breeze relaxed the tension in her body. *It all happened so fast. If I had had time to think about it, I never could have reached the child in time. I was definitely in the right place at the right time.*

The older woman situated the toddler on her lap and smiled. "My name is Anne Hutchinson and this is my daughter, Katherine. The baby's name is William, Jr. To whom am I indebted?"

The warmth of the infant against Martha's breast felt natural and fulfilling. She longed to hold a child of her own in her arms, but so far, her prayers had gone unanswered. "Martha...Martha Clarke," she stammered. "My husband is Randall Clarke. We are new in town.

Randall just opened a woodworking shop in an annex to our house at the end of the street next to the Weaver's."

Anne balanced her daughter with her left arm, reached for Martha's hand, and squeezed it. "It is nice meeting you. How can I ever thank you for saving my daughter's life?" she said once again. Tears of gratitude filled her eyes. "I hope we will become better acquainted through the coming months." She paused and studied Martha's youthful face. "I am originally from Alford, but we moved to Boston a few months ago. I will be glad to show you around town and introduce you to the shopkeepers and craftsmen I know. Right now, my husband is at the blacksmith shop with our other children. He should be along soon."

Martha looked down at the peaceful, mud-stained face of the sleeping little girl. She was amazed at how quickly sobs of terror had subsided into tranquil slumber once she was cradled in her mother's arms. "Your daughter is very lucky. The horses were so close that my skirt was brushed by the horse's front leg as I grabbed her."

"I am going to tell everyone how you saved my daughter's life. If you hadn't been there, Katherine would not be alive," Anne repeated. "The people of St. Botolph's Church will be amazed how once again God has protected my family."

Martha could feel Anne's deep, piercing eyes studying her. She squirmed and hesitated. *This woman makes me feel as if she is able to read my mind. Yet something is drawing me to her. She seems very ordinary, yet she possesses an air of confidence I have not seen before.*

"Have you ever been to St. Botolph's Church?" Anne asked. "It is the one with the tall steeple you can see for miles."

"No, I have never attended it, but my husband has talked about it often and is fascinated with its structure." She studied the grey stone spire in the distance. The windows and secondary spires enthralled her. Something unexplainable was drawing her to the magnificent building, accompanied by a feeling of foreboding.

Anne looked in the direction of the looming tower and smiled with pride. "I love that church. It is named after a seventh century monk who is believed to have founded a monastery at that location. The city name of Boston is just a contraction of St. Botolph."

Anne looked down at her sleeping daughter, and then shifted the child in her arms to a more comfortable position. "Since you are new in town, you may not have heard about Vicar John Cotton. He is extremely inspiring and thought provoking. People come from all over Lincolnshire to hear him. I cling to every word he preaches."

Martha nodded. "When I lived in London, I heard of the Reverend John Cotton. People said he can be very controversial at times."

Reverend John Cotton
(1585 - 1652)

Anne again looked off into the distance toward the tower of St. Botolph's Church looming over the city and nodded. "Yes, some people do not agree with John Cotton, but that is only because they do not yet understand the truth of God. I agree with everything he says. In fact, a group of women gather in my home every Monday to discuss his sermons."

"I have never understood what the controversy is about." Martha said. "I try to avoid any kind of conflict, religious or political. It leaves me too unsettled."

Anne took a deep breath. "Reverend John Cotton is working extremely hard to purify the Church of England and make it more like the church during Bible times. He speaks a great deal about absolute grace for all who believe in Jesus Christ. The bad thing is most of the other ministers think a person has to work his way to heaven and do not understand what he is talking about. I think it is the most freeing teaching I have ever heard."

Martha hesitated and tried to keep from wrinkling her brow. *I do not like the way this discussion is going. I scarcely know what she is talking about. If the ministers do not understand it or agree, how can I?*

She snuggled the baby in her arms closer against her breast as he whimpered in his sleep. "I do not understand theology. I would rather leave religion to the trained ministers. That is what they are hired to do. I like to read my own Bible, pray to God by myself, help my neighbors, and leave the controversy for others."

"The winds of change and controversy cannot be avoided," Anne stated confidently. "God expects us to stand firmly for what we believe. Many people do not think the king and his hirelings should control the church. Most of us want the local churches to be able to make their own decisions and to have the church be exactly as it was in Bible times. The Puritans feel so strongly about local control, they are willing to suffer all kinds of torture to be able to have the freedom to practice religion as they see fit."

Martha shifted her weight nervously. She could feel the roughness of the planks on the back of the bench through her dress. Her palms became sweaty.

When Randall and I moved to Boston in Lincolnshire, I thought this would be a peaceful haven. I did not realize there was so much conflict under the surface. I hope Randall does not want to become involved in the Puritan discussion. I want our children to grow up surrounded by peace and tranquility.

Trying to hide her frustrations, Martha chose her words carefully. "Does King Charles know about the activities of the Puritans? I would think he would be angry not having control over what is happening in the Anglican Church. After all, the king is the recognized head of the church in England."

Anne looked up and down the street. Apparently satisfied no one was listening, she replied, "Right now he is tolerating it, but things are beginning to get tense. I do not know how much longer it will be before something serious happens. The king has been sending his spies out among the people and into the local churches."

Anne paused, peered into the distance, and waved at a man with four children who appeared between two buildings further down the street. "There is my family. My husband and children will probably be ready to go home soon." She turned back to Martha. "I believe purifying the church is worth risking one's entire life. God can speak directly to anyone, not just the ministers, or the king. However, many church officials consider the claim, hearing directly from God, pure heresy. Why don't you come to the meeting in my house later this afternoon and we will discuss this further?"

Trying to mask her lack of enthusiasm, Martha forced a smile. "Thank you for the invitation, but I really need to be home with my husband. I did not finish all my household chores before I came to market and the hours are passing quickly. Maybe another time."

Tension filled the Clarke's small, thatched-roofed house. The fire in the hearth was burning down, and a cold chill filled the room. Martha laid her knitting aside, rose from her straight-back chair beside the fireplace, and faced her husband. "Randall, I absolutely refuse to go with you to St. Botolph's. The minister is crazy and is going to get everyone around him in trouble."

Randall Clarke scowled. Anger and love intermingled behind his hazel eyes. "Martha, how can you be so fearful? People are flocking from all over Lincolnshire to hear him. An exciting wave of religious understanding is sweeping the land. It is going to change the Anglican Church and purify it from all devilish ways. It is an exciting time. Just you wait and see."

"I see nothing wrong with the church the way it is," Martha stated firmly. "When I read from the prayer book and listen to the minister, I feel close to God. We were married within the walls of the Anglican Church with the blessing of the vicar. My parents are buried in the graveyard behind the St. Martin-in-the-Fields Church in London. Why would anyone want to stir up trouble and tear apart something that has taken centuries to build?"

The pitch in Randall's voice rose. His facial muscles tightened. "The Church of England must be purified from all influences of the Catholic Church and return to what the apostles had in the beginning of

Christianity. We can no longer let the church be controlled by foolish men or the devil."

Martha's heart pounded as she planted her hands firmly on her hips. "Why intentionally stir up strife? You know how much I hate conflict. I do not understand why people can't just live in peace with one another, especially Christians."

Randall shook his head with frustration. "Martha, you are such an idealist. Did you forget the Bible quotes Jesus as saying, 'I come not to bring peace, but to bring a sword?' If you can't cope with conflict, leave the fighting to the men, but don't be a stumbling block to their work."

"What if the men are fighting for the wrong thing and it accomplishes nothing?" she grumbled. "Today purification of the church is just an intellectual discussion, but what happens when the Reverend Cotton says something the king does not like? Sooner or later King Charles is going to clamp down on him and his followers, and then what?"

"We can address any resistance if and when it happens. If conflict comes, all thinking Christians realize we have to obey God rather than man." Randall took his hat from the peg on the wall. "I will be back later."

The heavy wooden door slammed louder than normal, and his worn boots stomped across the porch.

Martha slumped onto the straight-back chair at the crudely hewn pine table in the center of the room. She buried her face in her hands and sobbed. *I rarely disobey or challenge my husband's wishes. Why did I do it now? My mother taught me from a young age to obey my husband, but this time it was as if I could not help myself. I cannot stand to listen to pointless arguments about religious details and I do not like to go anywhere there will be disagreements and tension. God is going to do what God is going to do. What right do we have to try to change what God plans? What the church officials tell me is in the Bible is sometimes different from what I read myself. I want to be able to think for myself and make my own decisions without listening to long winded arguments. Who cares how many angels can dance on the head of a pin?*

Randall's aging grey mare plodded slowly down the street toward Saint Botolph's Church of Boston in Lincolnshire, England, more commonly known as the "Boston Stump" or simply "the Stump." The once proud horse of his youth could now scarcely bear his weight. *If only my woodworking business would become prosperous enough for us to retire poor Nell. She has served us well and needs a rest.*

The image of his beloved wife flashed before him. He had never seen her so angry until he told her he was going to hear Reverend Cotton speak. *I hope Martha never learns that a few years ago militant Puritans damaged this beautiful structure. She will never attend services here if she knows there has been violence at the church. She is so tenderhearted I hope she never has to face the harsh realities of Christian discord.*

By the time Randall reached the River Witham, fancy carriages began passing him, all heading in the same direction. Never before had he felt of such low estate. He looked down at the aging mare beneath him and felt the shame of an unprosperous business.

Locating an empty spot on the hitching rail, Randall slid to the ground, and tethered his horse. Wearing his only suit of clothes, he followed a finely dressed family into the church. He marveled at the majestic walls of stone, sculptures, and colored windows. How could there possibly be much conflict contained within the walls of such a beautiful place? How could militant Puritans even consider trying to destroy an exquisitely designed house of God? Randall found a bench in the back row of the sanctuary containing only two other men. He nodded politely and took his place on the end of the bench. He pretended to pray while he scanned the congregation. Women tried to pray while they hushed their children. Men sat stiffly with stern faces, their heads bowed.

A side door opened and a vicar donned in a black robe and gray wig climbed the steps to the pulpit. The congregation followed the order of worship led by the vicar. Randall bowed his head while Vicar John Cotton read from The Book of Common Prayer. In hearing the familiar prayers, Randall felt a twinge of understanding in how his wife received comfort from the formal prayers. Nevertheless, the ritual rang with hollowness within him. *People are merely reciting words without paying attention to what they are saying. Will God hear and answer prayers written hundreds of years ago?*

When the popular vicar began to preach, it stirred Randall's interest as no other clergy ever had. The words from the pulpit confirmed many of his thoughts. *I wish Martha were here. I think The Reverend Cotton's interpretation is something that would appeal to her and would remove her fears about the Puritan movement.*

As the sermon progressed, the man beside him shuffled restlessly. Randall watched the man's face redden when the vicar talked about the need to reform the Church of England and give authority to the local congregation. *It is obvious he does not agree with the vicar. I hope he is not a spy for the king.*

After more than two hours, the Reverend John Cotton gave a benediction and disappeared through the side door of the church. Before the congregation could file from the building, a loud voice echoed from the front. "If anyone is interested in learning more about the 'City upon a Hill', please gather in the grove beside the River Haven." With that, the man beside him nudged Randall aside and rushed to the door before anyone else had time to react.

Mystified, Randall studied the faces of the other men filing out of the church. They exchanged nervous glances and remained silent until they reached the fresh air. The congregation immediately gathered in small groups and began talking about the 'City upon a Hill.' Not certain what to do, He stood alone under the oak tree and watched people talking among themselves. *I wish Martha were here instead of stubbornly staying at home, working on her knitting. Maybe someday she will understand why it is important to make changes to the Church of England. Surely, The Reverend Cotton could inspire and motivate her. He is the most convincing speaker I have ever heard.*

As he hesitated in the churchyard not wanting to leave the glorious structure, a distinguished-looking man approached, followed by a woman whom he assumed was his wife.

"Randall Clarke, I presume," the man greeted.

"Yes. But how did you know my name?"

The stranger touched the brim of his hat and nodded slightly. "Your wife saved our precious Katherine from being trampled by a team of draft horses this past week. Our entire family will be eternally grateful to her. My name is Will Hutchinson."

"It is nice meeting you," Randall said. "It was fortunate Martha was there to help. God definitely had a protective hand around your daughter that day."

Will Hutchinson surveyed the young man dressed in humble clothing. "I saw your face light up when they announced the meeting about the City upon the Hill. Would you like to join us down by the river?"

Randall hesitated. *Surely Martha will not notice if I am a few minutes late.* He studied the older man and recognized heart-felt enthusiasm in his eyes he had rarely seen in others. "I am not certain I understand what the Reverend Cotton was referring to when he said 'City upon the Hill.' I assumed it was some sort of code."

Will Hutchinson nodded. "Yes, it is a code. City upon a Hill has become a rallying cry for those who are considering immigration to the New World. The Puritans would recognize the phrase John Winthrop used in a sermon on the way to the New World. He told the future Massachusetts Bay colonists that their new community would be a 'City upon a Hill' — a model of how a city could purge itself from evil and be entirely Christian. This city in the New World will become a New Eden. Adam and Eve sinned, and God had to make them leave the Garden of Eden.

Governor John Winthrop
(1587 - 1649)

John Winthrop is certain this time the Puritans will get it right and will not stray from the teachings of God, as the Church of England has. It is an exciting opportunity."

Randall's eyes widened. "Hmm. That does sound interesting, but is it realistic? The government and the church definitely need to be changed, but is this the way to do it? I would like to go and hear what it is about."

Leaving his mare tethered to the hitching post, Randall fell into step alongside Will Hutchinson and the other congregates. His hesitation quickly turned to eagerness.

"Pardon my rudeness," Will said. "I did not introduce you to my wife, Anne. We have been avid followers of John Cotton for some time. We cannot get enough of his teachings. We would follow him anywhere."

Randall nodded. "I agree his sermon was extremely thought-provoking and inspiring. I have never heard Scripture interpreted in such a way before. Now I understand why the king's officials might disapprove." He studied the couple's expressions for affirmation of his statement and was not disappointed.

"The Reverend Cotton says we can go to Heaven because of the grace of God and that we don't have to work for it," Anne Hutchinson said while Will took her arm to steady her when the path became steep and rocky. "I can scarcely wait for Sundays to come so I can learn more from him."

"But aren't you afraid King Charles will send his men to the gatherings and report back what is being said? They could cast us all into prison." Randall hesitated and sweat dampened his brow. "The man sitting beside me was acting very suspiciously and slipped out as soon as a gathering by the river was announced."

"We are willing to take that chance," Will Hutchinson stated with conviction. "We don't want to be reckless with our plans, so we are meeting by the River Haven instead of in the church."

"Wouldn't a king's spy have considered it treasonous when someone shouted out in church, 'Whoever is interested in becoming part of the 'City upon a Hill', please gather in the grove by the River Haven after the service'?"

A gentle rain began falling upon them while they trudged down the pathway to the clearing on the riverbank. Randall looked back and saw several families climb into their fancy carriages and hurry away while others had left their carriages at the church and continued toward the river with Reverend Cotton. *It is understandable that I would be searching for a better way of life, but why would the wealthy?*

The path narrowed and forced people to walk in single file. Will lifted low hanging branches for others to pass. "We are a close-knit congregation, regardless of the various social ranks. John Cotton knew everyone who was present today along with his or her views about reforming the church. He must have felt confident he was with like believers. Before he left the pulpit, he nodded to me to make the announcement."

Randall shook his head. "He must not have seen the three of us sitting on the back row. I have never been in church before so he would have no way of knowing my opinions. If that was a king's spy beside me, he obviously wouldn't have recognized him either."

Wrinkles deepened on Will Hutchinson's forehead and around his eyes, but he said nothing. They continued their walk in silence. When Randall and the Hutchinsons reached the grove, John Cotton was standing under a large oak tree while the others were taking seats on the grass, boulders, or fallen logs nearby. When the minister began to speak, a man on a rise above the grove shouted, "Three horsemen are turning the bend near the squire's house and are coming this way. They look like they are a part of the king's militia."

Without saying a word to each other, each person ran a different direction and hid behind trees, rocks, or tombstones in the nearby graveyard. Judging by their automatic reactions, Randall assumed this had happened before and everyone knew exactly what to do. Heart pounding, he too crouched behind a tombstone. *What if I am arrested? What would happen to my beloved Martha? I wish I had not left her angry.*

Randall watched the horsemen dismount and walk around the riverbank. He was amazed so many people could hide in such a close area without making a sound or being seen. He held his breath when they came within yards of where three congregants were hiding. Finally, the leader of the soldiers shook his head, motioned to the others, and turned back before discovering any ones' hiding places. The congregants waited in silence for several minutes. *Did they think we were not on the riverbank, or were they merely trying to frighten us and will return later to arrest us?*

After a few minutes, one by one the Puritans reassembled. Reverend Cotton took his place under the oak tree. Randall listened attentively when John Cotton explained the continuing development of the Massachusetts Bay Company. A world of opportunity lay before them, if they but trust God.

Randall listened intently. He thought of his beautiful wife he had left in anger earlier that day. *Martha would never consider such an opportunity. Her dream is to raise a family in peace and tranquility, and she would be afraid to take a risk with a group she did not understand. Would she ever realize Boston in the New World was founded on the very same principles as her dreams?*

Reverend Cotton's words echoed throughout the grove. "For those in the process of deciding whether to make the trip or not, passage will take approximately two years pay per person. However, local merchants may be willing to sponsor some; others can go as indentured servants and obtain their complete freedom after five to seven years of work. Woodworkers are in short supply in the new world, so the company itself would be willing to pay their passage if they agree to help with the construction of homes and buildings once they arrive."

Enthusiasm grew within Randall. *This sounds like a dream come true. I am not making a living wage here and my passage could be paid if we would decide to go to Massachusetts. If only I could convince Martha that life would be better and more peaceful in the new Boston as well as come up with the money to pay her passage.*

The Puritan's meeting ended an hour after they had reassembled. The congregation trudged slowly back to St. Botolph's; small groups discussed the possibilities of being able to be a part of the great experiment. When they neared the church, a man in the lead shouted, "All our horses and carriages are gone. The soldiers must have untied them and then swatted them to make them run away."

Panic and frustration spread throughout the group. From a distance, Randall could see the empty hitching post where he had tied his mare. *What will I tell Martha?* He trembled as he trudged home. *We do not have money to buy another horse. She was afraid of me attending church today and did not want me to come, but I did not listen to her. Now I have lost our only horse.*

When he turned the corner onto Elm Street, Martha emerged from the front door of their house and ran as fast as she could into his arms. "You are safe," she gasped. "I have been so worried. When the mare came home without you, I was certain something dreadful had happened."

"Praise God." he shouted and then swooped her into his arms. "I was afraid I had lost our only horse forever. You will never believe what happened."

Martha touched her fingers to his lips and caressed his hair. "There is no need to explain. I am just glad you are safe." She squeezed his hand and gazed into his eyes. "I am sorry I did not come with you. I should never have let you leave while we were angry with each other."

Randall's mind raced. *Is this a good time to tell Martha about the City upon a Hill?*

Chapter Two
The Visit

Boston in Lincolnshire, England - 1633

The whinny of a horse and the creaking of wagon wheels in front of their house caught Martha Clarke's attention. She stepped back from the hearth where she had been stirring soup for supper, hurried to the window, and pulled back the curtain. "Randall, come quickly. Whose wagon is that outside? Are you expecting guests?"

The couple peered through the side window while the man dressed in dusty traveling clothes pulled the horses to a stop, wiped the sweat from his brow with his handkerchief, jumped from the wagon, and tethered the team to a nearby tree branch. The woman stood, smoothed her grey skirt, and repositioned her bonnet to deflect the late summer sun.

"I do not recognize either of them," Randall said.

Martha watched while the man assisted the woman from the wagon. Suddenly, a smile of recognition spread across her face. "It's my sister, Mary!" she shouted racing to the door and down the steps of their thatch-roofed house.

The women nearly flew into each other's arms. They held each other and wept. "Mary, what brings you here? It's such a distance from London."

Mary pulled away from their embrace and motioned to her traveling companion. "I am sorry I wasn't able to get word to you sooner. I would like you to meet my new husband, William Dyer. We were married last week and he is considering opening a shop somewhere in Lincolnshire. He grew up in this area and still has distant relatives here." Mary turned back to her husband. "William, I would like you to meet my older sister, Martha."

Martha studied her new brother-in-law. His hands were calloused from heavy work, and his hair and beard were not groomed, but his eyes portrayed an air of authority, intelligence, and warmth. A long, low gasp escaped her lips. "I know you. You used to visit my mother when we were growing up in London."

William laughed. "Yes. I am your mother's cousin. I am surprised you recognized me. You were just a wee one when I visited your mother on occasion. You both were always busy at play and paid no attention to me. Our families drifted apart until recently. When I returned to London to serve my apprenticeship, I found your sister a beautiful young woman."

"I am happy for the two of you." Martha turned to her husband. "I would like you to meet my husband, Randall Clarke."

Randall stretched out his hand and smiled. "Welcome to our home. I am glad to meet you. Martha was just finishing a nice vegetable soup for supper, and we would love to have you join us."

William's shoulders slumped and a sigh of exhausted escaped his lips. He forced a smile and returned the greeting. "That is most kind of you to offer. We have not had a warm meal since yesterday."

Randall glanced over his shoulder at the team of sweating mares. "Before you come in and rest, let me help you take your horses to our barn where we can water and feed them."

While the men unhitched the horses from the wagon, the women walked hand-in-hand into the Clarke's home. Martha motioned for her sister to be seated at the plank table. "Make yourself comfortable while I warm a cup of goat's milk for you. It should help you relax after your exhausting trip."

Martha took eight biscuits from the tin, placed them on an earthenware plate, and set them on the table. She listened to Mary describe her trip from London while she poured the milk into a pot, hung it on the lug pole above the hearth, and stoked the fire. Before the milk was warm, the men entered through the backdoor and joined Mary at the table.

Randall smiled at his new brother-in-law. "We will do whatever we can to help you get set up in Lincolnshire, if this is what you choose to do. What business are you in?"

"I am looking for a place to build a millinery shop," William replied. "I just finished a nine-year apprenticeship in a branch of the Fishmonger's Guild, under milliner, William Blackburn in London. We like the London area, but we want to explore all possibilities before we make a final decision."

Randall took off his hat and set it beside him. "This area is open to all kinds of new businesses and ideas. I am certain we can find a place for you to get started. If one is not available, I could help you build a shop. Martha and I love it here, and I am certain our wives will enjoy living closer together."

Martha and Mary exchanged excited glances. This was more than Martha could have ever expected. Having her sister nearby would be the best cure for her loneliness. She set a plate of biscuits in the center of the table.

William reached for a biscuit and took a small bite of it. An expression of grave seriousness spread across his face. "What about the political climate? Rumors have reached London about the unrest in this area. When I was growing up in this town everything was peaceful and calm, but I have heard things have changed."

Randall hesitated. Martha held her breath. She realized he was trying to select his words with extreme care. *I hope my husband and my brother-in-law agree on major political and religious issues. It could become very uncomfortable, if not. I do not want anything to come between Mary and me.*

Finally Randall continued. "Many of the people in this area think the church has gotten too far from its original intent and want to go back to what they think the church was like during the time of the apostles. I have questioned if that is even possible, but Sunday I went to hear The Reverend John Cotton speak and he explained a lot to me."

William exchanged knowing glances with his wife before turning back to Randall. "I wish someone could explain the conflict to me so that we could understand it. Personally, Mary and I like to live above the confusion going on in the churches. Right now, we are attending the St. Martin-in-the-Fields Church in London. We try not to get involved in any side conversations. I do not want to offend either side." William finished eating his biscuit before continuing. "I am hearing a lot or talk in the street and taverns about purifying the Anglican Church of all Catholic influences. I do not know how that can possibly be done. That is our tradition and heritage going back for generations."

"It is a confusing situation," Randall said. "You are wise to check out the political climate before deciding to start a business in a different town. My opinion is, if the people are too fragmented, they will refuse to buy from anyone with opposing viewpoints. The conflict within the church is spreading across all of England. I do not know anywhere we can go to get away from it."

Martha set cups of milk in front of her guests and her husband and took a seat on the bench beside Mary. The warm aroma of the fresh goat's milk helped relax her uncertainties. She exchanged knowing glances with her sister, thankful their husbands were bonding well during their first meeting.

"That is true," William agreed. "Do you know specifically what is happening in Lincolnshire?"

Randall reached for another biscuit. "As you probably already know, John Cotton is one of the most well-known ministers in the area. Since we are new here, I wanted to hear him speak myself so I attended services last Sunday. I was greatly impressed with what he had to say. Having local control of the church instead of the government makes a lot of sense to me. Of course, he had to be extremely vague about the specifics from the pulpit, but after the service, he held a secret meeting on the bank of the river. Out of curiosity, I went to see what was going on."

A look of amazement spread across Mary's face. "That is unusual for a minister to do. What was their secret meeting about?"

Martha gave a nervous grin. *How can Randall possibly explain this complex religious environment to someone from out of town when many who live here do not understand?*

Randall made a quick sideways glance at his wife and gave her a reassuring smile before turning back to his guests. "Reverend Cotton wants the church to have an entirely new start. He is encouraging people to relocate to the Massachusetts Bay Colony where they could more closely follow the apostolic style of worship. He feels The Church of England has developed too many rituals that have nothing to do with God. They would like to purify the church of any remaining Catholic influence."

William nodded. "Just among the four of us, I agree that many of the current church rituals have little to do with God and Jesus Christ. Many of the statues, artwork, and prayers seem to have been made by man's own creativity and do not represent anything spiritual. The original church had none of these."

Mary leaned forward; her eyes became animated. "I heard at the marketplace that three years ago John Winthrop along with 700 followers went to Massachusetts Bay on a ship called the Arabella which was a part of a large flotilla. They said the letters that have been coming back from New England described it as the most healthful place in the world. They tell about the extraordinarily clean and dry air, springs of fresh water, magnificent woods along a shorefront complete with harbors and an abundance of islands. They claim more fish than one could haul, fat juicy turkeys in the woods, and pumpkins, carrots, turnips, and parsnips larger and sweeter than those grown in England. From what I know now, it is an extremely appealing idea."

Martha shook her head while she refilled everyone's cups and placed another plate of biscuits in the center of the table. "The description of the new world sounds inviting with the abundance of food, but why would one go there just to purify and change the church?"

She hesitated and reined in her temper, almost afraid to voice a dissenting opinion to the people she loved the most. The wounds from her argument with Randall were too fresh in her memory. "I personally like the rituals we have now. They help me focus my mind on God. When I am confused, the clergy explain the Bible so I can understand it. There is no reason for me to become involved in the conflict going on across the countryside...I abhor conflict."

Mary reached for her sister's hand, her voice soft and pleading. "But sister, don't you sometimes in the quietness of the night, feel God tug on your heart? Don't you occasionally hear a small voice within telling you to help the unfortunate?"

Martha blushed. "True...However, I am never sure if it is God talking to me or just my own thinking, so I put those thoughts out of my mind and listen to what the ministers have to say."

Martha watched William's face became stern and exchange knowing glances with Randall. *Are the men thinking the conversation is getting too personal?*

"Randall," William said. "Tell us more about the gathering on the riverbank last Sunday. Mary and I have never had a chance to experience such a thing."

Randall took another sip of the relaxing liquid. "Political opposition is building here in the Lincolnshire area. The government probably would have come down on Reverend Cotton months ago, but the locals seem to love him, so they try to avoid direct confrontation. After the worship services Sunday, things changed. One of the king's spies was present and heard the announcement about the gathering on the riverbank for those interested in making changes to the church. This must have angered the spy, even though the meeting was not held in the church building. After the people left the church and gathered by the river, three king's soldiers returned to the church and chased off their horses. They did not do anything to the people except harass them and leave everyone uncomfortable. We took it as a warning of something worse to come."

Mary's eyes brightened. She turned to her husband. "William, there is no harm in attending worship services and just listening. We could get a room at the local inn for a few days. We both need the rest, plus Martha and I have a lot to catch up on."

Before William had a chance to answer, Martha jumped in and said, "You will do nothing of the sort. We have plenty of room right here."

Shadows deepened in the Clarke home. The men relaxed around the fireplace while the women finished clearing the table from the evening meal and washing the dishes. Martha took a fresh candle from the candle tin, lit it at the fireplace, placed it in a holder, and set it on the table. "This is my favorite time of day. Work is done and we can relax a few minutes before retiring. Come and join me."

Mary took the bench at the table across from sister. "It is kind of you to take us in without any foreknowledge of our coming. Tomorrow I can help you make candles. Work always goes smoother when we do it together."

"We have had enough of political and religious talk for the day," Martha stated firmly. She leaned toward her sister with a smile. "Tell me about your wedding. What did you wear? Was it that beautiful gown you kept hidden in the wooden box under your bed while we were growing up?"

Mary's face reddened. "How did you know I kept a fancy gown under my bed? I thought it was far enough back, no one would ever see it. Mother made me promise never to talk about it. Now that we are grown and she is gone, I can see no harm."

Martha stared at her sister mystified. "You know how curious I was when I was a child. When no one was around, I looked through every box and sack that came into the house." She felt her face flush and took a deep breath. "One day when you were at the market with mother, I began snooping through your things...I was hurt and confused. I never understood why you never wore such a beautiful gown, why you never talked about it, or why I did not have one. I was positive our parents loved us equally, but you had something expensive that I did not have."

The candle flickered on the table before them while their husbands' soft conversation around the fireplace faded into the background. Martha held her breath. She finally had an opportunity to ask the question that burned within her since she was a child.

Mary hesitated and her gaze appeared distant. "Truthfully, my background has always been very confusing to me. To be honest, from an early age I have questioned if we were blood kin because we looked so different. You had hair and eyes like our mother and the strong, firm chin of our father while I did not look like either one of them. However, the bond between us was stronger than any sisters I had ever known. We had something special that would bind us together for life."

Martha wrinkled her brow. *What was her sister trying to say? Regardless of where we might live, we will always have an extra special sisterly love.* She turned back to Mary. "I always knew we never looked anything alike, but I never questioned it. What does not looking alike have to do with the gown?"

Mary cleared her throat; a pensive look crossed her face. "When I was a little girl, I never understood why I was invited to the palace as a guest of the court on three different occasions. I was even presented to the king himself, as if I was some kind of royalty instead of just a peasant girl from a lowly cottage of London. The gown you found under the bed was the one provided for me to wear at the palace when I was fourteen. I wished I could have worn it for the wedding, but it is much too small for me today."

"Did you ever find out why you went to the court and I didn't? We always went everywhere else together. Mother insisted we were treated equally."

"No one ever told me directly." Again, Mary hesitated. "Something strange happened the last time I was in the palace. I overheard Lady Olivia James tell a very strange story to her husband. She did not know I was standing behind a column within hearing distance."

William and Randall silenced their conversation to listen.

Martha was unable to mask her curiosity. "What did she say?"

Mary shuffled nervously and looked directly at her sister. "Lady Olivia said I was really the daughter of Arabella, a cousin of King James, and Sir William Seymour who was also a descendant of Henry VII. She said both Arabella and William Seymour were sent to prison and their baby girl was given to Arabella's lady-in-waiting who raised the child quietly in the countryside. They even told people my last name was Barrett so no one would be suspicious of whom I really was."

Martha's eyes widened. The story sounded preposterous, and yet it seemed to have an air of authenticity. "Things are beginning to make sense. Mother often talked about being a lady-in-waiting for royalty when she was young, but I never understood what she meant."

"In my eyes, she always appeared like royalty herself. We could not have asked for a better mother," Mary said. "I only wish she were here today to answer our questions. I kept my promise to her and she took her secrets to the grave. We will never know for sure who my birth parents actually were."

Martha gasped and reached for her sister's hand. It was not the possibility that her sister could be a descendent of royalty that touched the core of her being, but the fact she had been able to keep a promise to their mother for such a long time. "How could you live with such a secret? I could never have kept it quiet. I would have shouted it from the rooftops until someone told me the absolute truth about myself."

A faint smile spread across Mary's face. "It was easy to keep quiet. I did not think anyone would believe me and would consider me mad. I also felt uneasy about my safety if the wrong people found out who I was. There were too many powerful people with enemies involved."

"That might explain why our father always insisted we stay away from the entire political scene and not voice political opinions to anyone," Martha said thoughtfully. "Maybe that is where I got my need to avoid conflict at all cost and keep a low profile in the community."

Two days after their arrival in Boston in Lincolnshire, William finished building a wooden fence around the Clarke house and begged Randall for more tasks. Watching his brother-in-law work so intently, Randall became inquisitive about what was motivating him. Was he on a business quest...a religious quest...a family quest? He had only overheard a part of the conversation between Mary and Martha about their family life growing up. Could that be part of the real reason the Dyers came to Lincolnshire?

Later in the week while William was helping him in his woodshop, Randall asked, "Do you think there is a place for non-conformists within the Anglican Church?" He held his breath, waiting for an answer. There seemed to be an air of mystery hanging over the Dyers, something different that he could not put his finger on.

William shook his head. "I try to keep an open mind. I would rather leave the religious and political struggles for others. Right now, I am more focused on where to set up a business to earn a living for my family. However, even though Mary claims she is not interested in religious conversations, I watch her straining to hear any different teachings about God. It is like she is processing it, but not allowing herself to speak."

"In a way, I agree with you." Randall sighed with relief. "I try to have an open mind, as well. I am having trouble knowing the difference between what the Bible teaches, and what the church has added to it."

Randall noticed William begin to relax. *Maybe I will be able to understand the Dyers' point of view soon. I would not be surprised if we will be forced to make a public stand soon and I would like to be certain we stand together as a family.*

"I do not know if I am willing to trust the clergy entirely to be the only messengers from God," William admitted.

Randall raised his eyebrows. "Do you think God can speak through non-clergy, regular people like us?"

"That is an interesting question." William set the goblet he was smoothing onto the worktable and studied the expression on his brother-in-law's face. "I honestly do not know."

"This may be hard to believe," Randall said. "But I was recently introduced to a woman in the St. Botolph's Church who speaks with such knowledge and power that I wonder if she might hear the voice of God. She holds religious meetings in her home on Mondays to discuss the Sunday sermon. I do not know if she would be considered a prophetess or not, but she seems to be close friends with John Cotton."

A teasing twinkle appeared in William's eye. "Do you really think God could speak through a woman?"

Randall shrugged. "God is God. In the Bible God spoke through the mouth of a donkey named Balaam, so I assume He could also speak through the mouth of a woman."

"Hmm, interesting point."

Suddenly a loud rapping on the woodshop door interrupted their conversation. When Randall opened the door, he immediately recognized his acquaintance from the previous Sunday. "Will Hutchinson, it is good to see you," he greeted. "Do come in. What brings you to our humble abode?"

Will Hutchinson's eyes scanned the room and paused at the shelf containing the wooden goblets and bowls for sale. He took a bowl from the ledge and ran his hand over its polished surface. "You do beautiful work," he said and returned the bowl to its place.

"When I am in need of woodworking, I will have to return. However, today I came to see you for an entirely different reason."

Will Hutchinson studied the stranger at the worktable. "Hello, kind sir. I have not seen you before. Are you new to this area?"

Taken aback by the man's directness, William Dyer returned a cautious smile. "Randall is my brother-in-law, our wives are sisters. My wife and I are visiting from London, but are considering relocating here. When we learned John Cotton was minister of the local church we decided to stay until Sunday to hear him speak."

Will Hutchinson relaxed. "If that is the case, I assume we can speak freely before you." He cleared his throat and turned back to Randall. "Something has come up this week after the king's soldiers disrupted our meeting. It is extremely important that all those interested in cleansing the Church of England meet as soon as possible. Reverend Cotton has urgent news for us."

Randall hesitated, unsure how his brother-in-law would react. He regained his courage and said, "What is preventing the king from sending his spies to this meeting like they did last Sunday?"

"We learned our lesson last week," Will Hutchinson said. "I am going from house to house and personally inviting those who sympathize with our cause. There will be no public announcement. Saturday evening we will meet in the glen on the Jones farm further down the river from where we were this past Sunday. Everyone is to walk and leave his or her horses at home so we cannot be seen from the road. Can I count on you joining us?"

"Indeed you may," Randall assured him. "Perhaps my wife may want to accompany me this time."

"Mr. Hutchinson, even though I am not from this area, may I join you as well?" William Dyer asked.

The three exchanged nods of agreement. A spirit of camaraderie built in the room. Will Hutchinson said, "Anyone who is interesting in serving God and purifying the beloved Church of England is encouraged to attend. Like I said, this meeting is extremely important."

Saturday evening men and women from all over Boston converged at the appointed glen. The sheep grazing in the pasture seemed to ignore the extra movement around them. Curiosity mounted when Martha Clarke, her sister, Mary Dyer, along with their husbands hurried down the slope. They spotted Anne and Will Hutchinson sitting at the edge of the group and asked if they might join them.

"Please do." Anne motioned toward an open area of grass. "Martha, I am glad you are able to be with us. If it was not for your quick action, our little Katherine would not be with us today."

Martha blushed. "God put me in the right place at the right time. How are your children doing? You have such a precious family."

"Thank you for your interest," Anne said while the foursome made themselves comfortable on the grass close to them. "My children are all doing well. The young ones are thriving and the older ones help our fifteen-year-old servant so I can spend more time doing the Lord's work. Maybe you can come to the meeting at my house on Monday and get to know her."

Martha cringed at another invitation to Anne's home, but she said nothing. The Hutchinsons, Clarkes, and Dyers continued their conversation while twenty other men and ten women joined the group in the clearing. When everyone had arrived and seated themselves on the ground, tree stumps, or boulders, Reverend Cotton raised his hand for attention. "Let us open with prayer."

The crowd became silent. The minister's voice boomed words of praise and petition across the hillside. When he finished, he paused while anticipation mounted. "Fellow Puritans, as many of you know, ever since William Laud was appointed Archbishop of Canterbury, all Puritans have come under close scrutiny. I especially have experienced pressure from the church officials to the point of fearing for my safety and the safety of my family. This week I received notice that I have been removed from the ministry and threatened with imprisonment."

William Laud
Archbishop of Canterbury

When he hesitated, a low murmur spread across the crowd. Martha took a deep breath. *I was afraid something like this would happen.*

John Cotton raised his hands for silence and studied the wide-eyed faces of those before him who waited for an explanation. "Ever since John Winthrop began his Massachusetts Bay Colony experiment to build a second Eden —a

City upon on a Hill designed to be an example to the entire world—I have encouraged other believers to be a part of that community. Now it is my turn to leave Boston in Lincolnshire for Boston in the New World. This week my family and I will board the ship *Griffin* for Massachusetts. I would encourage all true Puritans at heart to consider following me. There will be ships traveling back and forth from our local harbor several times a year."

A shocked silence enveloped the group, followed by gentle sobs. Suddenly, Anne Hutchinson stood to her feet and shouted, "You can't leave without me. I thirst after every word you preach. You speak of the grace of God and not always the law. You speak of equality and not bondage."

Hearing Anne's nearly hysterical cry, John Cotton challenged her, "Why not join me in Massachusetts? If you are unable to afford the passage, there may be others who may be able to financially sponsor you."

Anne's sobbing subsided. "I can't leave now, my baby is due within weeks," she stated firmly, "but I promise to see you in the New World within a few months."

Chapter Three
Preparation

Boston in Lincolnshire, England, 1634

Exactly one week after the Reverend John Cotton announced his departure from Boston in Lincolnshire, a crowd gathered at the wharf while crewmembers loaded cargo, food, and livestock onto the ship *Griffin*. Friends and family bade farewell to their loved ones heading to the new world with promises to see them again someday, if not in this world, then the next. Passengers anxiously awaited their cue to board the ship. Tears flowed freely among them, but everyone stoically carried on.

Anne Hutchinson and Martha Clarke huddled together. Martha leaned over to hear the words of her friend.

"Where is Reverend Cotton?" Anne whispered. "I want to say good-bye and tell him how much I appreciated his teachings. Nothing made sense to me until I heard what he preached. I will truly miss him."

As the minutes passed, Anne became more and more desperate. Her tears gave way to uncontrollable sobs. "I want to go with him. There is so much I need to learn from him." She slumped to the ground, and buried her face in her apron.

Martha took her hand and knelt beside her. "You will be able to follow him to the Massachusetts colony soon, but now you must take care of yourself. You have to think about your unborn child and your precious little ones at home."

Anne shook her head. "Reverend Cotton's wife is with child and yet she is making the long ocean voyage. I have never had a problem delivering my babies, why should it make a difference whether I were on land or sea?" She hesitated while anger built behind her normally peaceful eyes. "Will insisted we wait until the baby is born. He said, with all the children, we couldn't get ready to go fast enough."

Confusion and frustration enveloped Martha when she tried to comfort her friend. She helped Anne to her feet and found two boulders nearby where they could sit. *What difference does all this make?* Martha pondered. *Why are they taking the details of religion so seriously? Why not trust the clergy to organize the church, plan the rituals, and preach about God? If Anne feels God is speaking directly to her, why does she depend so much on John Cotton?*

Anne and Martha continued sitting on adjacent boulders for another hour watching the men load the ship. The passengers around them organized their meager possessions while they waited to be allowed to board the ship. Time passed slowly and yet there was no sign of John Cotton and his wife. Surely, his tall frame and gray hair would stand out in a crowd. His presence always drew attention.

Suddenly Martha gasped and her eyes widened. She reached for Anne's hand. "Anne, look! Is that Randall and Will pushing wheelbarrows up the gangplank?"

Anne shaded her eyes against the noontime sun. "Yes, I wonder what they are doing. The ship must be short of deckhands and they are helping load the last minute supplies. The *Griffin* is supposed to set sail by mid-afternoon and they are well behind schedule."

From a distance, Martha heard a thunder of hoofs. The faint rumble gradually turned to a roar, a sense of confusion spread through the crowd, and people began to scatter. Anne and Martha stood to their feet and looked in the direction of the sounds. A soldier with a scar on his right cheek stopped his horse directly in front of the women. "Have you seen John Cotton?" he demanded. "He is wanted by the king immediately."

Martha's knees trembled. "No, I haven't seen him in several days."

The soldier waved his sword in her face. "Do not lie to me. You have been seen at Puritan gatherings. It is good riddance to the rest you, but John Cotton is not allowed to escape England."

Fresh tears began to flow down Anne's cheeks when the soldier turned his attention directly to her. "Honestly, I have not seen John Cotton. I am just here to say farewell to my friends."

The soldier spit on the ground and snarled at Martha and Anne while fear engulfed them and they trembled in their place. Suddenly, the officer in charge motioned for the soldier to ride ahead and join him. Martha watched nervously while the intimidating soldier dug his heels into his horse's side, shout an obscenity, and rode away.

After the soldier was gone, Anne held her stomach and took a deep breath. She wiped her eyes with her sleeve and sank back onto the boulder. "John Cotton must have been in more serious trouble with the officials than we realized," she whispered. "I hope he and his wife will be able to get aboard the ship before they are discovered. He does not deserve to spend time in jail just for preaching the truth."

Martha's heart gradually slowed to a normal rate. She returned to the boulder on which she had previously sat and continued scanning the crowd. "Look, our husbands are coming down the gangplank with their empty wheelbarrows. They must have the ship loaded now."

Martha and Anne watched the soldiers inspect each family before they were allowed walk the gangplank to the ship. Many of the children wailed and clung to their mothers who struggled under the weight of their possessions and fear of the soldiers.

Out of the corner of her eye, Martha noticed Randall and Will Hutchinson returning their wheelbarrows to the shed at the corner of the dock. She stood and waved to them and watched while the pair hurried to join them. She greeted her husband with a forced smile, trying to mask her tear-filled eyes. "Where are Reverend Cotton and his wife? The officers were extremely persistent about locating them. They're determined not to let him leave England."

Randall embraced his wife and whispered in her ear. "Don't worry about John Cotton and his wife. Will and I smuggled them aboard the ship in wheelbarrows while one of the other Puritans carried their personal items."

Anne looked around for soldiers and chuckled. "How clever. I knew there would be a way." She paused and gave a long sad sigh. "I wish you could have slipped me onboard, as well."

Will Hutcheson took his wife's hand and gave her a reassuring smile. "Hopefully someday soon, my love."

The foursome turned toward the ship and watched the last of the passengers board the ship. The crewmembers drew up the gangplank; the soldiers turned their horses around and left the dock in a cloud of dust.

"Thank God they are gone," Anne said. "I have never been so frightened before in my life."

As the ship slowly moved into the harbor, the remaining crowd moved closer to the shoreline. Each person waved and shouted their final good-byes to the passengers lining the railing of the ship. In their midst came a tall, stately gray-haired man. "It's him...It's him...," Anne shouted. "John Cotton is safely on his way to the New World."

The sky over London was growing dark when Mary and William Dyer approached the commons in the center of town. It had been a long, tiring trip from Lincolnshire and they yearned to feel the comforts of their own simple home.

They turned the corner to find a crowd gathering near of the commons. William slowed his horses to avoid the people mingling about. Suddenly, the crack of a whip shattered the evening calm followed by a man's scream of pain. Mary gasped, and her eyes grew wide. "What's happening?"

"That does not sound good." William stopped the horses and handed Mary the reins. "Wait here. I will find out what's going on." He jumped from the wagon and approached the nearest man. Mary watched their animated conversation and noted the worried look that spread across her husband's face.

Within minutes, William jumped back into the wagon and took the reins from his wife's hands. "A man is being flogged for stirring up dissent against the Anglican Church and the king. He is being used as an example to discourage others from doing likewise."

Mary muffled a scream. "How horrible! We thought the unrest was mostly in Lincolnshire County. Please take me home. I cannot bear to hear this."

Suddenly a soldier on a glossy black stallion came alongside the Dyer's wagon. "What are your names?" he snapped.

"William and Mary Dyer," William replied calmly, not wanting to stir any unnecessary ire in the officer.

"What is your reason for being in this area? Is the man at the stake a friend of yours?"

"No, sir. We were just passing through this part of town. We live in the neighborhood. We are returning home from Lincolnshire."

The soldier scowled and shouted. "You must be one of the Lincolnshire dissenters."

"We were just visiting kin folk," William tried to assure him, but to no avail.

"Lincolnshire is the center of unrest and non-conformists. You had better take note what happens to those who sow discord within the church. It is this man today, but it could be you tomorrow."

The soldier slapped the hindquarters of his horse with a whip. The horse lurched forward and Mary and William silently watched him disappear amid the crowd.

Mary trembled and reached for William's hand. Tears streamed down her face. "I am frightened. Please get me home as soon as possible."

William squeezed her hand. "I will do my best. It is only a little farther." William slowly worked his wagon around the crowd, which had now overflowed the commons onto the side streets. When a lane was clear, he urged the horses into a full gallop.

Mary clutched the bench of the wagon while they raced through the streets of London. When William turned the corner onto Front Street, she eased her grip on the seat. Mary stayed near his side while he unhitched the horses and took them into the stable behind the house. When they were safely inside their home, William bolted the door, and Mary collapsed onto a rocking chair beside the cold fireplace, buried her face in her hands, and sobbed.

Seeing her tears, William hurried to her side and wrapped his arms around her. "Mary, do not despair, I will protect you. We have done nothing wrong. We only went to listen to Reverend Cotton in the hope of understanding the Puritans' point of view, nothing more."

Mary dried her eyes on her apron. "I know you will try to protect me, but it is impossible to stand against the king's army. We are under suspicion just because we had been visiting Boston in Lincolnshire. I wonder what the soldier would have done if he'd known we'd actually gone to hear John Cotton speak?"

William's eyes became distant and his voice became firm. "One thing is settled in my mind. After what we have seen this last week, I am not going to open a millinery shop in Lincolnshire. There is too much political unrest there. I will have to see what kind of a business I can establish here in London, in spite of the competition."

Mary laid her head on her husband's chest and basked in the assuring strength in the scent of his perspiration. Her trust of his protection continued to mount. "That is not the only thing that concerns me. What if the rumor gets out that I might be related to the king? Could the opposition come and harass me next?"

Life in St. Botolph's Church of Boston in Lincolnshire was never the same after the departure of Reverend John Cotton. William Laud, the Archbishop of Canterbury appointed a minister who was loyal to the Anglican Church and the king, would not permit a hint of dissenting talk within his church. Members were required to pledge an oath of loyalty to the Anglican Church and the king. The attendance at the Sunday worship services declined to half what it had been under John Cotton.

Groups continued gathering in Anne Hutchinson's home on Mondays. Instead of discussing John Cotton's sermons, they discussed whether they would sign the loyalty pledge or not. Tension filled the air in Boston. Church members only talked with those whom they knew held the same viewpoint concerning purifying the Church of England.

Martha busied herself with the daily routines of life and avoided conversations with those she did not know. She tried to forget the fear she had felt on the dock waiting for the departure of the ship *Griffin* and the appearance of the soldiers, but those scenes continued to haunt her. Occasionally, she and Randall attended worship services but avoided personal contact with anyone. The only words the Clarkes spoke at the church were the words the congregation read together from the *Book of Common Prayers*. Whenever Martha was in church, she scanned the congregation for the familiar faces of their new friends, Anne and Will Hutchinson, but to no avail.

One rainy afternoon in mid-November, several weeks after the departure of the ship *Griffin*, Randall quit work in his shop early and joined his wife who was sitting in a rocking chair by the hearth in the main room knitting a shawl. "Martha, would you like to take a break from your work and walk to the Hutchinson's? We have not seen them in church or the marketplace in months. I hope nothing is amiss."

Martha laid the ball of flax on the floor beside her and hurried to her husband's side. "Excellent idea! I would love to see Anne again. I have truly missed her."

She went to the hook on the wall by the door and took down her bonnet and shawl. She placed the bonnet on her head and tied the strings under her chin. "Anne's baby should have arrived by now, and I would love to see the baby." Martha surveyed her husband's handsome face and trim physique. She forced a smile. "Anne continues to have beautiful children and is extremely efficient in organizing her household. I wish I were as fortunate."

Randall returned her smile and opened the door for her. "All in the Lord's timing. We must learn to be patient."

A cold mist blew against their faces while they walked the crowded streets of Boston in Lincolnshire. Dogs barked while they passed and children stopped their play to watch them pass. Martha reached for her husband's hand. *Even the children appear suspicious of those they do not know.*

Upon their arrival at the Hutchinson home, a fair-skinned girl who appeared about fourteen years of age opened the door. The girl smiled. "I remember you. You were the one who saved Kathryn's life. My name is Bridget. Would you like to come in and see mother and the new baby?"

Randall and Martha followed the young girl inside and found Anne bathing the baby in a large pot on the kitchen table.

Anne smiled warmly. "Martha...Randall welcome. We have not seen each other in a long while and we have a lot of news we need to share. Please have a seat and I will be with you as soon as I finish bathing Susannah."

Martha wrapped her arm around Anne, gave her a quick hug, and took a seat on the bench beside Anne. She watched while Anne gently wiped the baby's arms, legs, and the torso with a soft cloth while she supported the infant with her other arm. Martha admired the perfect features of the little girl. The sweet, clean fragrance of the child once again stirred her constant yearning for motherhood.

Martha could not take her eyes off the baby. "She is beautiful. I can hardly wait until I have a child of my own."

Recognizing the sadness in Martha's eyes, Anne reminded her. "All in due time...All in due time."

Anne took the baby out of the water and wrapped her in a towel and dried her, then pulled a gown over her head, and held her up. "I would like you to meet Susanna Hutchinson. She was born exactly three weeks ago today." Anne beamed with pride while she swaddled the baby in a small blanket, and laid her in a cradle next to the fireplace.

When she finished with the baby, Anne returned to the table and sat next to Martha. "William should be home soon. He has a great deal to do at the mercantile. A large order of shoes just arrived from Italy, and he must arrange them so customers can see what he has."

While Anne was bathing the baby, Randall had remained standing in the corner talking with Bridget. When Anne finished with the baby, he went to the table and placed his hand on Anne's shoulder. "Are there any chores you need to have done while I wait? I know Will is always busy and may not have time to get to them."

Anne set her jaw and pulled back her chin. "You are our guest. I would not consider putting you to work," she stated firmly and motioned for him to sit at the table with them. "We have too much news to share."

Randall obediently joined the women around the table. "The efficiency you and Will manage your household and business with is an example for all of us."

"We have been greatly blessed," Anne said and quickly changed the subject away from herself. "I am anxious to know if you have heard from your sister since they returned to London. I only met her once, but a special aura surrounded her. She seemed to be searching for something and had a depth of understanding and intensity that few possess."

Martha smiled. "She has always been that way. While she was growing up, she constantly wanted to know how and why things worked and what others were thinking. Her intellectual and religious appetite seemed insatiable. Since I was the older sister, I tried to protect her, but she was always high spirited and I often felt she was the one protecting me."

Suddenly they heard heavy footsteps on the path leading to the house. The front door opened and Will Hutchinson's large physique filled its frame. A smiled spread across his face and his eyes brightened when he recognized the Clarkes. "Welcome, dear friends." He extended his right hand to Randall. "I am so glad you came. I have thought about you often and wondered how things were going for you during this tense time."

Randall stood and shook Will's hand. "Good afternoon, Will. It is good to see you again. I too have been wondering about your family's well-being."

Will tipped his hat toward Martha, and placed a chair at the table with the others. "More specifically, I have been concerned about your safety."

Randall shook his head. "You needn't worry about my safety. The only places I have gone are to my workshop, the market, and occasionally to St. Botolph's Church."

"That is the point," Will stated firmly. "St Botolph's. Did you not hear what people were saying there?"

"We do not talk to anyone while we are at church," Randall said. "Martha and I refuse to sign the loyalty oath, but we do not want to give up the opportunity to worship God."

Will leaned back in his chair and took a deep breath. "It is wise not to sign the oath. It could lead to all kinds of problems later on, but I can understand why it is difficult not to attend Sunday worship services. By not talking with anyone, you probably miss the most dangerous part. However, I recently learned it was rumored around Lincolnshire County that we were the ones who had smuggled John Cotton and his wife onto the *Griffin*. So far, nothing has come of it, but we need to be cautious about where we go and what we say. The royal spies seem to be everywhere."

Martha felt her face blanch and a hollow pain gathered in her stomach. "What should we do? All I want to do is live my life in peace. Yet conflict seems all around us."

"Oh, Martha. You are such a dreamer." Anne patted her friend's shoulder. "We will never have complete peace while we are in this world, and especially not in England."

Martha hung her head and answered sheepishly, "I know. Sometimes I just want to get away from all the chaos and begin afresh before we start our family."

Will sat erect and turned to Randall. "Now that Susanna has been born, we are considering leaving this turmoil when the ship *Griffin* returns from its latest voyage to Massachusetts Bay. We want to be the first onboard when it next sails to Boston, Massachusetts— the new Eden."

Randall and Martha exchanged questioning looks but said nothing.

Seeing the nonverbal exchange between the Clarkes, Anne spoke up. "Why don't you join us? I heard the ship *Griffin* would be ready to make its next trip by the end of the summer. I could use help caring for the children while at sea since the servant I now have will be returning to her own family near Edinburgh soon. Martha, we would pay your passage, if you would help with the children."

Silence permeated the room. The baby began to cry in its cradle. Anne went to the baby, picked her up, and carried her back to the table where they were sitting.

Finally, Will turned to Randall. "I have heard it said the Massachusetts Bay Colony itself would pay passage for any carpenter if they would agree to help with the construction of houses and buildings once they arrive. Maybe you could check to see if that might be a way to have your passage paid."

Randall watched his wife's expression change. "We will have to give that some serious thought. We are having trouble building a profitable business here, in spite of how hard we work. Maybe we do need a fresh start."

That night sleep eluded Martha. Different scenarios kept running through her mind. After several hours, she reached over and touched her husband's shoulder. "Are you awake?"

"Yes. I cannot sleep either," he murmured rolling over to face her.

"I have been thinking about what Will said today. Do you think we will eventually get in trouble with the church and the government?"

Randall sighed. "I don't know, but I am feeling uneasy about the entire situation. I agree the Church of England needs to be purified from any Catholic influences, but I am not fully convinced that starting over in the New World is the right way to handle it. It is not right that we have to leave our homeland so we can worship how we choose. As long as the king is also the head of the church, we have few options."

Martha snuggled against her husband. "I agree. You know how much I do not like conflict, but I also do not want to live my life always looking over my shoulder for fear we might offend someone. I want to be able to think and speak openly. Would life be better for us in Massachusetts? Is that the plan God has for our lives?"

The couple lay in silence for a few minutes, each lost in thought. Finally, Randall said, "We must do the will of God. But sometimes God's will is hard to discern."

"I wish Mary were here. She always has a good understanding of the ways of God. Is there any way we can go to London and see them?" Martha's heart pounded waiting for her husband to answer. *If only God would speak directly to me with the answer...I need spiritual guidance from my little sister.*

Minutes passed while Randall stared into the darkness. "I need to go to London in a few weeks to get supplies. Maybe we could stay a couple extra days and visit with Mary and William. The change of scene would do us both good."

Rain pelted Randall and Martha Clarke as they entered London. The blankets in which they were wrapped had absorbed as much water as they could hold, and the temperature was beginning to drop. To make it worse, the wind had picked up speed.

Randall listened to the panting of the exhausted horse. "I am grateful the Hutchinsons loaned us one of their horses for the trip. I do not think our old mare would have made it through the muddy roads along the way."

"The Hutchinsons have been extremely kind to us," Martha said. "They must have understood how important this trip was to us and wanted to make sure we were able to get to London safely."

Being unfamiliar with the northern section of the city, Randall asked several people for directions and finally located the Dyer's house on Front Street. He stopped the wagon in front of the Dyer's front door, tied the reins around a nearby branch, and helped Martha to the ground. Randall waited nervously while Martha rapped on the front door.

"Martha!" Mary shouted when she opened the door. In spite of Martha's wet clothes, Mary embraced her. "I have missed you so. What brings you to London?"

"Randall needed to buy supplies for his woodworking shop. While we were here, we wanted to visit you and William."

Mary noticed her sister's chattering teeth and goose bumps on her arms. "Do come in. I will get dry clothes for both of you. William should be home soon and he will help bed down the horse."

Mary insisted Randall and Martha remain wrapped in blankets beside the glowing hearth while she prepared the evening meal. When William returned from work, he greeted them warmly, and insisted Randall stay by the fire while he unhitched Randall's horse and put the horse in the barn next to his mare.

Throughout supper, the conversation remained on light, general news. However, after they had shared an abundant meal of chicken, turnips, and bread, the tone of the conversation changed. Randall studied his brother-in-law's serious face. "William, what have you heard about the increased pressure on the Puritan movement? Has it affected London like it has Lincolnshire?"

William shook his head and sighed. "There is a lot of talk between individuals, but the officials try to keep a tight watch on what is said publically. I have noticed more floggings of dissenters in the town square and several of my neighbors have been taken to prison."

"That is what I was afraid of," Randall said. "It is not a good place to begin a business. Have you decided where you are going to set up your milliner's shop?"

William shook his head, a look of sadness crossing his face. "With the political climate what it is, I do not dare return to Lincolnshire County. I have started a small business down the street but with the extreme competitiveness in London, I do not know if I will be able to make enough money to support a family." William looked at his wife and winked.

Martha watched her sister's face redden. A smile spread across her face, and her eyes began to sparkle. "Mary is there something you have not told me?"

"I was going to tell you later," Mary said, "but I cannot wait any longer to share the good news. I am expecting a baby in the fall. We are so excited."

William reached across the table and took his wife's hand. "Before we knew she was with child, we were considering becoming a part of the Massachusetts Bay Colony, but I do not want to consider traveling until after the baby is born. I had an uncle in Lincolnshire die and leave me just enough money to pay for our passage."

Martha exchanged knowing looks with her husband and turned back to her sister. "Anne and Will Hutchinson are planning to go the Massachusetts when the ship *Griffin* returns next summer. They offered to pay for my passage if we would go with them to help with the children. I did not want to go without you and possibly never see you again. I wanted you to travel with us."

William rubbed his chin and hesitated. "That is a tempting offer, but we will have to wait. After the baby comes we can join you, but in the meantime, you must go ahead of us. If you do not go when it is first available, you may not have another chance. With the king's soldiers becoming suspicious of you, it is best you get out of England as soon as possible."

Chapter Four
The Voyage

The sails of the ship *Griffin* loomed over the harbor as the passengers, crewmembers, and friends approached the waterfront. The freshness of the salt air and the squawking of the sea gulls overhead increased the excitement of the day. This time the Hutchinson and Clarke families would leave for the Massachusetts Bay Colony. William and Mary Dyer helped Martha and Randall carry the few supplies they had purchased for their new home. Without the king's soldiers monitoring the loading of the ship as they did when John Cotton departed, all the passengers were in a holiday spirit. When the three families reached the end of the dock, the men walked ahead to help load the ship while the women hesitated, waiting for further instructions.

Martha watched her friend double-check every detail of her children's dress and every item in each of their bags. Anne had chattered incessantly all the way to the wharf. "In a few weeks I will again see our beloved minister, John Cotton. I have truly missed his profound teachings. He made me feel loved by God instead of always feeling I could never work hard enough to earn God's love."

Martha tried to imagine the beauty of the Massachusetts Bay Colony, the fresh air, beautiful vegetation, and luxurious fish and vegetables to eat. "What I'm looking forward to most in the New World is not having to look over my shoulder for fear one of the king's spies is watching me."

While the small band of passengers progressed toward the ship, Martha noticed her sister walking slower and slower, until she seemed not to be able to take another step and stopped. The wagon of food supplies she was pulling bumped against her ankles. Mary heaved a deep sigh. "I think I had better take a break for a few minutes. I am not able to work as I did before. I wish I were going with you, but I promise after my baby arrives, William and I will be on the next ship to America."

Tears built in Martha's eyes and she took her sister's hand. "I'm going to miss you. I so wanted to be with you when the baby was born, but I could not refuse the Hutchinson's offer to provide my passage if I would help with the children until they were settled. If we do not go now, Randall and I might never get to go. I will have a letter for you on every ship that returns from Boston."

"You do not have to keep explaining and apologizing," Mary reprimanded her gently. "We have discussed the departure many times and over-planned every detail. I will admit, now that the time has arrived, it is much more difficult than I expected." She reached into a tattered cloth bag in her wagon and handed a book to Martha. "I want you to take this with you to America. It is the most treasured possession our family has ever owned. When I join you in the New World we can share it."

Martha looked down. Her eyes widened and her hands began to tremble. "This is the *King James Authorized Version of the Bible*," she nearly shouted in excitement. "Very few common people are able to own these. How did you get one?"

Mary's eyes became misty. "It was our mother's. I do not know how she obtained it, but she gave it to me right before she died. She told me to treasure and guard it because there is a chance they will not print many more because of the controversy surrounding it."

Martha ran her hand over the smooth leather binding, gently opened it, and randomly turned a few pages. The musty smell tickled her nostrils. "I am grateful our mother had the skill and took the time to teach us both to read so we could read the Bible ourselves. I do not understand why a Holy Bible would be controversial within a Christian church?"

"I have no idea." Mary shrugged and looked mystified. "This version is easy for people to read and understand. I would think the clergy would want that."

Anne was unable to mask her frustration with the organized church. "The clergy do not always do what is in the best interest of the common people. Some Anglican ministers claim the only reason King James proposed a new English version was in response to the problems of earlier translations the Puritans discovered. They feel no Bible for the commoners is better than the wrong translation. Who knows what will happen with this version?"

Martha's eyes widened. She studied her friend's face, marveling at her wisdom. *Anne speaks with authority on nearly every religious topic that surfaces. How did she learn so much while taking care of such a large family?* From the corner of her eye, she saw their husbands weaving their way toward them through the throng of bystanders.

"I hope you are ready to get onboard," Randall said. "They have all the cattle loaded and are almost ready to load the passengers."

Martha scowled and wrinkled her nose. "You did not tell me there would be livestock on the ship. Will not it be kind of smelly?"

"If I told you pigs and goats were also going to be on board, would you have come?" Randall teased, before becoming serious once again. "Rest assured they will keep the animals' stalls clean. We have to have them to start our farms when we get to Massachusetts. Half the hold is sectioned off for them with a walkway in between so it shouldn't be too bad."

Mary smiled amid the tears building in her eyes. She gave her sister another hug. "I will see you next year in Boston, Massachusetts. I will be the first down the gangplank when we arrive."

Martha gave Mary one final embrace, tried to act brave despite her trembling, and walked up the gangplank. She stood at the ship's railing waving to her sister until she was merely a speck in the distance. The squawks of the sea gulls that had once been exhilarating to her now seemed to taunt her. *Am I doing the right thing? Will I ever see my sister again? Will my first niece or nephew be born strong and healthy?*

The ship *Griffin* rocked to-and-fro across the Atlantic Ocean while the days became long and boring for the passengers. The summer sun beat down on them mercilessly. Tempers became short when many felt others were intruding into their personal space. Besides the 30 cows that Governor John Winthrop had ordered from England along with scores of pigs, goats, chickens, and geese, the hold was crowded with furniture, and barrels of bread, cheese, butter, dried beef, peas, oatmeal, water, beer, and wine.

Designated crewmembers on the *Griffin* took turns standing guard peering into the distance with a refracting telescope; sometimes they would take a few minutes and let the children peer through what the children considered a magical device. Early one morning a shout went out. "Unknown ship in view on starboard side. All women and children to the hold and men on deck."

Martha helped Anne hurry her children to the ladder of the hold. Fifteen-year-old Bridgett Hutchinson began to cry. "What does this mean? Is there a pirate ship? I have heard pirates attack ships and rob them, kill the crew, and take the passengers prisoners."

Hearing Bridgett's comments, the smaller children began to wail. Martha tried to wrap her arms around as many children as she could while they lined up to go down the ladder below deck.

A look of concern spread across Anne's face, but she tried to make the tone of her voice reassuring. "God will protect us and the captain will take all precautions to keep us safe."

Martha and Anne gathered the Hutchinson children into the far corner of the hold. They huddled tightly together and held hands in the darkness. Grown women cried along with the children. Martha's urge to take each child in her arms to comfort them overpowered her apprehension. Quietly at first, then louder, and louder she began singing Psalm 23 to the tune they often used in their Sunday worship service. The crying ceased when one by one the others joined in song. Above them, they could hear men running across the deck and the crew firing one of the ship's guns. The smell of gunpowder filled the hold. Amidst the confusion, the passengers below deck continued singing for what seemed like hours.

Finally, a faint light appeared in the doorway overhead. "All clear...You may come out now. The unknown ship has disappeared."

The first few days at sea were tolerable for Martha in spite of the rancid hardtack they had to eat. She tried not to focus on food, but it was difficult not to recall the fresh vegetables and the scent of venison cooking over an open hearth. She had expected to have fresh meat to eat from the livestock brought with them, but she soon learned they were only for the farms after they landed. The meat they had to eat was hard and salty from being packed in brine. This only increased her thirst at a time when the captain rationed fresh drinking water and wine among the passengers.

Three weeks after leaving England, the *Griffin* entered stormy weather. Rain soaked the crew while they strained to work the sails. The ship tossed to-and-fro while the passengers remained below deck for several days without seeing sunlight. The smells became horrendous. Not only the people became seasick, so did the animals.

During the nights, Martha listened to sounds of coughing and vomiting while families tried to care for their own sick and ailing members. She would put her head under her straw-filled pillow to try to soften the sounds, but she could not escape the fact that at least a tenth of the passengers were ill at any given time.

One frightful night she took Randall's hand, rolled closer to him, and whispered, "Who will be next? Is this trip worth all the suffering? Will everyone's lives be better when we reach land, or will they be too sick to start anew?"

Randall wrapped his arms around his wife. "I think it is worth the suffering and risk. I am trusting God will carry us through and lead us safely to our destination.

Nothing could be worse than the way we were treated in England. However, I am beginning to hear some beg the captain to turn around and return to England."

Martha hesitated and basked in the warmth of her husband's embrace. "You are right. I may not understand a lot about the religious conflicts involved, but I do want the freedom to search and to think things through on my own."

"I am glad to hear you say that," Randall said. "Not many men appreciate women who think for themselves and not merely repeat what their husband's say. Your intelligence and openness is the very thing that attracted me to you. Together we can search for God's truth in a new land."

A week later in the middle of a cold, blistery night while the ship tossed violently in the waves, Martha could hear coughing coming from one of Anne's children. Following the sound, she crawled on her hands and knees until she came to Katherine. She reached out and put her hand on her forehead. Martha was shocked how hot the child's face had become. Suddenly, Katherine began to vomit and her body trembled. In spite of the darkness, Martha tried to comfort and keep her clean the best she could. Martha lay beside her and whispered comforting words in Katherine's ear while those around her continued to sleep.

"Am I going to die?" Katherine whispered in her four-year-old frightened voice. "Molly Green vomited and then she died."

Martha stroked the girl's hair. "No, you are not going to die. God protected you from an out of control team of horses nearly two years ago; he will protect you now. Please try to get some sleep. I will stay here with you until you are better."

During the voyage, Martha Clarke did her best to help Anne Hutchinson with her eight children. Not only did she assist with their physical needs, she worked to distract them from the harsh reality of life at sea. She sang songs and played simple games with any child on board who became restless. One sunny afternoon, children's laughter permeated the deck of the *Griffin*. Within minutes, a clergy person was standing over her. She tried to ignore him, but to no avail. The children became uncomfortable under the scornful eyes of the Puritan leader, their laughter turned to glum resignation, and they disbanded.

The next day, Martha gathered all the children around her and began reading the stories about Jesus from her treasured King James Bible. They listened with awe when the Bible characters came alive to them. They loved how Martha altered her tone or pitch each time a different person spoke. When Martha read about Jesus walking on the water, the children tried to imagine Jesus walking on the ocean toward their ship.

After over an hour of constant reading Martha's voice became hoarse. When she reached the end of a story she closed the Bible and said, "That will be the end of the stories today, but meet me here tomorrow and we will read more."

The children groaned in unison. "Please, just one more story."

She smiled and began opening her Bible. "This is definitely the last Bible story for today."

Suddenly a dark figure appeared beside her. Reverend Zechariah Symmes growled. "I see you have the King James Authorized Version of the Bible. I am certain it is the only one onboard."

Martha looked into his cold, dark eyes. "Yes, it was left to my sister and me when our mother passed away."

The minister reached for the book. "It is not seemly for women and children to be using a Bible not available to an ordained minister of the gospel. I must take your Bible for use by all passengers until we disembark in Boston."

Martha jumped to her feet, "But you cannot do that!" she screamed. "This is my mother's Bible."

Tears ran down Martha's face when the minister snatched the treasured book from her hand and walked away with it. The children sat in disbelief. *How can I possibly explain that the God I know is a loving God and not cruel and judgmental as the minister portrays?*

She studied the children's confused faces. "Don't worry, we will still meet in this same place every day, and I will tell you the stories of the Bible. I remember many of them because my mother told them to my sister and me every night before we went to bed."

Each day at sea, the Reverend Zechariah Symmes led services of worship, prayer, and singing which all the passengers were required to attend. Some days he would talk non-stop, up to four hours. Martha tried to ignore his lengthy preaching and sat imagining what life would be like in their new city, designed to be the perfect place to worship God. Colonists who had gone before had promised a place where the trees were full and lush, the air clean, the soil fertile, and the waters full of fish. They promised this would be just like the original Garden of Eden, only better. When she looked around, Martha saw many had also drifted into their own dream world during the lengthy sermons. *I wonder why Reverend Symmes took my Bible if he never planned to use it when he preached. I wonder if he reads from my Bible when he is alone or still reads from his own?*

One blistering hot afternoon while the passengers were forced to listened to Reverend Symmes preach about the laws of God, Martha watched Anne tighten her lips and clench her fists until the question period following the sermon. Martha had seen that expression many times before when Anne did not agree with what was being said. She admired the fact that Anne had the courage to speak the feelings and opinions Martha had trouble putting into words.

Defying the rule against women speaking during religious services, Anne Hutchinson said, "Your words bear a legal flavor, but they do not correspond with my understanding of the doctrine. I believe in a gospel of love and grace."

Reverend Symmes' face reddened. "As a woman, you have no right to question me. Remain silent."

"It makes no difference if I am male or female. You are not speaking the truth," Anne countered. She set her jaw and her voice became firm. "Jesus Christ came to free us from those laws. If you try to silence me, I will report you to the Reverend John Cotton as soon as we dock Massachusetts. You may not believe it, but in God's eyes men and women were created equal."

"That is not true," the minister snapped. "God has anointed certain men to speak for Him and to preach the gospel. God strictly forbids women speaking in church. On this ship, I am the only one appointed to speak for God. I demand you to be silent."

Anne's eyes blazed. She took a deep breath. "Many onboard are sick and may be dying. If God speaks through you, when are we going to arrive in Boston to alleviate their suffering?"

The tension mounted and the crowd pushed closer in order not to miss a word of the confrontation. Their presence emboldened the Puritan minister. "You have limited knowledge and do not understand that God no longer speaks directly to men. He has not done so since the days of the apostles. God now only speaks to His people through the Holy Scripture and I have been appointed to preach only what is in the Bible."

Anne's face became radiant while she proclaimed loudly for all to hear, "God told me directly we will land in Boston on September 18, 1634. I stand upon His words."

Reverend Symmes sneered and walked away.

When the *Griffin* docked in the Boston harbor on September 18, 1634, most of the passengers were too excited to remember Anne Hutchinson's prediction except for one—Reverend Zechariah Symmes.

Martha waited at the railing for Randall to carry the last of their belongings to the deck. To Martha's horror, she heard Reverend Symmes say to the ship's captain, "One of the first things I must due when I get ashore is to report Anne Hutchinson's offensive behavior and words to Deputy Governor Thomas Dudley. Any prophetic words she may have proclaimed must have come directly from the devil. The officials need to be made aware of the dangers and heresy entering their God-fearing colony. Boston must remain pure from all heresy."

Chapter Five
Decisions

Boston, Massachusetts, August 1635

Randall... Randall, they're onboard... they're onboard." Martha Clarke ran shouting to her husband.

Randall looked up from chopping wood outside their simple three-room home. He laid his saw on the pile of wood nearby and placed his hand on his wife's shoulders. "Slow down. Who's onboard what?"

"Mary and William are onboard the ship that is about to dock in the harbor. I went to the wharf to see if the fishermen had any fresh fish for sale, and I saw a ship bearing the English flag. One of the crew came ashore and read the passenger list." Martha took three deep breaths to calm herself, but she could not slow her racing heart. "Hurry, we have to be at the wharf to welcome them."

Randall grabbed a wheelbarrow and the couple rushed to the Boston Wharf. The tattered sails of the newly docked ship loomed before them while excitement raged through Martha's body. They joined the throng of colonists coming from all directions to greet the new arrivals and to learn news from their loved ones in England. Within minutes, passengers began descending the gangplank, each looking tired and worn, yet happy.

Martha watched intently until two familiar forms appeared at the top of the ramp. "There they are." Tears gathered in her eyes and ran down her cheeks. She shouted their names, waved, and ran to meet them at the end of the dock. The moment she had been waiting and praying for nearly a year had finally arrived.

Mary and William Dyer rushed toward them, piled their bundles on the side of the path, and fell into their waiting arms.

"We are finally together again," Mary sobbed and buried her face on her older sister's shoulder. "I have been so lonely without you."

Martha continued holding her sister and stroking her hair. "I missed you, too. Every day I said a prayer for you and your family." She stepped back, looked at William and back to Mary. "Where is your new baby? I thought it was due last October."

Mary froze and began crying even harder. "Our baby, William Junior only lived a few hours. He was the most beautiful child I had ever seen."

Martha looked up at her brother-in-law while she continued comforting her sister. "What happened?"

After a painful silence, William said, "It was a long, difficult delivery. The baby's first breath was a whimper and not a cry. He could scarcely breathe from the beginning and only lived a few hours."

Martha waited in silence with tears in her own eyes until her sister stopped crying.

After several minutes, Mary wiped her eyes with the sleeve of her dress and forced a smile. "We buried William Junior in the St. Martins-in-the-Field Church Graveyard October 27th. It was the saddest day of my life." She hesitated and took three deep breaths. "The good news is that I am expecting another child in the late fall. This time William let me travel while I was with child. He felt it was important that you be with me during the birth of this baby."

Martha ran her hand over her sister's stomach and noted the look of joy on William's face.

"Congratulations. God will surely bless you with a healthy baby this time. A new land always offers new hope."

A warm sea breeze refreshed the faces of the new arrivals while sea gulls squawked overhead. Martha continued clinging to her newly arrived sister. Never had she felt such a sense of fulfillment. "I too have good news. I am expecting a baby in October. Our babies will each have a cousin to play with while they grow up."

In the midst of the joyful reunion with her sister, Martha looked over her shoulder and smiled. The men had become restless with their discussion and were already picking up the Dyers' bundles and loading them into the wheelbarrow. "Come, we will help move your things to our house. Randall had the forethought to bring a wheelbarrow along to help."

Martha stooped and picked up a small gray bag beside her. "You can stay with us until your home is completed. Randall worked all winter on our house and made an extra room for you, trusting in your soon arrival."

William hesitated and turned to Randall. "It may not be that simple. I was told before I left London it would be difficult making a living as a milliner in the New World because the colonist were more concerned about food and shelter and had little money or time to spend on fashion needs. I brought my milliner tools with me in case I would ever have the opportunity to return to the trade. In the meantime, I decided to become a yeoman. I bought ten goats, eight sheep, six pigs, and twelve chickens with me on the ship. They will not begin unloading the livestock until tomorrow."

Martha looked at her husband. She wanted to say, *what are we going to do?* However, she was afraid of hurting her sister's feelings.

Randall lifted the handles of the wheelbarrow and began pushing it toward their home. The others walked beside him. "Being a yeoman is an excellent idea. We can modify our plans to accommodate the livestock. At the end of our street is an empty lot big enough to build a house and still have room for a fence in the back to contain your animals. We can check on its availability tomorrow."

William's face brightened. "That sounds perfect, but what do you suggest I do until I can get the fence built?"

Randall glanced at Martha who was unable to mask her puzzlement. He gave her a reassuring smile and turned back to William. "It will be no problem to rearrange our house. The animals can stay in the extra room since it has a dirt floor. We can make pallets for you and Mary to sleep on in the main room. It will not be perfect, but we can make it work. We can build a sturdy fence in two or three days with the help of a couple of neighbors."

Martha's eyes widened. *As thankful as I am to have my sister with me, how am I going to stand the stench of farm animals in the same house? That will be almost like when we were on the ship with livestock for over three months.*

Seeing Martha's look of horror, William said, "I appreciate all you are doing for us. I know it will be inconvenient, but we will make it up to you. We plan to share the milk from the goats and eggs from the chickens between our two families."

♟

Days passed quickly. William Dyer purchased the lot at the end of Summer Street and the neighbors helped him build a fence for his animals in three days. When they were finished, William approached Martha who was busy picking beans from her garden behind the house. "You will be relieved to know we finished the fence and can start moving the animals out of your spare room this afternoon. I am extremely grateful for your understanding. When the animals are gone, I will make sure to clean the room thoroughly. We will leave the door open for a few hours to air out and hopefully there will not be any lingering odor."

Martha stood, looked at William, and smiled. "I hope I did not show displeasure about the animals. You know I would do anything to help you and Mary get settled in Boston. I have been praying for over a year for your arrival."

With the fence completed, William turned his attention to building a house for Mary and himself. He offered milk to a neighbor in exchange for the use of the neighbor's two working steers to haul the fallen trees from the woods north of Boston to his future home site. The three-year-old steers often did not work together in a yoke and slowed the progress of moving the logs into town and the men were exhausted by the end of each day. It took a week of constant struggle before enough logs were on site to begin working.

Once the wood was available, Randall quickly planed the planks for walls. In the evenings, the men sat outside the Clarke's home until dark whittling wooden pegs to secure the planks together.

Usually the two men worked in silence, but after several weeks had passed, William could not hold back the obvious question. "Randall, have you joined the local church? Since we have been here I have noticed you haven't attended the Sunday worship service."

Randall shook his head. "Not yet. I am still trying to make up my mind. What's your opinion on becoming an official member of the Puritan church?"

William hesitated. His mind raced with memories and emotions. "Mary and I used to get a great deal of satisfaction from worshiping in our church in London, but in recent months, with all the political unrest and fear, we became overly cautious about becoming too involved. In coming to Boston, we are looking forward to begin worshipping at a church again."

Reverend John Wilson
(c. 1591 - 1665)

Randall sighed. He laid another finished peg in the wooden box on the floor beside him, went to the fireplace, and took the tongs to rearrange the logs. Within seconds, the fire in the logs was rekindled, and warmth filled the room once again. "Martha and I are still conflicted. We attended the First Church of Boston for a while, since it is within easy walking distance. The Reverend John Wilson is the minister and the beloved John Cotton is a teaching elder. However, something is wrong that I cannot explain. Martha does not want to attend worship services any more, but she will not miss a Monday meeting at Anne Hutchinson's house where the women gather to discuss the sermon."

William nodded his understanding. "Martha never did like conflict. I would think she would be glad to join a model church where all the people are supposedly in one accord."

"If only life were that simple," Randall said. "The major problem of the colony is the leadership of the church, and the government is nearly the same entity. It is an even tighter relationship than the King of England and the Church of England. The very issue we protested against while we were in England is even worse here."

William shook his head with disappointment. "How can people keep making the same mistakes? Won't we ever learn?"

"In the short time we have been in Massachusetts, many of us have become frustrated in the development of the laws of the colony," Randall said. "The church and the government both insist on everyone living by their strict, unrealistic interpretation of the laws of God. The officials hand out extreme discipline for the most minor infractions. If a law is not already on the books, the clergy will create one on the spot."

The sun turned to orange red and then disappeared below the horizon while the men continued whittling. The number of pegs in the wooden box multiplied during the evening. Finally William said, "That makes it hard to know what to do to avoid being in trouble with the clergy."

"It is very hard to anticipate their will," Randall said. "Martha ran afoul of one of the ministers on the ship on our way to the New World. She has never gotten over it."

William's irritation level rose. Sometimes he wanted to adapt his sister-in-law's philosophy of avoiding conflict at all cost. "The short time I have been here, I have heard several stories about the lack of individual rights. I cannot imagine mild-mannered Martha becoming angry with anyone. What happened?"

Randall paused. "Twelve months after Martha's encounter, the pain of the insult will not go away. No one has the right to treat my wife in such a manner."

"What happened?"

"Remember the King James Bible that Mary gave her before we left England?" Randall said. "It became Martha's most treasured possession and was her source of strength throughout the long voyage. She spent hours sitting on the deck reading it. Every day she would gather all the children onboard the *Griffin* around her and read Bible stories to them."

"Martha has always had a giving and nurturing spirit," William said. "How could anyone object to reading the Bible to children?"

Randall groaned with disgust. "When The Reverend Zechariah Symmes saw she had a newer version of the scriptures than he had, he confiscated it. He told her that it was more important for him to use the latest version to read to the adults during his daily worship services than for her to use it to read to the children. When we got to Boston, she had to beg the head minister at First Church to force Reverend Symmes to give her family Bible back to her. It was over three weeks before they reluctantly returned it."

The power of the local church and government was often the topic of conversation in many households across Boston every time new settlers arrived. While William and Randall were having their discussion, the same topic came up the next day between their wives while they washed clothes in a huge black kettle over an open flame in the backyard.

When Martha finished laying the last shirt across a branch, she turned to her sister. "Mary, why don't you join the group that meets at Anne Hutcheson's house every Monday afternoon? She leads a lively discussion over the sermon of the previous day. Even though I do not attend the church service, it is always interesting to hear people's different viewpoints. Sometimes I do not totally agree with Anne, but I appreciate the fact she accepts everyone's ideas and treats them with respect. We cannot meet within the church because the Puritans will not listen to any thing women say."

Mary looked up. Her eyes brightened. "The few days I was with Anne during our visit to Boston in Lincolnshire she impressed me with her spiritual understanding. I would love to go with you to a meeting." Mary dried her hands on a nearby towel. "Truthfully, I have been questioning the Puritans legalistic rules for some time. While I was on the ship I had a long time to think about God and religion, and I am having trouble believing all their regulations fit into the love that Jesus taught."

Martha breathed a sigh of relief. "I totally agree. I am beginning to understand and side with the free grace advocates," she said. "Anne promotes a person's experience of grace and love through Christ and the Spirit while the Puritans demand moral obedience, and teach good works and religious training is the only way to get to Heaven. Anne claims people go to Heaven because of Jesus' love and not by being good enough."

Randall pounded on the Dyer's front door and shouted, "Mary...Mary. Come quickly. Martha's baby is coming."

Seconds later, William opened the door. "Good afternoon, Randall. I am so sorry, but Mary is sick with typhus and is extremely feverish. She has not been able to get out of bed for over a week. Maybe Anne Hutchinson will be able to help deliver the baby."

Randall's eyes scanned the simple main room of the Dyer's home. Mary lay on a cot in the corner covered by a tattered quilt. Her face was pale and her eyes closed. "I am sad to hear that. We have always been able to help each other and now both of us need help. I will pray for Mary and will check back later if there is anything we can do."

"May God direct your path in finding a midwife," William responded and then turned back to his wife after hearing a low moan from the corner of the room.

Randall ran through the streets of Boston. The brisk autumn breeze stirred the falling leaves around his feet. Apprehension and excitement enveloped him.

He pounded on the wooden door to the Hutchinson's home on High Street. "Anne, come quickly. Martha's baby is coming and I need a midwife immediately."

Sixteen-year-old Bridget Hutchinson opened the door. A faint expression of recognition spread across her face. "Good day, Mister Clarke. I am sorry, but Mother is sick in bed with typhus. Come in and I will tell her you are here. Perhaps she will know who to get for a midwife."

Randall followed the girl into the home, removed his hat, and waited by the door while Bridget disappeared into a room in the back of the house. Seconds seemed like hours while he paced back and forth in front of the door.

At last, Bridget returned. "I told mother you were here, but she is so weak she can scarcely talk. She said

Jane Hawkins is an excellent midwife. She lives in the small house on the corner three streets north of here. It has a large oak tree in the front yard. When you meet her, the first thing she'll probably tell you is to call her 'Goody'."

"Thank you for your kindness," Randall said and hurried from the house. He turned and called over his shoulder. "Tell your mother I wish her well."

Although short of breath, Randall ran the remaining distance to the Hawkin's home. The vision of his beloved wife home alone during her labor haunted him. Mary had been too weak to help Martha, and now the desired midwife was sick. Upon arriving at the appointed house, he pounded on the door and waited nervously. A large, stern-looking woman opened the door. "May I help you?"

"I am looking for Goody Hawkins."

"I am she. What can I do for you?"

"My wife is having a baby. I went to get Anne Hutchinson to help with the delivery but she is sick in bed. She said to get you. Can you help?"

"Most certainly," Goody said. "Wait here while I get my bag of herbs and supplies. One never knows what we might need."

Within minutes, Goody Hawkins and Randall Clarke were hurrying back through the streets of Boston. The same dog barked and tried to follow them until his owner called him back. When they neared the Clarke home, they could hear Martha moaning with pain. Randall rushed through the unlocked door and turned to the midwife. "Wait here while I talk with Martha. She is expecting Anne Hutchinson, and I want to explain why she couldn't come."

Randall entered the bedchamber. Martha was trying to sit up in bed and reach for a glass of water on the table beside her. She forced a smile and reached out her hand. "Is Anne with you?"

"I am sorry to tell you, but Anne is sick in bed with typhus." Randall shook his head, unable to mask his disappointment. "And Mary is also sick with typhus."

Martha's eyes widened. A look of terror spread across her face. "What are we going to do?"

William took his wife's hand and pressed it to his lips. "Everything is going to be all right. Anne told me to get Jane Hawkins. She is supposed to be one of the best midwives in the colony."

"You mean you got Goody Hawkins?" Martha exclaimed in a sharp whisper. "The Puritans say she is a witch and possessed of the devil."

Randall took a deep breath and squeezed her hand. "If Anne Hutchinson recommends her, surely she is not a witch."

Another cramp engulfed Martha's body, she moaned, and lay back onto her pillow. When the pain subsided, she said in a soft voice, "If Anne says she is an excellent midwife; it is good enough for me. Have Goody come in."

Randall hurried to the main room where Goody was filling a bowl with water from a bucket by the door. "Martha would like to see you now. I will bring more water from the well and add another log on the fire so you will have enough hot water."

"Thank you. I will need as much hot water as possible." Goody entered Martha's bedchamber with a bowl of water in one hand and her bag of supplies in the other. "How are you doing, Martha? I am Goody Hawkins and I am going to stay with you until you have a bouncing new baby in your arms."

Martha forced a smile. "The pains are coming very close together, and I feel miserable." She gritted her teeth when another contraction swept through her body. Beads of sweat appeared on her brow. "I hope this will soon be over."

Goody set the bowl of water on the table and dipped a fresh cloth into it. "I know you've probably heard the rumors about me." She wiped Martha's forehead. "Most women in Boston have heard the stories and are able to understand my methods, but not the men. Do not be concerned if I need to mix what seems like peculiar substances with healing herbs to help alleviate the pain of childbirth. God often tells me directly what to use in different situations. The male clergy do not appreciate what may be necessary to deliver a baby and they accuse me of all kinds of strange things."

Martha laughed between her ever-increasing surges of pain. "You have my full confidence. In childbirth, I would definitely trust an experienced midwife over a male church official any time."

The hours passed slowly while Martha's pain increased in intensity. When it became almost unbearable, Goody Hawkins said, "Would you like my special potion to ease the pain?"

Martha nodded while perspiration soaked her body. Goody poured a spoonful of grey liquid into a spoon and guided it into Martha's mouth. Its bitterness stung her throat, but within minutes, the pain subsided and she was able to follow Goody's directions to help in the delivery the baby.

After several painful minutes, Goody lifted the newborn into the air. Martha could scarcely hear the baby's initial cry. A sense of terror enveloped her. "Is the baby all right?"

The midwife patted the baby on the back until she gave another slight whimper. "Yes, I think she is getting enough air into her system now. We will have to keep a close watch over her for the next few days, but I am certain she will be fine."

The midwife's words failed to comfort Martha. Tears started to roll down her face. She watched Goody wrap her daughter in a white blanket and place the baby in her arms. Martha snuggled the child next to her bosom. "Was it the herbs you gave me that is making it hard for the baby to breathe?" Her voice was weak and halting.

Goody shook her head and fluffed Martha's pillow to make her more comfortable. "No. When I gave you the painkiller, the baby was too close to delivery to be affected. Some babies are just stronger at birth than others. Try to get some rest. Randall and I will mind the baby."

The cool fall air nipped at Randall Clarke's nose while he walked through the Boston Commons on his way to the mercantile. He had remained indoors for nearly two weeks taking care of his wife and newborn daughter. When he finally felt confident Martha was strong enough to handle the struggling infant on her own, he went to share the news. While passing through the Commons, he noticed a small crowd gathering around a man in a tall, black hat who was preaching with vigor and enthusiasm.

Randall stopped and listened for a few minutes, then nudged the man next to him. "Who is that man? Isn't he afraid of getting in trouble with the church officials talking about a complete separation of the church and civil government?"

The stranger turned to him and smiled. "That is Reverend Roger Williams. He used to be a minister in the church in Salem until he encouraged them to separate from the other churches. This infuriated the General Court in Boston and he has been in trouble with them ever since."

"I like what he is saying. It takes a lot of courage to stand against the errors of the clergy," Randall whispered back. "I want my brother-in-law to hear this."

Leaving the crowd on the Commons, Randall hurried to the Dyer's home. After rapping loudly at the door, he was surprised when Mary answered it. "Mary, I am glad to see you up and about. How are you?"

Mary motioned for him to come in. Randall noticed that after weeks of Mary's illness, the Dyer's usually tidy home was in total disarray.

"I am much better, but still very weak. How is Martha? Has her baby arrived yet?"

"Martha had a little girl two weeks ago. We named her Sara Marie. The baby was very weak at the beginning and I stayed home and helped care for both of them. This is my first time out of the house to share the good news."

While they were talking, William entered through the back door. Randall quickly explained the news about the baby's arrival before changing the subject. "A minister named Roger Williams is preaching in the Commons right now, and I would like you to come and listen with me. He is presenting some interesting ideas."

William scowled. "I have heard about Roger Williams and I have been trying to keep my distance in case trouble breaks out. I don't want to be connected with it."

"Good point," Randall said and studied his brother-in-law's worried face. "Right now I have enough problems without being drawn into someone else's. What do you know about him?"

"Come sit by the hearth and we can discuss it," William said and motioned for him to follow.

William Dyer stoked the fire and added another log. They both pulled up benches. "All I know is that a few days ago Roger Williams was tried by the General Court and convicted of sedition and heresy. They declared he was spreading 'diverse, new, and dangerous opinions'." William shrugged. "However, when I heard him preach in the City Commons, I felt he was preaching only the truth of God."

"That conviction cannot be good. What did they do to him?" Randall asked. "It obviously did not seem to quiet him."

"Roger Williams was ordered banished from the Massachusetts Bay Colony, but the execution of the order was delayed because he is sick and winter is approaching. They are allowing him to stay in Boston temporarily providing he ceases his agitation."

Reverend Roger Williams
(c. 1603 - 1683)

"It does not look like he is obeying the order very well, does it?" Randall paused and the two men watched the flames leap in the fireplace when the new log began to burn. "Even though I do not think I would do it myself, something deep inside of me admires his courage."

The next three weeks, Martha kept her new baby at her side and tended to her whenever she whimpered. Each day she thought Sara was getting stronger until late Thursday afternoon while Martha was sitting by the hearth knitting she looked into the cradle beside her. The baby was still and her lips were blue. She grabbed the infant and nestled her close to her breast. "Randall, come quickly," she shouted. "Something is wrong with Sara."

Randall Clarke raced from their bedchamber where he was mending a broken table leg and took their daughter from his wife. The baby lay limp in his arms. Her face was ashen and her eyes fixed. Tears built in Randall's eyes. Martha wrapped her arms around both of them and sobbed. Minutes passed, but they remained frozen in grief.

Exhausted, Martha slumped onto the bench by the fireplace and wiped her face with the sleeve of her dress. "It is my fault...It is all my fault. I should never have taken the herb for pain Goody Hawkins gave me when I delivered Sara. The Puritans warned me about Goody, but I did not believe them."

Randall laid the infant's body gingerly in a plain household basket and knelt beside Martha. He took her hands in his, and pressed them to his lips. "Martha, that is not true," he insisted. "The painkiller Goody Hawkins gave you did not cause Sara's death. She used the same herb with many other women without ill effects. Sara's lungs did not develop properly from the very beginning. You must not believe all the gossip you hear in the colony."

Martha took three deep breaths before she murmured, "I know...I know, but those rumors will continuously haunt me. I will always live with the 'what if' thought in the back of my mind."

One brisk November afternoon while Randall Clarke and William Dyer were cutting trees in the nearby woods, Randall asked, "I know we have discussed this before, but, have you requested to officially join the First Church of Boston, yet? I know it has been a hard decision for both of us."

"Yes, after much prayer, Mary and I decided to be accepted into full membership in the very near future." William hesitated, afraid of upsetting his brother-in-law, but knowing if Randall did not hear it from him, he would surely hear it from someone else. "Reverend John Davenport told us baptism could only be administered to the children of full church members. He claimed only those who are baptized would go to heaven. Mary and I have trouble accepting that perception of a loving God sending innocent children to Hell, but we do not want to take any chances."

Randall hung his head. His voice softened. "I cannot believe our precious Sara is now anyplace other than with her Creator God. We did not have time to have her baptized. If the church is going to teach that baptism is the only way to Heaven, they should allow midwives to baptize the weak babies as soon as they are born."

William placed his hand on his brother-in-law's shoulder. An unseen bond strengthened between them. "I am in total agreement. The Puritans set out to purify the Church of England, but sometimes I feel we need to start another movement to purify the Puritan Church."

Randall nodded. "That is one of the reasons Martha has been attending the Monday afternoon meetings at Anne Hutchinson's house. Sometimes I attend myself. What Anne teaches makes much more sense to me than what the clergy teach."

Ann Hutchinson
(1591 - 1643)
Statue on the Lawn of
Massachusetts State House

William studied the frustrated expression on his brother-in-law's face. "I can understand her reluctance.... One of the reasons why I am choosing to take the Oath of a Freeman is I will be able to join the church, vote, and own land. I will not have any problem vowing to defend the Commonwealth, and not to conspire to overthrow the government."

Randall scowled. "I do not approve of the entire Freeman system. Most people come to the New World as indentured servants. Promising to work for five to seven years is the only way they can earn their passage. Men should be able to vote and be members of the church while they are fulfilling their contacts. They may not have as much money as the person who paid their passage, but an indentured servant is still equal in the eyes of God."

"I agree with you," William said, trying to ease the tension between them. "But since the laws are the way they are, I feel I am forced to abide by them."

Randall stepped back and stared at the pile of wood before him. He took another swing of his axe. "I hadn't thought about it in those terms." He paused, placed his axe handle on the ground, and leaned on it. "I have been concerned that fewer than half the people who leave England and come to Boston for a more democratic life are not eligible to vote or have any say in how they are governed. The majority of people in this colony are not even permitted to partake in communion or baptism services in the church. Without being able to vote in church or state affairs, they are like spiritual non-entities."

The wind howled around the Dyer's simple home on Summer Street. A baby's shrill cry pierced the evening calm. Anne Hutchinson hurriedly washed the newborn in warm water while Martha tended to her sister. When the baby was clean, Anne wrapped him in a soft wool blanket and turned back to Mary. "Would you like to hold your new son?"

Mary beamed and reached for the baby. "So it's a boy," She cried happily. "He is beautiful. He is the most beautiful baby I have ever seen." She uncovered the baby's right hand and stroked his tiny fingers.

Martha Clarke stood beside the bed immersed in the solemnness of the moment. *I admire Mary's strength during her greatest pain. When I was in the same situation, I cried out and begged for anything to kill that pain. She possesses an inner strength I will never understand.*

Martha pulled the loose strands of hair away from her sister's forehead and stroked the baby's arm. "Have you and William selected a name for the baby yet?"

Mary smiled and gazed into her child's innocent face. "We decided that if it were a boy we would name him, Samuel after the son of Hannah in the Old

Testament. He grew up to become a prophet and judge in Israel."

"That is a beautiful name," Martha said. "I am certain he'll grow up to do great things for the Lord and mankind, as well."

Mary continued beaming at her newborn son as if she could not get enough of his presence. After several minutes of tranquility, she looked up at her sister. "Would you get William for me? I want to share these moments with him."

When Martha opened the door to the main room, she saw William nervously whittling more pegs to use for building while he warmed himself before the fireplace. Before she could speak, the new father jumped to his feet. "How are they?"

"You have a healthy son, and Mary is doing well." She motioned for him to follow her.

William rushed to his wife's side and kissed her on the forehead. "How are you, my beloved?" He looked down at the bundle in her arms. "He is beautiful. Thank you for giving us another son after we lost our wee William in England. God has truly blessed us."

"That He has," Mary said. "I am glad we had decided on the name 'Samuel'. God has truly answered our prayers. The very meaning of the word Samuel is 'God has heard'."

Feeling intrusive in the privacy of her sister and brother-in-law's joy; Martha slipped quietly from the bedchamber and collapsed onto the crudely built bench by the hearth. Amid her joy and physical exhaustion, a sense of emptiness and longing for her own dead child overwhelmed her. Martha buried her face in her hands and sobbed. *Will I have a life of childlessness? Will Mary's children be the only children I will cradle to my bosom?*

Chapter Six
Crisis

Boston, Massachusetts, May 1636

Every Monday afternoon Martha Clarke and Mary Dyer hurried to Anne Hutchinson's home for her weekly meetings of those searching for the truth. Occasionally, The Reverend John Cotton joined them and added another perspective to the discussion. Martha and Mary were amazed at how often Reverend Cotton reinforced what Anne was teaching, even when she disagreed with Reverend Wilson's sermon of the week.

The second Monday of May a distinguished-looking family sat in the front alongside John Cotton when Martha and Mary arrived at the Hutchinson home. The sisters exchanged questioning glances, but said nothing.

After the opening prayer Anne said, "I would like everyone to meet my brother-in-law, John Wheelwright, my sister Mary, along with their five children. They recently arrived from Lincolnshire where he had been a minister for ten years. He will be a great asset to the colony and those who are searching for the true path to God. Until now, we have only had one minister in Boston who preached the pure truth, and that is Reverend Cotton. Now that Reverend Wheelwright is among us, he will add more strength and power to the ministry in our colony and to

The Reverend John Wheelwright
(c. 1592 - 1679)

[85]

the Natives around us. Until now, the Puritan clergy considered the Natives an inconvenience and were not interested in converting them to Christianity."

Reverend Cotton stood and stepped to the front of the room beside Anne. "God uses many different messengers with different gifts and talents to proclaim the gospel. I want to put my personal endorsement on the ministry of Reverend Wheelwright and the message of the grace of God he preaches."

Words of support and encouragement spread throughout the gathering. Reverend Wheelwright stood and faced the group. "I want to thank you all for your warm welcome. My family is looking forward to getting to know each one of you. If you would indulge me for a few minutes, I would like to share some of my experiences and religious thinking that brought us to Boston."

Martha and Mary sat spellbound while Reverend Wheelwright told of the work of God in Boston in Lincolnshire. Afterwards he shared specific news of family and friends the settlers had left behind when they left England and joined the Massachusetts Bay Colony.

Martha sat in amazement. *With so many Puritans from Boston in Lincolnshire coming to Massachusetts there will soon be more Puritans in the New World than England.*

The minutes turned into hours. The entire group sat spellbound, listening to Reverend Wheelwright's invigorating words. Martha thought of the clothes needing to be washed and the garden needing to be weeded, but quickly pushed those thoughts aside. *Work will always be there, but I rarely will have an opportunity to listen to such a fascinating speaker. I find myself agreeing with him even more than I do*

Reverend Cotton. She surveyed the faces of the other women in the group. *I am certain they also appreciate a few hours away from the drudgery of their daily chores.*

When the shadows began to lengthen in Anne Hutchinson's crowded home, Reverend Wheelwright ended his speech. One-by-one the guests thanked him and went their separate ways. Each complained about how much work they had to do when they got home and how unhappy their husbands would be about their being gone all afternoon.

Mary and Martha turned toward their homes on Summer Street. The streets soon emptied while each woman rushed to her own home to prepare the evening meal. Martha studied the peaceful smile on her sister's face. "You looked like you approved of what Reverend Wheelwright was saying this afternoon."

Mary smiled and nodded. "He was captivating. He made the gospel easy to understand. I do not know why the clergy tries to make it sound complicated and claim they are the only ones who can understand the ways of God. Someday I hope I will be able to comprehend God's love well enough to teach like Anne Hutchinson does."

Martha laughed. "Sister, you have always been a dreamer. However, I agree he was fascinating to listen to. I am beginning to understand what all the controversy is about concerning the gospel of works versus the gospel of grace. I used to think the controversy was merely an intellectual argument. Now I understand what a person believes can affect the way they live. The way Reverend John Wilson and most of the other clergy talk always seems harsh and judgmental. In their way of thinking, I could never be good enough to go to Heaven. "

"What Anne Hutchinson, and now her brother-in-law, teaches is what I crave to hear. I can never get enough of it," Mary said. "I want to experience more of God and be able to communicate with Him directly. Surely, God must live within people today and not just in the lives of the prophets in Bible times."

Only a slight ray of orange light remained in the western sky. The scent of burning oak from the fireplaces permeated the surrounding street when they passed. Martha increased her pace. "I appreciate listening to the discussions, but with so much work needing to be done in building homes, tending families, raising crops, and earning a living, I do not see how anyone can take the time to sit around and argue the finer points of religion. In the end, will it make any difference?"

"Sincere religious discussions and searching can make a big difference in people's lives," Mary protested, then took a deep breath. "I am excited about what God is doing through Anne. Many of the church and government officials may not like it, but the common people are attracted to what she has to say. I am certain eventually; you will feel the excitement of what Anne and her brother-in-law are talking about. It's more than merely an intellectually stimulating discussion."

Throughout the following weeks, Martha pondered the strange, yet exhilarating, ideas she had heard since she had become friends with Anne Hutchinson. They constantly dominated her thoughts while she went about her daily chores. Finally, late one Saturday afternoon after finishing her work, she walked to her friend's home on High Street.

Martha rapped on the heavy wooden door and within seconds, Anne opened it and greeted her with a smile. "Martha, come in. What brings you over this time of day?"

Martha stepped into the Hutchinson's large home, one of the few in Boston that had a loft for the children to sleep, plus an oversized fireplace. She marveled at the wooden plank floor Will Hutchinson had recently built to replace the dirt one. "I hope I am not interrupting anything. I have a few questions I wanted to ask you."

"I was cleaning turnips and carrots for supper," Anne said. "Sit here at the table with me; the girls can finish. It is more important for me to be about God's work."

Martha slid onto the wooden bench on the north side of the table. She smiled when she recognized one of the tables her husband had constructed with his own hands. She visualized what mealtime must be like at their household with all their children gathered around the long table at the same time. She thought of the work it must take to prepare meals for such a large family and marveled how Anne organized each of her children's tasks to contribute to such a lively household.

"Anne," she began hesitantly. "I have been listening to you teach for many months now, and am beginning to understand what you are saying, but I am getting more and more confused with what is happening in the colonies. A lot of hostilities are growing and many do not make sense to me."

Anne smiled. "There is a good reason it does not make sense to you. It does not make sense to any intelligent, clear thinking person. Many silly rumors and superstitions are being spread about town and the sad thing is people actually believe them."

Martha shook her head with disgust. "I must be too busy or ignorant to hear or comprehend them. My sister seems to understand, but she is not able to explain them in a way I can understand."

Anne smiled. "Which rumors are you referring to? There are stories the end of the world is coming, the Roman Catholic secret agents are plotting to undermine the colony, and boatloads of heretics are intending an invasion to massacre the clergy, and even a story of an 'American Jezebel' who will appear in Boston."

Martha laughed. "Those are ridiculous. How could anyone take them seriously? And what is the American Jezebel supposed to do?"

A serious expression spread across Anne's face. "Some are saying a woman as wicked as the biblical queen by the same name, will be raised up by Satan to overthrow the churches and the government of the colony."

Martha could not mask her amusement. "How could that happen? Women are not even allowed to speak or vote in the church or government."

"It does not make a particle of sense to me either." Anne's shoulders slumped. "The silly thing is some are even saying I am that American Jezebel."

Martha and Randall Clarke sat peacefully at their kitchen table enjoying their evening meal. Martha had spent most of the day preparing a venison stew and fresh baked bread to help lift her husband's fatigue after the long day he spent in the nearby woods felling trees. She was grateful the neighbor's working steers were getting used to their yolks and were now better trained than the first time Randall used them to drag the logs back to their house. He was not nearly as frustrated with them at the end of a day.

While the Clarkes were finishing the last bites of their stew, Martha reached across the table and took her husband's hand. "Randall, you know I did not want to go to church when Reverend Wilson is preaching, but I heard the congregation invited John Wheelwright to be one of their pastors." She hesitated and took a deep breath. "I would like to go with you this Sunday and hear him preach. I have agreed with what he taught on Mondays during the meetings at Anne Hutchinson's and I am certain his sermons will be an encouragement for both of us."

Randall smiled and squeezed her hand. "I have always shared your frustrations with the church. We simply approached it in a different way. I do not want to be like the Puritan men who insist their wife and family does exactly what they say. I want you to feel free to make your own decisions. I would be honored to have you accompany me tomorrow. I haven't had time to hear John Wheelwright speak yet, but I have heard many good things about him."

The next day, the cold late fall winds snapped at the Clarkes' noses and cheeks while they walked to First Church of Boston. Martha kept her hands tightly at her side to prevent the wind from whipping her skirt and exposing the calves of her legs. She smiled and nodded to her friends and neighbors who joined them on the dusty street. When they reached the church, Randall went to the men's side while she found a seat in the back on the women's side. Five pews ahead of her she saw Anne Hutchinson with her children.

Martha continued scanning the women's section, and she spotted her sister, Mary, holding little Samuel. How she wished she had seen her before taking a place alone. In the silence of the moment, Martha bowed her head and prayed until a rustling of robes and heavy footsteps caught her attention.

She looked up and could scarcely believe her eyes. The Reverend John Wilson was stepping to the pulpit. Her muscles tightened when she read the traditional prayers from the dirt-stained prayer book and listened to the scripture reading. She knew she would not like what he had to say and tried her best not to listen to the sermon, but bits and pieces of it still invaded her consciousness.

"We must work hard to please God if we want to go to Heaven.

We must discipline those in our midst in order to protect the holiness and purity of our church and keep each other on the path to Heaven.

Church discipline is the wall that protects churches from the corruption of the world.

In spite of the practices in England, no Puritan can take communion in our church or have their children baptized until they officially join a Massachusetts church.

Women must be obedient to their husbands."

Martha watched in amazement when Anne Hutchinson stood and walked out of the service carrying her newborn and followed by her other twelve children. Martha's shock turned to horror when her sister rose and followed Anne from the church carrying baby Samuel. Slowly, other women who attended Anne's meetings took courage and followed them down the aisle. *What should I do? I agree with what they are doing, but is it worth risking the discipline of the church to demonstrate my disapproval? What is going to happen to those who publicly demonstrate their displeasure?* Martha began to tremble when the words of condemnation and fear continued to echo from the pulpit in an even louder pitch.

"I realize this congregation invited John Wheelwright to be another pastor at this church. Many of you came today, not to worship God, but to hear him preach. The minority who invited Reverend Wheelwright were not aware of a church rule requiring all actions of the church be unanimous. The clergy was not properly consulted and he will not be preaching until this matter is resolved."

Confusion and rumors spread rapidly throughout Boston. Did the women commit blasphemy by walking out on The Reverend John Wilson's sermon? Martha refused to attend the meetings at Anne's house for several weeks following the walkout. Torn between the fear of church discipline and frustration with her own lack of convictions, Martha felt she could not face those who appeared firm in their beliefs and were able to stand for them no matter the risk.

Late one freezing November afternoon, while the wind blew the last of the dried leaves to the ground a loud knock at the Clarke's door startled Martha. Puzzled, she hurried to open it and found herself face-to-face with Anne Hutchinson. "Anne, come in out of the cold and warm yourself. May I heat some goat's milk to help warm you?"

Anne stepped into the Clarke's simple home, removed her mittens, and took off her coat. "Thank you, I would like that very much," she said. "It was colder than I thought when I left home."

Without hesitation, Anne took a seat by the fireplace to warm herself and got right to the reason of her visit, while Martha poured milk into a small skillet over the open flame. "You haven't been attending our meetings on Monday afternoon since many of us walked out of the church services. Is there a reason?"

Martha took a deep breath. She searched for the right words. How could she explain her confusion to the woman who appeared to have a direct link to God? Martha poured the warm milk into the cups, handed it to her guest, and took the bench opposite her. Fragmented thoughts ran through her mind. She measured her words carefully. "To be honest, I do not think I am a person of strong convictions like you and Mary. I am afraid of the church discipline. I am hearing more and more stories of people being thrown into prison and whipped on the Boston Commons."

Anne reached out and patted Martha's hand. "Someday you will experience what I have been talking about. You do not have to be good enough or prove anything to be accepted by God. You do not need to fight the religious battles when you are not ready. God will give you courage when it is necessary and not before."

Tears of relief began flooding down Martha's cheeks. "Thank you," she murmured, choking back sobs. "Thank you so much. Those are the exact words I needed to hear."

A sense of warmth emanated from Anne. "Martha, you are much stronger than you think. You must carry on in your unrecognized strength."

Gradually Martha calmed herself. "What ever happened to your brother-in-law and his family? It was extremely unfair John Wilson would not let him be pastor at First Church of Boston."

"Governor Winthrop assigned John Wheelwright to the Mount Wollaston Church which is ten miles south of here." Anne took a deep breath and forced a smile. "John found a simple cabin in the area for his family. Will and I along with our older children helped them move their few belongings to turn the cabin into a home. I know my brother-in-law. He'll be able to preach the gospel wherever he is."

"But what about you? Will you be given church discipline for showing your disapproval to Reverend Wilson and walking out of church?" Martha asked.

Anne wrapped her cold hands tightly around the mug and took another sip of milk before continuing. "God will protect me from their darts of evil. Last week several ministers held a conference with Reverend Cotton, me, and several members of the Boston church who supported me. Reverend Cotton took an extremely contrary viewpoint from me." Anne breathed deeply. She set her jaw while a pained expression spread across her face. "After all this time I thought he was a supporter, he now claims he does not agree with much of my doctrine. One of the other ministers even said I was 'a woman not only difficult in her opinions, but also of an intemperate spirit'."

Martha shook her head sadly. *The importance of standing up for what one considers right instead of running from all conflict is beginning to make sense.*

Some issues are too important to ignore. "It must have been difficult to listen to their absurdities."

"Their words were not nearly as bad as what the General Court did." Anne leaned across the table and lowered her voice. "Upon the clergy's request, the court dismissed from the church everyone who is closely linked with me. This even included my dear husband."

Martha gasped. "Anne, I am frightened for you. What will they do to you next? You have a family to care for."

Eight weeks later, Martha Clarke returned to the meetings held by Anne Hutchinson with new insight and understanding, confident she was gaining the strength of her convictions others seemed to have. Her conversations with her sister took on more meaning and depth. She marveled that while she had tried to avoid conflict, her sister had embraced the same discord and grown from it.

One afternoon while Martha was helping her sister with her baby, Mary said to her, "Martha, you must come with me to the Fast Day Celebration. It is going to be extra meaningful this year. After all the controversy last month, Reverend John Cotton asked John Wheelwright to speak."

Martha cradled Mary's baby even more tightly in her arms. Holding her nephew helped heal her yearning for her own baby who was lying in the cold ground of the church graveyard. "I have never paid attention to the Fast Day Celebrations in England and I did not realize they held them here in Boston. I am not sure what it is all about."

Mary picked up her knitting from a nearby basket where she sat and continued working on a scarf for her husband. She studied her sister's tired face. "It is supposed to be the reverse of Thanksgiving Day. On a Fast Day, the entire community is supposed to cease its daily work and go to church to repent and pray collectively for peace and order, civic health, and an end to sin and dissension. The clergy believe God protects those who obey His rules, and they encourage people to fast in order to avoid God's terrible judgment on those who do evil. After all the controversy in the General Court over Anne Hutchinson's teachings, they proclaimed a Fast Day for January 19th in the hopes of creating reconciliation and unity in the colony."

Martha shook her head. "I am not interested in hearing any more about God's judgment. I want to hear more about God's love. I would like to listen to John Wheelwright, but none of the other ministers."

"In that case, I will come by your house and we can walk to the church together," Mary suggested.

At the official Fast Day service, Martha cradled her nephew in her arms while she and her sister slipped into the back of the church. A few moments later, Martha observed Anne Hutchinson entering with her daughters and went straight to the front row. A few moments later, she noticed Will Hutchinson and the older boys come in the men's entrance. She scanned the men's section until she located Randall and William Dyer. Fearful others would see her looking at the men's section; she lowered her head in prayer and did not raise it until she heard movement at the front of the church.

After the traditional prayers and scripture readings, Reverend Wheelwright stepped to the pulpit. "Brothers and sisters," he began.

Martha's eyes widened. *This is the first I have heard a minister address the congregation with the greeting 'brothers and sisters' rather than simply 'brethren.'* She listened attentively while Reverend Wheelwright interspersed stories of Lydia, Deborah, Rebekah and several other women of the Bible into his sermon. *In all my years attending church services, this is the first time I have heard any minister credit a woman with public power. Perhaps someday they will allow Anne Hutchinson to teach the gospel in a public place.*

After two hours of sleeping nearly motionless in her arms, baby Samuel became restless and Martha handed him to his mother. Without the child in her arms, she concentrated even more on the words of the tall minister with curly hair, a mustache, and goatee. While John Wheelwright became more intense, Martha could scarcely believe the words she was hearing.

"It is important for the congregation to understand John Wilson and most of his fellow ministers fail to properly present Christ in doctrine and worship and are leading their flocks to damnation. Those among us who wish to return Christ into our presence must prepare for spiritual combat."

A subtle gasp was heard throughout the congregation. Before anyone could object, John Wheelwright gave a brief benediction and hurried from the church. Not knowing what to do, the surprised congregation followed him into the street while the other ministers watched in shock.

When the Fast Day service was over, Mary and Martha went directly to Anne Hutchinson's house.

Before they had a chance to knock on the door, Anne stepped outside.

"I am glad you came," she said. "I wanted to talk with you. Let's talk under the tree so the children will not hear us."

The three women walked silently to the large elm tree in the back of the house. When they were out of view of passersby, Mary said, "Reverend Wheelwright gave a very courageous sermon today. What do you think will happen next?"

"John has never been afraid to preach the truth," Anne said.

Uneasiness overcame Martha. "What do you think the Reverend Wilson and the other clergy will do? It was obvious they were extremely upset."

"I am expecting they will increase their surveillance on John and me and we will have spies at our regular Monday meetings the same as the king sent spies to the Puritan meetings in England. It wouldn't surprise me that he will be brought before the General Court the same as Roger Williams was."

"So what are you going to do?" Mary asked. "No one is going to speak openly at the meetings any more."

Anne smiled. "This is only a mild setback. God is still in control. We can have secret meetings on Tuesday mornings and only those who are personally invited can attend. Will the two of you go to the homes of the regular attendees and tell them our plans?"

Martha and Mary exchanged glances. "We would be proud to," Mary said. "Your meetings must go on as before. They mean too much to the women of Boston to stop them."

The unrest in Boston continued to increase until the middle of March. The people on the street took sides and argued about the freedom of speech and religion and the power of the church and government.

Just as Anne had predicted, John Wheelwright was order to appear before the General Court. On the day of the trial, the Hutchinsons, Dyers, and Clarkes along with Mary Wheelwright took seats directly behind the defendant. Martha smiled as she thought of Bridget Hutchinson taking care of the younger Hutchinson children along with the Wheelwright's children, and little Samuel Dyer at the Hutchinson home. *Bridget is going to make a fine mother someday. She is very quick thinking in planning activities to keep the littlest ones occupied.*

Reverend John Wheelwright's expression was firm and unflustered when he was led into the courtroom. He listened attentively to the charges and his answers to the magistrates were abrupt and concise. Martha could scarcely believe the accusations being heaped upon him. With each new charge she became even more convinced of the correctness of his and Anne's teachings as opposed to what the Puritan clergy taught.

By noontime, the head magistrate's face was red with anger. "John Wheelwright, we can no longer tolerate your teachings or disrespect for clergy or public officials. You refuse to abide by the civil laws or the basic tenants of the Christian faith as taught by the established church. Therefore, the General Court has no choice but to find you guilty of sedition and contempt of the civil authority for preaching a contentious sermon on a day the court had called for reconciliation. We will defer your sentencing until the next meeting. In the meantime you are forbidden to teach or preach anywhere within the Massachusetts Bay Colony."

Martha watched John Wheelwright walk stoically out of the courtroom. Confusion engulfed her as she joined a small group of Wheelwright supporters in the City Commons, eager to know the details. *I think the magistrates postponed his sentencing because they were afraid of all Reverend Wheelwright's supporters,"* she whispered to Mary.

As predicted, Anne Hutchinson was the most animated in defense of her brother-in-law. "We can never stand for this. You must keep preaching the gospel regardless of what the church officials do. When the Church of England censured you in 1632, it did not stop you; you simply came to Massachusetts and kept proclaiming the gospel of grace. Be of good courage and keep preaching wherever you may be."

Hearing his sister's words, John Wheelwright set his jaw and raised his hand to address the crowd. "Anne is right. Nothing will stop me from preaching the gospel. I may be forced to leave Massachusetts like Roger Williams was, but that is not defeat. God will use this situation to increase my mission field."

Few knew what to say and murmuring spread throughout the crowd. Finally, William Dyer shouted, "We can't let the court's action stand. We will start a petition protesting your conviction. The ministers and magistrates need to understand the support you have among the people."

The crowd cheered William Dyer's statement, but John Wheelwright raised his hand for silence. "I thank all of you for your enthusiastic support. I am certain hundreds would sign such a petition but they will only accept the signatures of 'freemen,' not women, indentured servants, or new arrivals to the colony. Only a small minority have a voice in the church or the government. Mark my words, with all the controversy, church membership and attendance will decline. Less money will come in and the clergy will have to use different tactics to support themselves and the church. They may become desperate enough to resort to demanding unbearable taxes. If you choose to take action, you must be prepared for their response."

Each time Martha came to help her sister with her housework or care for the baby, she noticed Mary becoming paler and having less energy. Knowing her sister was one who rarely complained, she often felt she had to force a response from her.

One Saturday afternoon while they were making soap together, Martha looked her sister straight in the eye and said, "Mary, what is wrong? You have been sick and vomiting for days on end. It has to be more than the normal stomach disorder. I do not mind helping with Samuel, but I do not like to see you suffer."

Mary took a deep breath and sighed. "I think I am with child again, but this time it feels different. I wonder if something is wrong."

"It must be the normal early months' discomfort," Martha tried to assure her. "In a few weeks, I am certain you will have the normal new mother glow."

Chapter Seven
Monster Child

Boston, August 1636

Every opportunity possible, Martha Clarke cared for her neighbor's children or her nephew, but nothing filled the emptiness for the baby she lost. Her happy face masked the hidden pain. She remembered the fun she and Mary had when they had laid side-by-side on their bed in London and shared their childish dreams. Would she ever be able to pass the same simple joy and contentment on to her own children?

One late summer afternoon while Martha was visiting Anne Hutchinson, the topic again turned to Anne's family. "Martha, you cared for the children extremely well while we were onboard the ship. I was wondering if you would teach my children to read. I have been too busy teaching adults, that I have neglected teaching my own children to read. It is vitally important each of them learn to read the Bible for themselves."

Martha hesitated. She had loved reading Bible stories to the children while they were onboard the ship, but she had never considered teaching anyone else. She appreciated her own mother who had insisted her daughters learn to read, while their neighbors were only concerned about educating the boys. "What exactly did you have in mind?"

"My boys are beginning readers and are being encouraged to go to the Latin School," Anne said. "However, the Latin School is designed to teach boys to learn Latin and Greek to prepare them to become

Puritan ministers. My sons do not need to waste their time learning Latin to be godly men. I do not want them to be taught the heresy the Puritans teach."

Anne paced around the room aimlessly before she continued. "I want my daughters to learn alongside my sons. They are equal in God's eyes. Widow James has openings in her Dame School, but she only accepts girls and spends most of the time teaching them cooking, sewing, and embroidering. I want all of my children to learn reading, writing, and numbers. Will and I can teach them basic life skills."

"I do not think I would have trouble teaching them to read and write," Martha said, "but I would have problems teaching arithmetic. I have difficulty remembering my addition and subtraction tables."

Anne smiled. "Don't worry, twelve-year-old Samuel is good at arithmetic, I am certain the two of you could manage teaching the basics to the younger ones."

Little Zuriel toddled up to Martha with his arms uplifted. Martha instinctively reached down and picked him up, then gave him a hug before placing him on her lap. She turned her attention back to Anne. "Do you have any books I can use? I only have my mother's treasured King James Bible. I am concerned it may wear out if I used it with children every day."

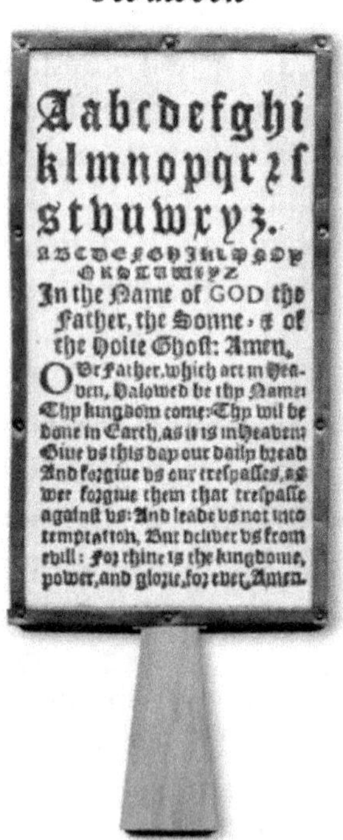

Hornbook

Anne blushed. "I have been able to make three hornbooks late at night after the little ones were asleep. I wanted them to use them to learn their letters, but when they were awake, I was too busy to sit down and work with them. Maybe the older girls can learn their letters by making hornbooks for the younger ones."

A gasp escaped Martha's lips. "How did you make your hornbooks? They are scarce in the colonies."

"Will did an excellent job making a perfect paddle shape and smoothing the wood for me," Anne said with pride. She gazed into the distance. "I had a lot of trouble making parchment myself, but I was able to make a few usable sheets."

"I have never known anyone to make their own parchment, much less a hornbook," Martha said. "How did you do it?"

Anne laughed and wrinkled her nose. "It was rather distasteful at times, but it worked. When the neighbor's goat died, they let me have its skin. I soaked the skin in lime to remove the hair and then washed, dried, stretched, and smoothed it. When it was dried, I wrote on the parchment and laid the parchment on the paddle shaped board Will had prepared. When I was finished I fastened a thin, translucent piece of cow's horn over it to protect the parchment."

"You are totally amazing," Martha said.

"Let me show you how they turned out." Anne went to a wooden box in the corner of the room, took out the three hornbooks, and laid them on the table in front of Martha. "I spent most of my free time last winter copying the letters of the alphabet, the Lord's Prayer, and the Roman numerals onto the hornbook. It is not the best, but I am certain it is clear enough to help them."

Martha picked up each hornbook one-by-one and studied it. "They're beautiful. You have excellent penmanship."

"I planned to make one for each of the children, but I am too busy to finish," Anne said. "I wanted each of them to treasure these and pass them on to their own children."

Martha ran her hands over the smooth surface of one of the hornbooks. "The children will be very proud of these. The cross you made on the top of each one is extremely detailed and should help them keep their minds on God while they're doing their studies."

"Then you will agree to teach them?" Anne persisted.

Martha lowered her eyes. "I am honored you have that much confidence in me. I have never been blessed with children of my own, and yet, you would trust me to help educate yours."

"Thank you. I appreciate your decision," Anne said with satisfaction in her voice. "Now to the details...Each of the children has chores to do in the morning, but if they could come to your house in the afternoon, I am certain you could accomplish a lot in three hours each day."

"That sounds perfect for me. I will have time to finish my chores and still have time to prepare lessons for the children."

"Of course, I expect to compensate you for your efforts," Anne assured Martha. "Since you will be spending your time working with my children, my hired help and I will bake all the bread for you and Randall. I bake bread for my family every other day and will make two extra loaves each time I bake."

Martha could not hide her pleasure. "I am certain Randall will be pleased with our arrangement. Would you like them to start this Monday afternoon?"

Anne scowled. "Of course not. You will not be able to attend the meetings here on Monday afternoon if they did. Let's have their school days be Tuesday through Saturday instead."

Martha readily agreed, said good-bye to Anne and the children, and left the Hutchinson home. While she walked the now familiar streets of Boston, the challenge of what she had just agreed upon began to overwhelm her. *Am I up to the task of educating the children of such a brilliant woman? Does Anne Hutchinson see more strength in me than I do?*

A brisk October wind chilled Mary and Martha and they wrapped their shawls tighter around themselves. The sun was high in the southern sky and their baskets of blueberries were almost full. Suddenly Mary groaned and clutched her stomach.

Martha hurried to her sister's side and took her basket. "What is it? Is the baby coming?"

Mary nodded. "I am not sure. The baby is not due for two months, but I had a very painful cramp. Let's go back to the house so I can lie down."

Martha draped the handle of both baskets over her right arm and wrapped her left arm around her sister. Together they trudged toward the Dyer home. Memories of Martha's own painful labor, delivery, and loss of her baby flashed before her. *Surely, things will go well for Mary. I have suffered enough for the both of us.*

When they arrived in the Dyer home, Mary had a burst of unexplainable energy. "I am feeling much better now. I will help wash the blueberries. I am certain our husbands will enjoy eating them for supper tonight." She filled a large bowl with warm water and emptied one of the baskets of blueberries into the bowl. When she was reaching for the second basket, she paused, grabbed her stomach, and groaned.

"Mary, forget the blueberries, go lie down and I will get Anne Hutchinson." Martha helped her sister into the bedchamber, covered her with a quilt, and brought a cup of cold water from the bucket on the counter. Before leaving, she stoked the embers in the fireplace and added another log.

Dogs barked and children stopped their play to watch Martha clumsily run the narrow streets of Boston. Panting with exhaustion, she pounded on the heavy wooden door to the Hutchinson home.

Within moments, fair-haired Samuel opened the door. His tall, muscular frame was a welcoming sight. An expression of joy spread across his face. "Teacher, it is good to see you. Are we late for school?"

Martha forced a smile. "I am afraid we will not be having school today. My sister may be having her baby. Is your mother at home?"

At those words, Anne Hutchinson appeared in the doorway. "Martha, come in out of the cold, sit down, and rest. Did you say Mary's baby is coming?"

Martha breathed deeply. She felt her heart pounding. "I am afraid so. She has already taken to her bed. The baby is not due for two months, but she is having severe pains."

"I will be right there," Anne said. "Would you fetch Goody Hawkins while I get my things and go on ahead?"

Martha's muscles tightened. She swallowed hard when a lump built in her throat.

Anne placed a comforting hand on Martha's shoulder. "After losing your own baby, I understand your fears, but Goody is not a witch sent from the devil which the Puritan ministers claim. She is a wise woman who listens to God and who may use strange methods to help make childbirth easier for women."

Martha lowered her eyes and her face flushed. "I know what the ministers are saying is silly, but I will never get over the fact she gave me one of her special herbs to ease the pain before my precious Sara was born. She was extremely weak when she was born and died a few days later. Since then, I have not been able to have any more children."

"Put that nonsense out of your mind," Anne instructed with a look of intense compassion in her eyes. "Hurry and get Goody, and I will meet you at Mary's house."

A half hour later, Martha and Goody rushed into the Dyer home. William was sitting by the fireplace entertaining little Samuel. In spite of the tension of the moment, Martha was amazed at the strange, unrelated thoughts bouncing through her mind. *It has been extremely confusing when both Anne and Mary named their first-born sons, Samuel. I do not think Mary thought about how difficult it would be for us when she named her son. At the time, we did not realize how much we would become such fast friends with the Hutchinsons and our lives would become this intertwined.*

Martha gave her nephew a quick hug and her brother-in-law a reassuring smile. "William, why don't you take little Samuel to my house and wait with

Randall? It will be much easier to care for him there. We will let you know when we have any news."

William Dyer said nothing, but nodded in appreciation and reached for a blanket to wrap around his son. Martha reached into a tin and took out six biscuits. She handed one to Samuel and gave the others to William to share later. Samuel smiled and clung to his father's neck when they disappeared through the front door.

When Williams was gone, Martha stepped into the bedchamber. She stopped in horror when she saw the intense expressions on Anne and Goody's faces. "What is wrong with my sister?"

"The baby is turned the wrong way," Anne said, pressing downward on Mary's stomach. "This is going to be a difficult delivery."

Goody lifted a spoonful of herbs along with a strange mixture of a bitter liquid to Mary's lips. Martha grimaced while she watched Goody follow with a cup of water to help wash away the bitter taste in Mary's mouth. Within minutes, Mary relaxed onto her pillow until another painful cramp enveloped her. Goody slipped a wet rag flavored with honey between Mary's teeth for her to bite against when the pain became too intense.

Martha tried to remain calm. She wiped sweat from her sister's brow and held her hand during each labor contraction. Goody continued administering pain relief throughout the day, but several times, Mary fainted from pain and exhaustion. While the shadows deepened, Mary gave an even more intense cry of pain. Gradually they could see two tiny feet and the baby's bottom.

"The baby's coming feet first," Anne said and pushed down on the top of Mary's stomach. "This will harder than we expected."

Martha continued encouraging her sister while she watched Anne and Goody worked quickly to deliver the baby. She waited for a lusty cry from the baby, but there was none. Panic enveloped her when she looked at the baby in Anne's work-weathered hands. Too many things were wrong. The baby had a face, but no skull. The body was twisted and deformed. She looked down at her exhausted sleeping sister, grateful she was not aware of the drama spinning around her.

Tears flowed from Martha's eyes. A wave of nausea overcame her. "How dreadful! Mary must never know how badly deformed her child was. It will break her heart. What can we do?"

Anne cleaned the baby, wrapped her in a white blanket, and laid her in a wooden box. In a calm assuring tone she said, "Martha, this is all in God's hands. Hurry and fetch William. We need to make plans."

Ignoring the uneasiness in her stomach, Martha grabbed her shawl from the hook beside the door and ran home. Tears streamed down her cheeks and sobs of grief and fear shook her body. Never before had the familiar path between the two homes seemed so long. When she burst through the front door, Little Samuel was sleeping on a pile of blankets in front of the fireplace unaware of the crisis the women were facing. Randall and William were relaxing on benches nearby. Randall looked like he was dozing, while William sat idly nearby whittling pegs from a piece of oak.

Rushing into the room, Martha gasped, "William, come quickly. Something is wrong with the baby. Anne needs to see you right away."

William jumped to his feet, grabbed his coat and hat, and followed Martha toward the door. Instinctively, he turned back to his brother-in-law. "Would you watch Samuel while I am gone? This cannot be good...Please pray for Mary."

"Don't worry about Samuel," Randall said. "I will take good care of him and will continue to pray for Mary and the new baby."

Dogs again barked seeing Martha and William running through the darkness. Martha's heart ached from grief and exhaustion. *What will poor Mary do when she learns she does not have a perfect baby like Samuel? What will the ministers do? I have heard the clergy claim a deformed baby is from the devil and it is an indication the mother is a witch.*

When William and Martha arrived back at the Dyer's home, Anne was waiting for them at the front door. She promptly led William into the bedchamber. "Mary has been through a lot tonight. She is not conscious of anything, but I am confident she'll recover in a few days."

William leaned over and kissed his wife lightly on the forehead before turning to the dresser in the corner where his child was lying in a box. Goody and Anne had dressed the baby in a simple white gown Samuel had used when he was born. William looked down, an expression of horror spread across his face. "How can this be? How could something this ugly be a result from the pure love Mary and I have for each other? She will be inconsolable when she finds out her baby did not live. We must never let her know how deformed her baby was." He began pacing aimlessly around the room. Tears of pain and confusion rolled down his cheeks.

Martha began to sob once again. "What are we going to do? What will we tell Mary? How will we bury the baby without the church officials finding out?"

Martha's words hung heavy over the room while the three stood helplessly staring at the child. "I wish I could bury the baby privately," Anne said in a slow, depressed voice. "Sad to say, in Massachusetts a midwife cannot lawfully deliver or bury a child in secret. The clergy are afraid midwives would attempt to hide abortions....They will not even let us baptize babies, even if it is obvious they are near death. At the same time, the clergy claim no one can go to Heaven without first being baptized. It isn't fair to a weak baby or their families."

Martha slumped onto a bench nearby and buried her face in her hands. "It is absurd," she said. "The Boston magistrates do not even trust the women whom their wives desperately depend upon."

William stopped pacing back and forth and turned to Anne and Goody. "After all that has happened in recent weeks, I am certain Governor Winthrop, John Wilson, and the other magistrates and ministers are looking for any faults or missteps they can use to condemn those who do not agree with them. They will interpret this birth as God's punishment against us for challenging Reverend Winthrop and Reverend Wilson's views. Mary will be condemned for the malformed baby. We need to bury the baby right away before word spreads."

Anne remained quiet for several seconds before looking upward. An expression of peace spread across her face. "William, you are exactly right...Wait here. I will go to John Cotton and see what he thinks we should do. He may have opposed my brother-in-law and me politically, but surely, he will remember our longstanding friendship and will help us. We have already been through much together."

Anne washed her hands, tied on her bonnet, and disappeared out the front door while the others exchanged blank, confused stares. William sat on the side of the bed, took his wife's hand, and held it gently in his own while Mary stirred under the quilt, faintly opened her eyes and closed them, and went back to sleep. Martha's sobs subsided and she remained motionless, lost in her own thoughts and prayers.

Goody Hawkins left the grieving family alone in the bedroom and tried to busy herself with routine tasks around the house. She stoked the fire, added more wood to the flames, and removed the ashes. Next, she swept the floor, dusted the furniture, and straightened the dishes in the shelf.

Minutes seemed like hours before they heard heavy footsteps outside. Anne Hutchinson thrust open the front door followed closely by Reverend John Cotton. They did not speak when Anne led the minister into the bedchamber. Reverend Cotton looked into the box on the dresser and shook his head. His eyes widened, and his jaw dropped. He turned to William. "I am sorry. I have never seen such a pitifully deformed child." He looked at the sleeping mother, back at the baby, and then to William once again. "I am concerned the news of Mary's baby will fall into the hands of the Boston magistrates and minister. I would advise burying her secretly."

"But we have no rights to bury a child in the church cemetery without clergy approval," William said.

Reverend Cotton studied Anne Hutchinson's pleading eyes. He turned to William and said, "Maybe I can help Anne with the burial, but it must not be discussed beyond the confines of this room." One at a time, he gazed at each person in the room and did not take his eyes off them until they nodded in agreement. "If we all agree to silence in the matter, I will help bury the baby in a far back corner of the cemetery."

"I will be forever grateful for your assistance," William said. "I will stay with Mary in case she needs help or asks any questions. There is a shovel on the side of the house, if you would like to use it. If anyone in the colony asks about Mary, we will tell them that the baby came prematurely and died."

Martha's hand trembled as she wrapped her newborn niece in a pillowcase and handed her to the minister. She hurried to the side of the house and found William's shovel. Together she, Reverend Cotton, Anne Hutchinson, and Goody Hawkins walked nervously toward the graveyard of the Boston Church. Faint lights flickered through the windows of the houses along the way. Fortunately, few people were on the streets.

Fear consumed Martha. *What if we meet the watchmen who patrol the streets every night? Would they ask questions and report Reverend Cotton to the Magistrates? Would they report Mary to the clergy?*

When they reached the graveyard, the foursome stayed in the shadows until they reached the far northwest corner behind a large elm tree. Tears ran down Martha's cheeks while she held her niece and watched Reverend Cotton dig her grave. *We will always be grateful to Reverend Cotton for the risk he is talking on behalf of Anne and Mary. Surely, we will be able to trust each other for life. October 17, 1637 will be a day I will never forget.*

The remainder of the week, Martha cared for little Samuel and helped William care for his grief-stricken wife. Whenever Mary asked about her baby, they gently explained the deformity of the child without going into detail. They were careful not to mention the seriousness of the event. Goody Hawkins and Anne Hutchinson visited Mary daily and brought food for the family.

On Sunday, Goody arrived at the Dyer home a few minutes after Martha. Noting the discouragement in Martha's countenance, Goody said, "You need a break and a few hours of rest and solace. " I will stay with Mary if you and William want to go to church service this morning."

Martha hesitated. It had been weeks since she had attended a worship service at the First Church in Boston. *Maybe it will bring relief. The only consolation I can possibly get is from the Lord.* She looked at Goody and then to her brother-in-law. "That sounds like a good idea. If you wish, I would like to take Samuel with me. It brings me such comfort holding him in my arms."

William smiled. "Of course you may take Samuel with you. I will walk with you to your house and ask Randall if he would like to join us."

Arriving home, Martha found her husband sitting by the fireplace with a blank stare on his face.

Martha took his hand, her voice intense. "Randall, I know I haven't been going to church lately, but it is been a difficult week for everyone. William and I would like to attend the worship service and wondered if you would join us?"

"Of course," Randall said without hesitation. "Please give me a couple minutes to wash my hands."

Within twenty minutes, Martha, Randall, and William Dyer arrived at the First Church in Boston. The men entered through the men's entrance while Martha followed the women though a door several feet away.

She slipped quietly into the back row of the church and nodded politely to those around her.

Near the front, Anne Hutchinson sat in her customary pew with her younger children. *How can Anne keep coming back to the church after all the mean, evil things the clergy has said about her?*

Martha surveyed the men's section and sighted Will Hutchinson sitting with his older sons. William Dyer was now seated in the fifth row, alongside her husband. How she longed to hold Randall's hand and feel the strength of his presence beside her.

Martha relaxed while she listened to the familiar scriptures and prayers. Truly this was the healing balm she needed to soothe the tension that had engulfed her body ever sense the stillbirth of her sister's baby.

The sight of Reverend John Wilson stepping to the pulpit caused her to tighten her muscles once again. *Maybe it was not a good idea for me to attend church today, after all. Reverend Wilson always seems to stir up fear and confusion within me.* Martha gritted her teeth when she heard his words of fear and condemnation. She longed to hear the words of God's love Anne Hutchinson talked about in her meetings.

Near the end of the sermon, her frustration with the preaching of condemnation turned to horror.

"The city of Boston has received an admonition from the Lord. One of the local residents named Mary Dyer, who became addicted to heresy, produced a monster in the place of a female child. God has intervened and pointed His finger at this woman at the height of her sinful opinions. May everyone in the colony recognize her sin in judgment and avoid such ideas lest God visit you with this same judgment. We must do all we can to document this evil and purge our city from the heresy that brought this upon us."

Martha choked back a gasp. She looked across the room and saw a pained expression on William Dyers face. Her heart pounded when several men nodded in agreement. *Thankfully, Mary is too weak to be here and is spared listening to this outrage. We thought things were bad in England, but the hatred and misunderstanding in this supposed 'city on the hill' is becoming unbearable. How can we ever escape it?*

Chapter Eight
The Trial

Are you sure the fire is hot enough to melt the tallow?" Anne Hutchinson asked. "Or should we add more wood?"

Martha peered into the kettle hung over the open flame in the Huchinson's backyard. "Yes, the tallow is beginning to melt around the edges." She wrinkled her nose. "I wish we had enough bayberries to make bayberry wax instead of having to use animal fat for the candles. When we burn the tallow candles, it smells up the house."

A cold fall wind blew around the women and Mary moved closer to the flames. "As soon as the tallow is completely melted, I will begin dipping the wicks."

Within minutes, the tallow was ready and the women began working. Even though candle making was their least desired task, working together made it tolerable and provided time for the friends to catch up on the latest news of their families and the colony.

Mary was unusually quiet while the other two talked about the activities of the Hutchinson children. Finally, she said, "ever since John Wheelwright was found guilty of sedition and contempt of civil authority, the clergy seems to be on a search for heretics. Everyone is under suspicion."

Anne shook her head sadly. "The clergy have decided that anyone who preaches the 'covenant of grace' must be a heretic and they are scrutinizing everything I say. They are even evaluating Reverend Cotton's sermons and teachings for signs of heresy."

Mary dipped a wick into the tallow, when it was completely coated; she pulled it out to harden for a few seconds. "I heard the magistrates are afraid the most recent immigrants might be John Wheelwright's followers from England and made passengers on the most recent ship from Lincolnshire disavow Wheelwright's doctrine or return to England within four months."

Anger rose in Anne. "It is hard for me to believe that could possibly happen in Boston, but it is true. I simply cannot understand how the officials admit blasphemers and profane persons to Massachusetts, but not accept true Christians. I must do something to make the clergy see the error of their ways."

Mary shook her head and took a deep breath. "I hope you are careful. William told me he heard nearly a quarter of the population of Boston have attended the religious meetings in your home. That is probably more than attend church on Sunday. The clergy are certain you are teaching heresy and Governor Winthrop may be developing a case against you."

Anne laid another piece of wood to the flame. A furrow on her forehead deepened. "I have not heard about formal changes, but it wouldn't surprise me. I will deal with the charge if it happens. In the meantime, I will continue teaching the covenant of grace and the love of God."

Just then, Martha looked up. "Shh...shh. That is one of the magistrate's wives passing by. We do not want to let her know we are doing anything but making candles on a cold afternoon."

The three women waved a greeting to the passerby, but the magistrate's wife looked the other way and continued down the street. "That was one lesson learned," Martha said. "From now on we will not speak of anything controversial while we are outside."

The remainder of the afternoon the women continued dipping and re-dipping the wicks into the hot tallow. When the candles were the desired size, they took them into the house and hung them to dry on a cord strung between two chairs. By the end of the day, they had made enough candles to last the three families throughout the winter months.

Word of pending charges spread quickly among Anne Hutchinson's supporters. When Mary Dyer heard the news about the charges against her dear friend, she wrapped Samuel in a blanket and rushed to her sister's home. Breathing heavily, she flung open the front door. "Martha...Martha. Have you heard what happened?"

Martha Clarke laid her mending in the wooden box beside her, rose from the bench in front of the hearth, and hurried to her sister's side. "What happened? I have been working inside all day and haven't talked with anyone."

"The Massachusetts General Court is going to try Anne Hutchinson for sedition November second in Shepard's Newtowne meetinghouse." Mary slumped onto a bench and tried to regain her breath. She had not run this fast since the birth of her stillborn baby. "Those charges are totally unfounded and ridiculous. Some are even talking of charging her with heresy...Martha, I must go to Anne Hutchinson's trial. She needs my support and encouragement."

Martha shook her head in disbelief. "Charged with sedition? What does that mean? She has not done anything wrong. "

Mary sighed and set Samuel on the floor. "It means Governor Winthrop is charging her with being 'one who troubles the peace of the commonwealth and churches'."

"That is the craziest thing I have ever heard." Martha gasped and continued. "All she does is hold meetings in her own home."

"Because the charges are absurd is why I must attend her trial." Mary studied her sister's shocked, puzzled expression. "Before I can consider going, I must find someone to care for Samuel. He is much too small for a lengthy trip. Would you care for him or do you know anyone who would be able to tend him while I am gone?"

Martha hesitated. "Do you think you are strong enough to make the long trip? Riding horseback can be extremely tiresome, especially if the winter winds begin blowing."

Unconcerned about his mother's conversation, Samuel toddled toward the burning embers in the hearth. Mary rushed to retrieve him and move him to another part of the room. She returned to her seat and smiled at her sister. "Martha, you needn't fuss over me. I will be fine. Since it is over three miles, William said he would drive a wagon to Newtowne for any of Anne's supporters who would like to attend. We will take a lot of blankets and fill the bed of the wagon with loose hay to keep warm. William has already talked with one of the farmers in the area who said we could sleep in his barn, if necessary."

"You know how much I love caring for Samuel, but I would also like to go to Newtowne to the trial."

Martha hesitated. She studied the quizzical look on her sister's face. "I know it sounds strange coming from me because I have never liked conflict. However, I am slowly becoming convinced some issues are important enough I need to take a definite stand, regardless of the price. Supporting Anne Hutchinson is one of those issues. If transportation is available, I want to go to Newtowne with you. Maybe we could get Goodwife Lancaster to care for Samuel."

Mary beamed and gave her sister a hug. Tears gathered in her eyes. "Having you attend the trial would mean a great deal to me. I would like nothing better than to share the experience with you. I will stop at the Lancaster's on my way home and see if she would be willing to care for Samuel while we are gone."

"Please explain what is going on," Martha said. "I am getting tired of the church and the magistrates treating people cruelly without a good reason. I want to do something to help, but I do not know what. Going to Anne's trial is the least I can do."

Mary's face reddened and her lips pursed. "The entire conflict these last few months is making me angry. The bottom line is both Anne Hutchinson and Reverend Wheelwright are accused of being heretics...Of course, their definition of being a heretic is very different from mine. William was able to get fifty-eight signatures from freemen in challenging the court's right to try a case of conscience before the church hears it. Of course, the petition in support of Wheelwright angered the magistrates and they immediately rejected it. I wish it had more signatures, but indentured servants, women, and non-members of the church are not permitted to sign petitions or have any other voice in the colony. Many freemen were afraid to sign it because of religious and political retributions. If everyone were treated equally, my guess would be three fourths of the population of Boston would sign the petition."

The first day of November, twenty supporters of Anne Hutchinson huddled together in the loft of Yeoman Leonard's barn with three horses, six cows, and three hogs below. The straw offered minimal comfort from the howling winds outside, but provided no comfort from the stench below. Sleep eluded Martha. She lay awake listening to others tossing in the hay, obviously not sleeping either. She was certain their lack of sleep was not only from their physical discomfort, but also from their concern for the outcome of the looming trial.

At the first ray of sunlight, William Dyer climbed down the ladder from the loft, found a pail, and brought water from a creek nearby for the supporters to drink and refresh themselves. One by one, they walked a few yards to the Leonard's outhouse behind their simple cabin home. After they finished eating a quick breakfast, the supporters climbed into the back of the Dyer's wagon. A cold wind blew around them as the horses pulled the heavy load across the frozen ground. The barrenness of the landscape matched the foreboding in their spirits.

When they neared the town, William stopped his wagon under a large elm tree at the edge of Newtowne and turned to the passengers. "I think it would be better if we separated here and entered the meetinghouse in groups of two or three. We do not want our numbers to be apparent to the magistrates. The meetinghouse is in the center of town next to the Commons. You should not have any trouble finding it. We can gather back at this site when the General Court session is over."

The men jumped from the wagon first and turned to help the women. Some began walking north right away, while others hung back until the next group was out of sight. When Martha Clarke arrived at the meetinghouse, she separated from the women with whom she was walking and stood idly in the back of the building near the magistrates' entrance hoping to hear any news of the proceedings. In a few minutes, Governor Winthrop approached the back entrance with Deputy Governor Thomas Dudley, both wearing a white periwig and a black robe. Martha slipped along the side of the building hoping she could hear their conversation.

"I intend these trials to be short," Governor Winthrop said. "The longer the trials last, the more time the heretics will have to stir up supporters."

Thomas Dudley's eyes appeared hard and his facial muscles firm with his lips tense and turned downward. "You are exactly right. We have to put a stop to these recent agitations within the church. I expect the trials to result in repentance and acknowledgment of the Court's authority. If not, punitive consequences will be swift and harsh. I would even consider banishment."

The governor nodded, opened the back door, and disappeared. Martha Clarke's knees trembled. *Surely, they would not consider banishing a mother of eleven children from the colony.*

Martha returned to the front of the meetinghouse. Not seeing any of the other Hutchinson supporters, she quietly opened the huge wooden door and took a seat in the far back row. Scanning the crowd, she cringed when she saw her sister in the first row, close to the defendant's table.

After the governor called the court to order. William Coddington, one of the Boston Deputies, rose to his feet. "I demand the April conviction of Reverend John Wheelwright be repealed. Not enough evidence has been presented to convict him."

A unified gasp spread across the courtroom. Martha watched Governor Winthrop's face redden while he pounded his fist on the table and shouted. "John Wheelwright was duly convicted by the court. William Coddington, for even questioning the ruling of this body, I remove you from your position as representative of Boston and demand you leave this courtroom immediately."

Without saying a word, William Coddington set his jaw and walked stoically to the back of the courtroom. Every eye followed him, some with sympathy, and others with contempt.

"Are there other objections before we proceed?" Governor Winthrop silently studied the expressions of the magistrates waiting for an approving nod from each.

Thomas Dudley broke the silence. "I vote to also remove two other Boston deputies, William Aspinwall and Sergeant John Oliver. It has been brought to my attention their signatures were on the Wheelwright petition."

Governor Winthrop stroked his goatee and hesitated. "If that is the case, your point is well taken." He turned to William Aspinwall. "Is it true you signed the Wheelwright petition?"

William Aspinwall stiffened and took a deep breath. "It is."

"It is," John Oliver echoed.

Governor Winthrop's eyes blazed. "You are henceforth removed from your position as deputy, but you are commanded to remain in the courtroom until the court has time to deal with your situation."

Martha's heart sank. Every magistrate and deputy she had hoped would come to Anne Hutchinson's defense was being eliminated from the panel. *Would anyone understand their position and have the courage to speak the truth and defend Anne?*

For three long days, the Hutchinson supporters listened to arguments and confusing debates in the Wheelwright sentencing trial. Prosecutors quoted scripture passages supporting the gospel of works and Wheelwright used scripture to support his position of the gospel of grace. Instead of providing support to John Wheelwright, the petition signed by his supporters became validation that Wheelwright was intentionally stirring up discord within the colony.

After the evidence was presented, Governor Winthrop's face became even sterner. He glared at the defendant. "John Wheelwright, it has been proven without a shadow of a doubt, you have been stirring up dissent and have been preaching heresy throughout the colony. Therefore, you are to be banished from the Massachusetts Bay Colony."

The governor hesitated and looked to the magistrates for their approval. His face softened. "Since winter is coming on, out of our sense of humanity, we will give you an opportunity to stay in the colony until springtime providing you do not preach to anyone in the interim. Do you understand?"

John Wheelwright stiffened his back and set his jaw. "I must obey God rather than man. If God calls me to preach, then I will preach, regardless of where I am."

Governor's Winthrop's face blanched. "I will hear nothing of your intent. The Court hereby orders you to leave the Massachusetts Bay Colony within fourteen days." With those words, the trial of John Wheelwright ended, and he left the courtroom in disgrace.

Anne Hutchinson's supporters sat nervously while the court next turned their attention to the Boston's deputies, John Coggeshall, Sergeant John Oliver, and William Aspinwall. Martha Clarke listened in shock while Aspinwall was sentenced to banishment for 'seditious libel' and ordered to depart Massachusetts by the end of March. She breathed a sigh of relief when the governor announced Coggeshall and Oliver were only to be disenfranchised and warned that if they disturbed the public peace, they, too, would be banished.

At the end of the day, the Hutchinson supporters gathered around John Wheelwright in a nearby house. A sense of gloom hung over the group. Many seemed to be in a state of shock and could not speak. If they banished Wheelwright, what might they do to Anne Hutchinson?

William Dyer was the first to break the silence. "Reverend Wheelwright, what do you plan to do? It is much too cold to travel and no ships will be leaving for Old England until the spring."

John Wheelwright stood and smiled. The confidence of his stance brought hope and encouragement to the group. "God will protect me. However, I cannot expect my family to leave the comforts of our home in the dead of winter to follow me."

Martha looked at the other women in the group and assumed they were thinking the same thing she was. "If you have to leave the colony, your family can stay in Boston and we will provide food and shelter for them."

A murmur of agreement spread across the room.

"I appreciate your thoughtfulness," Reverend Wheelwright said. "After what happened to Roger Williams, I was expecting such a sentence, but I do not want my family suffer on my behalf. I have been in communications with Reverend Williams and he has offered me a place in Providence Plantation, Rhode Island. However, I feel God is directing me north to New Hampshire. Take no care about my well-being. Our next biggest concern is now Anne Hutchinson's trial."

The next morning, Martha Clarke again took a seat in the back row of the meetinghouse while Mary Dyer took a seat in the front directly behind the defendant. The courtroom had been full of spectators during John Wheelwright's sentencing trial, but at Anne Hutchinson's trial, men and women stood around the back and side walls in order to gain a glimpse of the supposed Jezebel of Massachusetts.

When Anne was led into the courtroom, Martha was surprised how fatigued and worn she looked. She was no longer the young, vivacious mother she had met in England, but a middle-aged woman with locks of graying hair escaping from the side of her bonnet. It was obvious; her waistline was again expanding with another child. In spite of Anne's fatigue, she stood defiantly before the court.

Governor Winthrop did not attempt to mask his contempt. "Anne Hutchinson, you are charged with sedition and for troubling the peace of the commonwealth and

The Trial of Anne Hutchinson
November 1637

[129]

churches. You hold a great share of responsibility for promoting and divulging the opinions that caused the recent troubles within the colony. You have joined in 'affinity and affection' with those in the court already censured. You have slandered the ministers of Massachusetts and continued to hold meetings even after the synod condemned them. You have two choices. You can admit your errors or accept punishment and not trouble us again."

The governor paused; the weight of the charges hung heavily over the room. "Do you justify Mr. Wheelwright's sermon and the petition in his support?"

Martha studied the faces of the observers, most sat with wrinkled brows and clenched teeth. *This is a hostile crowd. If the trial were being held in Boston, the room would be packed with Anne Hutchinson's supporters. That question is not fair. There is no way she can honestly answer the question, without getting herself in more trouble.*

"Am I being charged with what I think about someone's sermons? I hear nothing legal laid to my charge," Anne replied in a strong, confident voice. "I have not participated in any public acts of preaching, made statements in the General Court, nor have I signed a 'seditious' petition."

The governor's eyes narrowed. "Being a woman, you may not have committed overt acts, but you have harbored and approved those who have," he sneered back. "Therefore, you are a co-conspirator."

Anne's normally tranquil eyes blazed. Her slumped shoulders straightened. "All I did was entertain Christians in my home. I did not conspire with anyone. If I am charged with entertaining John Wheelwright who is a brother-in-law of mine, than Reverend John

Cotton and everyone else who has entertained John Wheelwright should also be charged."

Martha watched Governor Winthrop slump in his chair and look down. *Anne made a very good point. Governor Winthrop must now realize he is not going to convict Anne for sedition. I wonder what tactic he will try next.*

"Anne Hutchinson, you are also charged with holding secret and unauthorized religious meetings and setting up a public ministry," Governor Winthrop shouted.

"I did not set up a public ministry," Anne snapped back. "It is scriptural for women to teach other women. Only a few men voluntarily visited in my home."

Throughout the day, Governor Winthrop continued pressing Anne with one charge after another, but she was able to provide clear explanations and could not be shaken. She freely quoted the Bible in her own defense. It was obvious she knew large portions of scripture by heart, more than most of the clergy in the room.

When Governor Winthrop began to tire, Deputy Governor Thomas Dudley took control of the trial. "Anne Hutchinson, you are also charged with slandering the ministers of the church. Numerous times you have been heard saying, 'none of the clergy except John Cotton were qualified ministers of the New Testament.'"

Anne scowled. "If I ever said that, I proved it by God's Word."

Thomas Dudley leaned forward and glared. "We have testimony from several clergy members who have heard you claim on numerous occasions that what the ministers of the Puritan churches were teaching about salvation was actually a 'way to hell'."

"If I said that," Anne replied, "it was in private conversation. The ministers had no right to make it public."

As the day continued, the prosecutors grew weary of battering charges and scripture back and forth with Anne. Finally, Governor Winthrop said, "We have labored all day to get Anne Hutchinson to acknowledge the error of her ways. Since it is getting late, we will let her consider her errors overnight for one last time and return to court in the morning with her answer."

After the meetinghouse emptied, the supporters trudged slowly to William's wagon under the elm tree at the edge of town. Words could not express their sadness and most remained silent during their ride back to the Leonard barn. They each ate from the small ration of food they had brought with them and crawled under the blankets in the loft in the hope of getting much-needed rest.

Martha tossed and turned in her makeshift bed throughout the night. *It would be much easier if Anne would just say the clergy's point of view was the right one. Then they would merely reprimand her and send her home to her family...However, I agree Anne must remain firm in what she believes is the true message from God.*

The next day the climate in the courtroom did not improve. Governor Winthrop opened the session by saying, "Anne Hutchinson, this is your last opportunity to acknowledge the error of your teachings and accept the official teachings of the clergy. Do you acknowledge your errors and repent before Almighty God?"

"I only teach what I am told to teach."

Governor Winthrop scowled and demanded, "By what authority do you teach?"

"I receive direct revelations from God," Anne replied.

A snicker spread throughout the courtroom and Deputy Governor Dudley ordered silence and leaned forward. A look of amusement spread across his face. "How do you know it is God speaking and not Satan?"

Anne's voice became firm and even more confident. "How did Abraham know it was God who asked him to offer his son to be a sacrifice, which was against the sixth commandment—Thou shall not kill?"

Thomas Dudley paused. He took a deep breath. "Abraham heard an immediate voice from God."

"So it is with me," Anne Hutchinson said. "I speak by an immediate revelation."

Governor Winthrop's face reddened. "I will not hear of such heresy. The only accepted mode of revelation from God is through scripture," he shouted.

"I hear the voice of God's spirit directly to my soul," Anne said. A glow spread across her face and a look of defiance was in her eyes. "You may have power over my body, but the Lord Jesus has power over my spirit and soul."

Martha listened with amazement while Anne lectured the court about the judgment of God. She emphasized mercy for the weak and the sinners and damnation for the church officials and Pharisees. In her conclusion, Anne's voice grew even stronger. "Therefore, take heed how to proceed against me. You have no power over my spirit. Neither can you do me any harm, for I am in the hands of the eternal Jehovah my Savior. I am at His appointment."

Martha trembled. The lines were drawn. Anne presented herself on God's side and against the state, while the magistrates also considered themselves on God's side in opposing her. The clergy viewed Anne

Hutchinson claiming a direct link to God equal to heresy. To magistrates, it was imperative for the court to punish Anne so the Lord would not punish the state in retribution for accepting her sin within their midst.

A hush fell across the courtroom. Spectators shifted their gaze from the defendant to her robed prosecutors, knowing neither side was going to back down. A single middle-aged woman was standing defiantly before the combined power of the church and state.

Magistrate William Bartholomew who had been sitting in silence for most of the proceedings cleared his throat and stared at Anne. "Do you remember me?"

Anne studied the robed magistrate. "Yes, I believe you were on onboard the ship *Griffin* when we sailed from England."

"That is correct," he said gruffly. "Your behavior onboard was bizarre and witchlike. Your strange revelations are something all passengers can testify."

Deputy Governor Thomas Dudley bit his lip, trying to hold back another question until it was time for him to speak. "Anne Hutchinson, in claiming to respond to the 'light within' are you claiming to be a part of the radical Anabaptist group or are you a part of the Familism sect?"

"I am not a member of either sect," Anne stated firmly. "I am only guided by the revelation God gives directly to me. I do not believe in the 'Covenant of Works' the Puritans believe. It is of the devil to try to approach God through the forms, practices, and laws of the church."

Deputy Dudley's face reddened. "Then how do you approach God?"

Ann Hutchinson smiled sweetly and lifted her gaze upward. "I believe in the 'Covenant of Grace.' I learn God's will by having it revealed directly to me."

Another shocked hush spread across the courtroom. At long last, Governor Winthrop said, "I am fully persuaded the revelation Anne Hutchinson brings forth is a delusion."

"We agree," the thirty magistrates said nearly in unison.

Not wasting any time, Winthrop addressed Anne. "After hearing what you freely stated without being asked, the court declares you guilty of 'sedition and for troubling the peace of the commonwealth and churches.' Now we must consider what is to be done to you."

The spectators scrutinized the magistrates while they huddled together and whispered loudly among themselves. They leaned forward, trying to hear the conversation among the magistrates. Time seemed to stand still.

Martha watched Anne shift nervously in place. *After standing all afternoon without relief, it must be nearly unbearable for Anne in her condition.*

After several grueling minutes of anticipation, the magistrates returned to their seats and sat erect. Governor Winthrop cleared his throat. "Anne Hutchinson, being a woman not fit for our society, the court sentences you to banishment from our jurisdiction. You shall be imprisoned until the court shall send you away and the church holds a heresy hearing."

Anne Hutchinson appeared unshaken. "I desire to know why I am banished. I have not broken any laws of God."

Governor Winthrop's face again reddened. "You have spoken too much. Say no more. The court knows why you must be removed from among our midst and it is satisfied with its decision. You will be returned to your cell and come before us tomorrow for the details of your banishment."

Martha Clarke lay awake under the quilts in the loft of Yeoman Leonard's barn starring at the dim light peeking through the slats in the roof. Sleep eluded her once again. She listened to the snoring and coughing of the other Hutchinson supporters. It seemed more were coughing and showing distress while they slept than the first night they arrived in Newtowne for the trial. Even the stench from the farm animals below seemed worse.

To Martha, the physical distractions seemed minor compared to the turmoil within. *Even if I have not studied theology, as an ordinary Christian, none of this makes sense. Don't we all worship the same God? I have stayed on the sidelines and tried to avoid conflict long enough. It is time I follow Mary's enthusiasm in searching for the truth of God. What the clergy is doing is Boston is definitely not right.*

After hours of staring at the slats of the roof, Martha finally fell into a restless sleep. It did not seem long before she heard William Dyer say loudly, "It is time to arise and go to the meetinghouse. We need to be early to make sure we have seats."

Martha was the first to her feet. She brushed the straw from her clothing and put on her bonnet. She watched as others stretched, stood, and greeted those around them.

Mary was soon on her feet and smiled at Martha. She turned to the others and raised her hand to get attention. "It has always been Anne Hutchinson who has led us in prayer and encouraged us. Since she is not with us, let us stand in silence and prayer for her and her family. Let us beseech God to make the magistrates lenient toward her."

They all stood and bowed their heads. Martha heard murmured prayers throughout the loft. After a couple minutes, Mary said a loud 'amen' and everyone gathered their few possessions and climbed down the rickety ladder to the dirt floor of the barn. Following their new routine, they refreshed themselves, ate a few bites of breakfast, and climbed into the back of the Dyer's wagon. When William parked the wagon under the large elm tree at the edge of town, the supporters climbed from the wagon and walked to the meetinghouse in groups of two or three in tense silence. Today would be different. Today they would learn the fate of their beloved friend and teacher.

An hour later, the Hutchinson supporters were scattered around the meetinghouse. The men were on one side and the women on the other. They waited in silence, many with bowed heads in prayer. When the magistrates entered the room, they rose with the others and returned to the seat when motioned to do so by the Governor. In spite of glares from the magistrates and the other spectators, the supporters stood when the guard led Anne Hutchinson into the courtroom.

Governor Winthrop scowled and shouted. "Would everyone be seated or you will be removed from the courtroom."

The governor turned his attention to the stoic woman standing before him. Without pause or introduction he said, "Anne Hutchinson, by testimony of your own words you have disgraced the ministers and the ministry of the church. You have brought this on yourself by voluntarily agreeing you claim to receive direct revelations from God. Therefore, this court sentences you to banishment from the Massachusetts Bay Colony. However, due to the severity of the weather and the humanitarian interest of the court, you will be held in house arrest at the home of Joseph Weld in Roxbury until the church tries you for heresy and disposes of you as they see fit."

Anne Hutchinson paused, looked toward heaven and back to her accusers. A peaceful expression spread across her face. "So be it. You may do what you will to my body, but nothing can separate me from the God that dwells within."

Chapter Nine
House Arrest

Roxbury, March 1638

Two months after Anne Hutchinson's trial, Mary and William Dyer joined Randall and Martha for an evening meal of boiled venison, carrots, and bread. After a hard day of work preparing her garden for planting, Mary was grateful not having to cook for her husband that night. She watched two-and-a-half year-old Samuel Dyer playing happily in the corner with a pile of sticks. Only Samuel was free of the cloud of disappointment and gloom hanging over them.

Mary admired her husband's strong facial features and weathered hands. "Things have gone from bad to worse since Anne's trial. It is completely unfair the seventy-five men who signed the Wheelwright petition have been ordered to be totally disarmed."

William shook his head with disgust. "They are trying to stamp out all remnants of Anne Hutchinson's and John Wheelwright's teachings. They even came up with a name for anyone who has any connection with them. I dislike being labeled an Antinomian. They are assuming if we believe in a gospel of grace we consider ourselves above any moral law and live perverse lives. Nothing is further from the truth."

Randall set his cup on the table, stood, walked to the hearth, and stoked the fire. "By giving people a label and assuming we are all in total agreement on every detail of religion is turning us into the enemy. They do not try to get to know us as individuals. The magistrates and clergy assume we all think alike, and if someone is labeled an Antinomian then they have the right to banish us from Massachusetts unless they repent."

Mary reached for her husband's hand. "William, yesterday I heard you referred to as 'the father of the monster baby'. We cannot put up with that kind of talk. What are we going to do?"

William's eyes became firm and he set his jaw. "We are still making our plans. It is bad enough that everyone they consider Antinomians will be banished from Massachusetts, but to take our weapons away from us is extremely cruel. How are we supposed to protect ourselves or hunt for food?" He joined his brother-in-law at the hearth. "I refuse to deny what I believe. Anne Hutchinson, John Wheelwright, and everyone else should have the freedom to teach and preach according to their conscience. I will turn my arms in at Mr. Keayne's tavern by November 30 as the court demands and throw myself on the Lord's mercy."

Martha gasped. "That is terrible. If those labeled Antinomians are forced to leave the colony, how are they going to be able to defend themselves without their weapons? The magistrates are now afraid of the Pequot War with the Natives and require all men over eighteen to carry muskets."

"It will be difficult," Randall said. "It takes courage to stand for one's convictions. I heard thirty-five petition signers have already acknowledged their fault and error to the clergy so they would be allowed to keep their muskets."

A worried expression spread across Martha's face. She turned to her husband. "Have you been accused of being an Antinomian?"

Randall forced a smile. "I am fortunate I haven't been accused, yet. I assume it is because I spend a lot of time in the woods and was not around when the church officials did their spying and made their charges. I was not an official member of the church so I could not sign the petition. But I will do everything I can to help the cause."

The embers in the hearth burned low while the four sat in silence, each lost in their own thoughts and fears. Finally William said, "This may sound strange, but in some ways I find our current situation rather liberating."

Randall gave his brother-in-law a puzzled look, but said nothing.

William continued. "Before the November trials, I had to mute my opinions or present them as 'questions' to protect myself against the legalism of the colony. Now that the decision has been made, I can say whatever I think openly. They have already done to us what they consider the worst thing possible to us."

"I am glad you said that, because I feel the same way," Randall said. "We are about to head in a better direction. My cousin, John Clarke, just arrived from England and I have seen him at all the trials. He was trained as a clergy and I am concerned he will take their side, so we have only had polite, vague conversations. Maybe I should be honest and open about our situation and perhaps he can provide a different perspective."

Suddenly, Samuel began whimpering in the corner. Mary rushed to his side and picked him up. She removed the sliver that had punctured his index finger and held him close. When he was calm, she set him back on the floor and returned to the table. "I plan to go to Anne's church trial in March. I heard they plan to hold it before all the clergy in Massachusetts, including the outlying towns like Salem and Ipswich. I am certain the ministers will admonish her, hoping to cleanse her of her sin, but knowing Anne like we do, she'll never waver on her beliefs."

"They say the rules of her house arrest are very strict," Martha said. "They are trying to break her spirit and convince her of the errors of her ways. She is not allowed to work or move about the area, yet her husband is expected to pay for her upkeep."

Mary smiled. "They do not know Anne. They will never be able to break her spirit."

Melancholy swept over Martha. "I really miss her. She had been such an encouragement to me. Her children are still coming to my house every day for classes and I hope I have been teaching them the way she would want. I wonder if there is a way we could see her while she is in Roxbury. It is only two miles from here."

Mary's face brightened. A smile spread across her face. "That is a great idea. I heard only her family is allowed to visit her, but maybe we could talk to Will Hutchinson and ride in his wagon the next time he takes the children to see their mother. If we stay hidden, perhaps we could talk to her through a window."

The Hutchinson cart headed southwest toward Roxbury. Will drove the team of horses while seventeen-year-old Francis sat on the bench beside him. Thirteen-year-old Samuel Hutchinson, ten-year-old Anne, nine-year-old Mary, seven-year old Katherine, huddled in the bed of the wagon surrounded by straw and blankets. Mary Dyer snuggled four-year-old Susannah next to her while Martha Clarke held one-year-old Zuriel in her arms. The road was long and bumpy and the cold wind blustered across their faces.

Mary and Martha encouraged the children to sing songs with them to keep them from thinking about the bitterness of their trip.

When they neared the last bend before Joseph Weld's house, Will stopped the wagon, handed the reins to his seventeen-year-old son, Francis, and climbed into the bed of the wagon with the younger children. "You must all promise me you will not speak a word about Mary and Martha being with us. No one is supposed to see your mother except the family. This will be a surprise for your mother, but it could be dangerous."

Grave expressions covered each of the children's faces. "We promise we will not say a word about them," Katherine said. "I am glad they brought warm clothing and food for mother. I was afraid she might get hungry and cold at night."

Little Anne clutched a parcel in her hand. "I brought mother her favorite book, *Herbal*. It tells her how to make medicine from plants. She will need it to heal people in Roxbury the same as she did when she was at home."

Will smiled at his daughter and squeezed her hand. "I am certain she'll appreciate the book. She is always looking for ways to help people." He turned his attention to all the children. "Mary and Martha will wait in the woods while we talk to your mother. You are to give their gifts to her, but make sure no one hears you tell who provided them. When we return, we will tell Mary and Martha what window your mother will be at. We will wait here for them while they sneak around the outside of the house and talk to her the window."

Mary and Martha nodded simultaneously. "Thank you," Mary said. "You have an excellent plan. I wondered how we could possibly get to talk with Anne in private." The sisters each wrapped themselves in a blanket and jumped from the wagon while Will climbed back onto the driver's bench, and took the reins from his son's hands.

Mary and Martha walked a few yards into the forest until they found a fallen tree. Locating two smoother spots on the trunk, they sat down. The cold November wind whipped around them and they wrapped the blankets tighter around themselves. Minutes turned into an hour before the familiar team of horses and wagon appeared around the bend in the road. The children waved and shouted when they spotted Mary and Martha hurrying toward the wagon.

Will pulled the horses to a stop and jumped to the ground. "I hope you did not get too cold while you waited. Anne is anxious to see you. She will be by the window on the northeast corner of the house. Tap lightly on the pane and she will appear."

"How is she?" Martha asked.

Will shook his head, unable to mask his concern. "She looked very tired. I do not think she is getting enough food and rest. I know she did not want to say much in front of the children, but if you get a better sense of how she is being treated, please let me know. We will wait here until you return."

Martha and Mary trudged along the rutted dirt road as fast as possible. When they turned the bend, a large, two-story house loomed before them. They moved to the shadows of the trees while increasing their pace toward the northeast corner of the house. Mary reached the window first and tapped lightly. Within seconds, Anne's smiling face appeared. Tears filled her eyes. "Good morning. I am so glad you came. I appreciate the clothing and supplies the children brought. It is getting colder and I definitely needed warmer clothes."

"If there is anything else we can do for you, please let us know," Mary said. "It is totally unfair the way you are being treated."

"Do not worry about me," Anne said. "God is watching over me."

Martha studied her friend's face. "How are you doing? You look tired."

Anne sighed and forced a smile of resignation. "Will said the same thing. I could not tell him in front of the children, but my time of waiting is not going well. The child I am carrying feels different. I have never been this tired and sick to my stomach as I have been this past month. What concerns me most is that I have not felt movement in my womb. The baby should be moving by now."

"Maybe it is because you are not getting enough to eat and not resting enough," Martha said. "Take care of yourself and we will continue to pray for you. Are they treating you well?"

Anne heaved a sigh of frustration. "Every day I attempt to do God's work by studying His Word and live in His way. At the same time, Joseph Weld tries to convince me of my errors. If dealing with Joseph Weld's comments is not enough, every few days I have clergy visitors. Ministers Thomas Weld, Thomas Shepard, Hugh Peter, and John Eliot take turns coming to visit. They preach to me what they think is God's Word trying to convince me to see the light and recant of my supposedly obnoxious opinions. They also record the supposed 'errors, spoken from my own mouth,' to present as evidence at my church trial in the spring. It is very unsettling. However, my will to serve God can never be broken."

Mary placed the palm of her hand against the vellum windowpane where Anne had her palm pressed.

"Anne, your faith and dedication is an inspiration to me. I hope I will become as sensitive to God's leadings as you."

Tears built in Anne's eyes. "I love and miss you all. I hope our group will be able to meet together soon to pray and worship. In the meantime, we must continue to support each other in prayer."

"That we will do," Martha promised.

Anne paused. Her eyes began to sparkle. "It hasn't all been bad. I have also received blessings, since I have been here. I was able to see my first grandchild the other day. My son, Edward, and his wife had their first child a few days before my trial began. The other day they were able to bring little Elishua to Roxbury. It always touches me deeply to hold each of my children in my arms for the first time, but holding a grandchild for the first time is an experience I cannot describe."

"It must be an unexplainable feeling," Martha said, thinking back to the few short days she was a mother. "And to think next month Bridget, will be presenting you with another grandchild while you are waiting for another child of your own. God has truly blessed you with children to carry on your legacy of faith and love."

Suddenly, Anne's face tightened. "Go quickly. Joseph Weld is coming."

Chapter Ten
Bodie Politick

Boston, March 1638

Eighteen signers of the Wheelwright petition along with ten male supporters gathered in the home of William Coddington late in the afternoon of March 7. A sense of uncertainty enveloped William Dyer accompanied by strong determination to do what was right. He surveyed the group preparing to leave Boston. A brotherly bond was strengthening among them. When everyone was seated, William Coddington rose and motioned for silence. "Faithful supporters of individual right of religious freedom and speech, I want to welcome you into my home. We all agree it is the time for us to make more detailed plans for our departure from Massachusetts. However, this plan cannot be taken lightly. Before we can decide on the supplies we will need, we must begin setting the framework for a foundation for our own government."

A murmur spread throughout the room while the men exchanged puzzled looks. William Dyer was afraid to voice the thoughts going through is head. *Why do we need an organized government now, when there are so few of us?*

"I wouldn't have the slightest idea how to begin," a voice from the back shouted. "All I know is the government in Boston is not fair and just. We need someone to guide us."

William Dyer shuddered at the man's boldness, but William Coddington seemed unaffected and motioned to a man sitting on his right. "Thankfully, God saw our need and provided an experienced leader to help us. John Clarke is a new arrival who has the

[147]

expertise we need. I will let him introduce himself and explain steps that need to be taken to establish our own community."

John Clarke rose. Every eye focused on him with curiosity. "I would like to thank everyone for coming today and especially my cousin, Randall. He wrote me

Reverend John Clarke
(1609 - 1676)

numerous letters extolling the benefits of this beautiful new world and encouraging me to join him. I must agree with him, Massachusetts definitely lives up to his glowing physical description."

Randall hung his head. "I am sorry I did not explain the turmoil in the government and the churches in Massachusetts. If I told you, I was afraid you wouldn't come."

"I understand," John Clarke said. "I did my own research before I came and made my own decision. I wanted to see and experience what was happening myself. I avoided making personal contacts and I sat quietly in the back and listened during the trials of John Wheelwright, Anne Hutchinson, and the others. When I arrived in Boston I was a devout Puritan, but after all the injustices I have observed, I am now a strong supporter of religious freedom."

With those words, William Dyer joined the others in spontaneous cheers.

William Coddington raised his hand for silence. "We appreciate John Clarke's stand on this principle. With his background as a minister and doctor, along with his study of the law, we can readily accept his leadership. John, how should we begin?"

"I have ink, a quill pen, and paper," John Clarke said. "I have already written the basics of what we will call the 'Boide Politick'. It reads:

The Seventh Day of March 1638.
We whose names are underwritten do hereby solemnly in the presence of Jehovah incorporate ourselves into a Bodie Politick and as He shall help, will submit our persons, lives and estates unto our Lord Jesus Christ, the King of Kings, and Lord of Lords, and to all those perfect and most absolute laws of His given in His Holy Word of truth, to be guided and judged thereby.

Those interested in leaving Massachusetts with us and organizing another settlement, please come forward and sign your name to this agreement. Do not feel obligated to join with us, if this is not your desire. You may want to consider going elsewhere."

William Dyer looked at Randall. "There is no doubt in my mind what I will do."

"Me either," Randall whispered back.

"I am standing with you," a man in the back shouted. "Let me be the first to sign."

A line formed around the kitchen table. One-by-one, twenty-three men signed their names or placed their personal marks on the paper. Several men exchanged nervous glances, but no one commented when two of their number slipped quietly out the front door without signing the compact.

After the last man laid the quill pen on the table, William Coddington announced, "Now that we are all of one accord, the next step is to keep meeting secretly and continue planning the details of our move. We need to study maps of American coastline and decide which area will best meet our needs. I think we can agree that the most important requirements for a new community will be good soil for farming, easy access to fresh water and wood, and less harsh climate than Boston's." The room darkened. He hesitated while his wife lit candles on the table, over the fireplace, and in the windowsill. "The day is getting late, let us gather again tomorrow, and continue making our plans."

With little discussion the men filed out of the Coddington home, William hurried to catch up with his brother-in-law. "Randall, I watched you boldly sign the contract, and yet, you have not been charged by the church or state. You are not being forced to leave Boston like the rest of us."

"I choose to go with you," Randall stated firmly. "I do not want to live and raise a family in a place where we are not able to think and explore different ideas from the clergy. Besides, Martha will want to go anywhere Mary goes. I do not think we will ever be able to separate them."

William smiled. "Thank you. Your dedication is admirable. Most signed the compact because they are being forced to leave Boston. You signed because of a principle for a higher good as well as your love for your family."

Sharp winds whipped snowflakes around them. "How are we going to tell our wives that they will have to leave their homes? They have worked extremely hard to make them livable and a pleasant place to rest after a long day's work," Randall said.

William remained silent for a few paces before he responded. "After they saw what happened to Anne Hutchinson and, even worse, not being allowed to bury Mary's baby properly, I am certain they will want to move on, in spite of the hard work it is to reconstruct another home. At least this time we will be able to take all our household goods and animals with us. When we left England, Mary was heartsick she had to leave her furniture behind."

William Dyer was the first to arrive at William Coddington's home the next day. A sense of responsibility weighed heavy on his shoulders. Within minutes, the other signers of the 'Boide Politick' began to congregating in groups of twos and threes. He watched each group carry on an animated conversation pertaining to where they might go and what they might need at their future home. *Any place would be better than Boston. This move could not possibly be as difficult as moving across the ocean, but we must be wise in our selection.*

After the twenty-third man arrived, John Clarke stepped forward. "I am certain we are all in agreement that our first concern is where we should go. Originally, I thought perhaps we should head south to Long Island or New Jersey. Those who have gone on hunting expeditions claim the climate and soil are much better there, but this morning I received a letter from Reverend Roger Williams. Most of you may already know him, but I have not had the pleasure of meeting him since he was banished from Boston before I arrived."

William Dyer nodded. *I would like nothing better than to join Roger Williams. He was reasonable in his teachings and cared about everyone, regardless of their station in life.*

John Clarke cleared his throat and continued. "Reverend Williams wrote a letter to all who are currently being banished from Boston and encouraged us to come to Rhode Island and become joint proprietors. He urged us to consider the Aquidneck Island since he has settled nearby at Providence Plantation."

John Clarke unrolled a crudely drawn map of the area. Excited affirmative nods and smiles spread throughout the group. "All in favor of moving to Rhode Island please say 'aye'."

William watched while each man in the room nodded and said, 'aye.'

"It is unanimously agreed we will go to the Rhode Island area," John Clarke declared

Again, the men cheered. Mister Clarke raised his hand for silence. "If we are in agreement, we must send word to Reverend Williams that several of us will be coming to Rhode Island to scout the area and make arrangements for the move before the month is out."

"But how can we travel through hostile territory?" William Dyer asked. "We had to surrender our firearms."

With that question, William Coddington rose and joined John Clarke in the front of the room. He took a deep breath. "We have remained stalwart and protested loudly while many of the others have recanted and acknowledge their thinking was in error. If we are to leave within a few weeks, I do not think we have any other choice than to recant ourselves. We would only be recanting to the clergy and not to God. We need to have our weapons for our own protection and to obtain food along the way."

A shocked hush spread across the room. Looks of bewilderment appeared on the faces of the men and they began murmuring to each other. William Dyer shuffled restlessly in his seat. *Will we need to go against the very principles of freedom we are struggling for?*

"I understand everyone's concern," John Clarke said. "This is not something you can choose to do lightly. Let us bow our heads in prayer and ask God's guidance." He hesitated until the men were silent, then continued. "Heavenly Father, we thank you for providing us the bounteous gifts of faith and love. We are now being forced into a situation in which we are not comfortable. We do not want to deny Your will and go against Your word, but we need our weapons for our survival. Please forgive us if we error. Let us use our weapons to spread religious freedom for all God's children. Amen."

"Thank you, Reverend Clarke," William Coddington said. "I am certain the Lord will bless our cause." He turned back to the other members of the group. "Those of you who are able to go to Rhode Island immediately to lay out our community should meet here early tomorrow morning to plan for our departure. It could be a long and tedious journey. Tonight each of us will need to inventory our food and tool supply and decide what we can take with us without shorting our families while we are away." He hesitated and looked directly at William Dyer. "We will need to have someone in our group who knows how to survey land."

"I would be honored to go with the advance committee," William Dyer said. "I haven't used my surveying skills since I left England, but I still remember the basic principles."

"But who will look out for our families while we are gone?" a man in the front row asked.

Again, a murmur spread throughout the room while the men exchanged looks of concern.

Without hesitation, Randall Clarke stood. "Since I am leaving Boston voluntarily and not being banished by the church and state, I will stay behind. I promise to check on each of your families every day and do whatever I can to help if a need arises. I am certain my wife can be a big help to the families left behind."

A thank you in unison spread throughout the room. William Dyer turned to his brother-in-law. "Randall, I appreciate all you are doing for the cause. I will see that we receive adjoining land so our wives can stay in close contact with each other."

Will Hutchinson put his hand on Randall's shoulder. "Randall, I too appreciate what you are doing. Even though it will be extremely difficult for my wife and children, I feel I must go to Rhode Island with the group in order to prepare a safer place for them to live. With my wife in house arrest, my children may need extra help. The older ones will be able to care for the younger, but they may have more challenges along the way."

Randall wrinkled his forehead and gave his friend a reassuring smile. "Will, I will check on your family every day and do whatever is necessary, but isn't your wife's church trial coming soon?"

Will shook his head sadly. "Yes, it is scheduled to begin March 12th and continue for several days. However, Anne and I have discussed the situation and we feel it is more important that I go to Rhode Island at this time to help get our future established. I know I can trust Anne into God's hands."

"Have no fear," Randall said. "If you do not get back, my wife and I, along with Mary Dyer, will be at the trial every day to support her."

After each man had a chance to express their concerns, John Clarke addressed the group. "One other thing before we leave. We need to select a treasurer of our group who will also care for the documents of the Bodie Politick.

William Coddington again looked at William Dyer. "Would you be willing to take on another responsibility and become the record keeper and treasurer for the Bodie Politick? You have always been accurate in your record keeping."

William Dyer felt all eyes upon him. *I fear they have too much confidence in my abilities, but I cannot let them down at such a critical time.* "I would be honored."

Again, a murmur of approval spread throughout the room. "Then I can safely say, William Dyer is unanimously approved for the position of treasurer," John Clarke proclaimed.

William Coddington rose and took a deep breath. "Now for the hardest part. We need to all go to Mr. Keayne's tavern together, recant our earlier statements, and reclaim our weapons."

Learning of the plans of the Bodie Politick, Martha hurried to her sister's home and rushed in without knocking. "Mary, do you think it is right Will Hutchinson goes with the advance committee to Rhode Island and possibly not be back for Anne's church trial?"

Mary stood up from the hearth where she was preparing dinner and gave Martha a quizzical look. "Don't you think that is a decision to be made between Will and Anne?"

Martha smiled and nodded. "Yes...You are right. We must trust their decision, whatever it may be."

"Let's talk with Will and see if we can ride to Roxbury with him the next time he goes to see Anne," Mary said. She removed the skillet from the open flame and set it nearby. "I am at a good stopping point. I will get Samuel and we can walk to the Hutchinson's and talk with him this afternoon."

Mary reached for a coat for Samuel, helped him put it on, and took her own shawl from the hook beside the door. The three of them hurried through the streets of Boston. Samuel clung tightly to his mother's hand while dogs followed them until distracted by chickens in a nearby yard. When they neared the Hutchinson's house on High Street, they could see Will working in the field nearby. They motioned to him and he hurried toward them.

"Mary...Martha. What brings you my way this day?" Will said.

Mary let loose of Samuel's hand and smiled at Will. "William told us the departure of the Bodie Politick advance committee may conflict with Anne's trial and you were considering going with them. We realize that is a difficult decision for your family so we will do anything we can to help. If possible, we would like to go with you the next time you visit Anne in Roxbury and assure her in person of our desire to help with the children and obtain any specific instructions she may have. We will abide by any decision the two of you make."

"She will appreciate seeing you again," Will said. "I am planning to go to Roxbury tomorrow without the children. Anne and I have a lot to discuss and we need to seek God's guidance together. Even if you are not allowed to see her, knowing you are in the background praying would mean a great deal to both of us."

The clouds over the Boston harbor hid the stars and a light rain began to fall. William Coddington and William Dyer quietly walked up the gangplank of a ship scheduled to leave for Barbados at the break of dawn. They peered through the fog. In the far corner, a torch showed the outline of two men rearranging barrels and one giving directions.

"Captain Cooley?" William Coddington said.

"Yes, here I am. Is that you, William?"

William Coddington gave a dry chuckle. "In person. I want to thank you for agreeing to take our group around Cape Cod. That will save us a lot of needless walking to Providence Planation to meet with Roger Williams."

Captain Cooley slapped his old friend on the shoulder. "Anything to help the cause. I am not much of a religious person myself, but when I learned what the church was doing to those who had any relationship with Anne Hutchinson I couldn't turn you away."

William Coddington became serious. "Captain Cooley, I would like you to meet my assistant, William Dyer. He is one of the primary organizers of the Bodie Politick and one of the hardest workers in the group."

"I believe in religious freedom and speech and will do whatever I can to help the cause," William Dyer said.

Captain Cooley reached out to shake William Dyer's hand. "It is nice to meet you." He turned back to William Coddington. "What do you have in mind for leaving Boston?"

A silence hung over the deck of the ship. Lights from the candles in the homes of Boston twinkled in the background. Dogs barked in a neighboring yard. "We do not want to let anyone know we are leaving," William Coddington said. "I would appreciate you letting us board under cover of darkness. Seven men are waiting nearby. They have agreed to board the ship one by one whenever they see a torch being waved. William will be a watchman for the group."

"Excellent plan. You have always been a conniving one." Captain Cooley laughed while he surveyed the deck to locate his officers. "I will have the first mate go to the railing and swing the torch whenever we are ready for another person to board. After one of your men arrives on board, the first mate can go back to the railing and swing the torch to alert the next one to start walking toward the ship."

With the exit plan in place, William Coddington and William Dyer hurried back to the simple wood framed house near the Boston Warf where the advance party waited. "Fellow members of the Bodie Politick," he began. "Captain Cooley is prepared to take us at least around Cape Cod. In a couple of days, we should be able to meet up with those who left on foot three days ago."

"I appreciate you making these arrangements," Will Hutchinson said. "Going by boat will be a tremendous time saver and we will be better able to relieve those who are exhausted from walking when we rejoin them."

William Coddington turned to Will Hutchinson. "We have asked you this before, but are you sure you want to come with us? I may not be back before your wife's church trial."

Will Hutchinson set his jaw. "Yes. As I said before, Anne and I have discussed it and we agreed it is more important I go and search for a better place to raise our family, than to be at her side during the trial. The clergy will do whatever they want to do whether I am there or not. I must trust her care to God and the strong women like Mary Dyer and Martha Clarke."

Each of the other men gave Will Hutchinson words of encouragement and concern.

When the talking had subsided, William Coddington again addressed the group. "If everyone is ready for the risk before you, the plan with the ship's captain is for us to watch for the waving of a torch from the railing of the ship to signal for only one man to slip quietly through the street to the ship until we are all assembled onboard. William Dyer will be our lookout and the last one on the ship. After the sun sets tonight, we will gather here with our belongings for the trip and execute our plan."

"I see the light from the torch on the ship," William Dyer whispered. "Stay in the shadows and when you arrive, tell the sailor with the torch that you are onboard and to wave the torch again to signal for another man to come."

Six members of the Bodie Politick received the same instructions and were safely onboard. When William Dyer saw the signal for him to join his comrades, he walked slowly through the shadows toward the ship. Suddenly, a stout night watchman appeared in front of him. He tried to remain calm and turned a corner away from the ship, but the watchman followed him.

"What are you doing out tonight?" the watchman snarled.

William took a deep breath and tried to act as composed as possible. "I was just returning home after visiting a friend. It was such a lovely evening I was enjoying the stroll."

"Hmph!" the watchman said. "A likely story indeed. Aren't you a follower of Anne Hutchinson? I am supposed to make sure the Antinomians do not gather together and stir up trouble."

"I am William Dyer. I was just helping a friend construct shelves for his house. It got dark before we were finished."

"Hmph! A likely story indeed." The watchman glared at William and hesitated before finally saying, "I will let you go home this time, but I do not want to see you out of doors after dark again."

"Thank you, sir," William said and slowly continued on his way. When the guard was out of sight, he hurried to the ship where worried companions greeted him.

Throughout the next day, the ship remained close to the shore while it tossed back and forth in the cold March winds. Many clung to the masts to stay upright.

A few miles past the Plymouth settlement, the captain turned to William Coddington, "Your men are welcome to go on further with us, but the gale winds are beginning to become dangerous. If I were you, the safer way would be to set out on foot. Rodger William's settlement could not be far from here."

William Coddington motioned for William Dyer to join him. They took out a water-stained map and studied it. After several moments, William Coddington looked back to the captain. "I agree with you. It is not worth us risking our time, much less our lives by going further in these winds. We are grateful for all you've done for us."

At the next available harbor, the men of the Bodie Politick waded ashore. After three days exploring the woods, following Indian trails and fording streams, the seven weary men arrived at the home of Roger Williams. Mary Williams welcomed the travelers, gave them blankets, and prepared warm food for them. They eagerly asked Reverend Williams about creating a colony and the availability of land in the area. They were anxious to meet up with those coming on foot to learn what they had found along the way.

Having shared the humiliation of banishment from the Massachusetts Bay Colony, Roger was eager to share his experiences with the new arrivals. "I never intended to start a colony when I left Massachusetts, but twelve families followed me. Most of them were freed servants. We divided the land equally with six acres for each family. We have a very trusting community with no boundary lines, no patent, no deed, no regular government, and no governor."

William Dyer shook his head. "That sounds ideal, but it will not be long before your little settlement will need some kind of administration."

"I suppose you are right," Reverend Williams said. "However, the people here are farmers with little education. I try to make the minor decisions of the settlement so they can be free to focus on providing for their families. Probably the most important thing I have done is to get to know the Narragansett Indians. They are worth a wealth of information about travel and

Roger Williams and the Narragansett Indians

survival in the area. The Massachusetts Bay Colony ignored the Natives and built homes on their land, but I felt the only honorable thing to do is to purchase the land from them and not claim it as my own without recognizing their rights."

"I totally agree with you," William Dyer said. "It is imperative we respect the rights of the Natives. Do you have any suggestions as to where we should settle?"

Roger Williams hesitated. "I think the two best places would be Souwamas and the Aquidneck Island. However, someone will need to go to the Plymouth colony to see whether another patent from England claimed either of these locations. I cannot stress how important it is to make sure land is registered properly in London. If you would like, I would be willing to go with you to Plymouth. I know the magistrates in the area as well as how to barter with the Natives."

"We would be honored to have you accompany us," William Coddington said. "We would like to leave first thing in the morning. With any luck we will meet up with the others from our group on the way."

Reverend Williams pointed to a wooden box in the corner full of beads. "It would be best if we could purchase land for your settlement before we return. I know exactly what has value to the Indians. We should take hundreds of "wompi" beads with us. They also like English made tools, especially hoes which they can use in their fields to plant corn."

The advance committee of the Bodie Politick along with Roger Williams worked well into the night packing supplies for their trip to Plymouth. It was a long, cold walk through the woods and they arrived mid-day of the second day. They immediately contacted the magistrates who, despite their differences, met with them.

After sharing a meal and news of the area, the head magistrate said, "The Souwamas area is a part of the Plymouth Patent and not available for others to settle. I would recommend settling on the Aquidneck Island. We will help you make the arrangements."

Early the next morning, the members of the Bodie Politick, and Roger Williams thanked the Plymouth Magistrates and headed south through the woods. Two hours later, they could hear men's voices in the distance. They listened carefully.

"That is English, we are hearing," William Dyer said. "Could it be the others from our group?" He fired a musket into the air and shouted.

Within minutes, the two groups reunited in a clearing near the riverbank. They thanked God for their protection and each reached into the bags they had brought with them to share their meager food and water. Everyone appreciated the fresh supplies from Providence Plantation.

"This is an excellent spot to spend the night," Roger Williams said. "Tomorrow we must find Chiefs Canonicus, and Miatonomo who live in Narragansett. It is fortunate we met up today and could combine our resources to be able to pay the Indians for their land."

The next day, March 24, 1638, William Dyer and seventeen other members of the 'Bodie Politick' watched in amazement while Roger Williams discussed the terms of the agreement to purchase a small portion of the Natives' land. In the end, the Narrangansett chiefs accepted forty fathoms of white wampum beads, ten coats, and twenty hoes as a "gratuity" in exchange for the slender, fifteen-mile-long island of Aquidneck. The deed was signed with the bow and arrow symbols of Canonicus and Miantonomo and the signatures of Roger Williams and members of the Bodie Politick.

After signing the deed for the purchase of Aquidneck and the Native chiefs had disappeared into the woods, Roger Williams addressed the group. "I am ready to return to Providence Plantation, but there is a ship that routinely docks in this area to obtain fresh water. They may be willing to provide you passage back to Boston."

The men bade Reverend Williams farewell and spent the next few hours resting on the bank above the harbor. Much to their delight, two hours later the white sails of a small ship came into view. After the ship docked and the sailors were ashore, William Coddington approached the captain.

William Dyer strained to hear their conversation and was greatly relieved when he heard the captain say, "You most definitely may join us. Our crew is getting tired and we could use the extra help on the last portion of our trip."

As they sailed past a tiny island near Aquidneck Island, William Dyer fell in love with it. "Captain, could we land for a few minutes so I can explore that little island?" he begged. "I am certain William Coddington would permit it."

The ship's captain looked questioningly at William Coddington who nodded an affirmation. "It is nearly meal time and we could take a break."

Several members stayed on board and rested while others waded ashore. The sandy beach was lined with mussels and clams. Birds flew up from the marshy grasses and inland ponds as they passed. "Mister Coddington," William Dyer said. "Since the deed we signed with the Indians included this outlying island, I would like to take possession of it for my very own. My family and my wife's sister and husband could live on this island."

William Coddington smiled. "You've been extremely helpful to the group, but it is not the value of the land that I would grant you your request. It is because of your love for the island that I grant it to you."

While the others walked around the small island, Will Hutchinson became restless. When they neared the ship, he fell into step beside William Coddington, William Dyer, and the ship's captain. "Now that the purchase of land is settled, I would like to get back to Boston as quickly as possible. I cannot get Anne's plight out of my mind. I wonder if we hurry it might be possible to arrive in Boston before the trial is over. I am certain it will lift her spirits to learn of the new area that is available to us."

The men nodded and the captain shouted for everyone to come onboard. When they were presented with the possibility of getting back to Boston sooner, they all agreed to work extra hard to arrive early and hoped the prevailing winds would be with them. Could they possibly make it to Boston before Anne Hutchinson's trial before the church officials ended?

Chapter Eleven

Church Trial

Boston, March 12, 1638

Warm early spring winds blew across Boston. Snowmelt turned the roads to mud that caked Martha's and Mary's shoes and skirts, while they made their daily visits to each of the families whose menfolk were searching for a better place to live. Mary and Martha had become the communication link between the women of the Bodie Politick. They helped arrange for the caring of each other's children when someone was sick, the sharing of household chores, and providing food for those in need.

In anticipation of the Hutchinson church trial, the intensity of the political climate within the Boston continued to mount. Every time Martha would go to the mercantile, she would overhear conversations about Anne Hutchinson. One day she came home particularly angry.

She slammed the door behind her and dropped her basket on the table. "Randall, you never would believe what happened in town today. Two men actually got in a fight over Anne Hutchinson."

Randall looked up from the table where he was sorting pegs. "I knew the emotion was getting pretty intense, but I cannot imagine people actually coming to blows over it. What were they saying?"

Mary slumped onto the bench on the other side of the table. "One was convinced the clergy knew the absolute word of God from the scriptures and they had to be obeyed to preserve the power of the church. He was totally convinced that women should have no voice in religious matters."

Randall sighed. "I am afraid that viewpoint is much too common in the Massachusetts Bay Colony. Too many feel threatened if anyone is allowed to think for themselves and reach their own understanding of God, especially if it is a woman."

"The man who lost the fight felt all the so-called Antinomians should be banished from the colony and Anne should be hung as a heretic," Martha said. "Fortunately not a lot of the bystanders agreed with him."

On the day of the trial, the Boston church was crowded with onlookers from all over the area. Mary and Martha found a seat on the back row of the church alongside the wives of the assembled ministers and magistrates.

When Anne was led to the front, she stared straight ahead with her head held high and her jaw clenched. Martha and Mary exchanged nervous glances when they noted the pale, exhausted look on Anne's face along with her expanding waistline. *What would the clergy do if she would not humble herself and agree with them?* Martha pondered.

Martha's eyes widened. Anne's grown son, Edward Hutchinson, and her son-in-law, Thomas Savage, were seated on the front bench on the opposite side of the room. *I wish Will Hutchinson could be here to support Anne. I know it would mean a lot to her, but I understand she would rather have him searching for a new home than spending his precious hours sitting in a church court.*

Anne took her place at the defendant's bench and stood with the others when the church officials entered and took their places at the presiding table. When the audience was seated, the Reverend John Cotton snapped, "Edward Hutchinson and Thomas Savage, would you step forward."

The two young men stepped forward with their heads bowed. They tried not to make eye contact with their mother. Reverend Cotton continued to glare at them. "You are both grown men. You should be insightful enough not to believe any of the teachings of your mother. You should have strength of character to challenge her nonsense and convince her of her error."

Edward and Thomas stared at the floor while John Cotton continued glaring at them. "Do you promise to control your mother's speech?"

"I promise to care for my mother," Edward stated firmly.

"Caring for your mother consists of keeping her from evil thoughts and speech," John Cotton retorted. "If you cannot control your mother, you will also be brought before the church and the court on charges of supporting heresy. Now return to your seats. I expect not to see you in this place again."

Reverend Cotton turned to the women's side of the church. His gaze settled on the back row where Mary Dyer and Martha Clarke were sitting. "To the women of this congregation, many of you have been seduced and led astray by Anne Hutchinson. I admonish you in the name of the Lord not to believe anything but the word of God spoken by the clergy. Anne Hutchinson is but a woman and subject to error. You are putting your very souls in danger."

Anne sat on the defense bench barely ten feet from her accusers and quietly observed the minister whom she had followed and served for more than twenty years. When Anne's head was turned slightly, Martha could see the pain in her eyes. The minister who had once been a strong supporter was now the chief of her accusers.

Finally, Reverend Cotton turned his attention to the defendant. "Anne Hutchinson, step forward and take your place before the ministers of the gospel."

Slowly and defiantly, Anne stepped forward. Her jaw was set and her back was erect.

"Anne Hutchinson, you have been accused of heresy against the church," The Reverend John Cotton snarled. "What do you have to say for yourself?"

Anne took a deep breath. "The only error the clergy have ever stated that merits excommunication for heresy is the denial of the resurrection of the body which is stated in the 39th Article of Religion. I have never denied the resurrection of the body."

John Cotton scowled. "I have heard upon proper authority about your inappropriate sexual activity and that you encourage other women to do likewise at your weekly meetings."

A gasp spread throughout the spectators. A look of disbelief spread across the faces of Edward Hutchinson and Thomas Savage.

"That is furthest from the truth," Anne retorted. "I have only been with one man, my husband Will Hutchinson. I have always encouraged absolute marital faithfulness to the women who attended the meetings in my home."

The ministers and judges continued to toss accusations upon her, scarcely giving time for her to answer. Each time, Anne responded with fierce defiance, despite her weakness and the formidable forces marshaled against her. Nothing they said could shake her firm resolve.

When the day ended, Reverend Wilson said, "Anne Hutchinson, in the name of the church, I order you to return to this place in seven days to finish giving an answer to the charges this church and the elders of other churches have concerning your opinions. During this week, you will not be allowed to return home, but must remain at Reverend John Cotton's house. Hopefully, he will be able to show you the error of your ways and you will recant of your heretical opinions."

With those words, Reverend John Wilson ended the session and the judges and ministers filed out of the side door. Anne was led down the aisle flanked by two guards. Martha watched her eyes scan the spectators and their eyes met briefly. She was certain she saw Anne's little finger rise in her direction in the form of a greeting.

Solemnly, Martha and Mary trudged along the muddy streets of Boston toward home. When they were safely away from the others, Martha said softly, "the clergy are trying to make Anne Hutchinson an example before the entire church and the elders of the colony. That trial was merely a performance, with the intent of shrinking her influence, not discovering the truth."

"I agree," Mary said. "They are trying to make her a scapegoat. Anne is encouraging people to think for themselves, and the clergy feel threatened."

Martha nodded, unable to hide her frustration. "They can't accept the fact that God might use women to preach the gospel."

Mary walked a few paces in silence. Pain to permeated her soul. Finally, she said, "Anne confided in me that of all the cruelty that has been said about her, the thing that hurts the most is the betrayal of John Cotton. She was such a loyal supporter that she followed him to the New World. It is almost unbelievable he would accuse her of such ghastly things while she was teaching most of the same opinions he was."

A week after the beginning of Anne Hutchinson's church trial, Martha and Mary again waited nervously for Anne Hutchinson to be brought into the church. This time they sat on the front row behind the defendant's table. When Anne entered, Martha studied her friend from head to toe. Months of in-house arrest had taken a toll on her. "She looks even more tired and drawn than she did when we saw her last," she whispered to Mary.

They waited restlessly for the ministers and judges to enter. Martha surveyed the supporters, accusers, and the curious who had gathered in the church meeting room. The muscles in her shoulders tightened. The sisters watched with concern while Reverend Cotton led Anne through a series of questions and instructions with more intensity than the week before.

This time during her interrogation, Anne altered her tactic in answering the questions. She acknowledged some of her errors in wording and tried to use scripture to explain her opinions, but courteously deferred to the minister's leadings. When she finished, she summarized her position with the words, 'my judgment is not altered though my expression does' and took her seat.

The ministers dismissed themselves while the audience waited in hushed silence. Mary and Martha leaned forward in the hope of reading their lips while they whispered with great animation in the corner of the room. Several minutes later, the clergy took their seats at the presiding table once again. Reverend John Cotton turned to the defendant. "Anne Hutchinson, step forward to receive your sentence."

Anne complied. The look of defiance was again on her face.

Reverend Cotton cleared his throat and surveyed the onlookers before turning back to the defendant. "Anne Hutchinson, the ministers of the Massachusetts Bay Colony convicts you of not only lying, but also for espousing doctrinal errors while teaching and preaching heresy. You are sentenced to excommunication from the church. You will leave this building as a leper."

Without looking back at Martha, Mary Dyer rose, walked to Anne's side, and took her hand. The pair walked out of the church together. When they reached the back, Anne shouted, "Better to be cast out of the church than to deny Christ."

When Anne and Mary descended the church steps hand in hand, several women who were not able to obtain seats were waiting outside. Martha shifted nervously when she heard one ask loudly, "Who is that woman accompanying Anne Hutchinson?"

The other woman answered loud enough to be heard in the front of the church, "She is Mary Dyer, the mother of a monster child!"

Martha watched with horror as the expressions on the ministers' faces hardened. Governor Winthrop's face reddened. "Reverend Cotton, what are they referring to when they say Mary Dyer is the mother of a monster child?"

Reverend Cotton's face blanched. A silence fell across the room before he stammered, "Last October

Anne Hutchinson and Midwife Jane Hawkins delivered Mary Dyer's grotesque child."

Governor Winthrop's eyes flashed with anger. "And why was I not notified of this devil child being born within our colony? Where is it buried? I need to confirm its existence and bring charges to the witches who delivered it."

Shock spread throughout the room. Never had the people of Boston seen such an open challenge between the governor and a clergy member. "The monster child is buried under the elm tree in the northwest corner of the church cemetery," Reverend Cotton said, in a hushed and shaky voice.

Governor Winthrop pounded on the table. "I demand the corpse be exhumed, regardless of how corrupted it may be, and brought to the shed behind my home by next Friday. I want all the clergy of Boston present when we examine the monster child."

Martha shrank back in horror. *Mary must never know Reverend Cotton betrayed her secret and they are going to disturb the grave of her daughter. Why couldn't they let the child rest in peace?*

The shadows were lengthening the following Saturday when Martha raced to her sister's home. "Mary...Mary," she shouted, thrusting open the door to her sister's immaculate house. The smell of cooking meat permeated the room. "I just heard the most dreadful thing."

Mary rose from the hearth where she was preparing stew to share with the neighbors. She hurried to her sister, and put her hand on her shoulder. "Slow down and tell me what happened."

Martha slumped onto a nearby bench. "Governor Winthrop was not aware of the baby you lost in October until you walked out of the church with Anne Hutchinson at her trial. Reverend Cotton told him Anne and Goody Hawkins had delivered your 'monster baby'."

Mary sat next to her sister on the bench and sighed. "I guess the truth was going to come out sooner or later. What happened?"

"Governor Winthrop was furious when he learned Reverend Cotton had secretly helped bury the baby. He is going to demand Reverend Cotton repent in front of the entire church."

Mary hung her head. "In spite of everything, I do not want Reverend Cotton to get in trouble on my account. He is the only clergy in the colony who has demonstrated a particle of compassion toward us."

Martha took a deep breath. *It is going to be painful, but it is more important Mary learn the harsh reality from me before she hears it from anyone else.* "It is worse than that," she said. "When Governor Winthrop examined the corpse, the official report claimed the child was greatly corrupted, yet it still had the horns, claws, holes in the back, and even some scales. He claims that over a hundred people actually saw the baby. Governor Winthrop and several ministers concluded the baby was a satanic mix of woman child, a fish, a beast, and a fowl, all woven together in one, and without a head."

Mary buried her head in her hands and sobbed.

Martha wrapped her arms around her sister. "Have no fear, Mary. God loves you. He will give you strength to walk through this. In a few weeks, we will be moving far away from Boston and out of the reach of the clergy and the magistrates. Hopefully, William and the others will be back in a few days and we can begin making plans to leave."

Mary and Martha held each other and cried. Gradually Mary's sobs began to subside, and she lifted her head from her sister's shoulder. "How can I tell my beloved husband that the clergy believe he is married to a mistress of the devil?"

A week after the sentencing of Anne Hutchinson, while plodding through the muddy street to visit one of the families of the Bodie Politick, Mary Dyer turned to her sister. "I heard Goody Hawkins is going on trial tomorrow. Would you be able to attend the General Court session? Since I am perceived as the mother of a devil's child, I am certain my presence would only make things more difficult for Goody."

A pained expression spread across Martha's face. "Of course I will go to Goody's trial. What is she being charged with?"

Before Mary could answer, a horse thundered past them. Mary and Martha jumped aside, but not before their coats and faces were coated with mud. They stopped and wiped the mud off each other's faces. When they regained their composure Mary said, "The crimes Goody Hawkins has been charged include giving barren women fertility potions of herbs, being 'notorious for familiarity with the devil,' occasionally falling into trances when she spoke Latin, as well as bringing a monster baby into this world."

Martha shook her head with frustration. "That is crazy. The current laws have no regard for women. They prohibit midwives from using anything men consider witchcraft, charms, or sorcery to ease the pain in childbirth. Although I questioned Goody's methods at first, I am grateful she gave me painkilling herbs during my delivery. I was close to passing out from the agony of the travail. The herbs had nothing to do with why my baby died."

Mary forced a smiled. "Martha, thank you for attending the trial in my place. I know how much you do not like harshness and conflict. We must spread the word. The women in Boston must let the clergy know how much they appreciate Goody Hawkins' help and medicine."

"Even if you had not asked, I wouldn't miss Goody's trial," Martha assured her. "Women have to support each other during these trying times."

The day of Goody Hawkin's trial, Mary Dyer waited nervously in her home. She checked the window every few minutes watching for Martha's return. At the end of the day, she saw her sister coming up the path to her house. Mary flung open the door. Without a formal greeting, she cried out. "Tell me what happened."

Martha walked the last few steps in silence. Her shoulders were slumped and her face was grim. "It was what we expected. The clergy used the argument that since Goody and Anne Hutchinson assisted with the birth of your baby, she, too, was of the devil. Goody Hawkins was also convicted of heresy and banished from the Massachusetts Bay Colony. It looks like she will be coming with us when we leave Boston."

Mary smiled for the first time in several days. "This may sound strange, but I am glad Goody was convicted. We will need a good midwife in our new settlement since Anne Hutchinson's baby is due in a few short weeks. Anne is already saying this time it feels different from when she was previously with child. If Goody were not with us, it would be up to you and me to deliver Anne's baby. I do not think either one of us have the skills to deliver a normal baby without the guidance of a midwife, much less a child or mother who may have difficulties."

Chapter Twelve

The Departure

Boston, April 1638

Martha Clarke trudged home. Her body ached and her head throbbed. She had promised to help the families whose fathers were in Rhode Island searching for a place to settled, but today the task seemed overwhelming. She had spent her entire day helping two different families with their laundry after their mothers became ill and had baked bread with children in still another family.

When her house came into view, the door opened and Randall appeared. He hurried to meet her. "You look exceptionally tired tonight," He gave her a quick hug. "I want to let you know your hard work is not going unnoticed. Everyone is talking about what a help you have been to everyone."

Martha sighed. "I wish the men would be home soon. Even though those in the Bodie Politick who remained in Boston have bonded together to help each other, on some days the work seems almost overwhelming without them."

Suddenly, she saw thirteen-year-old Samuel Hutchinson running down Summer Street shouting to anyone who would listen. "They're coming...They're coming...I just saw my father and the other men at the edge of town. They are pulling carts and carrying bundles and are moving very slowly."

Women and children began gathering in the street to discuss the news. Martha forgot her fatigue, raced toward the Dyer's home, and burst through the door without knocking. "The men are back. Samuel Hutchinson saw them on the edge of town. Grab little Samuel and let's go meet William and the others."

Mary set the plate she was drying on the shelf, threw the towel on the counter, and reached for her bonnet on the hook by the door. "I am so excited they are back safely. I can hardly wait to see William."

Martha picked up her nephew, and they rushed down their path, joining the other excited families who were hurrying toward the Boston Commons. Tears filled Martha's eyes when she spotted the tattered band of men trudging down the path toward the Commons. This was the beginning of a new chapter in their lives.

When the women and children in the crowd spotted their loved ones, shouts of greetings rang out while they ran into the arms of their fathers and husbands. Little Samuel clung to his mother's hand until he saw his father in the middle of the group. As soon as he recognized him, Samuel dropped his mother's hand and raced toward William with Mary close behind.

Mary waited patiently while William greeted his son before hugging her husband and kissing his ragged beard. "Welcome home, my beloved. I am glad you are back. I have missed you so."

The commons filled with excitement and laughter, even the arrival of the city watchman did not dampen their spirits. After the families had time to greet their loved ones, William Coddington lifted his arms and shouted for silence. When everyone was quiet he announced, "I know you are bursting with questions. It will be easier if we tell everyone at the same time and answer the common questions you may have. I invite everyone involved in the move to my house where we will describe the land we purchased from the Natives."

Martha was glad when Randall worked his way through the crowd and squeezed her hand in greeting before turning to help carry William's bags. Excitedly the assembled band followed William Coddington to his home. When they arrived, most of the women and children sat on the floor while the men lined the back wall of the crowded main room. The odor of wet leather intermingled with sweaty body odors from men who had not bathed in days.

After watching the guests shuffle to make room for late arrivals, John Clarke raised his hand for silence. "I cannot tell you how good it is to be home. It was a difficult trip, but extremely fruitful. We know the main questions on everybody's mind are where and when will we be going?"

Everyone in the room nodded simultaneously. Martha leaned over and whispered to her sister, "I know our departure date can't come soon enough for you." Seeing a quick smile spread across her sister's face, Martha turned back to John Clarke and continued listening intently.

Reverend Clarke continued with a strong, firm voice. "We were able to purchase the entire fifteen-mile-long island of Aquidneck in the Rhode Island area from the Narragansett Indians. It is a fertile land with an excellent harbor with an abundance of fish."

An enthusiastic cheer of approval erupted throughout the group. When the excitement subsided, John Clarke continued, "William Dyer will be responsible for surveying the land and dividing the plots equally among the families. Each man will receive a lot for his house along with two or three acres for gardens and outbuildings. These lots can be supplemented with larger plots of several hundred acres for farming, slightly to the south. The cost of the land will be two shillings per acre. Because we were told we had to be out of Boston before May or appear in the General Court once again, we need to begin packing immediately and leave by the middle of April."

"But how are we going to get there?" a worn, frail woman seated in the front asked. "Our single horse will not be able to pull our belongings and we have too many farm animals for my husband and me to drive a long distance."

"Have no fear," John Clarke assured her. "We will all work together and share the workload. I am going to arrange with boat owners in the harbor to take the animals and some household goods around Cape Cod. We can take the rest of the household goods overland with horses and wagons. The most important thing everyone must do is put an identifying, permanent mark on each of their animals before they board a ship."

With those words, William Coddington stepped forward. "Until we depart, we can meet in my home at the end of each day to share the progress of our plans. We each need to know what the others are bringing so we can make sure we have everything we need without duplications."

Reverend Clarke smiled and nodded with approval. "William, thank you for offering your home. We definitely need a central gathering place." He turned back to the group who were waiting for further instruction. "Those of you who prefer to head north and join Reverend John Wheelwright in New Hampshire are free to do so. However, Reverend Wheelwright cannot guarantee you land in New Hampshire. Many decisions remain, but those who just returned from Rhode Island are exhausted and need to go home and rest. We will meet here tomorrow at three o'clock to sign an agreement to establish a new colony and answer further questions at that time. We will call this new document the Portsmouth Compact."

The gathering at the Coddington's disbanded and the families headed for their separate homes. Randall and Martha walked alongside Mary and William Dyer and helped William carry his supplies. Their steps were slow and determined. After a few yards, William turned to his brother-in-law. "Randall, you know you do not have to come with us? You and Martha were not among those being banished from the colony. We are going into an area that has not been settled by Europeans, and life will be extremely primitive at first."

Randall straightened his shoulders and took a deep breath. "No, we choose to go with the others. We came to Boston for religious freedom like everyone else, but found it worse than in England. Religious freedom is more important to us than daily comforts."

After a few paces, Mary turned to her sister. "Martha, I know you hold Anne Hutchinson in high regard, but you have also questioned many of her teachings. Are you sure you want to come with us when you do not have to?"

Martha wrapped her arm around her sister. "When we left England, we agreed to stay together through good times and bad. I cannot leave you now. I want the same freedoms you do. I am willing to make the sacrifice."

William's steps became slower and slower. In spite of his weariness, he turned to Randall. "I admire your dedication and am glad you have decided to come with us. It will make the transition much easier, but it is going to be difficult for both of us to sell our houses in a short time and get everything packed."

"Don't worry about a thing," Randall said. "You just rest for a few days. I will begin making arrangements for all of us right away."

The following day, the Dyers and the Clarkes strolled happily along the muddy streets of Boston toward the Coddington home. William Dyer carried little Samuel who clung tightly to his father's neck. An air of anticipation surrounded them. "I wonder if the Hutchinsons will come with us to Rhode Island or go with her brother-in-law to New Hampshire," Martha said. "Their families have always been close."

Mary's jaw dropped. "I certainly hope Anne does not go to New Hampshire. She has meant so much to all of us. She explains the ways of God much better than the church ministers do."

William Dyer moved closer to his wife and took her hand. "Will Hutchinson took an active role in arranging for the settlement in Rhode Island and building a new home for his family there. I am positive they will be coming with us. I doubt if many will go their separate ways. It is safer to travel in a group than for individual families to take off on their own."

Mary smiled. "That is comforting news. I don't know how our new community could get along without her."

The two families walked in silence, basking in the presence of being together again. Suddenly they heard a shout from behind. "Mary...Martha, wait for me." They turned to see Anne Hutchinson trudging toward them.

Anne's strides were slow and labored. Mud caked her shoes with each progressive step. "Isn't this exciting? God is blessing us with our own colony where we can live in peace and worship God in the manner he leads. I am looking forward to going to Aquidneck Island."

Mary Dyer reached out and took Anne's hand. "I am glad you decided to come with us. I can hardly wait to leave. How are your moving plans coming?"

Anne sighed and forced a smile. "That is why I wanted to talk to both of you. I may need help during the trip. The younger children will be going to Aquidneck Island with us, but some of the older ones will be staying in Boston. Richard's wife is five months pregnant and does not want to move into a primitive area until after the baby is born."

Martha noticed the pained expression on Anne's face and said, "After being in house arrest last winter, it must be difficult to leave part of your family behind."

"It is more important my children become independent, God-fearing people without feeling obligated to live close to their father and me for the rest of our lives," Anne stated firmly. "I am grateful Edward is able to help the family move and then return to Boston to be with his wife and baby. Six days of walking is going to be taxing on all of us."

When they neared the Coddington's home, they saw Will Hutchinson waiting outside for his wife. The three couples exchanged greetings, slipped quietly into the main room, and stood against the back wall. They watched the others enter the room, all talking among each other.

After everyone was assembled, John Clarke stepped forward. "One of the first things we need to know is exactly who will be going to Rhode Island with us and who will be going to New Hampshire." His eyes scanned the room. "Would those who plan to go to New

Hampshire or return to England, please raise your hand."

Martha glanced around a silent room. Cautiously four men raised their hands. A look of sadness seemed to spread across the faces of the others.

"We wish you all Godspeed," Reverend Clarke said. "If there is anything we can do to help each other in the transition, we will all work together during this difficult period. When you see John Wheelwright, please give him our regards. If we do not meet him again in this life, we will see him in the next."

John Clarke turned back to the entire group. "I assume the rest of you will be coming to Rhode Island with us." He surveyed the group. When he was assured the others agreed, he continued. "I ask everyone heading south with us, to give the names and ages of all your family members to William Dyer. Those who will be bringing livestock will need to draw a picture of the marking you intend to use to identify each of your animals. No animal will be allowed on the ship without the owner's mark and all poultry must be in crates."

The conversation continued while the sun dropped behind the horizon and darkness settled over the Boston. William Coddington's wife lit a series of candles and arranged them on the table, fireplace, and windowsills. Little by little, the plans for their departure began to take shape.

The following Saturday afternoon a loud rapping on the door to the Dyer's home interrupted Mary and Martha's packing. "Who could that be?" Mary hurried to the door and cautiously opened it. "Mister Coddington, Reverend Clarke, please come in."

"Is your husband at home?" John Clarke asked.

"William is in the shop. Ever since he got back from Rhode Island, he has been spending all his waking hours constructing boxes for those who are leaving. Have a seat and I will get him."

Mary hurried through the front door to the shop and within minutes, William Dyer appeared in the doorway. "What brings the two of you to our humble abode this fine day?"

"We hate to interrupt you at such a busy time," John Clarke said, "but we need to get a few things settled before our meeting this evening. More families than we anticipated are planning to come to Rhode Island with us. Many who were not banished are leaving voluntarily because they support our principle of religious freedom. How many have officially signed up at this time?"

"Just a moment and I will check." William Dyer strolled to his crude wooden desk in the corner. He removed a sheet of paper and returned to the table where the guests were sitting. He studied the paper in silence for several minutes. "Over sixty men have given

me the names of their family members. That is more than we planned for when we bought the Aquidneck Island."

William Coddington shook his head is dismay. "In that case, your record keeping is going to be even more important. We will have to make Friday the deadline to sign the Portsmouth Compact if they plan to come with us. With so many going, it makes it even more important that you get to Rhode Island ahead of the group to survey the land. How soon do you think you will be able to leave?"

William Dyer shook his head, frowned, and took a deep breath. "I have over fifty wooden boxes I have promised to build for others. They will have trouble packing and moving without them."

Martha laid the blankets she was packing into the box and joined the men at the table. "Randall has been busy building boxes himself, but if you have to leave early, he might be willing to work overtime and build all the combined boxes ordered."

"Thank you, Martha," William said. "I will talk to Randall tomorrow and see if he is willing to do additional the boxes. It will make it easier for me to get things set up in Rhode Island, if I leave as soon as possible."

At dawn the first day of April, Randall Clarke stopped their horse and wagon in front of the Hutchinson house. He turned to Martha before jumping to the ground. "Wait here with our wagon. I want to go back and help Mary. I admire her determination to drive their own wagon, and I know she is an expert handling the horses, but she may not have the physical strength to get thc horses hitched to the wagon."

Randall sprinted the five blocks to the Dyer home. When he arrived, Mary was getting ready to hitch the horses to the wagon. "Let me help you." He checked the bridle, collar harness, backed the horses to the wagon, and secured the harness to the wagon tongue. When he was finished, he lifted little Samuel and Mary into the wagon before he climbed up himself. "I will drive you to the Hutchinson's. John Coggeshall's family is coming with us and I have made arrangements for their son, Nicholas, to help you drive your wagon when you need a rest."

When the wagon began to move, Mary turned and took one last look at her home. "I am glad we were able to sell the property for a good price, but it is bittersweet. William and I worked hard to build the house and adjoining shop, and now we have to start over again."

Randall gave his sister-in-law a sympathetic look. "It may be difficult at first, but in the end, I am certain we will all be happier in Rhode Island."

When the Dyer's wagon turned the corner toward the Hutchinson's home, three wagons were already lined up with the Hutchinson's wagon in the lead. The adults were gathered under the oak tree on the front yard while the children played nearby. Mary jumped from the wagon and approached the group. She could hear Edward Hutchinson say, "We will have to follow an Indian trail to Mount Hope. I have never been this way before, but my father gave me detailed directions so we should not have any problems finding our way. When we get to Mount Hope, we should be able to see Aquidneck Island. It will probably take us five or six days of to get there. We will wait near Mount Hope for those coming by ship and they will help us get across the bay. Are we all ready to leave?"

In spite of the day of her delivery drawing closer, Anne Hutchinson said, "I prefer to walk. The older children are welcome to walk with me. We will stay between our wagon and the Coggeshall's wagon in case anyone gets tired and needs to ride."

"That is a good idea, mother," Edward said. "No one should wander from the path without a musket.

There are wolves in the woods and it is rumored small bands of hostile Pequots are occasionally seen in the area."

All the children over the age of seven hurried to Anne's side and shouted excitedly. "I want to walk with you. I am strong and I am not afraid of the Natives."

Anne put her index fingers to her lips. "Hush. We must remember to keep very quiet until we are out of town. We do not want people to know the precise time we are leaving."

Sensing Anne's frustration with the children's exuberance, Martha turned to her husband. "I think I had better walk with Anne. She is going to need help with the children."

Moments after Martha joined the children, she felt a small hand envelope hers. She looked down at eight-year-old Katherine Hutchinson's tear filled eyes.

"Are you afraid, too?" Katherine whispered. "Do you think the officials will follow us? The clergy have been mean to mother when all she wanted to do was teach about God."

Martha wrapped her arm around the child. "We are going to a place we will be safe. God will protect us, but we must be strong."

"I know," Katherine whimpered, "but I still do not want to leave our home."

In the midst of her clouded emotions, Martha could hear Edward Hutchinson shout 'giddy up' and slap the reins against the rumps of the horses in the lead wagon. She forced a smile and squeezed Katherine's hand. Of all Anne's children, it was little Katherine she held a special fondness for. If Katherine had not been rescued from the path of racing draft horses five years before, she would not be with them today. "We are off," Martha said. Let's consider this the beginning of a new adventure, not an ending to our life in Boston."

Slowly the four families traveled the streets of Boston for the last time. Women working in their front yards recognized Anne Hutchinson and her followers. They gathered their children around them and hurried inside. The families of the signers of the Portsmouth Compact held their heads high while they silently exited the city and disappeared into the surrounding forest.

When they first entered the woods, every sound made the children jump. Little by little, they relaxed and enjoyed the new sights and sounds around them. They tried imitating the chirping of the various birds in the trees above them, when they tired of chirping, the children tried to make the sounds of wolves howling at night. In the middle of the children's frivolity, a band of Pequot Indians approached from the west without warning. Edward pulled his wagon to a stop while the others did likewise. The children huddled around their mothers.

Each man jumped from his wagons and exchanged nervous glances. Anne Hutchinson stepped forward and said softly, "Raise your right hand with the palm forward to show there are no weapons in your hand."

When the six Natives saw their gesture of peace, they responded with a wave and took a few cautious steps toward them. The younger children began to whimper and clung tighter to their mothers.

Anne wrapped her arms around those closest to her. "Don't be afraid. These are friendly Natives. Maybe we could share our food with them."

The frightened travelers remained cautious while the Natives approached. The leader of the Natives moved his partly closed hand downward past his mouth and back up. He pointed to the group then pointed to a large wooden bowl held by the shortest of the braves.

Anne stepped forward, peered into the bowl, smiled, and turned back to her friends. "I think they want to share food with us."

The brave put a handful of unfamiliar substances into her hand. She cautiously placed a small amount in her mouth. "Umm, this is good. It tastes like cornmeal with wild, dried strawberries."

The Natives nodded with pride when seeing Anne's look of approval and moved from person to person giving each a handful of strawberry cornmeal. The frightened children relaxed and found a fallen tree to sit upon to enjoy their nourishment. The bowl was nearly empty when the brave reached Edward Hutchinson. Before accepting the food, Edward handed the brave a string of colored beads. The Natives made an unknown gesture, but from the looks on their faces, everyone could understand it meant thank you.

Martha watched while the Natives examined the horses and looked inside each wagon with curiosity. When the travelers had eaten their fill and rested, Edward motioned for everyone to get into their wagons. Much to their surprise, the Natives did not leave, but walked alongside them through the forest. When they reached a fork in the trail, Edward hesitated and took out the map his father had drawn for him. When he began turning to the left, the six Pequot Indians in unison pointed to the right. Edward turned toward his mother seated beside him with a questioning look.

Anne studied the map for a few minutes and looked heavenward. "We need to follow the Natives. They must be sent by God to help us along the way."

Martha tried to mask her apprehension when the path became narrower and the trees more dense. *Are we being led into a trap or an ambush?*

Having no other choice, Edward led the caravan down the Indian trail. The shadows lengthened and the evening calls of owls were heard in the distance before the caravan reached a clearing in the woods. In the middle of the clearing stood six crudely built wigwams. Before anyone could react, the Natives disappeared back into the forest.

Each of the travelers stood in silence filled with amazement and fatigue. Finally, Anne shouted, "God does provide."

The men unhitched the horses, tied them to low hanging limbs, and began repairing the wigwams while the children gathered firewood. By the time darkness had descended upon them, the preparations for night were complete and the weary travelers huddled around the blazing fire wrapped in blankets.

Katherine Hutchinson laid her head on Martha's lap while Martha stroked the child's hair. "Today was just like I said it would be — an adventure," Martha said. "I wonder what tomorrow will hold."

"But what if friendly Natives don't come to help us tomorrow?" Katherine asked. "How will we know where to go? What if fighting Natives come instead?"

Chapter Thirteen
Aquidneck Island

Aquidneck Island, Spring 1638

The morning songbirds awakened Martha Clarke. She rolled over in the bed of the wagon and faced her husband. Randall's eyes were closed and his mouth slightly ajar. For a few moments, she lay watching him sleep, memories of the love and happy times they shared flooded over her. This move was going to be a new adventure they would experience together. She then slipped quietly off the wagon. Since she was the first one to the fire, Martha stirred the embers covered with ashes from the night before to obtain a little heat. She warmed a small amount of goats' milk and poured it into a cup.

The moist grass squeaked beneath her shoes when she approached her sister's wagon. Martha stood on her toes and peered into the wagon bed. Mary rolled over, forced a weak smile, and moaned.

"Mary, are you all right?" Martha whispered. "You are extremely pale."

Mary looked at her sister. "I am so tired. It has been a hard four days on the road and whenever Samuel was not sleeping, it seemed like he was crying. I thought I could handle the team myself when William went on in advance, but there is no way I could have done it without Nicholas taking over and driving the team for me."

Martha climbed onto the wagon, sat beside her sister, and handed her the cup. "I brought you some warm milk which should make you feel better." When her nephew awoke, she picked him up and cradled him in her arms. "Hopefully, we will see the ships soon. It must be miserable for them as well, trying to keep the animals calm in a confined space. I wish we could cross the bay on our own, but we will need their help."

Mary remained on her back in the wagon bed and stared at the fluffy clouds in the grey sky. "I am anxious to get to Aquidneck Island. I do not think I can take another hour bumping along in the wagon through mud and ruts with low hanging branches hitting me in the face."

"Hopefully the ships will be here today," Martha tried to assure her. "In the meantime, try to get some rest before the others awaken." In the distance, the sisters heard movement and talking in their encampment. "It sounds like the men are trying to get a good fire started. I hope they are successful. It was too wet last night and everyone was much too tired to keep a fire going. Fortunately, several men caught fish last night before they went to bed. Rest here and I will help with the cooking and bring your breakfast back to you. I will take Samuel with me, so you can rest."

By now, the women were comfortable sharing chores and instinctively knew what the others were going to do. Martha squatted over the open flame and began frying fish in an iron skillet. Anne Hutchinson and Mary Coggeshall spread butter on the dry bread and took out a container of water and drinking cups. The smell of frying fish brought the children scrambling to the campfire.

When everyone had finished eating, the younger children wandered to the shoreline to play. Suddenly, they began shouting. "I see a ship...I see a ship."

Hearing their shouts, Mary laid down her plate and jumped from her wagon. She and Martha raced to the shoreline along with the others. At first, all they saw were seagulls soaring through the air and the whitecaps beating against the shoreline, but soon white sails were seen in the distance. Within minutes, the ship was in shallow water close to the bank.

Martha and Mary watched the six men climb over the side and wade toward them. After the excited greetings subsided, William Coddington addressed the group. "We are so glad to see you all. We have been concerned about your travels. Did you have any major problems along the way?"

Edward Hutchinson stepped forward. "No. We are all tired, but in good health. We met a band of Pequot Indians who helped us part of the way, and provided food for us."

William Coddington surveyed the weary group. "We are glad to hear all is well. I am certain everyone is anxious to get settled. We will begin helping you cross over to Aquidneck Island as soon as we can. William Dyer is already on the island surveying the family plots."

"The Natives seemed to already have had contact with the English," Edward Hutchinson said. "They spoke a few words I thought I recognized. They kept pointing south and saying 'Pocasset'."

William Coddington smiled. "The Natives call the area we are going 'Pocasset', which means 'where the stream widens.' Since we will be living there, we thought we should Anglicize the name and call it Portsmouth."

Martha smiled while she watched the younger children begin chattering excitedly among themselves. It was obvious Katherine Hutchinson was selected their spokesperson. "We can hardly wait to get there. Can we leave on the ship with you?"

"I wish you could," John Clarke said, "but the ship is full of animals." He looked over the children's heads to the adults standing behind. "If a couple of the men would come with us to help unload the animals on the other side and tend to them while we come back to get the others, it would be a great help."

John Coggeshall stepped forward. He looked at his son and back to John Clarke. "My son, Nicholas, and I will be glad to go with you. That will leave Randall and Edward here to protect the women and children."

"I appreciate your offer," John Clarke said and turned his attention to the women. "We should be back by mid-afternoon. When the tide is out, the men will be able to get the horses and wagons across the bay. With the livestock off the ship, we can load it with what is now in the wagons. Hopefully, we will have everything across by dark and all of us will be able to sleep on Aquidneck Island tonight."

As the hours passed, those left on Mount Hope waited restlessly at their campsite. Mary returned to her wagon for much needed sleep while Martha watched Samuel play with the older children.

Two hours later, Mary awoke and rejoined the women and children. "Thank you for minding Samuel for me. I feel so much better. At least now I will have the strength to cross over to our new home."

"You needed the rest," Martha assured her. "You look so much better. Anne has been reminding us that in spite of the hardship and sacrifices we are going through, we will be much better off away from the Puritan clergy. We can always trust God to guide us."

The sun was high overhead when the ship returned. Martha and Mary watched the men throw a raft into the water and guide it ashore. Much to Mary's delight, William was in their midst. He waved to his family and shouted, "Mary, you will love your new home. This land is more beautiful than you can imagine."

When little Samuel saw his father approaching, he ran to him and wrapped his arms around his father's leg. William leaned over, picked up his son, and hugged him tightly against his chest while he talked to his wife. "I have most of the land surveyed for the first arrivals. However, I have selected an adjacent, small island for our home. It is not named yet, so I am going to call it Dyer Island. Randall and Martha can build their house next to ours and we can share the grazing land for the animals."

Mary laughed. "Keeping the animals on an island, we won't have to worry about building fences. I can hardly wait to see it."

William set his son on the ground and turned to Randall. "I am grateful for your help moving my family and household goods. It is going to take us several hours to get everything across the bay and will probably be dark before we finish. We will have to spend the night with the others on Aquidneck Island, but first thing in the morning, we can begin moving our livestock and household goods onto Dyer Island."

Everyone worked together unloading the wagons and placing the household goods on the raft. As soon as it was full, the men pushed it to the ship, unloaded it, and returned to shore for another load. When the last of the household goods was on the ship, the children excitedly climbed aboard followed by the women. With the wind behind them, the ship slowly moved toward the other shore.

When the wagons were empty, the men on Mount Hope took the reins of each of the horses and cautiously led them into the water. Step by step, the horses entered deeper water, pulling the wagons behind them. When the water came up to their shoulders, the horses instinctively began to swim with a man swimming beside him holding onto the bridle. When the water reached the base of the wagon beds, they began to float behind the horses. When each horse and wagon reached the opposite bank, the men led them to shore surrounded by the loud cheers from the children and women.

❡

Shelter was the settlers' primary concern the first night on Aquidneck Island. Thankful to have at last reached their new home, everyone seemed as awed by its beauty as Mary felt. However, they trembled in their beds at the sustained howling of wolves.

Little Samuel snuggled against Mary and sobbed while the terrified cries of the other children could be heard throughout their encampment. "William, something must be done about the wolves. No one will be able to rest until they are gone."

William pulled his wife closer to himself. "We will meet with the others at daybreak and discuss it. We may need to send someone to Providence Plantation and see if Roger Williams knows how to get rid of the wolves. We cannot live with our children terrified whenever the sun goes down."

Before the women and children were awake the next morning, the men gathered around their campfire. "Not only are the wolves scaring our families," John Clarke said. "They are a danger to our livestock. We will have to keep an armed guard with the livestock until we figure out how to get rid of the wolves. Hopefully, Roger Williams will have a solution for us."

Randall Clarke stretched his long legs and pulled his woolen blanket tighter around himself. "If someone will tell me how to get to Providence Plantation, I will leave at the break of dawn. We have a settlement to build and cannot risk the wolves harming our livestock."

William Dyer drew a quick map to Providence Plantation. Before the women and children were awake, Randall Clarke and Nicholas Coggeshall packed a few supplies and left to seek advice from Roger Williams at Providence Plantation. When the others awoke, they quickly ate their breakfast and began organizing their belongings. William Dyer helped each family locate their purchased plot of land where they could build their house and fences for their animals.

When all the livestock and household goods had been removed from the ship except for the Dyers and the Clarke's, Mary began an inspection. "I am glad all the sheep are accounted for. William and I have agreed the sheep are going to be my responsibility while he tries to earn a living in his woodshop, like he did in Boston."

Martha stacked the box she was carrying in the corner of the deck on top of another and turned to Mary. "With William's surveying responsibilities and record keeping for the colony, he is going to be extremely busy. We came with you to help in any way we could." Martha hesitated and sighed, unable to mask her frustrations. "Hopefully, I will be having a child of my own soon."

The women worked nearly non-stop throughout the day. As the shadows began to lengthen, Martha and

Mary sat on the deck of the ship to rest while Samuel played nearby. In the distance, they could see two men approaching the encampment. When the men drew closer, they recognized Nicholas and Randall.

When Nicholas spotted his parents' wagon, he left to join them while Randall climbed onto the ship. He looked around with amazement. "I cannot believe the two of you have rearranged this all by yourselves. You must be exhausted."

Martha smiled a weary smile. "We definitely are. I am still feeling every heavy box in my back."

Randall affectionately rubbed the small of Martha's back without saying a word. She breathed deeply and felt her back and shoulders relax.

When it was obvious Martha was feeling better, Randall turned to Mary. "Do you know where William is?"

"Not specifically," Mary said. "He has been busy helping families locate their plots all day. It is a good thing he came before the others so he had the majority of the work done and people can begin settling in right away."

"I have good news for everyone, but I need to talk to William first," Randall said.

Martha looked at her husband quizzically. "What is your good news?"

"Since he has learned their language, Roger Williams is certain he will be able to convince the Narragansett Indians to come to Aquidneck Island and get rid of the wolves. The Natives love him and will do almost anything for him. Roger thought the Indians should be here sometime tomorrow," Randall reached into an open sack on the box beside the women, removed a carrot, and took a bite. "I need to find William as well as William Coddington and John

Clarke to let them know about the Natives arriving tomorrow. We do not want to have anyone frightened of their appearance."

"They will be glad to hear the good news," Martha said. "We will have supper ready for you when you return."

Randall hugged his wife. "I will ask William what he has planned about moving to Dyer Island. It is obvious we will have to spend another night here. You both look tired. I appreciate all your hard work today."

Midafternoon the next day, three tree-trunk shaped canoes carrying twenty-four Natives appeared on the northern shore of Aquidneck Island. They wore only loincloths made of deerskin, while their arms and legs were decorated with wampum bracelets; some had bone pendants or beads. Their bodies carried a strong smell of raccoon fat, used to grease their bodies.

The men hurried to the shoreline to greet the Natives while the women watched from a distance and the younger children clung tightly to their mothers' skirts. Fortunately, one of the braves spoke a few words of English, so accompanied with sign language the Natives and the English were able to communicate. Using crude shovels, the Natives dug a deep pit by the sea. Once they appeared satisfied, they disappeared into the woods.

Martha watched until they were out of sight and then turned to her sister. "I wonder what they are doing. It does not make sense to me."

"I have no idea," Mary replied. "However, under the circumstances, we have to trust whatever they have planned."

The women continued murmuring among themselves for a few minutes trying to figure out what the Natives were doing, and then returned to their work. An hour later, the Natives returned from the woods carrying a wounded deer on a long stick. The women and children watched while they placed their lure into the bottom of their freshly dug pit. The Natives again disappeared into the woods. With whoops, hollers, and flying arrows, the Indians rounded up a pack of wolves and stampeded them towards the trap. The normally quiet woods turned into a screaming jungle. The children clasped their hands over their ears to dull the shrieks. The commotion did not last long. The pit became a wolf grave and Aquidneck Island had twenty fewer wolves to prowl around the settlers at night and disturb their livestock.

When the Natives were nearly finished, Randall and William Coddington approached Martha while she was preparing fish for the evening meal. "Martha, do we have sugar that is easy to get to?"

"Yes, I think the sugar is in one of the last boxes we put on the ship. Why do you ask?"

"Roger Williams told me the Natives like sugar. If we want to keep a good relationship with them we will need to give them a gift that they treasure," Randall explained.

William Coddington nodded his agreement. "This is only a temporary solution to the wolves. We will eventually need a more permanent protection and will have to plan for the fences around a common pasture for the entire town and individual barns and outbuildings for each farm. In the meantime, we should be able to rest in peace and tranquility tonight."

The settlers on Aquidneck Island excitedly set to work establishing their homes. William and Randall's experiences in Boston provided them both with skills and techniques to build two houses and a shop in less than half the time their Boston house had taken to build. Mary and Martha took turns tending the sheep, caring for little Samuel, and sharing household chores.

One late afternoon Mary joined her sister in their freshly plowed garden. "Have you heard the news?"

Martha stood up and smiled. She was always amazed at her sister's enthusiasm for any new development, no matter how small. "What news?"

"Next week we are going to hold our first town meeting," Mary said. "William said they are going to allow women to attend, but he wasn't sure if they would let us vote, yet. Do you want to go with me?"

"That is a silly question," Martha teased. "Of course I would love to attend. I have never been a part of planning for our future before. Others have always done the planning and I have done whatever I could just to get along."

Mary sat on a nearby tree stump while Martha laid aside her crudely built hoe and sat on the ground. A cool ocean breeze blew in from the bay and dried the perspiration on their foreheads. "After serving as the secretary of the Bodie Politick, William expects he will be elected clerk, which means he will have to plan and conduct the meetings. He said William Coddington and John Clarke have drafted a few proposed laws for the settlement and will present them at the meeting for approval."

The week passed quickly for the Dyers and the Clarkes. Martha and Mary completed planting the garden and helped deliver three new lambs into the fold while their husbands put the final touches on their houses and woodshops. When the day of the town meeting came, the two couples and little Samuel crowded into their canoe and the men rowed from Dyer Island to the main island.

When they arrived in the clearing that was to become the City Commons, Mary and Martha took Samuel and sat under a tree while William and Randall joined the men. A table and two chairs were set in the front of the assembly. As predicted, William Dyer was elected clerk and William Coddington was selected judge. After the vote, they took their places at the presiding table under the oak tree.

"The first issue we need to address," William Dyer began, "is who should be allowed to vote in our colony. A discussion of the women's vote will be done later. Our first concern is the rapid growth of our settlement. Word is spreading of our endeavors, and new families are moving here from Massachusetts who were not a part of the original Bodie Politick."

Up to this time, Randall had been kneeling at the edge of the men's section listening intently to the proceeding. He rose and said, "Since only a third of the colonists of Boston are allowed to vote, because they were either indentured servants or did not own land, I think we should be more lenient with newcomers. I suggest all men, whether free or indentured, who are living within the settlement be allowed to vote."

A spontaneous applause erupted throughout the gathering. William Dyer smiled. "There is obviously no need to take an official vote on the matter, but record that all men in the settlement will have the right to vote." William surveyed his friends sitting around him. "The next on our agenda should be the safety of our settlement. Are there any suggestions?"

After much discussion, the men voted to require every man between the ages of 18 and 50 years to bear arms and drill for militia service and anyone found two miles from town unarmed or, attending a meeting without their firearms, would be fined. Shadows lengthened and some became restless while the men developed a detailed alarm system in which drums would be steadily beaten while a messenger ran from house to house alerting the inhabitants of impending danger.

When their protection system was agreed upon, William Dyer again surveyed the group. "Due to the lateness of the day, I suggest we disband and meet together next week to decide if we want to relocate the center of the town and construct a building to function as an inn, brewery, and grocery store. I appreciate your valuable input today and will look forward to everyone's attendance next Wednesday at two o'clock at the same place."

The day following the first town meeting, Martha approached Mary as she was tending to her new lambs. "I did not see Anne Hutchinson at the meeting yesterday. She would never miss such an event unless something was wrong. I know it is getting close to when her baby is due. We have a lot of work to do here, but I would like to visit her and make sure she is all right."

Mary set one of the lambs on his feet next to his mother and continued checking the others for any injuries. "As soon as I finish here, let's get Samuel and we can take the log boat across the bay. Since we have been busy getting settled, I have missed visiting with

Anne on a regular basis and hearing her encouraging words."

An hour later, Mary and Martha were rowing their hollowed out log boat to Aquidneck Island with little Samuel smiling in the back. He seemed to love nothing more than to have the wind blow through in his hair and hear the splashing of the oars in the water.

"It is going to be good to see Anne again," Martha said. "She always has the right words to lift my spirits. Maybe there is some way we can help her after all she has done so much for us."

Mary made two powerful strokes with her oar. "She is an amazing woman. I cannot imagine the strength it took to bear fifteen healthy children in twenty-five years, maintain her busy household, and still have the energy to teach the Bible the way she does. However, since her trial, she continues to put on a strong face, but I get the impression she has not felt well during this entire pregnancy. She never complained, but moving from Boston has been very hard on her."

Reaching the sandy shore of Aquidneck Island, Mary and Martha pulled their primitive boat onto the bank, anchored it to a nearby branch, and climbed the incline toward the Hutchinson's home. When they reached the top, Martha stopped to readjust her bonnet to reflect the noontime sun. "After all the work they have done for the settlement, I hope people are paying the Hutchinsons back in one way or another."

Mary took off her shoe, dumped out the sand, and put it back on her foot. "William is doing his best to see that they are rewarded. They received six lots on what they call the Great Cove. With such a large family, they need the extra land for garden space and grazing their animals."

When Mary and Martha approached the Hutchinsons' home, eight-year-old Katherine came bounding toward them. "Martha...Martha. I am glad you came. How did you know we needed your help?" She stopped for a moment to catch her breath. "Mother is very sick. She told me not to get help because it wasn't time for the baby, but we are scared."

The sisters exchanged knowing glances. "God has a way of spreading the news," Martha said.

Martha and Mary followed Katherine into the Hutchinson's hastily constructed home and knelt beside their friend who was lying on a makeshift rope bed. Samuel went to play in the corner with two-year-old Zuriel Hutchinson.

"Anne, how are you?" Mary asked.

"Praise God," Anne murmured. "You came without anyone asking. You are both angels of mercy. I do not know what is wrong. It isn't time for the baby." A severe cramp surged through Anne's body, and a loud groan escaped her lips. Sweat beaded her forehead. When the pain subsided, she turned to her friends. "I think the baby is coming. Would you have the children take all the buckets they can find to the ocean and get water? The older girls can heat it in the kettle at the side of the house. "

While the children hurried back and forth from the ocean shore and started a fire in the pit beside the house, Mary and Martha tended to their friend. Anne began to sob. "Something must be wrong. I have had fifteen babies, but this pregnancy has not been like the others. I have not felt this baby move the entire time I carried it."

Mary held her friend's hand while Anne's pain increased. When it was time to deliver the baby, the sisters worked methodically together. Suddenly Mary gasped and tears rolled down her cheeks. "I am so sorry, Anne. This is not a baby. It is a mass of tissue that resembles a handful of transparent gooseberries."

"Please let me see it." Anne begged. She stared at the mass. A look of shock spread across her face while tears rolled down her cheeks. "Mary, we both had malformed pregnancies. I wonder what this means?" Within minutes, she lay back with exhaustion while she was still bleeding profusely.

Martha went to the front door, opened it, and scanned the cove. "Bridgette," she shouted. "Hurry...Fetch your father. Tell him to come quickly."

Bridgette gasped. "Is mother all right?"

Martha swallowed hard. A lump built in her throat. "I hope so. Just hurry."

All of the children followed Bridgett to find their father. While the children were away, Martha and Mary sat on the floor beside their weak friend, tending to her the best they could. Time seemed to stand still until they heard heavy footsteps outside and the front door burst open. Will Hutchinson and John Clarke stood in the doorframe.

Will knelt beside his wife and took her hand. She roused and opened her eyes. "Anne, how are you? Why didn't you tell me you were feeling badly when I left?"

Anne turned her head slightly and moaned without answering. Her eyes fluttered and closed.

"Anne, John Clarke is with me," Will said. "He is not only a minister, but also has received medical training. He will be able to help you."

John Clarke examined Anne while the others sat at the table in silence. He felt Anne's stomach and saw the amount of blood she had lost.

When he was finished, Will asked, "She is going to be all right, isn't she?"

John Clarke shook his head sadly. "I hope so. It is a dangerous time for her. It is not uncommon for older women to have unnatural births. However, this situation is very unusual. Normally, when a baby does not develop right, the woman will miscarry in her early weeks. In this case, the malformed tissues kept growing until near her term. Anne must have been very miserable and knew something was wrong the entire time."

While Will and the clergy doctor talked and tended to Anne, Mary and Martha solemnly found a shovel and went to the backyard to bury the mass of tissue. "I hope the clergy in Boston never hears of this," Mary said. "They will say the pregnancy was from the devil, similar to what they said about my child. They will claim it is the judgment of God for her sin of teaching heresy and not obeying the clergy of the Puritan church."

Chapter Fourteen
Portsmouth Exodus

Portsmouth and Newport, Summer 1638 - Spring 1639

Randall and William carried two benches from near the fireplace outside and placed them under a large shade tree. The evening sun was approaching the horizon, while night owls called from a distance. "We should be more comfortable out here," William said.

Martha and Mary followed their husbands outdoors, each carrying two cups of cool water from the nearby spring. Each handed a cup to her husband sat beside him on the bench. "This is my favorite time of day," Mary said. "What work did not get done today, can be done tomorrow."

"That is a good way to look at it," William sighed. "Sometimes I feel like my work is never done. I want to make sure our settlement is developing the right way. If we make organizational mistakes, we will have to live with them for years to come."

Randall swatted at a bug and looked across at his brother-in-law. "From what I can see, you are doing great as town clerk."

"It is interesting you say that," William replied. "Portsmouth is developing much differently than Roger William's settlement at Providence Plantation. I am not sure what model would be the best for us."

Mary looked at her husband with puzzlement. "How are things different in Providence?"

"Roger Williams places the wishes of the individual ahead of the concerns of the group," William said. "He tries to shoulder most of the responsibilities of his settlement so the others can concentrate on the physical work that needs to be done. They have a very casual evolution of security."

"But how is that different from what you and William Coddington are doing here?" Martha asked.

William shook his head and his shoulders slumped. "Whenever we have a discussion and vote at our town meetings, the men decide to make the welfare of the group their primary concern and the interests of the individual secondary. They try to anticipate any emergency and require all men to bear arms. This method will encourage them to make laws they may not need. There is still so much work that needs to be done."

Martha reached out and patted William's arm. "Like Mary said earlier, what did not get done today, can be done tomorrow."

"I know," William said, "but simple things are becoming very frustrating. Before we even moved here we decided to call the town Portsmouth, but most of the people are still calling it by its Indian name. We haven't even had a formal vote on the matter."

The four sat in silence and watched the sun slowly disappear below the horizon while Samuel gathered sticks from beneath the tree and pretended he was building a campfire. As the moon rose in the sky, Martha said, "I hate to go inside, but I guess it is getting about that time. I do not think anything can be more peaceful than evening time in Aquidneck Island, far away from the stern eyes of the Puritan clergy. What could possibly disturb such a peaceful locale?"

[211]

June 1, 1638, while Martha and Mary, along with a dozen other settlers gathered for prayer in Anne Hutchinson's home, the earth began to tremble. The walls shook and pegs holding the wooden slats in the walls together began to pop out of their holes from the strain. Women and children screamed as they ran outside. Martha watched in horror when a neighbor's outhouse swayed back and forth and collapsed. Neighbors from surrounding houses joined them in the street. Many held onto trees while the earth continued shaking for a full three minutes.

"It is the end of the world," someone shouted. "God is punishing us."

The children cried hysterically along with some of their mothers. "Why is God punishing us," a neighbor sobbed. "What have we done to displease Him? He led us out of Boston to this beautiful island. Why would he punish us now?"

As calm settled over the group, everyone remained in his or her places wondering what might happen next. Rumors and speculations ran rampant. Anne raised her hand for calm. "I don't know what is happening, but God is not punishing us. He wants good for us and not evil." Anne's words provided little reassure to the frightened colonists.

Finally, Martha took a deep breath, trying to calm herself. "When I was young and still living in London, I heard a scientist tell about an earthquake that shook London and the east of England way back in 1601. I wonder if this is what is happening to us today."

Mary smiled. "Of course. The Bible tells about a number of earthquakes. I am certain we have nothing to fear."

When the shaking stopped, Anne Hutchinson again raised her hand. "Peace be with all of you. This was the spirit of God coming to reassure us of His protection over us. However, God is telling me Boston and its churches will soon be destroyed. Tomorrow I must write a letter to the Reverend John Cotton warning him of their coming doom and ask the next traveler to Boston to deliver it to him."

Martha and Mary exchanged puzzled looks. "How can this be?" Martha whispered. "How can we be sure it is God speaking to Anne? How can the shaking earth be a sign of protection for us and doom for Boston?"

"When we walk close to God we will learn to recognize His still small voice," Mary whispered. "In the meantime, we need to accept Anne's leadings."

"But what if a word from God is confused with wishful thinking?" Martha whispered back.

It took weeks of stillness before the people of Rhode Island re-established a trust in the ground upon which they walked. They were relieved to learn from travelers from the Massachusetts Bay Colony that Boston, and all the other towns along the coast, also felt the earthquake and it was not limited to their island alone. The travelers relayed rumors about fields in Connecticut being under ten feet of water and the people were starving.

Anne Hutchinson's prophecy for the destruction of Boston haunted the new residents of Portsmouth. Many of them still had family and friends living there. Although some were still angry about their harsh treatment from the clergy and magistrates, they could not wish ill will on the entire community. For weeks afterwards, every traveler and hunter from the outside was immediately quizzed about the wellbeing of Boston.

Three weeks after the earthquake, Martha and Mary again rowed their log boat to the main island to attend a meeting at Anne Hutchinson's. While they walked the newly packed streets of Portsmouth, they marveled at the changes made in such a short time. The woods around the settlement chimed with the sinking of axes and the falling of trees. New fences and houses appeared in nearly every clearing.

Suddenly Martha stopped, gasped, and pointed. "Look! The meetinghouse is almost completed. I do not care if it is made of mud and wood, it is ours. It will be the best church we have ever attended, even better than the 'Stump' in Boston in Lincolnshire, England."

Instinctively, Martha walked to the side of the meetinghouse and peered into the open window frame. "I hope Anne will be allowed to teach here. Her house is much too small for those who want to attend her meetings."

Mary seemed to ignore her sister and continued down the street surveying the changes with added curiosity. A look of shock spread across her face. "That cannot be," she nearly shouted.

Martha ran to join her sister, halted with astonishment, and stared at the latest addition to the town.

Mary's voice faltered. "Portsmouth is beginning to look like Boston. Among the first things built are stocks, a whipping pole, and a jail. How dreadful...We left England to get away from this kind of punishment. We were forced to leave Boston because of persecution. When will we ever be free of this kind of cruelty?"

Martha walked to the stocks and ran her hands across the rough wood. A splinter punctured her finger. "Hopefully, they will not punish anyone for what they believe. I cannot imagine any person among us committing any serious crime to need these."

Mary sighed. "I do not understand what is happening. William has started to comment on mounting tensions here in Portsmouth. Even though William is the clerk, he is not able to convince others to include the women in the town meetings and give us a vote."

Martha and Mary continued slowly down the street. Sea gulls fluttered overhead and landed nearby to scavenge for food. The sisters watched the birds in silence before Martha said, "Since we came to Portsmouth, fewer people are attending Anne's home meetings. I wonder why that is?"

Mary shook her head. "I have noticed the same thing and I do not understand. Anne seems to have lost a lot of the fire and determination she had in Boston. Perhaps it is because she was not feeling well while she was pregnant and had to spend the winter in house arrest away from her family. She has been through a lot these last few months."

"That is a possibility," Martha said. "However, I had another theory about why fewer people are coming to hear Anne." She paused and took a deep breath. "I hope this will not offend you, but I wonder if it is because most people like to hear John Clarke speak. His sermons are too sensible to criticize and too down to earth to excite and stir up controversy. There was always conflict after hearing many of the Boston clergy talk. People liked to come to Anne's meetings to debate the sermons. It became a form of entertainment for some. Without a lot of controversy, the less dedicated may not feel the desire to attend."

Mary's face reddened. "That could be true, but people should come and hear Anne speak whether there is controversy or not," she stated firmly. "Anne has a lot of fresh ideas. She must be getting discouraged about no longer having a dramatic impact on the spiritual lives of her neighbors. Even if only a few people attend, I still think she should be allowed to speak at the meetinghouse."

Martha put her hand on her sister's shoulder. "Mary, don't be angry. I agree with you. Not only should women be allowed to speak in church, I believe God does talk directly to women. If there were women prophetesses in Bible times, couldn't there also be women prophetesses today?"

"In my eyes Anne Hutchinson is a modern prophetess." Mary hesitated. She stared into the distance. "I am glad you are open to the idea of modern day women prophetesses. To be honest, sometimes I think God is speaking directly to me. I have not told anyone when that happens, not even William. I am afraid some might consider me mad."

Martha did not share her apprehension while she watched her sister's stomach gradually expand. She made sure Mary got plenty of rest, nourishing food to eat, and did not allow her sister to do any heavy chores around the house. *Please God, let this baby be normal. Mary will surely die of a broken heart, if it is not.*

Tears of relief streamed down the faces of both Mary and Martha when the newborn gave a blustering first cry. "It's a beautiful baby boy," Martha said while she cleaned the baby, wrapped him in a blanket, and placed him in his mother's waiting arms.

Mary snuggled the infant next to her bosom. "Thank you, God for my beautiful baby boy." She lay silently examining each minute detail of her son. "He is perfect."

Seeing her sister in complete peace, Martha sat on the chair by the bed. It had been a long, stressful night and she was exhausted. She recalled how William had pounded on the door to her house in the middle of the cold February night, asking her to come quickly to help Mary. This was the first baby she had delivered entirely on her own and she was grateful the labor was short and the delivery uncomplicated. "Mary, what are you going to name your son?"

Mary continued stroking her baby's head. "I want to name him William. I am fortunate to have a husband who is kind and gentle, yet strong and wise. He suffered a great deal of heartache after of the birth of our poor, deformed daughter more than two years ago."

"William is an excellent role model," Martha said. "Any son would be proud to bear his name."

Mary sighed. "I named my first son, William, after my beloved husband, but he only lived a few days, and we had to bury in the graveyard of St. Martin-in-the-Fields Church in London. I want to have a living son to honor my husband."

Hearing the baby cry, William rapped on the chamber room door. "May I come in?"

"Most certainly," Martha said.

William went directly to his wife's side and gazed down at his beloved wife and new son.

"I would like you to meet William Junior," Mary said.

William beamed with pride. "Thank you," he whispered. "I am honored to have two beautiful sons and a loving, dedicated wife."

"I love you, William," Mary whispered before her eyes closed.

William leaned over and kissed Mary on the forehead then then turned to Martha.

"Thank you for helping. If you like, I will take the baby so you can get some rest."

"I appreciate your offer," Martha said as she took the baby from Mary's arms and handed him to William.

After the new father had left the bedchamber, Martha made a pallet beside the bed for herself. She dropped onto it in exhaustion, and quietly sobbed. *Dear God. When will my turn come? I want children like other women, yet my womb seems to be closed. I know my faith has not always been the strongest and I have not always tried to serve you the best I could, but please grant me just this one desire.*

During the following weeks, Martha and Mary concentrated on their housework and children, while Randall worked in the woodshop and helped the women tend the animals. William modified his millenary skills and prepared vellum and oiled cloth for window coverings for his neighbors' newly constructed homes.

One afternoon while Mary was preparing a venison stew over the hearth and William was stretching a young calf's skin on a frame to dry, they heard a loud rapping. William went to the door and was surprised to see William Coddington and Nicholas Easton.

"Welcome," William greeted. "Do come in and have a seat. What brings you to our humble home?"

William Coddington and Nicholas took a seat at the Dyer's table and exchanged nervous glances. William Coddington cleared his throat. "You will never believe what happened."

William Dyer wrinkled his brow. "No, I have been busy with our new baby and trying to meet the demand for window coverings and haven't gone into town for several weeks."

William Coddington's eyes blazed. "This is hard to believe. I went back to Boston to tend to business for a few days and when I got back to Portsmouth, Will Hutchinson had been appointed judge in my place. It was a coup d'état. They completely ignored the original election." He shook his head with disgust. "The way it is going, they will probably make Anne Hutchinson the minister of our church next. Samuel Gorton even dared to question the right of the Bodie Politick we had drawn up and claimed we shouldn't exist without a royal charter from King Charles I."

"That should never stand," William said. "What do you suggest we do?"

Nicholas Easton looked at his traveling companion and back to the Dyers. "Some of us have begun to think the time has come for our town to divide. Already we have had to reduce the land portions for new settlers and have increased the price the town receives for the use of public land. Yet, more and more inhabitants keep arriving every month."

"I have noticed at the last few meetings our government is becoming extremely cumbersome to administer," William Dyer said. "When we first arrived it worked fine to have every act voted on by all the men in the town. Now that we are growing, it would be better if we delegated some of our responsibilities to representatives of the people. Do we need to move to another location to accomplish this? Couldn't we just modify our laws?"

William Coddington's face became stern. "I think we have no other option. It has become a power struggle. There are too many in Portsmouth to maintain a pure democracy of each man needing to vote on each proposal. Those who support Will Hutchinson would not approve delegating their power to representatives."

Mary studied her husband's face from across the room, and anxiety rose within her. *We just got settled on Dyer Island surely William would not consider moving again.*

William Dyer sat in silence for several minutes. His jaw tightened. "The fact a single group had the majority of the votes and put someone else into an elected position when the current officeholder is away cannot be tolerated."

"I agree," Nicholas Easton said. "It troubles me that some feel we do not need elected officials at all. Our friends the Hutchinsons are among them."

Mary trembled. *How could anyone talk against my dearest friend's husband? It was bad enough to be separated from Anne when she was under house arrest in Roxbury. Surely, I will not have to leave here and start again in a new place less than a year after we arrived.*

Tensions continued to mount in Portsmouth during the coming weeks. The community divided between the supporters of Will Hutchinson or William Coddington. The division in their small settlement crushed Martha Clarke and Mary Dyer. They agreed with their husbands that it was time for the colony to split, but to leave the one who had been their spiritual guide and mentor was devastating. However, when they listened to Anne speak; her messages became more about herself and power in Portsmouth and less about the power of God.

The followers of William Coddington chose Nicholas Easton and his two young sons, Peter and John to explore the southern tip of Aquidneck Island and determine the best location to build their new community. The day after the return of Nicholas and his sons, he and William Coddington paid another surprise visit to William Dyer.

Mary was busy mending clothes beside the fireplace and paid special attention to their conversation. When the three men were seated around the Dyer's table, William Coddington began, "Nicholas Easton and his sons found an excellent site for another settlement. They described an area with an exquisite harbor lying between the embracing arms of two points of land. They claimed the water was deep enough that any small ship could sail right up to the banks and moor to a tree."

"A good harbor would be a necessity. I would definitely trust their judgment," William Dyer said. "I do not think we explored that area when we were here initially. We want to make sure we have legal claim to it."

William Coddington cleared his throat. "The members of the Massachusetts Bay Colony have always chided us for inventing a settlement without the authority of a Royal Patent from England. The only authentic claim we have to Aquidneck Island is the deed signed by Miantonomo."

"That is true," William Dyer said. "I have custody of all the agreements made by the original Bodie Politick and the deeds for individual grants of land."

William Coddington breathed a sigh of relief. "I assumed you did. It is critical you hide the official documents among your personal possessions when we leave. We do not want them falling into the wrong person's hands."

William Dyer nodded. "I have them saved in a water-proof pouch. I will make sure I carry them on my body when we leave."

"Excellent," William Coddington said. "Those remaining in Portsmouth have no idea how to set up a government and what we have organized so far will be lost. Aquidneck Island could turn into chaos."

Mary cringed as the men finished planning the details of their move and agreed to leave in secret at dawn on the first day of May. *We are just getting settled in Portsmouth, even though it may be necessary, I do not want to gather all our worldly possession and again move to an unknown territory to begin a new settlement. Martha and I both will be devastated to leave without saying good-bye to our friends, especially Anne Hutchinson.*

Chapter Fifteen
The Founding of Newport

Newport, 1639 - 1643

The seagulls squawked overhead while the forty-two people who had left Portsmouth gathered on the southern shore of the bay Nicholas Easton had selected. Martha Clarke and Mary Dyer sat on the grass among the women while the children played on the sandy beach nearby. "I hope the men have our home sites selected soon," Martha whispered to her sister. "This move has been even more difficult than when we left Boston. I did not mind sneaking out of Boston, but I did not like having to sneak out of Portsmouth without saying good-bye or explaining why we were leaving."

Mary snuggled her newborn baby tighter against her breast. "I am very conflicted about the entire situation. I wish the men could have agreed upon the type of administration to have in Portsmouth and the town could keep growing without us needing to move. However, with all the disputes involved, I agree it was time for a change. I also miss the old Anne, the one who had been my spiritual mentor for all those years."

"Maybe when things settle down after the town is built, they will allow us to go back to visit our friends." Martha reclined on the grass, stretched her arms and legs, and sighed. "I hope they get our houses built soon. I am tired of sleeping on the ground or in the bed of the wagon. I do not think they realize how much more difficult it is cooking over an open campfire than even the crudest built hearth."

Samuel became tired of playing with the other children and returned to where the women were sitting.

He laid his head on his mother's lap and was soon fast asleep. Martha tried not to envy her sister with a baby in her arms, and a toddler sleeping on her lap, but an air of sadness overcame her. She lay and watched the clouds drift overhead and imagined herself cradling a child of her own in her arms.

As the men's conversation became more animated, Martha sat up and listened intently. "I am not surprised William Coddington was elected judge and William clerk," she whispered to Mary, "but I do not know how William will find the time to earn a living, survey the territory, and be the town clerk."

"He will find a way," Mary assured her. "He always has...I am glad they agreed to allocate each family ten acres of land to raise their crops and animals. Nearly every family in Portsmouth needed more land and there was scarcely enough room for everyone's gardens."

With the men finished selecting their leaders, the next topic on the agenda was the selection of a name of the town. Men, women, and older children all had an opinion and shared their ideas in private conversations with those around them. William tried to silence the group, but to little avail.

It was not long before the name discussion began to bore Martha. *The only thing they can agree upon is that they want to change the Indian names to names of our English heritage.* In frustration, she whispered to Mary, "Why don't they call this place Newport after the town on the Isle of Wight and move on to another topic? They will never get anything decided with all the side conversations."

Much to Martha's amazement, William Coddington looked her way. He raised his hand to silence the group. "I do not know who said the name

Newport, but it's an excellent idea. All those in favor of Newport as the name of our settlement say 'Aye'."

All the men simultaneously said, 'Aye'.

While the meeting continued, the women swatted the insects buzzing about them. Soon red bumps appeared on everyone's exposed skin. A long skirt, shawl, and bonnet were insufficient to protect them from the insidious sting of the mosquitoes. Martha shuddered when she saw the shoreline containing thickly interwoven brambles and thickets. "No wonder there are so many mosquitoes. The brambles and thickets on both sides of us make a perfect hatching ground."

A warm spring breeze blew through Martha's hair while she stood before an open window of her new home in Newport. She marveled how a few weeks before, the land on which her house was built was swampland. *Roger Williams was right. It is extremely important to make friends with the Natives if we are to live in their land. Our men would never have known how to fill in the swamp with sand gravel until it was firm enough to support a building.*

Mary opened the front door of the Clarke's home and walked inside unannounced. "You look deep in thought. Would you care to share?"

Martha jumped and turned to face her sister. "I am sorry; I did not hear you come in." She reached for her nephew in Mary's arms. "I was just thinking about how much we are learning from the Natives. I was watching the Native women show our men how to plant crops. It must be hard for them to incorporate Indian methods into English farming techniques."

Mary walked to the window and looked across the newly plowed field. "Watching the Indian women teach the English men is rather amusing, but with the braves spending their time hunting and fishing, it is the women who know the techniques of farming."

"The Indian practices of farming are fascinating," Martha said. "I am glad we have better tools and do not have to attach clamshells to sticks to dig furrows, but the Natives make it work. With such crude tools, I understand why they do not plow entire fields. Making parallel furrows six feet apart and cross plow at the same intervals would be less work, but it is going to be hard for our men to change."

Mary laughed. "William came in at dusk yesterday and expressed that very same thing. He said the multi-seed planting the Indian women did, makes a lot of sense. He like the way they interspersed corn seeds with peas, beans, and pumpkin seeds, but no one else agreed with him."

The baby began to cry, and Martha handed him back to his mother. "I am convinced we would not have survived here without the Indians. What has amazed me the most is that they want to help us. They were even willing to help drain the swamp for fifty brass buttons."

Mary took a seat at the bench by the fireplace and began to feed her baby. "In spite of all the Natives have done, I am most interested in their religion. I wish I could speak their language so I could understand their relationship with God. They seem to live so close to the earth that they are worshipping their surroundings and confusing the creations with the Creator, but maybe they know a part of God I do not know."

Martha joined her sister near the fireplace. "I have a great deal of respect for the Indians' religion, whatever it is. My concern is that William Coddington is taking an offensive attitude towards them. He seems more concerned the Natives do not interfere with the lives of the white settlers. He is making a lot more stringent rules about what the Natives can do than Roger Williams did in Providence."

Mary scowled. She shifted her baby in her arms, and reached over to pat Samuel's head when he came to her side for reassurance. "William is very disappointed, that after all the Natives have done for us, Coddington and his assistants do not want them idling in our settlement except for trade, messages, and in their travel. On the other hand, Roger Williams has been known to house at least sixty Indians at a time in his home."

Martha beamed as Samuel crawled into her lap and laid his head against her shoulder. "I wish we could all live together without so many rules. It is difficult enough to settle in a wilderness, without making extra man-made rules."

"I do not understand why we can't be more relaxed with the Natives," Mary said. "Chief Miantinomi has the confidence, respect, and admiration of all the settlers. He is not only the symbol of the finest qualities of Indians, but of men everywhere."

The location of Newport turned out to be as fortunate as Nicholas Easton had predicted it would be, and the town prospered. The soil was fertile and fed them well. After a year of living apart from the settlers in Portsmouth, one evening there was a sharp rapping on the Dyer front door as the Dyer and Clarke families were sitting at the table enjoying their evening meal.

William Dyer hurried to the door. "William Coddington," he said. "What brings you out at this time of day?"

William Coddington stepped into the Dyer's three-room home. He stomped the dust from his shoes and nodded to Mary, Martha, and Randall before turning back to William Dyer. "You will never believe who is spending the night at my house," he said with a mysterious look at his face.

William Dyer wrinkled his forehead and shook his head. "I haven't a clue."

"Will Hutchinson himself, along with two of his assistants."

The eyes of everyone in the room widened. "And what brought Mister Hutchinson to our settlement after over a year of separation and a great deal of hard feelings?" Randall asked.

"He said the inhabitants of Portsmouth became aware Newport was taking the lead in commerce and thought it would be beneficial for both settlements to unite. They would like to meet with everyone in Newport first thing in the morning to discuss the idea. As clerk, you will need to be there, especially since the treaty and ownership papers are in your protection."

William Dyer looked at the others who were nodding in agreement. "We all will be there at dawn. I can hardly wait to hear what they have to say." He hesitated for a few moments before continuing. "In the meantime, did they have other news from Portsmouth? We have been through so much together and still consider them our friends."

"He said the Boston church sent a delegation to Portsmouth a few months ago to try and convince his wife of her errors and restore her to the church." William Coddington took an extra chair and set it at the corner of the table. He stretched his long legs in front of him and relaxed. "As you might expect, Anne was not interested in repenting. The Boston delegation then went from house to house trying to find people interested in being a part of the Boston church, but no one was."

Mary gave a dry laugh. "After the way the Puritans treated us, I do not think anyone will ever want to return to Boston. Why don't they just leave us alone?"

Everyone in the room nodded. William Coddington rose to leave. "I need to get back to my house guests. I will see everyone in the morning."

Promptly at nine o'clock the next morning, William Coddington called to order the Newport General Court of Election. Women gathered in the back to listen while children played in the grass nearby. His voice boomed across the open field. "The first thing we need to agree upon before we proceed is whether the communities of Portsmouth and Newport should be united. If that is not agreed upon, there would be little need to continue the meeting."

With no hesitation, the assembly voted to unite and turned their attention to the issues that had so bitterly divided them over a year before. As they reconsidered those concerns, none seemed nearly as serious as they did the year before.

Again, Mary and Martha watched the men conduct the town's business. They grew weary as the day wore on and the men agreed on other rules and name changes. They voted that the chief magistrate would no longer be "judge" but "governor" and William

Coddington would be the first governor of the united settlement. They decided upon a joint treasury with equal amounts for each town. Mary and Martha were ecstatic when the assembly agreed upon free passage between the communities. Finally, they could visit their friends in Portsmouth and share ideas with Anne Hutchinson.

With the uniting of Portsmouth and Newport, Mary Dyer and Martha Clarke took the opportunity to have several visits with Anne Hutchinson during the next two years. However, their relationship was never the same. Anne Hutchinson's teachings had become different from what they had been in Boston. Mary did not challenge her, but quickly changed the subject of the discussion when she was in disagreement.

June 25, 1642, Mary and Martha traveled to Portsmouth with their husbands to visit friends and sell wool from their herd of sheep. As they neared the town, Martha said, "Do you want to visit Anne while we are here even though the last visit with her did not go well?"

Mary shook her head sadly. "After all we have been through together and all the things she has taught me, I do not feel right about giving up on our friendship now. As soon as we have sold our wool, I think we should go and see her. We do not have to stay long."

Much to their delight, their wool was gone by lunchtime. Martha and Mary joined their husbands under a tree and ate the bread and apples they had brought with them while the boys played nearby. A concerned look spread across Mary's face and she turned to her husband. "William, would you mind watching the children while we visit Anne Hutchinson? It would be easier to concentrate on our visit if they were with you."

William looked at Randall, smiled, and turned back to Mary. "We would be glad to. We were planning to rest here under the tree for a while anyway."

The sisters hugged the children and their husbands and headed toward the Hutchinson's home. As they neared their house, Kathryn Hutchinson came out to meet them; her shoulders were slumped and her lips downturned.

Martha wrapped her arms around the child. "Why the sadness?"

Tears began rolling down Kathryn's cheeks. "I am sorry. You had no way of knowing. Father died last week and mother has not been the same since then."

Mary and Martha gave simultaneous gasps and exchanged mournful looks.

"May we go in and see your mother?" Mary asked.

Katherine nodded. "Most definitely. I hope someone is able to cheer her. She has scarcely stopped crying since father died and she refuses to leave the house."

Mary and Martha followed Kathryn Hutchinson into her home. Anne was sitting on a bench staring into space. She did not stand when her friends approached and barely acknowledge their presence.

Mary and Martha leaned over and hugged her. "I am sorry to learn of William's death," Martha said. "Is there anything we can do to help?"

Anne forced an unconvincing smile. "There is nothing anyone can do. I just want to get away from here as soon as I can."

"But why would you want to leave your friends and grown children who could help you with the younger ones? Where would you go?"

A silence hung over the room. Anne heaved a painful sigh. "The Dutch are more tolerant of religious beliefs than the English. I am going to go to New Amsterdam."

Martha took Anne's hand. "But without Will, how will you move your belongings and earn a living once you are there?"

Anne's eyes flashed. "I can take care of myself," she snapped. "I am fifty-one years old; I do not need outside help. Besides, Long Island is only 130 miles away. I plan to send my furniture and heavy belongings over land along with our horses, cattle, and hogs. We can hire boats for part of the trip, if necessary. Seven of my children will be moving with me along with six or seven neighbors. We can work together to become self-sufficient."

Mary scowled. "I do not want to discourage your plans, but I heard the Dutch and the Indians are in constant conflict in that area. I would hate for you to get involved in the middle of Indian wars."

"I don't know why you are so worried about me," Anne said in a tone more defiant than Martha had ever heard. "I will treat the Natives with love and respect. When they realize we trust them and do not keep firearms in our house, we will not have a problem with them. If the Dutch would follow that example, there would not be Indian wars."

Mary and Martha continued trying to convince Anne of the folly of her plans, but without success. Completely disheartened, they returned to their homes in Newport. What had happened to their beloved spiritual advisor and mentor?

The next few months passed quickly for Martha and Mary following the death of Will Hutchinson. William and Randall completed a smaller house near the Dyer's home for Martha and Randall. No longer were the two families crowded into the same house. Their herd of sheep grew and Mary and Martha spent many long hours knitting shawls, hats, and stockings to sell to their neighbors and occasional seaman who docked in the Newport Harbor.

One hot August afternoon less than a year after Anne had moved her family to Long Island, Martha raced toward her sister who was tending the sheep in the pasture beyond their houses. Tears flowed down her cheeks. "Mary...Mary. I have terrible news."

Mary set the lamb she was holding on the ground and hurried toward her sister. "What has happened?"

"While I was in town getting supplies, a ship landed from Long Island. One of the sailors told the shopkeeper the Indians murdered and scalped Anne Hutchinson and all her family except eight-year-old Susannah who was away picking berries at the time. The Siwanoy Indians kidnapped Susannah and they don't know what happened to her."

Mary's face blanched and she could not hold back a gasp. "But Anne had only kindness for the Natives. She would never consider arming herself or her children. What could have happened?"

"The sailor said Anne and her family had set up a comfortable home on Pelham Bay, but because of her location, she was caught up in the Dutch/Indian War. The Natives told her not to settle among them, but she was certain it was God's divine will and she built her house there anyway. Not knowing who she was, a band of Indians scalped all of the family, except Susannah, put their bodies in the house, and burned the house down. They said sixteen people died during that raid."

Mary collapsed onto the ground and sobbed. "This is awful...just plain awful...I must go to Providence and see Anne's sister, Catherine Scott...I need to have a time of prayer and remembrance with her. Catherine is all we have left of our beloved Anne."

Martha sat on the ground beside Mary and cradled her head in her lap. "But you cannot go now. Your new baby is due in a few days. Samuel and little William are too small to travel. Maybe after the new baby is born, we can plan a trip to Providence."

Tears streamed down Martha's checks. "Dear little Katherine. Ever since we met on those muddy streets of Boston in Lincolnshire, I have always had a soft spot for her in my heart. I had such high hopes and dreams for her and now they are cut short."

On a hot July afternoon in 1643, for the second time in three years, Martha laid a newborn son in her sister's arms. "You have another beautiful boy. He is perfect in every way. What will you name him?"

Mary shook her head. In spite of the joy of the moment, she was not able shake off her grief. "I am going to call him, Mahershallalhashbaz and call him Maher for short."

Martha gasped. "What kind of a name is that?"

"Mahershallalhashbaz is the name of the prophet Isaiah's first son. It means 'quickly to plunder.' Since Anne Hutchinson died, my heart and soul has been plundered. I don't know if I will ever recover."

Martha knelt beside her sister and stroked her hair, still damp from hours of travail. "God will heal your pain, but it may take time. He has blessed you with three healthy sons who will be the joy of your life."

Mary caressed her new son. Tears ran down her cheeks. "I am proud of my sons, but Anne Hutchinson helped me feel close to God. How will I ever replace that connection? Will I feel separated from God for the rest of my life?"

After the birth of Maher, Mary's depression deepened to the point some days she was unable to get out of bed. Each morning, Martha rushed through her own household chores, and then hurried next door to help Mary with her three sons. Gradually, the cloud of gloom that enveloped Mary faded and life returned to normal once again.

One afternoon while Martha Clarke was stirring the stew over the hearth in the Dyer's home, Randall and William Dyer stomped through the door. Their brows were wrinkled and their shoulders slumped.

She straightened and turned to them. "What has happened? Why are you both so worried?"

The men pulled out the benches at the table and sat. William took off his hat and rested is elbows on the table. "We just came from a general meeting. The Massachusetts Bay Colony is continuing to encroach upon the lands we purchased from the Narragansett Indians. Before long they will be on our doorstep."

Mary laid her knitting beside her and took a seat beside her husband. "But how can they do that? We paid for the land."

"True, but we do not have sanctions from England and the only constitution we have is what we wrote ourselves," William said. "We are in such a desirable location; the other colonies would like nothing better than to take advantage of our beautiful bays and fertile farmland. Roger Williams is extremely upset and is leaving for England this March to obtain one charter to unite the towns of Providence, Portsmouth, Newport, and Warwick into a single colony. His goal is to maintain regional independence from Massachusetts."

"I hope the Massachusetts colony will leave us alone until he gets back," Martha said. "We left Boston for a reason and we do not want to live under their bondage of church rules again."

William Dyer took a chair at the kitchen table, put his head in his hands, and sighed. "Worse than that. The Boston magistrates and minister could put us in jail again. I hope Roger Williams can gain immediate favor with the king and Parliament before we are absorbed by Massachusetts. We have always accepted religious dissidents, but the very essence of freedom is shaky without the blessing of a royal charter from England.

Chapter Sixteen
The Colony of Rhode Island

Rhode Island, 1644 - 1651

One warm summer afternoon, while Martha and Mary were working in their garden and the boys played nearby, Mary stood erect and rubbed her back. "I wonder why our husbands insisted we not come into my house this afternoon, but put the children down for their naps in your house. William has been acting very peculiar lately."

Martha laughed. "I have noticed that myself. Maybe it is because the general assembly finally gave an official approval of Roger Williams' charter. They have been so concerned the United Colonies of Boston will take over our settlements. It is good to see him happy and relaxed again."

Mary gripped her hoe and continued removing the weeds around the beans. "When we left England, we had no idea how complex it was to start a new colony. William has worked extremely hard trying to make sure it is set up and organized right. If mistakes are made now, it will take years to undo them. I do not know how he could have accomplished what he has without your and Randall's help."

"We agree with the same principles he does," Martha said. "Randall and I feel the best way we can support our town is to do the farm work to free William to do the work for the colony."

"William seems to be working night and day," Mary said. "I was impressed last night when I saw him sitting in the dim light by the fireplace studying the book *A Key into the Language of America* by Roger

Williams. This Indian word phrase book coupled with observations about life and culture can be a tremendous aid in communication with the Natives. I agree with Roger Williams, we have much to learn from them."

When the shadows lengthened, the children became restless and the women were no longer able to work. Martha took the hands of the older boys while Mary picked up Maher from the box where he was sleeping at the end of the row. Mary looked longingly at her own home before turning back to her sister. "I wish I could take the boys into my own house to give them supper, but William insisted I not come back until he says to. It must be important, but I don't understand the secret. It is unusual for him to do something without explaining why."

"No problem," Martha said. "I have plenty of food and goats' milk and we can make pallets on the floor where the boys can sleep."

Mary and Martha took the children to Martha's house, and prepared their supper. The boys were just finishing eating a bowl of porridge when William and Randall opened the front door. They both looked exhausted, but smiling. Samuel and little William ran to their father, expecting hugs. After greeting his children, William turned to Mary and Martha with a childlike grin. "It is completed. You may now come home."

"What is completed?" Mary asked as she followed her husband through the door and down the path to their home while Martha carried Maher. Samuel and little William followed close behind.

When William opened the front door to their home, Mary's eyes widened and she gave a gasp of delight. "Wooden floors. You mean you both worked all day building wooden floors for us. We will no longer have to worry about the boys playing on the dirt floor. Thank you, thank you, thank you." Mary embraced her husband while Samuel and little William scampered around the room with excitement.

William basked in the approval of his wife and sister-in-law while they inspected every corner of the new floor. When Mary and Martha finished admiring the floor, they took seats on the benches at the table. William said, "I have other good news to share, as well."

Mary looked quizzically at her husband.

"We just received word from a traveler that Roger Williams has arrived in Boston from London," William said. "He was able to obtain a complete charter for The Providence Plantation along with all of Rhode Island. He should be here in a couple days. I have invited everyone in Newport to come to our house to meet with him on Thursday."

Mary smiled while she surveyed the new floor. "With the new floor, our home will make an excellent meeting place."

Mary Dyer served as a gracious hostess the following Thursday afternoon when nearly every resident of Newport crowded into her home. She was proud, not only of her new floors, but also of her husband who took the time from his busy schedule to build them. Many preferred sitting on the new plank floor rather than on a bench.

When all were assembled, Roger Williams stepped forward. "It is good to be home in the newly formed Rhode Island Colony."

The crowded erupted into cheers of welcome. Reverend Williams waited for silence before he continued. "It was extremely difficult, but I was able to finally obtain a charter for our colony, in spite of the civil war going on in England and the Puritans being in charge of the government."

When Roger Williams hesitated, William Dyer said, "We applaud your success. The military alliance of the United Colonies of Massachusetts, Plymouth, and Connecticut has made us very uneasy. Those of us who escaped Boston for religious freedom are frightened of their desire to extend power over what they consider our heretic settlements."

Roger Williams surveyed the group crowded into the Dyers home. A look of conviction spread across his face. "I believe there should be a distinct separation between the church and the government. Every person has a natural right of freedom of religion. Rhode Island must be a safe haven for people being persecuted for their beliefs."

The next two hours, Reverend Roger Williams shared his hopes for the Rhode Island Colony. When the settlers of Newport left the Dyer home, they were overjoyed with the charter Reverend Williams had obtained and were determined to protect the religious freedom of all people.

After Roger Williams returned from London, Martha and Mary were more determined than ever to welcome those fleeing religious persecution into their homes. Every week or two a traveler appeared with a tale of woe as to their treatment in Boston or the surrounding area. The women helped new settlers become established in Newport. Randall took even more responsibilities with the livestock, while William traveled from town to town and house-to-house explaining the importance of the Roger William's charter and the advantages of being united as one colony.

At dusk on a cool October day in 1747, while Martha was preparing a meal over the Dyer's open hearth, and Samuel was watching his two younger brothers, William Dyer returned home. When he opened the door, Martha stood and smiled, the ladle was still in her hand. "Welcome home, William. How was your trip to Portsmouth?"

"Very tiring, yet productive," William said. "Where is Mary?"

"In the chamber room resting. Her baby will be here any time and she has been extremely tired these last few days."

While Martha was speaking, Mary opened the chamber room door and saw her husband. "Welcome home, William. I have missed you more this time than any other."

William hurried to his wife, kissed her, and helped her to a bench at the table. "How are you my beloved? I am glad I am home, I did not realize it was so close to your time."

"I am doing well," Mary said. "I am more tired and clumsy than previous times, but all is well. Tell me about your trip to Portsmouth."

William went to the water pail on the counter, filled two cups with water, returned to the table, and set one in front of Mary and one in front of himself. "We finally got all four towns to approve the charter Rogers Williams brought back from London three years ago, but it has been a long slow process."

Mary shook her head with frustration. "The charter process has been difficult for me to understand. When

Roger Williams returned from London, everyone in Newport was enthusiastic about Rhode Island being a haven for religious freedom. I don't understand what has changed."

William sighed. "The way I see it, the biggest problem was the divisions between the towns and powerful personalities. That is the reason why we felt Newport had to separate from Portsmouth in the first place. It is no secret William Coddington never liked Reverend Williams, nor did he like being subordinated to his new charter government. He has been spreading confusion throughout the colony ever since."

"Now since the charter is accepted, I hope things will calm down and we can move beyond all the conflict." Mary grimaced and reached for her stomach. She gritted her teeth and said, "I think I better lie down again."

William wrapped his arm around his wife and walked her to the bed while Martha followed close behind. After Mary was comfortable in the bed, Martha turned to William. "I have delivered two of Mary's babies by myself, but I may need help this time. Even though she has been feeling well, Mary is extremely large and there could be more problems. Would you fetch Goodwife Easton for me?"

While William located a midwife, Martha remained by her sister's side and encouraged her when the pain became intense. When Elizabeth Easton arrived, Martha made sure enough water was warm and enough towels were available to care for Mary. That evening William fed the boys and made pallets beside the fireplace for them to sleep.

Time passed slowly. Three hours later, Elizabeth delivered a baby boy who entered the world with a lusty cry. When Martha finished washing the baby and was ready to lay the infant on Mary's chest, she was surprised Mary was not focused on the new child.

"What's happening?" she whispered to the midwife.

Elizabeth smiled. "Another baby is coming. Mary is having twins."

Martha laid the baby boy in the box and helped Elizabeth deliver the second baby. Within minutes, a beautiful baby girl appeared. Mary laid back and closed her eyes in total exhaustion. The women finished washing the baby girl and each carried an infant into the main room.

"Congratulations, William. You have twins, a boy and a girl," Martha said.

William beamed. "Thank you. Is Mary all right?"

Martha handed the baby girl to William. "Mary is sleeping. She did a lot of work today and is exhausted. Do you know if she had two names picked out, yet?"

The new father stroked the baby's head and uncurled her fingers. "If it was a boy we had decided on the name Henry after Henry Vane. He was the one who helped Roger Williams get the charter for Rhode Island." William walked to Elizabeth's side and admired the infant in her arms. He smiled and looked back at the baby in his own arms. "Since we also have a girl, I would like to name her Mary. I am proud of my wife and want to give her due honor."

News about the Dyer twins spread quickly among the women in Newport. Within hours, the women developed a rotation plan for someone to come and help Mary with her growing family. On the third day after the birth of the twins, Elizabeth Easton arrived at the Dyers' before Martha had left for the afternoon.

"Martha, have you heard the news about Mary Coddington?" Goody asked.

"No," Martha said. "Outside of Mary, you are the first person I have talked to today."

Elizabeth became serious and her forehead wrinkled. "I just learned Mary Coddington died this morning. She has been feverish for a couple of days, but no one knows what happened. William Coddington is extremely distraught."

Martha stood in shocked silence. "Mary Coddington was a gracious, loving woman...I could understand why her husband would take her death so hard. It was a double blow for him. He was already very disappointed when the four towns voted to unite to form Rhode Island. Losing his beloved wife must make it unbearable for him. I hope he will be able to bear the strain."

Late one May afternoon in 1648, William Dyer returned home from the General Assembly of Rhode Island in Providence. Martha was washing dishes and putting them on the shelf, and Mary was caring for the twins when he opened the door. "How was the meeting?" Mary asked. "You look exhausted."

William embraced her and then hugged each of the older children, before he sat on the bench at the table and took off his hat. "Even though William Coddington did not attend the meeting, he was elected President of the entire colony. I think there is going to be trouble."

"Why is that?" Martha asked.

William Dyer scowled, but his expression softened when little Henry began to cry. He leaned over and picked up the baby. "William Coddington makes no pretense that he does not support the charter. I heard he wanted to have Portsmouth and Newport become a part of the New England Confederation instead...That is the worst idea I have ever heard. Both towns have well-organized governments in which civil and religious liberty are clearly defined and fully recognized. These liberties would be lost in a government under Plymouth."

Mary studied her husband's worried face. "So what can we do about it? Is there a way to get William Coddington out of office? He used to be a dear friend, but now he is totally different from when we first established Newport."

Governor William Coddington's House in Rhode Island

"There is a move afoot to replace Coddington with Jeremy Clarke as Governor. At least, he supports the Rhode Island charter Roger Williams obtained. We will have to see what happens."

While most of the women of Newport paid little attention to the affairs of the local government, since many of the meetings were held in the Dyer home, Martha and Mary became deeply involved. Instead of sitting in the background listening, they began sharing their ideas, which the men soon came to respect.

On a cold February afternoon, the leaders of Newport once again gathered in the Dyer home. Mary and Martha greeted each man warmly when they arrived. Before the meeting began, Martha asked the group. "Does anyone know what has happened to William Coddington? Ever since his wife died, I have been checking on their daughter to see if there is anything she needs. Yesterday when I went by, the house was locked, and when I looked in the window it appeared like they had moved."

The men exchanged nervous glances. "He has been acting rather peculiar since his wife died," one said.

"I heard he left his farm and business interests in the hands of an agent, but I don't know where he went," another said.

Other questions and comments were heard around the room. Finally a soft voice in the back said, "I live next door to the Coddingtons, and when the windows were open I could hear their conversations. Several weeks ago, I heard William Coddington discuss with a friend that he was taking his daughter and going to England. He said he wanted to present a petition for an independent colonial government on Aquidneck Island, free from union with Providence. His charter would make him 'Governor for Life'."

Martha shuddered. She heard shocked gasps around her. *How can he do this to us? Aren't we all on the same side in favor of individual freedom?*

William Dyer stood and motioned for attention. "This is extremely serious. We need to talk with Roger Williams and see if Coddington can actually obtain a new charter making himself governor. Reverend Williams will be in Newport next Wednesday to see me. I want to invite everyone back Wednesday afternoon to discuss this new development."

Following the meeting and before Roger Williams' visit, the days passed slowly for Martha and Mary. They went about their household chores and cared for Mary's five children with worried expressions on their faces. Any time they were working in the same area, they discussed the possibility of William Coddington successfully obtaining a new charter and Rhode Island becoming a part of the United Colony.

"I certainly hope William Coddington's charter does not go through," Mary said while she bent over the open hearth. "Plymouth may not be as oppressive as Boston, but I want my children to grow up where they have freedom of religion and they are not controlled by one particular church and clergy."

Martha nodded. "I agree." She finished bathing and dressing Henry and then picked up his sister and set her on the table. She dipped the washcloth into the basin of water nearby and rubbed soap onto the cloth. Little Mary cried and wiggled in Martha's hands while she was being washed.

Mary watched the entire scene with amusement. "As high spirited as my children are, none of them would last long under Puritan rule."

The following Wednesday, an air of gloom hung over the Dyer home as the supporters of Roger Williams' charter began to assemble. When the room was full, Reverend William rose from his bench. "I understand many of you are distressed about the news of William Coddington's trip to London. I would hope he would not be able to get a new charter, but with a civil war going on in England, it is possible for anything to happen. The best thing I can do is to write to Sir Henry Vane who helped me obtain our original charter and explain the situation. My concern is that by the time my letter gets to London in six to eight weeks, William Coddington will have already made headway in convincing the Colonial Commissioners of a need for a new charter for Rhode Island. I have heard that Governor Josiah Winslow of the Plymouth Colony is also in London at this time. He might encourage Plymouth's claims to Rhode Island."

"So what do we do?" Martha asked. "It will take weeks before we have an answer back from England

and by then irrevocable damage could already be done."

"All we can do is watch and pray and hold firmly to our principles," Reverend Roger Williams replied.

Letter after letter from numerous leaders from Rhode Island were sent to officials in London, but there was rarely a response. In the meantime, the settlers continued growing their crops and livestock, fishing, and expanding their homes. Government intrusion into their personal lives was kept to a minimum. Underneath the relative calm was an air of uncertainty for those supporting Roger Williams' charter.

Mary and Martha continued participating in the meetings regularly held in the Dyers' home. They especially looked forward to the times Roger Williams could join them. He spoke with such confidence and authority.

Much to the Dyers' joy in September of 1650, Mary delivered her sixth child; a boy they named Charles after the king of England. Martha found herself helping Mary with the children several hours every day. After a turbulent beginning, life in Newport was settling in to a peaceful routine.

One bright June afternoon the following year, Martha rushed down the path to Mary's house and flung open the door. "You will never guess who I just saw on the City Commons."

William was sitting by the fireplace whittling pegs while Mary stood at the table slicing vegetables for the evening meal. She laid her knife on the table and went to her sister. "I have no idea, but this sounds serious."

"It is," Martha said, still trying to catch her breath. "William Coddington is back in Newport and he brought a new wife with him."

Hearing those words, William jumped to his feet. "Never mind the wife. Did you hear anything about a new charter?"

Martha frowned. "Yes...A large group of people gathered about him were cheering. I was able to work my way into the crowd and heard someone say Sir Henry Vane recognized Coddington as a wise and effective chief magistrate, and helped him get a charter that allowed him to serve in his new role as governor for an indefinite period, subject to the will of Parliament. They said that he was to have a council of six men, elected by popular vote of the freemen."

William's face reddened. He pounded his fist on the table. "This shall never stand," he shouted. "I am leaving immediately for Providence to see Roger Williams. I will be back as soon as we know what to do."

Hearing their father's anger, Charles and the twins began to cry. Mary cradled the baby in her arms, while Martha comforted Henry and little Mary. William hurriedly placed three apples, six carrots, three biscuits into a bag, filled a jug of water, bade everyone good-bye, and left.

The days passed slowly while William was away. Randall helped Mary and Martha care for the children. They took turns going to the City Commons in the hope of learning more as to the plans of William Coddington, being careful not to mention where William was.

Six days later, William Dyer walked into his home just as the others were gathered around the table for their evening meal. Mary kissed her husband while the older children huddled around him for a hug. Martha filled a bowl of stew for him and set a glass of goats' milk before him.

"Thank you for such a warm welcome," William said. "I am certain you are all anxious to know what Roger Williams had to say."

Randall smiled. "We most definitely are. No one else outside the four of us realized how important your trip to Providence was."

William hurriedly took three bites of his stew before continuing. "Roger Williams said there is no way to settle this issue without returning to London himself. He feels several others from the colony should go with him to strengthen the cause."

"That makes sense," Randall said, "but who would go with him and how could they pay for their travels? Settlers in Rhode Island are scarcely able to feed their families and provide shelter, much less take several months from work and pay their passage."

William took several more bites before answering. "Roger Williams is willing to sell his Trading Post near Providence to finance the trip. He felt it would be best if John Clarke from Portsmouth and I accompany him. He thinks we should be ready to sail by November."

Mary's face blanched. "How long would you be gone?"

William reached for Mary's hand. "It could be about a year. I will miss you and the children, but someone must make the sacrifice. We cannot let Rhode Island be in bondage to the colonies who do not believe in the separation of church and government and religious freedom."

William finished his stew and Mary refilled his bowl. "Randall, I know this is a lot to ask of you, but if I go to London would you be willing to care for the animals and tend to my shop while I am gone?"

Randall leaned back in his chair. He looked at his wife for approval and then back at William. "Of course, I would. Roger Williams' charter is a vitally important for our entire Rhode Island Colony and we all must work together. It is the least I can do for the cause."

Mary stared out the window. After a long silence she said, "I want to go with you...I want to be involved in making sure we have a charter to guarantee our freedoms. Women are the ones primarily raising the children; we should have a voice in their future."

"But what about our six children?" William protested, "Is it fair to leave them behind?"

Martha and Mary's eyes met. Each seemed to understand what the other was thinking. Martha reached across the table and took her sister's hand. "I have loved your children as if they were my own. I will take good care of them until you return."

Mary squeezed Martha's hand. "I am so blessed to have you as a sister. To be honest, not only do I want to support the men in obtaining a separate charter, I would like to meet with the newly formed group called Quakers. Several travelers have told me about them and I have a yearning to learn more about their teachings. I heard a revival was building in England and I want to be a part of that revival."

Chapter Seventeen
Back to England

London, 1651 - 1652

After a difficult passage from England to Boston in 1635, sixteen years later the Dyers found their return trip much less challenging. The crew had a more systematic way to preserve food and water and distribute it among the passengers, fewer livestock were onboard, and the crew was better trained to handle the sails. Mary and William spent many long hours on the deck with Roger Williams and John Clarke discussing what a charter for Rhode Island should contain and how they should present their requests.

Roger Williams appeared to be the most apprehensive about obtaining a new charter. Mary

grimaced when she heard his words. "As soon as we get to London, we need to go directly to Sir Henry Vane and explain our situation. It makes me angry when I think of his involvement in William Coddington's charter, but I want to give him the benefit of the doubt. He must have been swayed by misinformation and political pressure from the parliament."

William Dyer leaned back against a wooden box on the deck and stretched out his legs in front of him. "I am certain having the governor of Plymouth present at the same time as Coddington, increased the pressure and misinformation Henry Vane received. I hope it is not too late to rectify the situation."

William looked at his wife who was relaxing beside him. He reached for her hand. "Mary, we appreciate all your valuable input on political issues. You provide a balanced perspective on the organization of the colony, but I am concerned the parliament and political figures in London are not as accepting of women as we are in Rhode Island. Would you mind waiting at the inn the first time we talk to Sir Henry Vane? We will explain your wise counsel and ask if they would allow you to participate in the discussion."

John Clarke nodded in agreement. "We do not want to hurt your feelings and I wish you could have more of a voice in the matter, but we need time to get a sense of the political climate. If they will not let you participate in the discussion, we will seek your counsel in the evenings."

"You are not going to hurt my feelings," Mary assured them. "I am grateful you let me accompany you to London. While you are in meetings, I will try to learn as much as I can about the Quaker revival. After following Anne Hutchinson for so many years, she convinced me of the necessity of searching for God's specific leading in my own life."

December 25, 1651, the ship *Truelove* docked in the London Harbor. Roger Williams, John Clarke, along with William and Mary Dyer gathered their few belongings and walked down the gangplank into a crowded wharf.

The fresh salt breeze from the ocean refreshed Mary's spirit; she increased her pace to keep up with the men. When they got to the end of the harbor, she looked around and said, "When I lived in London growing up, I came to the harbor often, but I don't recognize anything now. It has changed so much since then."

Roger William hesitated while he surveyed the surrounding buildings. "It has been eight years since I was in London getting the first charter and it has even changed a lot since then. I think I can still find the way to the Ox Bow Inn. I stayed there when I was here before and found it very comfortable and with good food. I hope it is still open."

In the weeks that followed, Roger Williams, John Clarke, and William Dyer spent a great deal of time with Sir Henry Vane and the Colonial Commissioners. Much to everyone's disappointment, Mary was not allowed to participate in the discussions. William tried to make Mary feel she was an important member of the group. When they returned in the evenings, he and Mary would sit up and discuss the events of the day into the early morning hours.

After William left in the mornings, Mary soon discovered the men from the neighborhood came to the Ox Bow Inn to drink ale and tell stories. She could hear their conversations from a distance and found their stories distasteful and would retreat to her room as soon as they arrived. Within a few days, she became restless from staying alone in her simple room all day. The straight-back chair was hard and there was little to do. By the third day, Mary decided to walk around the side streets and the local market.

Memories of her early life in England when she visited the marketplace encircled her. The sights and sounds were still the same. While examining a display of vegetables at a vendor's booth, she overheard two customers talking and paused to listen.

"Did you hear George Fox speak last night at the City Commons?" one said.

The other woman scowled. "I stayed for a few minutes and left. George Fox speaks heresy when he talks against the clergy and calls our churches 'steeple houses.' What is worse, he claims to hear directly from God. How can he possibly think he is more special to God than the rest of us?"

The first woman put down the turnip she was examining and shook her head. "I thought George Fox spoke as one who knows the truth and not one who could be easily swayed by self-righteous clergy."

"How could you be so foolish?" the second woman said and stormed down the street.

Cautiously, Mary approached the frustrated woman beside her. "Excuse me," she said. "I couldn't help overhear your conversation. Could you tell me more about George Fox? Is he still teaching in the area?"

The woman looked at Mary suspiciously. Her eyes seemed to pierce into Mary's soul the way Anne Hutchinson's did the first time she had met her. "You do not look familiar. Are you new to London?"

"I used to live here but my husband and I emigrated to the Massachusetts Bay Colony sixteen years ago. We now live in the Rhode Island colony. My husband is here clarifying the charter for that colony."

"Then you do not know about George Fox?"

Mary shook her head. "A few traveling Quakers have visited our town and told us about some of the teachings of their leader, George Fox. But I know little else."

The woman relaxed and smiled. She motioned for Mary to step away from the vendor's booth to a more private area and spoke in a soft, low voice. "Part of what my friend just said is true. George Fox does have a sharp tongue, but you must hear him speak to become convinced of the underlying truths he proclaims. George Fox talks of God not only being with us, but also *in* us. He tells us we have to listen to His Inner Voice to know His will."

Following the stranger's lead, Mary whispered. "Do you know where I could hear George Fox speak?"

The woman looked in both directions, and then said, "He will be preaching tomorrow afternoon across the street from my house."

"And where do you live?" Mary asked.

Mary sensed unusual warmth from the stranger when she said, "To get to my house go to the end of this street and turn east. My house is four houses down on the south side of the street. People will gather to hear George Fox in the large house on the corner. When you turn the corner, you will see a crowd of people assembling. Just follow them into the house. I hope to see you there."

Suddenly, she heard the sound of pounding hooves when two king's soldiers approached the marketplace. Without saying a word, the woman disappeared amidst the crowd. Mary shuddered. *Some things in London have not changed.*

Mary tucked her parcel of purchased peaches under her arm and headed back to the inn. When she arrived, the men were just returning from another meeting with Sir Henry Vane. She smiled and waved as they approached. John Clarke and Roger Williams entered the inn while Mary signaled William to remain outside with her. When the door closed behind the others, she said, "I heard the most exciting news today about an itinerant preacher named George Fox who is speaking in the area. Will you be able to join me tomorrow afternoon to hear him?"

William shook his head. "I am sorry. Tomorrow afternoon we are to dine with a member of the Colonial Commission. His influence is extremely important for our cause. Feel free to go yourself; it will spare you spending another afternoon alone."

Mary's shoulders slumped. *I wanted William to hear George Fox so we could discuss it afterwards. It will be hard for me to explain everything I hear, and I know William will ask about it.*

The following afternoon, knowing that the meeting was nearly a mile away, Mary left the inn early. She wanted time to think, and fresh air always seemed to clear her mind. She walked through the littered streets of London, scarcely conscious of the puddles of muddy water in her path, and the rats that scurried away as she passed. As she approached the house, caution overwhelmed her. *What if they do not welcome me? Before I left London for Massachusetts, private religious meetings were often spied upon and raided by the government. I wonder if that has changed.*

Mary walked back and forth in front of the large house on the corner hoping she would see a familiar face. Men and women of all stations in life greeted each other and went inside. When she was almost ready to give up and go inside by herself, a woman behind her said, "Hello. Remember me? I met you yesterday at the market."

Mary turned and smiled. "Oh, yes. You are the one who told me about the meeting. It is good to see you again. I was hoping you would be here."

"My name is Sarah Leonard," the woman said. "Please come in and join us. I am certain you will like hearing George Fox preach."

"I am grateful you invited me. My name is Mary Dyer. I heard about George Fox when I was in the colonies and never imagined I would ever have a chance to hear him speak."

When the women entered the house, a sense of peace enveloped Mary. Seated around the room were more than two dozen people talking among themselves. Standing in the corner was a man with a broad brimmed hat shading his piercing eyes. His piercing eyes resembled those of Anne Hutchinson, and Mary found it hard to look away from him. *That must be George Fox.*

Since all the benches and chairs were taken, Mary and Sarah sat on the floor by the unlit fireplace. When George Fox began to speak, Mary felt her spirit leap.

"The light of Christ, or a measure of His Holy Spirit, is given to every person," he proclaimed loudly. "It is to this Light or Spirit that everyone must bring his thoughts, words, and deeds, to be judged. For God directly teaches His people about Himself. The Lord has created thee for His glory, and it is to Him that thou must give account of all thy words and actions."

For two hours Mary sat fixed on the words of the preacher. It seemed as if he were addressing each word to her. *It is hard for me to imagine that the Light of Christ can live within me. George Fox is extremely eloquent and his words provide an understanding and truth I had never known before.*

When the meeting was over, Mary could scarcely wait to tell her husband the exciting words she had heard. However, much to her chagrin, when William arrived back at the inn that evening, he stayed up late discussing the future charter with Roger and John and showed little interest in the excitement that was churning within her.

Mary slept little that night as the words of George Fox replayed through her mind. *The spirit of God resides within both men and women. He is not just a God somewhere out there who makes sure we follow every single law He has ever proclaimed. People can receive guidance directly from the Inner Light God puts within all believers....What George Fox is teaching is similar to what Anne Hutchinson taught, only much deeper and more personal.*

Early the next morning, William greeted Mary with a smile. "I am sorry I was not able to go with you yesterday and was not talkative when you returned. We are within weeks of completing the charter, and it has become very intense. I am interested in hearing what you have learned, but we agreed to start work early this morning, but we will not have to work late tonight. I promise you, we will talk tonight. I do want to know what George Fox had to say."

Mary bit her lip. Her shoulders slumped while she forced a smile. "I understand. The entire colony of Rhode Island is depending on your work here."

William reached for an envelope lying on the table beside their bed and handed it to her. "A letter from your sister arrived yesterday. I need to leave now, but when I return I will be anxious to learn the news from home."

Mary's hands trembled as she tore open the envelope and began reading.

"My beloved sister,

I send you all my love and affection. We are all well. The children and I miss you. Samuel has been a great help to Randall in tending the sheep and planting the crops. They are teaching Will how to tend to the sheep so Samuel can spend more time in the shop.

This spring fifteen new lambs joined the flock and they are growing extremely fast. They are fun to watch frolicking in the pasture.

You would be proud of little Mary. For such a young girl, she is able to do most of the work a grown woman would do. She is a big help with the younger boys.

Charles has learned to walk since you left and tries his best to keep up with Henry and Maher. He gets extremely frustrated when he cannot. You will scarcely recognize him when you get back.

Samuel, William, Henry, and Mary have all become excellent readers. I am teaching them the same way I taught Anne Hutchinson's children and it seems to be paying off. I still have trouble teaching them to add and subtract, but we have made special charts on vellum to help them remember.

Do you know when you and William will be able to come home? We all miss you greatly and pray for your safety every day.

Your loving sister,
Martha"

Mary slumped onto the side of the bed. Tears filled her eyes. *How I miss my children. I wish I could take each one of them into my arms and hold them...Yet, something even stronger within me is pleading for me to know God better, before I return home. I have only heard George Fox speak once, but I must hear more from him. In just one sermon, he answered many of the questions I have struggled with for years.*

One evening after nearly a year in England, William rushed into their room in the Ox Bow Inn. He grabbed Mary and whirled her around with joy. "We are successful at last," he shouted. "Our mission is complete. The British Council of State ordered the vacating of the commission given to Coddington and directed the four towns of Rhode Island to unite under our new charter. We can now return home with the news. With good fortune we could be in Rhode Island by the end of January."

Mary pulled out of her husband's embrace. Her muscles stiffened. Tears filled her eyes. "But I cannot leave England now. I cannot leave George Fox and my new Quaker friends. I have so much more to learn."

William scowled. Mary could see a flash of anger in his eyes. "What do you mean, you cannot leave? It was you, who chided us for months about the length of our business. You claimed you wanted to return to Newport and your family. Now that we are ready to leave, you tell me you cannot leave."

Mary began to sob. "I am sorry...I am so sorry." She gasped for air. "It is true, William. I cannot leave. I still yearn for the children, our home in Newport, and the clean, fresh air from the sea, but something has happened. I am changed."

"Changed?" he snapped.

Mary stopped crying. A sense of determination spread over her. "Yes, I have become convinced the Quaker way is the true way to God. I have found a mission here with the Quakers that I cannot give up. God has spoken to me and told me I must join the Quakers in England and to help spread His word."

A look of confusion and anger spread across William's face. "Can't you spread God's word just as well in Rhode Island as you can in England?"

Mary tried to hug her husband, but he stood frozen in place. "God willing, I will return to Rhode Island, but the time is not right for me to do so. I love you and the children, but I must put God first. I wish you could understand."

William walked across the room and stared out the window. "But I must leave as soon as possible. The future of Rhode Island rests with the papers I carry. Every day we are delayed, Coddington's power will become more deeply rooted and harder to remove. You have had many weeks to learn from the Quakers. Now your place is with me and the children."

Mary reached for her husband's hand. "I have prayed that I would not be separated from you, dear William, but the Lord will not take this burden from me. It is only in England I can be strengthened in the faith. I will follow you as soon as God will permit."

"Roger Williams has sacrificed so much and has booked passage for him, you, and me to leave on the *TrueLove* ship this Saturday," William protested.

Mary became solemn. "Then John Clarke could use my passage."

"John Clarke will be staying in England as the colony's agent. Someone must be available to speak for our colony and make sure someone like William Coddington does not come and convince the Colonial

Commission to change the charter that was just granted to us."

"We cannot let my passage go to waste," Mary insisted. "I know several Quaker missionaries who are ready right now to go to the colonies and preach God's word. I will have them contact Roger Williams to finalize the arrangement."

Two days later, Mary and William Dyer stood near the wharf of the ship *TrueLove*. They gave one final embrace before William pulled back and walked stoically up the gangplank. The seagulls squawking overhead taunted the pain in Mary's heart. *Will I ever see my husband and children again? Why is God asking me to make such a great sacrifice?*

Chapter Eighteen
Life without Mary

Newport, Rhode Island, February 1653

Aunt Martha," William Junior shouted as he raced into his house. "A ship was spotted in the bay. Do you think mother and father might be one it? They said they would be gone about a year, and it is time for their return."

Martha looked up from the dishpan she was using on a shelf under the side window. "I hope so. We can walk to the dock and see, but we have done that several times before and came back disappointed."

Martha Clarke gathered the younger children and then went to the woodshop where Randall and eighteen-year-old Samuel were working on a new bed for Charles. For the last year, Martha had thrived on taking care of her sister's family, but seeing her tall, attractive husband seated on a bench behind a worktable, she imagined herself and her husband alone with their own large family. She quickly shook the thought from her head. "Randall, a ship is about to dock. Let us take the children to the harbor and check on it without getting their hopes up, only to be disappointed again. William's last letter said they would be here in the middle of February. It is possible that Mary and William will be on it."

Without saying a word, Randall laid his chisel on the table and followed Martha out the shop door with Samuel close behind. Snow flurries blew around them and their boots crunched on the frozen mixture of snow, salt, and sand. Seeing how tired two-year-old Charles was becoming, Randall picked him up and carried him.

When they approached the dock, people were coming from all directions to join them. Minutes later, William Dyer came bounding ashore. One traveling bag was thrown over his shoulder while he carried a large wooden box in his arms. Before Martha and Randall could get to him, the eager crowd pressed around him begging for answers from England. Seeing his children amongst the crowd, he set his box on the ground and quickly hugged each of them before turning to the impatient crowd.

"It is good to be back in Newport," William shouted above the howling winds. "I come bearing good news. The British Council of State has ordered the vacating of Coddington's commission and provided us with a new charter directing the four towns of Rhode Island to reunite. The first of March, freemen from the four towns will need to meet in Portsmouth and reinstate the officers who were displaced by the Coddington Commission."

Hearing those words, the crowd gave a resounding cheer while the few Coddington loyalists shrunk silently into the background.

William waved good-bye to the crowd and turned to his children. Henry clung to his legs while Samuel picked up his father's traveling bags.

William Junior looked up into his father's eyes with a look of bewilderment. "Where's mother? Why isn't she with you? I was looking forward to seeing her again. I really miss her."

William Dyer's gaze became distant and Martha was certain she saw tears welling in his eyes. *Surely, nothing has happened to Mary*

"She will be coming on a later ship." His voice sounded weak and pained. "When we get to the house, I will explain everything to you. It is much too cold to tarry outside."

The biting cold wind increased its speed as the Dyers and Clarkes trudged toward their homes. The children's cheeks reddened with the cold and they curled their hands as close to their bodies as possible. The two men fell into step beside each other while Martha and the children followed close behind. Randall studied his brother-in-law's sea weary face. "Tomorrow Martha and I will move our personal belongings back into the little house so you can spend time alone with your children. They have talked about you and Mary constantly since you left."

Martha increased her pace until she was beside William. She was unable to mask her conflicted feelings. "I am anxious to learn when she will be coming back. I will continue to cook for your family and care for the children until she returns."

When William entered his front door, he hesitated and gazed around the room. He turned to his sister-in-law and her husband. "You have put up new shelves and built a new mantle for the fireplace. You have put up new curtains on the window. The children seem happy and healthy. I do not know how I can ever repay you for your faithfulness."

"It was an honor and a joy," Martha said, "and also our way of helping the cause of freedom for the Rhode Island colony. Please make yourself comfortable at the table, and I will warm goats' milk for everyone."

The children took their places on the benches around the table. Charles snuggled up to Randall, seemingly unsure of the stranger who had joined them.

"Father, please tell us where mother is?" Maher begged. "I hope she is not ill."

Again, Martha noted a distant, sad look in William's eyes when he said, "this may be hard for you to understand, but your mother felt she needed to remain in England for a while longer."

"Why," Mary begged. "Doesn't she love us anymore?"

William wrapped his arm around his only daughter. "She loves you all very much. However, as much as your mother loves you, she loves God even more. She feels God wants her to stay in London a while longer, and she must obey His guidance."

"I don't understand," eleven-year-old William Junior said. "What will she do in England?"

William took a deep breath. "Your mother has always had a deep yearning to know and understand God better. That is why she used to spend as much time as she could with Anne Hutchinson. She wants to stay in England to learn more of the beliefs of the Quakers from George Fox."

Martha watched William study the expressions on his children's faces. The older ones seemed to understand while looks of confusion remained on the faces of the younger ones.

Samuel wrinkled his forehead. "How is what the Quakers believe different from what we believe in Rhode Island? Didn't we leave Boston so we could believe whatever we wanted to? Couldn't she believe like the Quakers do here in Rhode Island?"

"You have wisdom beyond your years, son," William said. "Your mother is learning new things about God. The easiest way I can explain it is that the Quakers believe that God lives within each person. They call the God that lives within the Inner Light.

Your mother wants to learn how to obey that Inner Light better."

"But where will she live and what will she do to earn a living while she is in England?" Samuel persisted.

Martha watched the dismay on William's face as he struggled to explain to his children what he obviously did not understand himself. "Before I left London, your mother made contact with a Quaker woman named Margaret Fell who lived at Swarthmore Hall, the main gathering place for the Quakers. They grow a lot of sheep in the area. Perhaps she could earn her board and room by helping spin the wool for them."

Little Mary began to cry. "I want my mother to come home. I can hardly remember what she looks like."

As the months passed, Martha would visit every vessel from England that docked in the Newport bay to see if there was a letter from her sister. Each time she returned home disappointed. Would God ever send her sister back to her?

One late October afternoon, eight months after he had returned from England, William burst through the front door of his home. "It came...It came," he shouted.

"What came?" Martha said as she looked up from stoking the fire.

"A ship just docked and there was a letter from Mary. Would you go outside and get Samuel, little William, and Randall? I want to read it to everyone at the same time."

Martha put the fire poke into its holder and hurried outside to find the others. Within minutes, they were all gathered around the long kitchen table.

The children's gazes seemed glued on their father who stood at the end of the table. He slowly unfolded the letter and read:

"My dearest husband and children,

My heart overflows with love for each of you. I am looking forward to the time when God deems it suitable for us to be reunited. Until that time, be assured that God is teaching me great truths and leading me in the Quaker ways.

I am learning the power of shared silence of individual inner voices of the Quakers along with the equality of all people: male or female, rich or poor, king or peasant. Because of these beliefs, I need to change many customs I have taken for granted all my life. Since everyone is equal, I can no longer use the formal 'you,' but like all other Quakers, I will address all people regardless of their status, with the familiar "thee." I am learning that because Quakers believe all people are equal, men will not remove their hats for anyone or anything, except in prayer since God is the only superior who warranted such an act of respect. I like that practice very much, but it makes the king of England angry.

The issue that is getting the Quakers in the most trouble is they refuse to take an oath when the law requires every British citizen to swear his allegiance to the government. Several times, I have been among the Quakers when they were herded to the local jail and left there to fall prey to illness, cold, and hunger. Do not grieve for my plight because, through it all, I have learned a deep richness of spirit.

Please write to me at the Swarthmore in the Furness area of Cumbria in North West England, and Margaret Fell will see that I get the letter. I am anxious to hear from each one of you.

William, thank you for caring for our children in my absence and thank Martha and Randall for helping us. I am certain the children are growing into fine young men and woman. I am blessed to have such a loving, understanding family.

Your loving wife and mother,

Mary Dyer"

A hush fell across the room as William folded the letter and placed it in his pocket. Maher was the first to speak. "That was a strange letter. I scarcely remember my mother. Aunt Martha has always been here to care for us."

A look of shock reflected on Samuel's face. "Maher, your mother is a good and loving mother. We have to understand that serving God is more important than being with her family."

"When Mother says God is telling her to stay in England does that mean God does not like us?" Maher said while tears began running down his cheeks.

Martha knelt beside her seven-year-old nephew and wrapped her arms around him. "God loves you very much. Even though your mother has not been able to be with you, hasn't God met all your needs? Haven't you felt love from your Father and Randall and I?"

Maher laid his head on his aunt's shoulder. "Y...y...yes," he mumbled. "I know my family loves me very much. I just want to know my mother."

Martha exchanged a panicked look with William before she responded. "All in due time...all in due time."

As the Rhode Island colony grew stronger and more productive, the colonists felt it necessary to take  active measures to protect themselves against the Dutch who were sending exploring parties and making claims in the area. In preparation for possible military action against the Dutch, William Dyer received a commission from the General Assembly.

Randall often accompanied William to patrol the shoreline looking for Dutch scouting boats. The men would paddle back and forth into each of the coves peering into the darkness wondering if the Dutch might be hiding, waiting to take possession of their small island.

One cold winter night while on patrol, Randall stood up in the canoe to survey the shoreline across the cove. Suddenly, he lost his balance and the canoe capsized throwing the two men into the freezing sea. William thrashed about in the biting water, knowing the human body could not survive long in such temperatures. Images of his children and his beloved Mary flashed before him. *How can they get along without me? They are so young and innocent and their mother is not here to help them.* Struggling against the current, William's feet settled upon a boulder and he was able to stand. The chilling water was at his chest, but one painful step at a time he made it to shore. Within minutes, he collapsed onto the beach where he lay exhausted and semi-conscious until daybreak.

Through his fog, he heard a faint child's voice. "Mister...Mister. Are you all right?"

"I am cold...I am so cold," William moaned. "Have you seen my brother-in-law?"

"You are the only man I see," the child said. "I will go home and get my father to help you. I will be right back."

William closed his eyes and faded into semi-consciousness once again. Time seemed to stand still. The next thing he knew a man and older boy wrapped a blanket around him and lifted him onto a wagon. "You are William Dyer, aren't you?" a gruff voice said. "We will take you home."

"Yes, I am," William mumbled. "Did you find my brother-in-law, Randall Clarke?"

"Not yet," the gruff voice said, "but several people are looking for him."

Lying in the wagon bed, William felt every rut in the road. When they stopped in front of the Dyer home, Samuel came running toward them and peered into the back of the wagon. "Father, what happened? We were so worried when you and Randall did not return last night."

William tried to sit up, but was too weak. He took a deep breath in the hope of gaining more energy. "Our canoe capsized last night in the cove by the Brown farm. Please go look for Randall."

Samuel helped carry William into the house while the younger children looked on in horror. He removed his father's wet clothing, pulled a dry nightshirt over his head, and laid him on his bed. "I will leave you in Martha's able care and go look for Uncle Randall."

Terror filled Martha's face. "Please find Randall. It is too cold for anyone to last long out of doors." She took a deep breath, whispered a prayer, and began making hot milk for William. When he was strong enough to hold the clay mug, she returned to the hearth and began heating broth. Her hands trembled when she placed the bowl on a tray and carried it to the bed.

Hearing the commotion, the younger children bounded from their beds. "What's wrong? What's wrong?" they clamored.

Martha shook her head sadly. "Your father's canoe capsized last night. Early this morning a little girl found your father lying on the beach, but no one has found Randall yet."

Little Mary rushed to her father's bed and reached over to touch his arm "How are you? You look very pale."

William reached out and took his daughter's hand. "I am feeling better now. I just need to rest. Please pray they find your Uncle Randall soon."

After making certain William was resting comfortably, Martha took her shawl from the peg beside the door and grabbed a blanket from Mary's bed. "Mary, stay and take care of Henry and Charles. Will and Maher will need to come with me to help in the search."

As Martha and the boys started down the trail toward the sea, a horse and wagon rounded the bend.

"Is it Randall?" Martha shouted.

"Yes," the gruff voice said while he stopped the horse. "I am so sorry."

"No," she shouted. "It can't be Randall." Martha ran to the wagon. In the back was a body covered with a homespun grey blanket. She pulled back a corner and wailed. "No. It cannot be. Randall can't be gone."

"I am so sorry," the gruff voice repeated. "We did the best we could."

"I am certain you did," Martha said between sobs. "Please bring him to our little house behind the Dyers. We will have to make plans for proper burial."

The man with the gruff voice and his son carried Randall's body into the Clarke's home and laid him on a cot in the corner. "I am so sorry...I will get my wife to help you," he said and then turned and walked out of the house with his son closely behind him.

Martha slumped onto a chair beside the cot. "God, why did this happen? I cannot go on without my husband. He has always been my strength. The new world is too rough and unsettled for a woman alone. If only Mary were here...She is so strong...She is the one who understands the ways of God; she would know what to do...I am totally lost and empty."

Chapter Nineteen
The Quaker

Newport, Rhode Island, October 1656

Gloom and depression settled over Martha Clarke following the death of her beloved Randall. First, her sister had left for England and had not returned and now her husband was gone without leaving heirs. Every day she went next door to her sister's house and cooked, cleaned, did laundry, worked their garden, and taught the six children to read. She loved the children as if they were her own. Each evening she returned to her own simple home and felt a loneliness that could not be filled.

In the middle of a brisk autumn afternoon, Martha returned to her house to rest following frustrating hours of laundry in the backyard. The wind had kept blowing the clothes from the branches and rocks where she had spread them out to dry. Little Mary would fetch them for her so she would wash them again, hoping they would stay in place long enough to dry. By mid-afternoon, she was exhausted and needed a quick nap. She had just fallen asleep when there was a knock on the front door and a voice said, "Martha, are you here?"

Martha quickly arose, opened her chamber room door, and saw William Dyer standing by the door. *This is strange. William rarely comes to my house since Randall died.*

"I hope I did not disturb you," William said, "but a traveling Quaker missionary named Peter Hooker just arrived in Newport from London. He said he knows Mary."

Martha stood in shock. "Did he say how she is doing? She has been gone nearly five years. Is she planning to return soon?"

William shook his head. "Peter Hooker said Mary has become a Quaker minister and God has not given her an immediate call to return to Newport."

"The poor children," Martha said. "They may never get to know their mother."

William gazed at the dirt floor. "I know. Her absence is very hard for them to understand."

Martha gave a dry smile. "I sometimes have trouble understanding Mary's actions myself. I would like to know what it is about Quakerism that she is willing to sacrifice so much."

Martha could sense the pain in her brother-in-law's voice when he said, "I feel much the same way. Maybe Peter Hooker will help clarify it for us. He is speaking in the Easton's home this afternoon. Would you like to go and listen to him?"

Tears welled in Martha's eyes. "Of course," she stammered. "I miss Mary so. Ever since Randall died, I have felt empty and alone. Maybe I can find hope again and restore my faith in God."

"The Quakers have a peculiar belief system," William said. "Maybe Peter Hooker will have words of encouragement for both of us. If we leave now, we should have time to talk with him privately before the others arrive."

Martha took her bonnet from the hook beside the door, placed it on her head, and tucked the stray strands of hair beneath it before she tied the white strings. She then took her shawl from the next hook, wrapped it over her shoulders, and followed William out the door. An air of anticipation was in her steps.

Together the pair hurried down the path to the Easton's home. The crisp afternoon breeze whipped Martha's skirt and nearly blew William's hat from his head. *Even if I cannot be with my sister, maybe this man will help me understand why Mary feels her quest for God is more important than her family.*

Much to Martha's amazement when they arrived at the Easton's home, it was already filled with their friends and neighbors. William stood along the back wall with the other men, while Martha took a vacant chair in a corner.

It was obvious Peter Hooker had been speaking for some time. His voice was clear and concise. "Many of thee have asked why there is such a conflict between the Puritans and Quakers. I will do my best to explain what is happening."

Martha leaned forward to hear better. *Mary wrote about the Quaker's persecution in England. I did not know the Puritans in the new world also had a problem with the Quakers.*

Peter Hooker hesitated; his face became serious, as he scanned the group. "The real Quaker/Puritan conflict is political instead of religious. In both England and the colonies, the conflict focuses on power. The Quakers maintain that God created all men and women equal while the Puritans preach God's design his hierarchical and the clergy should control the religious thinking of the people. The Massachusetts governor is afraid to let the Quakers express their views for fear the Church-State partnership might collapse and they would lose control over the people."

Out of the corner of her eye, Martha could see William become restless. When Peter Hooker hesitated, William said, "The Puritans did not like what Anne Hutchinson taught either. They labeled her a heretic and forced those of us who followed her to leave the Massachusetts Bay Colony nearly eighteen years ago."

Peter Hooker nodded. "I applaud thy efforts. Because thee worked and sacrificed to allow freedom of religious thought in Rhode Island, the Quakers would like to visit thee and share our views about God."

Martha gazed out the window. The face of her beloved husband came before her. *I wish Randall could hear this. While we were in Boston, he never understood why the Boston clergy went to such extremes to persecute Anne Hutchinson or why the Puritan clergy were so fearful of people having different religious ideas. We learned while establishing Rhode Island, power and control is often the basis of most conflicts and not the religion itself.*

Much to Martha's surprise, William said, "When we left Massachusetts John Winthrop was governor. It was obvious he would not accept any thinking that did not agree with the Puritan clergy, but I was hoping the new governor would be more understanding. Several of our colonists have gone to Boston on business and no one bothered them."

An uncomfortable gasp echoed from the far side of the room and a silent pause enveloped the room until Peter Hooker responded. "Yes, there were a few months of relative calm, but Governor John Endicott has proven to have a volatile disposition and often displays explosive fits of rage when confronted by those who do not agree with him. With Anne Hutchinson

Governor John Endicott
(c. 1601 - 1665)

and the so called Antinomians out of Boston, the governor is beginning to focus on the Quakers."

William's face reddened. "I did not know there were Quakers in Boston. While I was in London, only a few believers ascribed to the teachings of George Fox. My wife became so captivated by the Quaker religion; she chose to remain in England to learn more about it than to return to her children in Rhode Island. And now you tell us Mary has become a Quaker minister?"

Peter Hooker appeared unfazed by the challenge. "If you are referring to Mary Dyer, I understand your confusion. However, she has chosen the higher ground. God is preparing her for greater service."

William shook his head with exasperation and leaned back against the wall.

Peter Hooker gave William a sympathetic look and turned back to the others. "To further explain what is going on in Boston, last summer two Quaker women arrived in the Boston Harbor. No sooner had they disembarked than they were led to the Boston jail for three weeks before being sent back to England. On August 9 when a small ship called *Speedwell* entered the Boston Harbor, the port authorities were alerted to search the ship before anyone landed. The passenger list had "Q's" beside the names of four men and four women, indicating they were Quakers. Those eight were ordered directly to the Boston court."

William's countenance hardened. "That shouldn't be allowed. They did not even have time to do or say anything illegal. They were being persecuted just for being a Quaker."

"That is exactly right," Peter Hooker stated firmly. "Two of the Quakers knew the law and immediately demanded their release, claiming there was no law that justified their imprisonment. Governor Endicott was so threatened by their knowledge of the law he manipulated the General Court to pass severe anti-Quaker laws. From now on Quakers who dock in

Boston will be punished and immediately sent back to their own land."

William's face blanched. "If passenger lists to Boston are being tagged for Quakers, how will Quakers like Mary come to the new world? The ports in Rhodes Island are too small for the large ships."

"That is the problem," Peter Hooker said. "It will be months before we can get word back to the Quakers in England not to come to Boston. It may be too late for some who are already in the process of coming to America."

Chapter Twenty
The Return

London, 1656

The gray drab walls of Swarthmore Hall in North West England loomed before Mary Dyer as she hurried to the gathering where George Fox was to preach. Instead of seeing the drabness of the grey walls, she felt exhilaration watching people come from all directions to hear the leader of the Quaker religion speak.

SWARTHMORE HALL.

Finally, I have found what I have been searching for. I have experienced the true Inner Light. Everyone is grateful Thomas and Margaret Fell permit their mansion home to be used as a gathering place for Quakers. It has such a peaceful setting with large gardens and fields for sheep. Even more, I am thankful they let me stay in an attic room and help tend the sheep in the pasture to earn my board and room. Sometimes when I am caring for the sheep I think of my time of tending our sheep in Newport. I think of my dear husband and my children who are growing up without me. I miss them terribly.

When Mary found a seat in the corner of the grand room where George Fox was about to speak, she surveyed the group. *A woman in the corner looks strangely familiar. However, I do not think she is someone I have met recently here in England.* While George Fox spoke, Mary was unable to keep her eyes off the petite woman with graying strands of hair dangling out from under her bonnet. Occasionally their eyes met and Mary looked down with embarrassment.

When the meeting ended, Mary watched the woman hurry in her direction. "Mary Dyer, do thou remember me?"

Mary continued studying her features and finally exclaimed, "Anne Burden. How wonderful to see thee after many years. How have thee been?"

Anne Burden shook her head sadly. "When my husband and I were forced to leave Boston, we chose to return to England. However, things did not go well for us. He recently died, and now I am completely alone. I wish we had gone to Rhode Island with you and the other supporters of Anne Hutchinson."

Mary Dyer wrapped her arms around her old friend and held her close. She felt the frailty of Anne's body against hers. "After these many years, imagine meeting each other in England. Are thou a Quaker now?"

Ann Burden gave a slight smile and hung her head. "Yes, my husband and I were some of the earliest followers of George Fox. What little solace in life I have, I find among the Quakers. Since my husband died, I have been destitute."

"I am certain the Quaker community is happy to provide thy support," Mary said.

Anne set her jaw. "I do not want to be a burden to anyone. When my husband and I were in Boston the fortune he had was in debts owed to him. However, having to leave in a hurry, we were not able to collect those debts. This money is still due his estate, but I cannot benefit from it since I cannot go back to Boston alone and collect it."

Mary hesitated. Images of her six children as they looked six years before crossed her mind. "Letters from my husband and sister tell me how much Rhode Island is changing. I do not know what is happening in Boston."

A look of puzzlement spread across Anne's face. "Could I be so bold to ask why thou are in England without thy family?"

Mary gazed out an open window onto the fields of grazing sheep. A restlessness stirred within her. "Six years ago I came to London with my husband, Roger Williams, and John Clarke when they were applying for a charter for the Rhode Island colony. While I was waiting for them to do their work I met George Fox."

Anne's eyes brightened. "Then thou are a Quaker as well?"

Mary smiled. "Yes. I have been staying at Swarthmore Hall, praying and listening to the Quaker teachers, especially George Fox and Margaret Fell. I have heard the Inner Light convince me to become a minister and George Fox has confirmed that leading. Since then I have been traveling around parts of England preaching God's Word and Quaker testimonies. When I am free, I help with chores at Swarthmore Hall. Now I am waiting for the Inner Light's direction as to where I am to go and minister next."

Day by day, the friendship between Anne Burden and Mary Dyer was not only rekindled, but also strengthened. Mary became concerned for Anne's frail condition and her refusal to take outside assistance for others in the community of Quakers. Finally, Mary confronted her. "Anne, thou cannot keep doing laundry for others to make a few meager pennies to support thyself. It is too hard on thy body."

Anne sighed and sank onto a bench at the kitchen table. "I only have two choices. Either I continue doing laundry or I go back to Boston and try to collect the debts that are owed my husband. I do not have money to pay for the passage. I may have to ask the Quaker community for help."

Mary studied her friend's face and asked softly, "And what is God telling thee to do?"

Anne looked confidently into Mary's eyes and smiled. "I have been praying about this for several weeks and feel God is leading me to return to Boston."

"Then I will go with thee if we can obtain money for our passage," Mary insisted. "I too have been praying about returning to Rhode Island. I feel my work in England is nearly over and am anxious to see my family. Let us agree to conclude our affairs in London and secure passage on the next ship for Boston."

On a cold January afternoon in 1657, eight weeks after leaving England, Mary Dyer once again stood at the rail of a ship in the Boston Harbor; this time with frail Anne Burden at her side. In the distance, she watched a small boat leave the shore and approach the *Speedwell*.

Mary turned to Anne. "That boat must be the one to take us ashore. In a few days I will be reunited with my family."

The women watched as a uniformed marshal stepped aboard the ship while another remained in the boat. The marshal talked with the captain of the *Speedwell* and crossed the deck where Mary and Ann were standing.

"What are your names," he snapped.

"I am Mary Dyer."

"And I am Anne Burden."

"Are you members of the Quaker group?"

Mary and Anne exchanged bewildered looks. "Yes," Mary said. "We are proud to be Quakers."

"Then come with me," he commanded.

Mary's muscles tighten. "Why are we being taken into custody? We have just arrived. Certainly membership in a particular religious group is not against the law in Boston!"

The marshal glared at Mary and snarled, "Religious groups are not against the law, but it is against the law for a Quaker to enter Boston."

Mary trembled. "In that case, I wish to be taken to thy superiors immediately for a full explanation of this outrage. My friend and I are only transients. She is in Boston only to collect just debts due her late husband. I assure you my only intent in being in Boston is to take the first opportunity to leave for Rhode Island where my family awaits me."

"Tell that to the magistrates," the marshal snapped. "I have been ordered to seize any Quaker upon arrival and hold them in confinement until I receive further orders. In the meantime, you are not to speak or communicate with any person except the officer who has you in charge. Do you understand?"

"I understand only that this is an outrage," Mary said. "I must be permitted to notify my husband of my whereabouts, lest he think I have vanished from the face of the earth."

"Your husband is no concern of mine. Your obedience is. We would all be better off if all Quakers vanished from the face of the earth." The marshal turned to the ship's captain. "Will you retrieve all personal possessions of these women? Any Quaker books and pamphlets must be immediately burned. The rest will be impounded."

Mary's heart sank. *Those materials were to be used to spread the word of God to help the non-convinced understand the tenets of being a Quaker.*

Ropes were tied around Anne and Mary's wrists and they were led down the gangplank of the *Speedwell* in disgrace. The officer in the marshal's boat, rowed the boat to shore, docked it, and joined them at the end of the wharf. The marshal grasped Mary's arm while the officer took Anne's. Children and women stopped to stare as they were led through the streets of Boston to the local jail.

Cold dampness enveloped the women when they descended the steps to the jail below. As soon as they entered the dirty cell, Anne collapsed. Mary gathered as much straw as possible to cover her and then lay as close to her as possible, hoping her own body heat would ease her suffering. Throughout the night, Anne had continual fits of coughing. Each craved for water to soothe their parched throats, but none was provided.

The following day, Mary and Anne were brought before a magistrate for questioning. Anne was first, but she was too weak and hoarse to respond. Mary watched with dismay while the guards drug her from the courtroom to a holding cell in the corner of the hall and dropped her on the floor.

Mary's muscles tightened as the magistrate glared at her and snapped, "You are next. Step forward at this time."

Mary stood erect and walked defiantly toward the magistrate.

The magistrate surveyed her dirty dress and mud-stained face. "Are you Mary Dyer?"

"I am."

"Do you know why you are here?"

Mary scowled, yet tried to force herself to be pleasant. "Indeed I do not. Yesterday my friend and I were seized and imprisoned for some law of which we know nothing about."

"Then you shall know it now," he replied as he filed through a pile of paper beside him. He cleared his throat and began reading.

"At a General Court held at Boston, October 14, 1656: 'WHEREAS, There is a cursed sect of heretics lately risen up in the world which are commonly called Quakers, who take upon themselves to be immediately sent of God and infallibly assisted by the Spirit to speak and write blasphemous opinions despising Government and the order of God in Church and Commonwealth, speaking evil of dignitaries, reproaching and reviling magistrates and ministers, and seeking to turn the people from the faith and gain proselytes to their pernicious ways. This Court taking into serious consideration the promises, and to prevent the like mischief as by their means is wrought in our native land, doth hereby order, and by the authority of the Court be it ordered and enacted, that whatever master or commander of any ship, bark, pinnacle, catch, or of any other vessel that shall henceforth bring into any harbor, creek, or cove within this jurisdiction any known Quaker or Quakers, or any other blasphemous heretics as aforesaid, shall pay, or cause to be paid'...."

Mary's mind wandered. Anger boiled within her as the magistrate continued reading. *That is pure nonsense and does not make any sense.*

"...The Quakers were to be whipped, sentenced to labor in the workhouse section of the prison, and permitted to speak to no one. Quaker books were to be confiscated and a fine levied on those who brought them to the colony. Anybody defending Quaker opinions was to be fined for the first two offenses and thereafter banished. Finally, any disrespect to a magistrate would result in whipping and a fine."

"Mary Dyer, you and Anne Burden are both sentenced to the fullest punishment of this law," the magistrate said. He turned to the three guards standing beside her. "Take both women to the prison yard and administer their punishment."

In obedience to those words, the guards took Mary roughly by the arm while another set of guards went to the holding cell for Anne. The guards dragged them both to the prison yard. Before the eyes of several men loitering about, Mary and Anne were stripped to the waist.

Anne was the first to be tied to the whipping post and received her lashes. By the time she received half a dozen lashes, she slumped unconscious in her bonds. The guard doing the whipping gave a questioning look to the head guard.

Mary watched in horror when the head guard snarled, "The law is the law. She must receive the prescribed number." When Anne's whipping ended, the guards untied her from the pole, and dragged her limp body down the steps into her cold, damp jail cell.

Mary cringed as they tied her to the whipping pole, but tried to remain stoic. She prayed to the Lord to keep her conscious despite the searing pain of the thongs that struck her skin. Blood flowed from the crimson welts across her back and breast when she was led back to her cell. Entering the cell, she saw her friend lying bloody in a corner. "This edict is of the devil and I intend to spend my remaining years working repeal this vicious law."

The days were long and the nights were even longer for Mary while she lay or sat on the prickly straw on the floor of her cell, wondering how she could let William know where she was. She prayed constantly for Anne's health and wisdom. Mary used part of her drinking water to cleanse Anne's wounds and shared a portion of her own rations with her. She rejoiced when strength began to return into her friend, but she did not know how to contact the outside world.

One rare sunny afternoon Mary and Anne were allowed to exercise in the prison yard. They stretched and slowly walked around the grounds under the careful watch of the prison guard, Mary admired each rock and pebble beneath her feet. Simple things of nature took on an entirely new meaning. Suddenly she spotted a small piece of charcoal with several pointed edges. *This will make a perfect writing tool. Now all I need is a piece of paper or vellum.* When the guard was looking the other way, she picked up the charcoal and hid it in the folds of her mud-stained dress.

Two days later, Mary and Anne heard a loud turmoil at the top of the stairs. The prisoner continued shouting and cursing while the guards threw him into the cell next to them.

"He's obviously drunk," Anne whispered.

"I wonder what his story is," Mary said. "In spite of how obnoxious he may be, he is still one of God's children."

As soon as the cell door clanged behind him, the new prisoner fell asleep. Loud snoring and a foul odor drifted from the man's cell into the women's. He did not awaken until the next morning. When he did, he edged to the side of his cell next to women's. He smiled at Mary. His eyes were clear and bright. "This is not a very pleasant place for women. Why are you here? You do not look like the threatening type."

Mary moved closer to the bars that separated the two cells. "The only charges they have against us is that we are Quakers and proud of it. Why are thee here?"

The stranger shook his head and gave a dry, sad sigh. "I was charged with breaking the seventh commandment. The owner of the mercantile was certain I had spent the night with his daughter and called the officials. This is farthest from the truth. I do not even know his daughter. However, I was drinking too much and I guess I might have gotten a little belligerent, but I did not harm anyone or take anything that was not mine."

"Maybe thy family will come and plead thy case and thee will be released soon," Mary said.

The stranger sighed. "I hope so. Too often in Boston, the punishment does not fit the crime."

Mary shook her head; sadness was in her voice. "It is hard for me to understand the cruelty of the Puritans while they try to follow all the laws in the Bible. God is more than just a list of laws. That is why I became a

Quaker. God is love and lives within all believers. He forgives us when we do wrong."

The man hesitated. "That is an encouraging thought. You should be out of here telling people your view of God."

"I obviously wish I could," Mary said, "but my husband is in Rhode Island. I do not have any way of getting word to him to let him know where I am."

The stranger reached into his pocket. "I have a piece of paper you could use to write a letter to him." He paused a moment. "You probably do not have anything to write with."

Mary crawled to the corner of her cell and dug through the straw. "I found this piece of charcoal in the prison yard last week. Perhaps I could get this to write well enough for my husband to read. The next problem would be finding someone to take it to Newport, Rhode Island."

"If you can get a letter written with the charcoal," the stranger said, "when I am released, I could take your letter to Rhode Island. I need to get as far away from Boston as I can. Once the magistrates consider a person an undesirable they are known to keep harassing them until they leave. I cannot promise anything, but I will do my best to find your husband."

Chapter Twenty-One
William Dyer to the Rescue

Newport and Boston, 1657

The winds whipped around Martha Clarke as she piled another log on the fire beneath the kettle in the backyard. Laundry days were always a challenge, but the springtime brought extra work. William's and the children's clothes were especially coated with mud from working in the garden and fields and caring for the sheep. Months before, Samuel had strung a rope between tree branches to provide more space for her to spread the clothes to dry which had saved her a great deal of time each week. Martha looked up when a stranger approached the Dyer home. Instead of knocking on the door, he came around the side of the house to talk with her.

"Good day," the stranger said. "My name is Henry Lott. I have a personal letter for William Dyer, do you know where I might find him?"

Martha Clarke surveyed the tall, slender visitor. His sunburn, holes in his britches, and bug bites on his arms indicated to her he had been traveling for some time. "He is in the field with the cattle, I could have one of the boys go and get him. Would you like to come into the house and have some fresh water while you wait?"

"That would be most appreciated," he said. "I have been walking most of the way from Boston and I could use a comfortable rest."

Martha laid her laundry stirring stick down and motioned Henry Lott to follow her. As they approached the house, Maher was leaving by the front door.

"Maher, please go to the back field and tell your father he has company."

Maher stopped and studied the tattered strangers. "Yes, Aunt Martha. I would be glad to." With that, Maher leaped a fence and began running across the nearby field while Henry Lott and Martha smiled with amusement at his eagerness.

Martha opened the front door and pointed to the bench at the table. "Have a seat and I will get you a cup of water." She dipped the ladle into the water bucket on the table under the window, poured it into a cup, and handed it to him.

Henry finished the water in three gulps and said, "Thank you so much for your kindness. It has been weeks since I have had clean water to drink."

While Martha was pouring the weary traveler his third cup of water, the door opened and William Dyer entered. He smiled and approached the guest with his right hand extended. "Good day. I am William Dyer."

Henry stood and shook William's hand. "I am Henry Lott. I thank you for the fresh water and for letting me relax in your home." He reached inside his pocket and handed him a folded sheet of paper. The corners were bent and tattered. "I brought a letter to you from Mary Dyer."

Martha watched William's face whiten.

"Do you know Mary?" he stammered. "Is she well?"

Henry nodded. "She and a friend are in prison in Boston. She wanted me to let you know where she was. Mary is in good spirits, but both women have been beaten several times."

William sank onto the bench beside Henry. He studied the paper in his hand. Martha saw tears well up in his eyes. "But why would Mary be in prison? She is a good woman. When did she arrive in Boston?"

Henry shook his head. "The women are in prison only because they are Quakers. I met them when I was imprisoned on false charges. Mary said she was on her way home to Rhode Island. They did not know about the new law claiming it was illegal for Quakers to enter the Massachusetts colony when they landed in the Boston Harbor."

William's hands trembled. He gave Martha a sad, pleading look. "After all these years away from home, and to think prison is the way Mary is welcomed back into the colonies. I must leave immediately for Boston to plead for her release."

"May I have the pleasure of traveling with you?" Henry Lott asked. "I must go back to reclaim my possessions so I can establish myself elsewhere. It is always easier with a companion."

William's eyes widened and his jaw dropped. "You mean you walked all the way from Boston to bring me this message from Mary and are now ready to return?"

"Yes. Your wife was so good to me while I was in prison; it was the least I could do."

William looked to his sister-in-law. "Martha, would you assemble enough food and water for Henry and me to get to Boston as well as enough for Mary and my return trip? I am glad we have several extra blankets we can take with us."

William Dyer drove his horse and wagon down the once familiar streets of Boston with Henry Lott at his side. "I can scarcely believe the changes to Boston I am seeing. When I was forced to leave Boston nineteen years ago, it was a small town and now it is a thriving city."

Henry shook his head. "It is amazing. I have seen tremendous growth in just the few years I have been here. When I first arrived, my house was at the edge of town and now several streets have been built beyond it."

Henry directed William to his house. Before he jumped from the wagon, William attempted to pay Henry for his time and sacrifice, but Henry gently pushed William's hand away. "You have a loving, spiritual wife who encouraged me a great deal while I was it prison, it was the least I could do. I plan to move to Rhode Island as soon as I close out my business here."

William thanked him once again and turned his horse and wagon toward Governor Endicott's home. Much to his surprise, the once familiar house was now three times its original size. He tethered his horse to a nearby tree and knocked on the governor's front door.

When the governor opened the door, William waited uncomfortably while the governor surveyed him up and down before speaking. After several tense moments, the governor's eyes widened. "William Dyer, I presume. What brings you from Rhode Island?"

"I understand my wife is in the Boston jail," he said firmly.

"I have heard so," the governor said coldly. "A law had been passed that no Quakers are allowed to enter Boston. She was banished from Boston many years ago with the Antinomians, and now she was trying to enter the harbor as a Quaker. She also had numerous Quaker pamphlets, tracts, and books in her possession.

William tightened his fists behind his back. "Mary was on her way back to Rhode Island. The Newport Harbor is not developed enough for the larger ships from London to dock. Any law banning Quakers from crossing through Boston is totally unjust, and I demand her immediate release."

John Endicott's face flushed. "Your wife has broken a law that was passed by the General Court of Boston. Quakers are not allowed within this jurisdiction." After pausing a few moments, his features softened. "Boston has experienced many changes since you left. I learned you are now clerk and judge in Newport. In order to maintain harmony among the colonies, I will make arrangements for you to plead your case with the head magistrate tomorrow and set the conditions for her release."

William Dyer forced a smile. "I thank you, sir. I will be at the magistrate's office at dawn."

Unsure of the reception he might receive at the newly constructed Boston Inn, William chose to drive to the edge of town and sleep in the bed of his wagon. He tossed restlessly throughout the night with the anticipation of seeing his beloved Mary. The moment he had been praying for during the past five years could be just hours away.

When the court convened the next morning, William Dyer took a seat near the front. Hours passed as he listened to one trivial ruling after another. *How can they ignore an important case like mine while they make trivial rulings on drunkenness and perceived petty thefts?*

When the last case was finished and the room was empty except for William and the magistrate, the magistrate said, "William Dyer, you may now state your concerns. Do keep it brief."

William walked to the front. "Gentlemen," he began. "I am here to ask for the release of my wife, Mary Dyer. She meant no harm. She was unaware of the newly passed law that Quakers were not allowed in Boston. She was here for no other purpose than to return to our home in Rhode Island. Had you let her pass through, you would not have had to deal with her nor have her punishment on your conscience. Surely, there can be no further purpose in holding her. I beg you to release her along with her friend, Anne Burden."

The magistrate scowled. "William Dyer, you yourself are not blameless in this matter. When you resided in Boston, you also caused mischief and concern to the point you were disarmed and banished from us. We owe you no favors. It is the opinion of this court, however, that your wife has had sufficient punishment to convince her not to set foot upon the soil of this commonwealth until she has completely forsaken here grievous errors. Therefore, the court will release both Mary Dyer and Anne Burden to your custody on the following conditions. First, you must leave this jurisdiction immediately without stopping to rest or seek lodging until you are out of the Commonwealth of Massachusetts. Second, you must not permit your wife to speak or hold conversation with any person except yourself while on the journey. And finally, you are informed that severe penalties will be invoked against you should you fail to adhere strictly to the terms and conditions of this order."

William sighed. "I agree." His heart raced. *How can I possibly agree to keep someone else from speaking, especially Mary? She has always had a strong-willed, determined spirit.*

The magistrate scowled. "After signing this agreement, you will be able to meet Mary Dyer and

Anne Burden at the jail tomorrow morning at dawn and promptly remove them from this jurisdiction, never to return again."

Chapter Twenty-Two
Homecoming

Newport, Rhode Island, April 1657

They're coming...They're coming," Henry Dyer shouted as he raced out the front door with Charles close behind.

Martha Clarke looked up from the black kettle on the hearth where she was preparing a stew for the evening meal. She followed the boys to the door. In the distance, she could see a familiar horse and wagon with a driver and two women. She ran to the road and waved frantically. "Mary...Mary," she shouted. "My precious sister is finally home."

As soon as William Dyer pulled his mare to a stop, Mary jumped from the wagon and bounded into her sister's arms. "Martha, Martha. It is good to see thee again. I have missed thee so."

Martha held her sister close while tears streamed unashamedly down her cheeks. She noticed her sister's thin frame, dark circles under her eyes, welts on her hands and neck, and a foul odor from being in prison. "Mary, how are you? It is good to have you home. You look as if you have been through a great deal."

Mary pulled back, but continued holding her sister's hand. "The Boston prison is an evil place and they are doing horrible things to the Quakers. I am grateful William came to rescue me, but I must not forget the Quakers still in prison there."

"Come in and rest and tell us all about it," Martha said and then looked quizzically at her sister's traveling companion.

Mary smiled and motioned for Anne to join them. "Martha, do you remember Anne Burden? She and her

"

husband were also among the followers of Anne Hutchinson who were forced out of Boston the same time we were. They decided to return to England instead of coming to Rhode Island with us."

Martha took Anne's hand. "Welcome to Newport. You may stay with us as long as need be. I have an extra room in my house you may use." Martha studied Anne's frail body and sweet face. *Why would anyone leave England and return to a place where they might not be welcome?*

As if her sister reading her mind, Mary said, "Anne's husband died a couple years ago and she was left without any means to support herself. Several leaders in Boston owed a great deal of money to her husband's estate, but because they had to leave Boston so hastily, they were unable to collect all that was owed them at the time. Anne intended to collect that money and return to England as soon as possible. Little did she know Quakers could no longer enter the Massachusetts Bay Colony. William made arrangements for mutual friends in Boston to collect that money for her and see that Anne receives safe passage back to London from another port."

One by one, Mary's children gathered around them. Martha watched the awkwardness as Mary greeted her own six children. She felt the children were accepting their mother more like a visiting aunt than a mother. The younger children were polite, but they had no memory of their mother, only the stories that their father and Martha had told them. Charles, who was but an infant when she left, was now a mischievous seven-year old. Nine-year-old Henry was a constant companion to Maher who was now eleven. Sixteen-year-old Will had trouble masking his conflicted feelings toward his mother who had abandoned him at a tender age. Little Mary at nine had tried to make herself the mistress of the household. With her mother's return, she became reserved and non-accepting and received her mother back as a peer and a competitor.

After hugging and greeting each of the youngest, Mary turned to twenty-two-year-old Samuel who was standing beside a young attractive woman. She reached out with both arms and hugged him. "Samuel, thou have grown to be a strong man in my absence. I have prayed for thee constantly during our separation. I missed thee so."

"I have also missed you," Samuel said. "I thought I would never get the opportunity to introduce you to my betrothed." He reached out and took the young woman's hand. "Mother, I would like you to meet Anne Hutchinson; she is the granddaughter of your once best friend and mentor."

Mary reached out and hugged her son's betrothed. Tears ran unashamedly down her cheeks. "Thou look so much like thy grandmother. I am truly blessed to have thee join the family...and to think my grandchildren will share a heritage with my dearest friend."

Martha had been standing back watching Mary greet her children after more than five years of being away from them on a mission they did not understand. Concerns began to envelop her. *Mary calls them, "thee," but their response to her is always "you." Will this combination of "thee" and "you" ever again feel like "we?"*

For the next few days, Martha hovered over Mary and Anne Burden. She made sure both rested and received extra nourishment. She spread salve of bees'

wax and herbs on their backs to help heal their wounds. She provided them with new clothing, burnt their old dresses in the backyard, and helped wash their hair to make certain all bugs and lice were removed. Day by day, the color gradually returned to Mary and Anne's faces and their strength returned.

Late one afternoon William rapped on the door to Martha's house with a broad smile. "Martha, is Anne asleep? I have good news for her, but I don't want to disturb her."

Hearing her name, Anne opened the chamber room door. "I am awake and I always anxious for good news."

"Come, sit at the table and I will explain," William directed with a mysterious voice.

Martha and Anne took seats across from William before he continued. "I just came from the dock and a small ship just docked from Boston and a man was inquiring about you. He was shocked about the treatment you had received in Boston. He gave me a satchel for you and told me his ship will be sailing to Long Island in three days. He said you would be welcome to go with them to Long Island and catch the next Dutch ship to England."

William handed her the worn leather satchel and Anne immediately opened it. Her eyes widened and her lower lip began to quiver. "There is enough money here to pay my passage and to support me for the rest of my days. I will not need to take in laundry in order to survive. How can I ever thank thee?"

Anne turned to Martha with a broad smile. "I must go to the dock right away to thank the sailor who did this for me and tell him I would like to sail to Long Island with them."

Anne's departure from Newport left both the sadness of missing a friend and the joy of answered prayers. Martha now had more time to spend with Mary. For several days, they quietly walked around the town and nearby fields and beaches, relaxing in the beauty of nature. Martha marveled how well Mary remembered the details of the town she left almost six years before.

When her sister was stronger, Martha took her to visit their neighbors and help reacquaint her with the people and ways of Newport. Everyone was anxious to learn the news from England and Mary was more than willing to share whatever she knew. While in England, she had been in a multitude of towns and villages telling the stories of the Quakers and the ideas of George Fox, so was able to provide welcome news for many families separated from their loved ones.

Within weeks, Mary began preaching the Quaker beliefs in the Newport Commons. At first, only Martha was there to listen, but gradually the numbers grew and Mary became more energized. She shared the values of simplicity in worship, the belief that most of the ordinances of the church such as baptism and communion were unnecessary. She stressed the importance of inner dedication and communion with God's spirit over the legalistic following of every detail of scripture.

One day while Mary was preaching the local magistrate shouted, "By whose authority do you speak?"

Martha watched intently as Mary turned to him, not with anger but an angelic expression of love. "If thou are asking me if I have been approved by the clergy who preside over the steeple churches, the answer is 'no'. My words come from the God who resides within me."

"Are you saying the words you speak are not from scripture? If that is the case, I do not want to listen to what you have to say," a man leaning against an elm tree said.

Again, Mary seemed unshaken. "Yes, the Bible is the inspired Word of God, but that same spirit that inspired the Bible also lives within an individual. It is what Quakers call the Inner Light. What the Inner Light is telling us today outweighs what the spirit told the believers in Bible days."

The magistrate took several steps toward Mary. His eyes became harsh and his jaw firm. "Since you do not speak with the authority of the organized church, you should not be allowed to speak. You must return to your home."

The crowd became loud as individual groups broke into side conversations and arguments. Some supported Mary's ideas and others did not. In the distance, Martha saw William Dyer approaching the commons. Never before had he been present at his wife's preaching sessions. Voices hushed in the presence of one of their most respected leaders.

William stepped onto a tree stump so everyone could see him. He looked directly at the magistrate. "What was the reason most of us were forced to leave Boston?"

The magistrate's face reddened. "We would not accept all of the teachings of the clergy and wanted to think for ourselves. Anne Hutchinson and John Wheelwright encouraged us to do so."

"Exactly right," William Dyer said. "Lest we forget, Roger Williams welcomed us with open arms even though some of us did not believe exactly as he did. These principles of religious freedoms are the very ones on which Rhode Island was established. Therefore, I challenge any person who would deny the rights of a Quaker to speak to remember our treatment in Boston and the very reason we started a new colony." With those words, William stepped from the tree stump and turned toward the path toward his home.

Anger rose within Martha when she heard the man behind her whisper to a friend, "Poor Mary, she is ill in both mind and body. When she recovers her faculties, these strange ideas will pass away."

"I do not view it that way," the friend whispered back. "I like what Mary is saying and I want to hear more of it."

As soon as her husband was out of view, Mary stepped onto the tree stump. "I want to thank my husband for what he said. One of the core beliefs of the Quakers is the right to search for God within one's own spirit and not permit others dictate to you. Religious freedom is a principle I am willing to die for. I will be here tomorrow at the same time and will share more of the Quaker ways and teachings."

As Martha and Mary walked the narrow path toward their homes Mary said, "I am annoyed how the crowd reacted to what William said."

Martha looked at her sister with amazement. "Why do you say that?"

Mary shook her head. "What William said was the absolute truth that I have been trying to explain to them for weeks, but few would listen. Why would many in the crowd listen to him and not to me? I am the one who is a minister."

"The Quakers are one of the first religious groups to have women ministers," Martha said. "Of course, people will look on you with suspicion. Just be thankful

William backed your freedom to have a voice and to speak what you believe. The wives of most Puritans are still considered property and subject to the will and desires of their husbands."

Mary walked in silence for several minutes. The shadows lengthened and storm clouds began to build in the west. "It is much more complicated being a Quaker in America than I expected. Don't people realize all people are equal and should be listened to regardless of whether they are male or female? As much as I appreciate William coming to Boston to plead my case, it was also very humiliating. Why was it necessary for my husband to plead my case for me as if I were a misbehaving child?"

Chapter Twenty-Three
The Quakers Are Coming

Newport and Providence, 1657 - 1658

The sun was beginning to dip below the horizon when Martha Clarke and Mary Dyer reached the end of the bean row in their joint garden and stood up. "I think it is time we go inside and prepare supper for the children," Martha said. "Do you know when William will be home?"

Mary shook her head. "When he left, he did not think his meetings would be over until late. It may be dark before he returns."

Walking around the corner of the Dyer home, Martha and Mary noticed a man taller than William approaching their house. They exchanged puzzled glances.

"Good afternoon," he greeted. "I am Nicholas Coggeshall. I have recently moved to Newport from Portsmouth. I recently became convinced of the Quaker ways and I am anxious to help in any way I can. I have heard thee speak in the Newport Commons but have not had an opportunity to talk with thee privately."

Mary beamed. "I am always willing to share with another Quaker. Please come in and have a cup of milk with me and my sister."

When the three were comfortable around the kitchen table with warm cups of milk before them, Nicholas said, "Dost thou remember Mary Fisher and Ann Austin?"

Mary hesitated. "Yes, I knew them well when I was in England. We often traveled the countryside together sharing what George Fox had taught us."

"They landed in Boston a few months before your ship did," Nicholas said.

Mary felt a tightness in the pit of her stomach. "I wish I had known this earlier. I hope they did not get the same treatment I did."

Nicholas sighed. "I'm afraid they did. One by one, their Quaker books were cast into a large fire in the  Boston Commons, all one hundred of them. Mary Fisher and Ann Austin were then taken to prison. The officials were not content examining their opinions with which they did not agree, they also stripped them naked on the pretense of examining their bodies for tokens of witchcraft. They held them in prison for five weeks and then were taken directly to the *Swallow,* which was still in port and shipped back to England.

Martha and Mary exchanged looks of horror. "Nicholas, something must be done about the law preventing Quakers from landing in Boston," Mary stated firmly, "but I do not know what we can do from Newport."

"Even though we are scattered, Quakers are beginning to take action," Nicholas said. "I have written letters and sent word by one of our people returning to England, to notify Quakers who wish to come to the new world to take the smaller ships headed for Newport where they will be welcomed. The smaller ships will be able to dock in our harbor with little problem and the mid-sized ones should be able to maneuver in with a little more seamanship."

Charles entered the house from the garden to ask his mother a question, but Mary motioned him away. His shoulders slumped as he went back outside without speaking. She turned back to her guest. "I appreciate thee sending an invitation and welcome for Quakers to come to Newport. I am certain there are those who will wish to take advantage of it, but it does nothing to change the law in Boston. I am willing to work single-handedly to see that the anti-Quaker laws in Boston are changed."

Nicholas shook his head. "Mary, I am not sure thou are right. If these laws are to be defeated, thou cannot do it alone. There are legions of Quakers willing to help, and Newport can be their headquarters."

Martha and Mary exchanged glances. Martha was certain her sister was in agreement. "I have an extra room in my house," Martha said. "Any traveling Quaker is welcome to stay there as long as needed."

"Our main room is large enough for Quakers to assemble regularly for meetings," Mary added. "We do not always need to meet in the Newport Commons, especially during foul weather."

The three continued sharing ideas how they might help the Quaker cause in Rhode Island and eventually make changes to the anti-Quaker laws in Boston. When the shadows began to lengthen, Mary's children returned from the field and the shop for their evening meal. Nicholas bade everyone farewell and agreed to return whenever he had news and ideas to share.

Every two or three days, Mary went to the Newport Commons to share her beliefs in God and the Quaker faith. Sometimes only one or two of their neighbors would attend and other times twenty or more would be there. If their daily chores were completed, Martha would accompany her; otherwise, she stayed behind and finished their work. Much to Mary's disappointment, only her son Will showed serious interest in what she was teaching and made every effort to finish his work early and join her on the Newport Commons.

Three weeks after Nicholas Coggeshall's visit with Mary and Martha, he returned to the Dyer home. Not finding anyone there, he went to the small house next door and rapped on the door. When Martha appeared in the doorway, he said, "Martha, do you know where Mary is? She wanted me to let her know whenever I heard of new Quakers coming to the area. I just learned a ship named *Woodhouse* docked in Providence with Quakers onboard. I do not know anything about them and I am not able to leave my work to greet them."

Martha's heart began to pound. "Thank you Nicholas. I will go to the pasture and let Mary know right away. I am certain she will want to go to Providence as soon as possible."

"Thank you," Nicholas said. "I wish I could do more to help, but my best milk cow is about to give birth and I need to be there in case something goes wrong. Give Mary my regards."

Frustrations overtook Martha as she hurried toward the garden. *I hope Mary will not be disappointed again. Every time a ship has appeared in the Newport harbor, she went to the wharf to see if any Quakers were onboard. With each one, she became more and more discouraged, and more determined to fight the anti-Quaker laws in Boston by herself. I hope this time will be different.*

Seeing her sister in the distance, Martha shouted, "Mary...Mary...Come quickly, I have good news."

Mary gripped her staff and hurried toward her sister. "What is it? I could use good news for a change."

Martha took a deep breath and tried to relax. "Nicholas Coggeshall was here and he said a shipload of Quakers docked in Providence two days ago. He knows nothing more about them and is concerned he is not able to greet them himself and offer Newport hospitality."

Mary could not contain her excitement. "I will go myself," she shouted. "I will have Maher keep tending the sheep and little Mary will be able to do the cooking. Tomorrow, I will take the ferry to Providence. Would thou like to come with me?"

Martha hesitated. *The Quaker cause is Mary's passion, not mine. However, I agree with her that everyone should have religious freedom and be able to live and travel wherever they like without being mistreated. Since she has returned from England, I am beginning to feel as if I need to protect Mary from herself.* She reached out and put her hand gently on her sister's shoulder. "Yes, I will go with you to Providence. I will work extra hard on the farm when I get back to catch up with what didn't get done while I was away."

Martha studied the Quaker men and women gathered in the large living room of Catherine Scott. She remembered Catherine from many years before in Boston as the sister of their beloved friend, Anne Hutchinson who was constantly at Anne's side. Martha remembered how distressed both were when circumstances led Anne to Portsmouth and Catherine to Providence. *I wonder what Anne would say today if she knew her sister had become a Quaker?*

When the room was full, a thin, yet muscular, man arose. "I am Christopher Holder. I want to welcome everyone here today. This is a most important time in which we plan how we will spread the principles of the Quakers and of George Fox to all the colonies. I especially welcome Mary Dyer and her sister, Martha, from the Newport settlement."

Martha shifted her weight nervously and nodded an acknowledgement to the group. Mary appeared much more comfortable and smiled warmly to each of the guest and said, "I remember many of you from my recent years in England and am looking forward to working together to bring justice to all Quakers, wherever they may be."

I thank thee, Mary Dyer," Christopher said and then turned back to the entire group. "I am very distressed I must begin this discussion with bad news. I personally gave a letter from George Fox to Roger Williams yesterday, but it was met with a very cold response. The only part of Fox's letter Roger Williams would agree with was 'every creature, Black or Indian, deserves liberty and freedom.'"

Martha grimaced when her sister said, "That is strange George Fox could not convince Roger Williams to become a Quaker. Roger Williams has always believed in freedom of speech and religion. He was forced out of Boston for that very reason and later encouraged everyone who was banished with Anne Hutchinson to settle in Rhode Island. Now that we have found the source of truth, I do not understand why he will not become a Quaker along with us."

"Roger Williams said he has no intentions in his entire lifetime of ever becoming a Quaker," Christopher Holder stated emphatically. "He claims Quakers do not allow any interpreter for the spirit of God except the spirit that dwells within the individual. Reverend Williams feels man's humanness can distort the truth of God. He maintains the scripture is the only source of the Word of God and that claiming the Word of God in the form of the Inner Light can live within each believer is total fallacy and erroneous."

Martha watched the shocked expressions spread across the faces of the Quakers. *After all Roger Williams has done for everyone, both Indian and Europeans, it surprises me that he will not accept the Quaker beliefs. At least he will allow others to believe differently than himself. That is much better than what they do in Boston.*

In spite of her frustrations, Martha listened with intense interest as the seventeen passengers on the *Woodhouse* retold their adventures of navigating 3,000 miles without a compass. They considered their safe passage a miracle and confirmation of God's protection. As the discussion continued, she noted a fearless loyalty and determination develop among those involved in the Quaker faith. Martha smiled to herself when she noticed how Christopher Holder kept looking at Catherine Scott's oldest daughter, Mary, and edging across the room to be closer to her.

Before the meeting ended, most of the Quakers who arrived on the *Woodhouse,* felt called to go to New Amsterdam while others went south to Maryland and Virginia to preach the word of God. A few chose to go to the Dyers' home in Newport to continue their search for God's direction as to which parts of New England the Lord might direct them.

During the next few weeks, the number of Quakers in Newport and Providence increased greatly. Regular home meetings were established where the members drew strength from one another. It was not long before the members of the new meetings became impatient to share their faith in places where the welcome might not be as cordial as it was in Newport.

One glorious Sunday morning when the Newport Quakers gathered for their weekly First Day meeting, Christopher Holder stood before their period of silence began and said, "John Copeland and I sense a call to spread the Quaker message throughout the Massachusetts Bay Colony. Because of the 1656 law preventing ships with Quakers on board from landing there, it would be foolhardy for us to enter by ship." His eyes scanned the room before he continued. "We have found someone who is willing to take us as far as Martha's Vineyard. In our silent prayers, would each of thee seek God's guidance for us?"

The group nodded in agreement and bowed their heads. Mary Dyer felt especially touched by Christopher's request. The silence of the room enveloped her as she drew deeper and deeper within, trying to listen to the Inner Light. *Dear God. It feels right for Christopher Holder and John Copeland to go to Massachusetts via Martha's Vineyard. What about me? Where should I go to spread the Quaker message?*

As the days passed, Martha Clarke watched the restlessness build within her sister while they went about their daily tasks. The Dyer's home had become a gathering place for returning Quakers who had met resistance on their travels. Many had been beaten or starved and needed a place to rest and be restored.

Seeing the pain the Quakers were suffering, Martha approached William Dyer. "Would it be too much to ask if you and Samuel could build a small addition to my house? I could then move into that room and reserve the rest of the house for use by the Quakers. The main room can be used for gatherings and my current bedchamber could be occupied by those who are traveling and need a place to refresh."

William thought for a few moments. "It would only take a few days to build such a room. Even though I may not agree or understand everything the Quakers are preaching, no one should be treated the way they are. I will work my hardest to support a person's right to seek God in their own way." A teasing twinkle appeared in his eye and the corner of his lips turned up. "Even if it is my own wife."

On a cold January afternoon a week after Martha had moved into the back room of her newly remodeled home, there was a knock at the door. When she opened it, a man nearly collapsed into her arms. She supported his weight the best she could and helped him into the bedchamber. She removed his shoes, fluffed the pillow, and covered him with a quilt. Without saying a word, the stranger fell asleep.

Martha returned to the main room, stoked the fire, and began preparing a stew for when he awakened. Minutes later, Mary burst through the front door. "Who was the man who just came in?"

Martha shook her head. "I do not know. He appeared too exhausted and beaten to speak, so I helped him to the bed and he is sleeping now. Judging by his bruises and torn clothing, I am certain he has quite a story to tell. I noticed the letter 'H' was burned into the back of his hand."

Mary's face blanched and she sunk onto the chair by the fireplace. "I heard the Puritans were burning the letter 'H' on Quakers to mark them as heretics, but I have never seen it done before." Her eyes flashed with determination. "I am not going to go back to my house until I have had a chance to talk with him."

Mary remained with Martha throughout the day and helped her clean and straighten the house. "Martha, if thou would come to the Quaker meetings with me, thou would learn how badly the Quakers who enter the Massachusetts Bay Colony are being treated."

Martha looked at her sister and then lowered her eyes. "All in due time. I still have too many questions. Maybe someday I will understand and become a Quaker."

When the sun was setting, the stranger appeared in the doorway to the bedchamber. He looked around the room. "Hello. I thank thee for taking me in and giving me a bed to rest upon. Not everyone would have taken in a total stranger."

"Come and sit at the table," Martha said. "We have a warm stew for you which should help you regain your strength."

While Martha served the food, Mary took a seat across from the stranger. "Thou look very familiar. Have we met before?"

The stranger nodded. "I am Humphrey Norton. I was one of the passengers on the ship *Woodhouse* with Christopher Holder. On my way to New Amsterdam to preach the word of God, I had to pass near New Haven. I was apprehended and without being given a chance to explain I was taken into New Haven and thrown into prison."

A look of concern spread across Mary's face. "I am so sorry. Were thou mistreated?"

Humphrey devoured his bowl of stew before he responded. While Martha was refilling the bowl he said, "I was confined for twenty days with little food or heat. On January 11, I was brought before a magistrate to be examined. They asked many questions, but before I could answer, a large iron key was tied across my mouth so I could not talk. I was found guilty of heresy, and that afternoon the people of New Haven were assembled with beating drums to witness my punishment. I was stripped to the waist, tied to a pole, and lashed more times than I could count."

"What about the 'H' on thy hand?" Mary asked.

"I was branded a heretic plus fined twenty pounds for being a heretic. There was no way I could pay any fine, but a kind Dutchman who witnessed the cruelty offered to pay the fine for me. I did not want to accept his generous offer, but the magistrate accepted it and released me. I think I surprised everyone when I fell to my knees and prayed for them after I had received such harsh treatment."

Mary slammed her fist upon the table. "This cannot stand. I must go to New Haven to protest thy treatment."

Just as Mary made her dramatic declaration, William opened the door. "Why do you want to go to New Haven?"

"Did thou hear what they did to this man?" Mary said. "Quakers have to bring this to the people's attention. I am certain the people of New Haven would object if they understood what their magistrates were doing to innocent people. I must go to New Haven to protest."

William took her hand and pleaded, "But Mary, do you think they will listen to you?"

"I must at least try to help," Mary said. "I have to stand for what is right."

"But Mary, you must not take the weight of the world on your own shoulders. You have already been away too much. Now that you are back and your health restored, it is foolish for you to leave again. We need you here...The children need you...I need you."

Mary smiled and squeezed her husband's hand. "My dear, sweet husband, I know what a trial I must be to thee. I know I may appear irresponsible to thee, but the choice is not mine. I am God's, and when He commands, I must obey."

William shook his head. A touch of anger could be seen in his eyes. "But Mary, it is the coldest time of the winter. You cannot walk in this snow."

Mary straightened her back and set her jaw. "Then I will take the horse."

"But you cannot venture into the wilderness by yourself."

Mary looked toward Martha who slightly nodded her head, and back to her husband. "Then Martha can come with me."

Martha's mind raced. *I would do anything to protect my sister. I just do not know if peaceful confrontation is the best way to change the situation. If they would not listen to Humphrey Norton, why would they listen to a woman?*

Mary spent that night with Martha. Before going to sleep, they packed food and blankets for their trip. At dawn, they tied their bundles to the mare and both climbed onto its back. Mary had always been an excellent horse handler and during Mary's long absence, Martha likewise became confident with horses. However, neither realized the challenge that was before them. Snowdrifts slowed their travel, while wind whirled around them.

When the sun became low in the sky, they stumbled upon an abandoned cabin. Martha pushed in the door and Mary led the horse inside. Lacking dry wood for the fireplace, they huddled together in a corner for warmth. The floor was hard, but at least they were out of the wind.

Early the next morning, Mary and Martha arose, ate two rolls each, gave three apples to the horse, and packed their blankets into the bag tied to the mare.

The second day was not nearly as cold as the day before and the depth of the snow seemed less. By noon, the path widened and houses could be seen in the distance. To their surprise, six riders appeared from among the trees.

"They must have learned of our coming," Mary said. "I hope we will soon be warming ourselves around someone's fireplace and eating warm food."

Martha nodded. "I do not think I would be able to travel another day like this."

The horsemen did not slow their pace until they were within feet of the Dyer's mare. "Halt," the leader shouted. "Are you Mary Dyer, the Quaker?"

"Yes I am," Mary replied as the six horsemen lined their horses so passage would be impossible. "I am on my way to New Haven to preach the word of God and explain the power of the Inner Light."

"We do not allow Quakers preaching in our town. Turn around immediately or suffer severe consequence."

Martha trembled while she watched her sister pull herself more erect on the horse and set her jaw. *Surely, Mary will not challenge them. Didn't she suffer enough in Boston?*

Mary hesitated then slowly began to turn the horse around. "Woe to thee for not listening to the word of God. Woe be unto thee, for Humphrey Norton's sake and the cruelty thou showed to him."

Martha watched tears flow down Mary's cheeks as they started the long journey home. "What will I tell

William?" Mary sobbed. "He didn't want me to go to
New Haven, but I had to follow God's voice and not
my own desire. Why were we not successful?"

Chapter Twenty-Four
Persecution

Newport and Boston, 1658 - 1659

Discouragement enveloped Mary Dyer during the remainder of the winter. The humiliation of her rebuke in New Haven hung over her like a cloud. Martha tried to cheer her, but to little avail. Mary quit preaching in the Newport Commons and withdrew into herself.

On a cold March afternoon, while Martha and Mary were doing laundry in the Dyer's side yard, Martha said, "I heard Christopher Holder had his mouth stopped by the magistrates stuffing a handkerchief and glove into it while he was in Salem. Something needs to be done as to how the other colonies treat the Quakers."

Mary nodded sadly. "I know....I tried to follow God's leading when I went to New Haven to protest Humphrey Norton's treatment, but all it accomplished was a lot of suffering on our part. William was angry with me, and the New Haven magistrates were amused that two women came alone to plead the Quaker cause and mocked our presence. They claimed I was mad."

Martha finished laying a shirt across a rope to dry and put a comforting hand on her sister's shoulder. "At least you tried. That is more than most have done. I do not understand all you are struggling with, but you must stay true to your convictions and do what you feel God is telling you."

"Thou are right, Martha," Mary said. "Regardless of the outcome, I must keep following the Inner Light."

When all the clothes were hung to dry, Martha put out the fire under the kettle just as two men in tattered clothing appeared in the distance. As they came nearer, Martha gasped. "That is Christopher Holder and John Copeland. Are those bloody rags tied around their heads?"

Martha and Mary ran to meet them. "What has happened?" Mary said. "Who has treated thee so badly?"

Christopher mumbled an unintelligible response and slumped his shoulders even further. The men's strength seemed to wane and the women took them by the arm to support their weight as they neared their destination.

"Please come into my house and rest," Martha said. "We will give you warm food and fresh water."

When Christopher and John entered Martha's simple home, they nearly collapsed onto the benches at the table. Mary poured cups for fresh water for them while Martha dished up bowls of stew that had been simmering over the hearth since mid-day.

After they had eaten, Mary persisted. "What happened to thee? Who did this?"

John shook his head sadly. "We went to Boston to share the Quaker ways and were whipped and banished. We left for a few weeks and then felt God wanted us to return to Boston to continue preaching. When we did, the magistrates had us arrested and our right ears cut off."

A wave of nausea flooded over Mary and she collapsed on the opposite bench. Tears filled her eyes while she listened to their terrifying story. "If they treated thee this way, how are they treating the other Quaker men?"

"Every report I have heard has been bad," Christopher said. "We know of three other Quakers who had had their right ears cut off. Whippings and banishments happen regularly. One of the passengers with us on the *Woodhouse* was severely whipped, locked in irons, and his body bent double for sixteen hours a day."

"You may stay here and rest as long as you need," Martha said. "William Dyer enlarged this house to serve as a restoration place for Quakers. The bed is in the room to the right. While you are resting, Mary and I will try to find fresh clothes for you to wear."

Martha and Mary cared for Christopher Holden and John Copeland for nearly three weeks before they felt well enough to travel again.

A week after the men left while Martha and Mary were cooking the evening meal, Mary said, "What right do I have to stay here in the security and comfort of my own home when other Quakers are suffering and risking their lives for their faith?"

Martha's spirits dropped as she searched for words of comfort. "Mary, don't you understand how much you are needed here? Don't you think you can better serve God by meeting the needs of your family and comforting the traveling Quakers by helping nurse their bodies to health and strengthening their spirits?"

Mary sighed and her gaze became distant. "Sometime I feel that way, but most of the time all I can think about is how the unjust laws are applied only to the Quakers. I must do something; until then my soul will find no peace."

As weeks passed, Mary seemed more and more like a kettle about to boil over while Martha's frustration grew as she tried to be a voice of reason for her sister. *How can Mary be so confident she is hearing*

God's voice and not her own? I wish I could hear God speaking directly to me so I can better help her.

Late one spring afternoon a knock at Martha's door interrupted her knitting. She hurried to the door; there stood Catherine Scott from Providence, her daughters, Mary and eleven-year-old Patience. Two men stood behind them who seemed strangely familiar.

Before anyone could speak, Patience wrapped her arms around her. "Martha, I am so glad to see thee. We are on our way to Boston and we wanted to visit you and Mary before we left."

Martha hugged the child and then turned her attention to the others. "Come in and rest. I hope you will be able to spend the night before you travel on. We have so much news to share. I'm certain Mary will be here soon, if she saw you walk by her house."

Catherine hugged Martha and then motioned to the men behind her. "Do thou remember Marmaduke Stevenson and William Robinson? They arrived on the *Woodhouse* with Christopher Holder."

"Yes, I remember them from the meeting at your home in Providence when they first arrived." Martha smiled at the two men. "Welcome. This home is designed to be a haven for weary Quaker travelers."

Just as Martha had predicted, the front door opened and Mary rushed in.

"Catherine, it is good to see thee once again." Mary greeted Catherine and her two daughters with a hug before turning her attention to the men. "Marmaduke...William, welcome. What brings thee to Newport?"

"A child named Patience," Marmaduke replied while he rested his hand on the child's shoulder.

Both Mary and Martha gave Patience a quizzical look.

"And how did you manage that?" Martha asked.

Patience smiled. "I merely said I believed God wanted me to go to Boston to plead with the governor and councils not to execute their unrighteous anti-Quaker laws against us."

Catherine shook her head trying to show frustration, but an intense pride glowed from her face. "I tried to persuade Patience that she was too young, but she would not listen. Hearing her persistence, Marmaduke and William agreed to take her. Of course, I could not let my daughter go without me."

Tears filled Mary Scott's eyes. A pained expression spread across her face. "When I heard of the suffering my fiancé, Christopher Holder, experiences every time he goes to Boston, I felt I needed to go to help plead his case."

"I wish I could go with thee," Mary Dyer said, "but I am still recuperating from pneumonia which I contracted after my trip to New Haven. I am still weak and would slow thy travels."

Mary sat in silence and stared at the floor for a few moments. "As soon as I am stronger, I will join thee in Boston. I want to try their bloody law to the death."

Through the coming weeks, Martha watched color gradually return to her sister's cheeks and strength and endurance in her step. She hoped Mary had given up on any plans to return to Boston. However, in midsummer, Mary joined her in the garden and the long dreaded words came from her mouth. "I am much better now. I feel the Inner Light leading me back to Boston. Will thou come with me?"

"Are you sure God is leading you back?" Martha sighed and leaned against her hoe. "Didn't William sign a document promising you would never return to Boston?"

Mary hung her head and then an angelic expression covered her face. "I love my husband dearly, but I must follow God rather than man."

Martha remained speechless, unsure what to say. Before she thought of a response, Mary continued, "Will thou come with me? Since thee will not be recognized as a Quaker, thou could be a great help to us."

"Dear Mary, I wish you would not go," Martha pleaded. "Your family needs you here and you are such a help and nurturer to the traveling Quakers who pass through."

Watching Mary's stubborn determination, Martha knew she would soon be leaving for Boston in the hope of once again trying to protect her younger sister. She looked skyward. *Please God, let me hear your voice. Let me know how to protect my sister. Nothing I can say will convince her to stay away from Boston.*

Mary gave Martha a hug and then pulled back and looked directly in her eyes. "Promise me thou will not tell William. I will write him a note explaining where we are going, and we can sneak out at dawn before he is awake. We will have to travel very light since we will be walking instead of taking the horse."

Martha spent a restless night. *How long will it be before I feel the comforts of my simple home again? Will I need to spend my entire life trying to protect my sister from the consequences of her determination to follow the Inner Light?*

Just before dawn the next day, Mary tapped on the door to Martha's bedchamber and opened it slightly. "Are you ready to go?"

"I will be right with you." Martha rose from her bed and slipped on her dress, bonnet, and shoes.

Mary and Martha wrapped apples, carrots, bread, and a jug of water in two separate blankets and each tied a bundle onto her back. As they headed down the path, Martha turned and took a long, sad look at their homes.

The first few hours they made good time, but gradually the heat of the summer sun began taking a toll on their energy. They ate little and drank only when they came to a spring. The first night, they came to Portsmouth and slept in the home of friends. The other nights friendly Indians gave them food and shelter. In five days, Mary and Martha reached the first houses of the Boston settlement.

Martha marveled at the changes in the town since she had moved to Rhode Island. Yet, her sister's silence concerned her. *What could possibly be going through her mind? Now that she is in Boston, I wonder what she plans to do.*

When they neared the Boston Commons, Mary said, "The first place I want to go is to the prison gate and see the Scotts, Marmaduke, and William Robinson."

Martha gave a quizzical look. "How do you know they are even in jail?"

"The Inner Light is directing me," Mary said.

Martha shrugged. *I will know if it truly is the Inner Light leading her if the Scotts are in the jail when she arrives.*

When they came in sight of the prison, Mary said, "Wait here. I do not know what is going to happen and

I do not want the guards to know who is with me. If I do not return, it will be because they remembered me."

Martha sat under an oak tree in an empty field near the prison and watched Mary knock on the door of the jail.

"What do you want?" she heard a gruff voice respond to Mary's knocking.

"I would like permission to visit some unfortunate souls you have confined here," Mary said.

"Whom would you visit?" the gruff voice demanded.

"Catherine, Mary, and Patience Scott and the men who accompanied them," Mary said calmly. "Are they here?"

Martha watched the big prison door swing open; she strained to hear the conversation. "They have been here a fortnight," she heard another male voice say. "You may come in." There was a long pause.

"Mary Dyer," the gruff voice shouted. "You are one of the cursed Quakers. Because of this visit, you have violated our laws once again, and you must answer for it."

"It is what I expect," Mary said and disappeared from Martha's view.

Martha slipped around the corner of the building. Rows of narrow barred windows were at ground level looking into basement cells. Lying on her stomach, she peered through the windows to the cells below. She was shocked to see Catherine, Mary, and Patience Scott huddled against the wall. Tears filled Martha's eyes when the cell door opened and her sister was shoved inside.

"Mary...Mary," she whispered when the guard was gone. "Are you all right? What can I do to help?"

Before greeting her friends, Mary went to the window. "I am all right. Do not worry about us. God is our protector."

Martha began to tremble. "Someone is coming, I must go, but I will pray for all of you. I will be back tomorrow and see if there is anything you need."

Mary Dyer, Catherine, Mary, and Patience Scott, as well as Marmaduke Stevenson and William Robinson remained in jail for five weeks before they were brought before the Court of Assistants on September 12.

On the day of the trial, Martha waited near an open window in the hope of hearing the proceedings. When no one was around, she peered into the window. The courtroom was small. Across one end of the room stretched a long table where Governor John Endicott sat. He wore a black cap, a broad starched collar, and a black robe. His bearing was stiff and his manner curt. Six robed assistants flanked him, three on each side. The prisoners sat on a long bench facing the court, the men on one end, and the women on the other.

After everyone was assembled, the magistrate stood and read the charges. "Every person of the cursed sect of Quakers who is found within this jurisdiction shall be apprehended without a warrant and committed to prison where he or she is to remain without bail until the next Court of Assistants. At that time they shall have a legal trial and being convicted to be of the sect of Quakers shall be sentenced to be banished upon pain of death."

The reading continued, but Martha had heard enough. *It used to be a religious heresy to preach*

Quakerism in Boston, but now it is a crime just to be a Quaker.

"Patience Scott, come forward," the governor commanded.

With dignity well beyond her years, Patience took her place before the court.

"What is your age?" the governor snapped.

"I am eleven-years-old," Patience answered simply.

"You have done a foolish thing and have listened to very dangerous people who have taught you many heresies." Governor Endicott took on a fatherly tone. "This court does not want to punish you, but these people have led you astray. You could not know that those who claim to be your family and friends are in truth trying to stir up mutiny and rebellion against this government and the establishment of church and state. We want to help you. Tell us in your own words, why you came to Boston."

Patience stiffened her back and stood as tall as she possibly could. "I came to Boston to bear witness against thy persecuting spirit toward Quakers."

The Governor wrinkled his brow and his lips tightened. "Don't repeat the words you have heard from heretics. You cannot possibly understand their meaning."

"I know their meaning well," Patience said firmly. "Thy filthy prison has taught me the meaning of thy unrighteousness and unjust laws. All thy cruelty will avail thee nothing, for God resides within the inner being of those who believe. I beg thee to see the evil of thy ways and repeal these sinful laws that thou have passed against the Quakers."

Governor Endicott's face reddened. He turned to the magistrate. "There is a spirit in this child greater than any woman. It must be the devil. Satan is making use of this child who is not old enough to judge the principles of religion. She is discharged to return home."

Turning back to Patience, the governor said, "You are free to go. Just take care with whom you associate. Your future will be very dim."

Patience turned, smiled at her mother, and walked out the door of the courtroom.

Martha Clarke stepped around the corner of the building. "Patience...Patience," she whispered. "I'm over here."

Patience ran into Martha's arms. "It was awful...just plain awful. I am worried about everyone else. Hopefully, they will release mother and my sister today, but I could tell the jailers were extremely upset with Mary Dyer and they tried to make her life in prison as miserable as possible."

Martha took Patience by the elbow and led her around the corner of the building. "Let us get as close as we can to hear what is going on."

Huddled outside the open window, Martha could hear Governor Endicott's loud voice, "Mary Scott, step before this court."

Patience and Martha watched Mary cautiously step forward. *Since Patience was released, surely, he will let Mary go as well,* Martha thought.

The governor paused and studied the innocent face of the young woman. "Mary Scott, are you a part of the heretical group who call themselves Quakers?"

"I am."

"And why did you come to Boston?"

"I came to see my fiancé, Christopher Holder, but I was unable to locate him before I was put in prison."

"You are a foolish woman," the governor said. "Christopher Holder has been banished from this jurisdiction and must never return."

Mary Scott stood motionless while a silence enveloped the courtroom.

Martha held her breath. *Please God, let them release Mary as well.*

The governor consulted the assistant beside him and then turned his attention back to the prisoner. "Since this is the first time you have been before the court, I will release you with the promise that you will never again set foot within the Massachusetts Bay Colony. If you do, you will be immediately arrested and brought before the court. Do you understand?"

"I do."

"Then go immediately. You must be out of Boston before sundown."

While Mary Scott walked out of the room, the governor announced, "Catherine Scott, step before the court."

Martha watched Catherine walk to the front.

The governor again studied the face of the woman before him. "Are you a member of the heretical group known as the Quakers?"

"I am a Quaker...and proud of it."

Governor Endicott scowled. "And why may I ask did you come to Boston?"

Catherine hesitated. "My daughters were determined to come to speak against the unjust anti-Quaker laws. I could not let them travel alone."

"Were you in support of their mission?" the governor asked.

"I am."

"Your daughters received their foolish ideas from your satanic teachings. I have half a mind to throw you back in prison, but since this is your first offense, I will also release you with the promise that you will never again set foot within the Massachusetts Bay Colony. If you do, you will be immediately arrested and brought before the court. Do you understand?"

"I do," Catherine immediately replied.

"You may go," the governor snapped. "May we never see you again."

Outside the courtroom, Catherine rushed into the waiting arms of her daughters. "We must praise God for protecting us." She looked over Patience's head at Martha. "I hope Mary gets the same sentence, but the way she was treated in jail I am concerned they will not go lightly on her."

"Every time I visited her at the window, I was concerned about her treatment," Martha said. "I am afraid she is pushing their patience too far."

The four women huddled around the window to the courtroom. Much to Martha's chagrin, her sister Mary, William Robinson, and Marmaduck Stevenson were standing before the governor and his six assistants. Each assistant was pelting the prisoners with accusations and questions for over an hour. When they tired of the interrogation, Governor Endicott proclaimed, "By your own confession, words, and actions, you are Quakers; therefore you are sentenced to depart this jurisdiction on 'banishment on pain of death.' You will be returned to your jail cell until a proper day for your release is selected."

As Mary Dyer and her two companions were led away, Martha, Catherine, Mary, and Patience moved to a nearby tree in the hope of avoiding attention. Patience's eyes were wide and frightened looking. "Mother, what does 'banishment on pain of death' mean? How is that different from the governor telling us to leave tonight and never return to Boston?"

Catherine Scott took a deep breath and stroked her daughter's hair. "Patience, I am afraid it means if any one of them is ever found within the Massachusetts Bay colony they will be executed." Catherine looked over her daughter's head to Martha. "Do thou believe Mary will now be willing to stay away from Boston?"

Chapter Twenty-Five
Mary's Return

Newport and Boston, October 1659

As Martha and Mary trudged the familiar path in the twilight shadows, they could see the faint outline of the Dyer home. It had been seven weeks since they had left for Boston and everything seemed exactly the same as it was when they left. Suddenly the front door opened and William Dyer raced toward them. He grabbed his wife and pulled her close to his chest. "My beloved Mary, I was so afraid I would never see you again. I'm glad you are finally home where you belong."

Mary collapsed against him. "It is good to be home with thee once again. While I was sitting in the filthy jail, memories of thee lifted my spirit."

The couple pulled apart, and William wrapped his arm around Mary to help support her weight while they walked toward this house. "Why must you subject yourself to such cruelties, when they could be easily avoided?"

Martha knew exactly how Mary would answer. "I must move at the call of the Lord, even when others do not understand."

William opened the front door of their home and led his wife to the bench at the table. "I appreciate your devotion to God, but I am having trouble explaining your absence to the children. Samuel especially cannot understand why you are gone as much as you are. Young Will is the only one who has accepted the

Quaker ways and embraces your missions. The younger ones are lonely and confused."

"Tomorrow I will explain to them about the treatment of the Quakers in Boston," Mary said. "They have not experienced such suffering in Rhode Island, but they need to learn that Christians must help carry each other's burdens. When one suffers, we all suffer."

Mary rested in bed for over two weeks after her return from Boston and only got up to eat the warm food little Mary and Martha had prepared for the family. Martha bathed her sister and tended to the wounds and bug bites Mary had received while in prison.

After Mary had finally regained her strength, she turned to Martha and said, "It has been months since I have visited friends in Newport and shared the word of God with them. Would thou come with me this afternoon?"

"I would like that very much," Martha replied. "I would especially enjoy seeing Elizabeth Easton. She has a sweet spirit and I always come away feeling better after I visit her."

As soon as the day's chores were done, Martha and Mary walked into town. They marveled at the amount of work and the new buildings that had been constructed in their absence. After greeting friends along the way, they went to the outskirts of town and rapped on the door to the Easton's home. As soon as Elizabeth opened it, the three women cried with excitement while they exchanged hugs.

"Do come in," Elizabeth said. "It is good to see thee. I am anxious to learn of thy experiences in Boston."

Elizabeth heated milk while her guests arranged chairs around the fireplace. She handed cups to each of them before turning to Mary, "I am sorry for your treatment in the Boston jail. When Catherine Scott and her daughters came through Newport they explained what thee and other Quakers were going through. Thou are looking very well for only having been home for two weeks to rest."

Mary nodded. "Yes, it was difficult, but there is no better honor in this world than suffering for our Lord."

Martha took a deep breath and closed her eyes. *There is no deeper pain than watching a loved one suffer. Sometimes I get a faint understanding of what Jesus' mother must have felt when she stood at the foot of his cross.*

"Thou have a very positive outlook on the plight of Quakers," Elizabeth said. "We are protected here in Newport and have the freedom to worship God as we see fit. We have little understanding what the Quakers who have had the courage to go to Boston have suffered."

"We must work together to challenge their bloody law," Mary said. "If Quakers are banished from Boston under 'pain of death,' then no one of any faith will have freedom of speech or religion."

Elizabeth rose and walked to the window. She starred outside in silence for several minutes. Finally, she turned and said, "I admire those who are working to change the anti-Quaker laws. I just learned Christopher Holder is back in the Boston prison. He must have been put in jail a few days after thou were released."

Mary Dyer jumped to her feet. "What! That is terrible! Christopher has already suffered so for the cause. He has been whipped; his right ear has been cut off; what more can they possibly do to him? I must go back to Boston to help him."

Martha's eyes widened and she put her hand on her sister's arm. "But Mary, you were banished from Boston under pain of death."

"I must go wherever God leads me," Mary stated matter-in-factly.

Exactly one month after Mary's banishment from Boston, Martha once more walked reluctantly down the Boston streets with her sister beside her. "Mary, you must be careful. Sooner or later someone is going to recognize you."

"I must put my fellow Quakers needs over those of my own," Mary insisted. "I have to find Christopher Holder and help him. If he is in prison, he will have no one to bring him food and he will be existing on spoiled vegetables and moldy bread. I will search for him there first."

Martha stared at her sister in amazement. "Don't you think going to the jail would be a foolish thing to do? They will surely recognize you and put you back in prison. I will inquire of the guards while you stay in hiding."

Mary shook her head adamantly. "I cannot let thee take such a risk for me. Thou have not completely accepted the Quaker ways. Yet thou have been a faithful sister and have risked thy own life for my beliefs."

"I may not yet be totally convinced in the Quaker way," Martha said, "but I agree that everyone should have the freedom to seek God without punishment or interference from the clergy or government."

Mary and Martha continued slowly down the street. The sea gulls squawked overhead and the fresh salt air blew around them. A fisherman passed pulling a wagon of fresh fish. "I have always loved the excitement of docks and the activities all around," Mary said. "Before we go to the prison, let's walk around the wharf area and enjoy the sights and sounds."

Martha smiled to herself. *This is one of the first times I have heard Mary want to do something for the pure pleasure of enjoying life without the intensity of being productive or being in service to others.*

As they walked, Martha watched a smile cross her sister's face while she breathed in the fresh salt air. When they neared the dock, a familiar figure appeared. Martha asked, "Is that who I think it is?"

Mary gasped. "It is...That is Christopher Holder." Mary waved and hurried to catch up with him.

When they neared their friend, Mary said, "Christopher, what a surprise to see thee. I am glad thou are no longer in prison. What are thou doing here?"

Christopher smiled at the sisters and turned sternly back to Mary. "Mary Dyer, what are thou doing in Boston? I heard thee were banished on pain of death."

Mary hung her head while a familiar look of determination spread across her face. "When word reached Newport that thou were back in prison in Boston, I could not stay away. I felt the Inner Light lead me back to help thee and encourage the Quakers who are suffering for what they believe."

"Thou are a very brave woman," Christopher said, "but thou take extra-ordinary risks for the cause." He hesitated while he surveyed Mary's radiant face. "I was released from prison a few hours ago and I am here trying to book passage back to England."

Mary wrinkled her brow. "It is unusual the magistrates released thee after all the persecution and threats thou have received."

"The magistrates are becoming afraid of me due to my high connections back in England," Christopher explained. "It is rumored the Massachusetts Bay Colony Charter is already at risk because of their cruel treatment of Quakers. The magistrates decided it would be preferable to insist on my departure instead of a hanging. However, William Robinson and Marmaduke Stevenson are still in prison."

Martha listened to Mary and Christopher's conversation and then asked, "Why are William and Marmaduke back? They left Boston the same day we did. In fact, they walked to the outskirts of town with us. From there they said they were going to Salem."

Christopher nodded. "That was the problem. They left Boston, but not the Massachusetts Bay Colony. In Salem, they made new followers and continued their Quaker teachings. They had several good meetings in the outlying woods of Salem before Governor Endicott's scouts learned of this and brought them back to the Boston jail."

Martha's heart sank when Mary said, "I must go to the jail and encourage them. Maybe I can get food to them through the windows."

October twentieth Martha Clarke took a seat in the crowded courtroom as close to the prisoners as possible. She scanned the audience and recognized a number of men—some clergy, some town officials, and some curious citizens. The panel of magistrates was the same as those in Mary's previous trial. Governor Endicott seemed to be trembling and his face was ashen. Martha watched her sister along with William Robinson, and Marmaduke Stevenson being led into the room. Mary was thinner than she was after her last imprisonment, but her face was strangely radiant.

"Remove your hats," Governor Endicott commanded the men.

William and Marmaduke did not move or acknowledge they had even heard the order.

Turning to the guard who had brought them in, the governor shouted, "If they will not obey, take off their hats for them."

"We have to obey God, rather than man," Marmaduke Stevenson said.

Governor Endicott scowled, his voice quavering. "Marmadule Stevenson and William Robinson, you have remained in the Massachusetts Bay Colony after banishment on pain of death. I do not desire the death of anyone, but you have made this decision yourself. Therefore, you shall be taken to your cell and on the appointed time taken to the gallows where you will be hanged by the neck until you are dead."

Mary Dyer before the Boston Magistrates

Marmaduke turned to the magistrates seated at the table with Governor Endicott. "If you put us to death you will bring innocent blood upon your own heads, and God's swift destruction will be upon you."

Governor Endicott glared and motioned to the guard. "Return the male prisoners to the cell."

The courtroom grew silent. Mary Dyer was left standing alone before the governor and magistrates. Again, Governor Endicott's voice rang out, "Mary Dyer, you have returned to Boston after banishment on pain of death. You, too, shall be returned to your cell and from there to the gallows where you will be hanged until you are dead."

"May the will of the Lord be done," Mary replied and looked radiantly toward the ceiling.

The governor's face reddened. "Marshal, take her away."

An angelic expression continued across Mary's face. "Yea, joyfully I go."

The Marshal roughly grabbed Mary's arm and turned her around.

"Thou can let me alone, Marshal," she said. "I would go to the prison without thee. I go in service to my God."

A wave of nausea enveloped Martha. Her knees were weak when she tried to stand. By the time she was able to leave the courtroom, a crowd of Quaker supporters was already beginning to gather. Martha worked her way to the edge of the crowd where she saw one of the newly convinced Quakers from Newport. "We must get word of the execution to William Dyer right away. There must be a way it can be stopped."

The man from Newport nodded. "I am a fast runner and am friends with many native Indians along the way. I can be in Newport in a couple days. In fact, I have friends who also know the trails. They can help spread the word of this gross injustice to all the colonies."

Martha moved with the crowd as they marched from the courtroom to the prison. People came from all directions to join them. The crowd chanted. "Let them free! Let them free! Let them free...."

Although the Massachusetts officials tried to prevent the colonists from conversing with the prisoners, the sympathy of the people grew stronger during the week before the hanging. They flocked to the prison windows to hear the victims speak. The guards were unable to hold them back. Chaos continued to build around the Boston prison.

When word reached Newport that Mary was back in the Boston jail, William Dyer was overwhelmed with both anger and grief. Two years before, he had gone to Boston himself and signed a document promising she would never return. Now she was sitting in the Boston jail for the second time since he had made that agreement. He had to find a way to rescue his unpredictable wife. He went to his desk and began penning a letter to the Boston magistrates pleading for his wife's life. He had to find someone to hand deliver the letter to the governor—someone who would speak highly of his wife and understand her position, and yet someone the magistrates might respect. But could a courier arrive in Boston before Mary's trial?

The following week Martha stayed in the grove across from the prison, watching who was coming and going and if they supported the Quaker prisoners or not. Much to her surprise, Governor John Winthrop, Jr. of Connecticut, son of the late Governor of Massachusetts, appeared at the Boston jail. Martha hid in a clump of trees to listen to his conversation with the guards. *That governor banished Mary Dyer from Connecticut a year ago. I wonder why he wants to see Mary now.*

Martha could not hear the entire conversation, but she could tell Governor Winthrop was pleading for mercy for Quakers. As he turned away from the prison, Martha shouted from the shadows of the trees. "Governor. Over here."

The governor peered into the shadows and moved toward Martha.

Martha stepped from the shadows and said, "Thank you for coming to support my sister, Mary Dyer."

Governor Winthrop shook his head in frustration. "I may not agree with the Quaker ways, but I cannot go along with these executions. They have done no harm. If I thought it would do any good, I would have crawled on my bare knees from New Haven to Boston begging that the condemned would not be hanged and offering them shelter in Connecticut."

"But what can we do at this late date?" Martha asked.

Governor Winthrop set his jaw. His eyes took on a stern expression. "I am going directly to Governor Endicott and try to point out the fallacy of his decision. Travesties that happen in one colony will affect all of us in the end. Parliament will not be pleased with this kind of bizarre treatment toward the Quakers. The last thing the colonies need is to fall into displeasure with the English Parliament."

Martha smiled. "Thank you for your assistance. I wish you well."

Throughout the remaining days of Mary's imprisonment, Martha remained vigilant outside of the jail. Scores of people, Quakers and non-Quakers, came to protest or to participate in the excitement. Much to Martha's dismay, she never saw Governor Winthrop again, nor learned the outcome of his meeting with Governor Endicott.

Two days before the scheduled execution, Martha Clarke sat glumly on a tree stump near the edge of town. Her options seemed to have run out. Men, women, and children passed by her, but she paid no heed. After nearly an hour, she looked up. Much to her amazement, she recognized a young man walking down the street.

Martha jumped to her feet and raced toward him. "Will, what brings you to Boston?"

Eighteen-year-old William Junior embraced his aunt. "My father has written to letter to Governor Endicott begging for mercy for mother. He was afraid to come to Boston for fear of being arrested since he had already signed a document stating he would never set foot in Boston again. I am on my way to deliver the letter directly to the Governor and beg for mother's release."

Dismay shuddered down Martha's spine. She had helped raise Will since he was a baby and the fear of him spending time in prison was more than she could consider. "Please be careful. Do not let them know you recently became a convinced Quaker. They are putting Quakers in jail simply because they are Quakers."

Will patted Martha's hand trying to reassure her. "I promise I will be careful. If thou will wait here, I will report back when I am finished talking with the governor."

"May God be with you." Martha hugged her nephew and he turned to leave.

Time passed slowly for Martha as she fluctuated from intense, trusting prayer to anxious worry. After what seemed like hours, William Junior returned. His pace was slow and his shoulders slumped. "That was a strange meeting," he said.

Martha wrinkled her brow. "In what way was it strange?"

"Governor Endicott asked Reverend John Norton to join us. The two politely listened to my plea. They then ordered me to leave and said the execution would take place as scheduled, but they wanted to make modifications. I have no idea what they are talking about."

Chapter Twenty-Six
The Boston Martyrs

Boston, October 27, 1659

Amid a growing crowd, Martha watched the jailer lead William Robinson, Marmaduke Stevenson, and her sister from the jail. Soldiers and guards surrounded them, but the prisoners walked unshackled and almost joyfully. It was a mile's walk to the gallows and Martha followed as closely to Mary as possible shouting words of encouragement over the rat-a-tat of the soldier's drums. On every corner, town criers stood announcing the news. People streamed in from outlying towns. Women sobbed. Some men mocked and jeered while others removed their hats in respect. Children darted about and called to each other with little understanding of the gravity of the situation.

Captain James Oliver lead the prisoners down the crowded street, escorted by a band of 200 armed men beating drums to drown out any attempts to speak to the prisoners. The two condemned men, with Mary between them, held her hands. All three wore peaceful expressions as they walked toward the gallows. A peaceful expression was on each of their faces.

Captain Oliver turned to Mary with a sneer. "Are you not ashamed to walk hand in hand between two young men?"

Mary smiled and looked toward heaven. "It's an hour of greatest joy. No eye can see, no ear can hear, no tongue can speak, no heart can understand the sweet and refreshing spirit of the Lord."

Martha shrank back in horror when she saw the great elm on the Boston Common that constituted the gallows. Even more shocking, directly under the ladder she recognized Reverend John Wilson. He was now old and bent, but standing proudly in a long black robe holding a Bible. She remembered happier days twenty-four years before when she was present to watch Reverend Wilson baptize Mary's oldest son, Samuel.

As the prisoners approached the tree Reverend John Wilson shouted, "I shall carry fire in one hand and fagots in the other, to burn all the Quakers in the world. From the devil they came, and to the devil let them go!"

Amidst Reverend Wilson's taunts, the hangman placed the noose around William Robinson's neck while the jailer yanked William's hand from Mary's and bound his hands with a rope. William slowly ascended the ladder. Before they tied a handkerchief over his face and the ladder jerked from beneath him, he proudly shouted, "I suffer for Christ, in whom I lived, and for whom I die."

A wave of nausea swept over Martha as she watched William's lifeless body dangle before her. She watched in horror, when his body was cut down, and the ladder was again laid against the branch on the elm tree. *What could lead people to such cruelty in the name of religion?*

Marmadule Stevenson's hands were similarly bound and he climbed to the top of the ladder. In a loud voice he proclaimed, "Be it known unto all this day that we suffer not as evil-doers, but for conscience sake." Before he had finished, the ladder was kicked out from under him and his lifeless body dangled before her.

Through the crowd, William Junior approached his aunt. He put one arm around Martha's shoulder and took her trembling hand in his while they watched Mary confidently stepped forward. The hangman secured her skirt, her hands bound, and the noose was slipped over her head.

Reverend John Wilson stepped forward. "The birth of the devil's child should have been enough to convince you of your sin. Since you refuse to repent of your heresy, God's judgment is upon you. You will now spend eternity with your monster child." He reached into his pocket and tied a handkerchief over her face.

Martha remained nearly paralyzed and leaned against her nephew. Suddenly a stir was heard in the back of the crowd and a white horse came galloping across the Boston Commons headed for the gallows. Its rider was wildly waving his hands and crying, "Stop! She is reprieved!"

The crowd picked up the chant. "Stop, for she is reprieved...Stop, for she is reprieved...Stop!"

William Junior turned to Martha. "Now I understand what the governor meant when he said he wanted to frighten mother by bringing her to death's door. This was a prearranged, cold-blooded refinement of cruelty to shake her faith and overcome her fortitude. It is the most diabolical scheme I have ever heard."

Martha nodded, but remained silent as she stood trembling beside her nephew. *How can Mary retain her sense of faith through all of this?*

The messenger handed the note from the Governor to Captain Oliver. He hesitated. His muscles tightened. Captain Oliver shouted to the hangman, "Unbind the prisoner."

Martha's heart pounded while she watched her sister's hands and legs being unbound and the kerchief and noose removed. However, Mary did not move.

"Come down," Captain Oliver ordered.

Mary did not move. She looked up to heaven and said, "I am willing to suffer as my brothers have. I am happy to do so, unless you repeal thy wicked anti-Quaker laws."

"Bring her down," someone in the crowd shouted. The people began pulling her and the ladder down together.

Someone caught Mary before she hit the ground. She stood abruptly and faced Captain Oliver. A look of anger was in her eyes. "Why was I reprieved?"

The captain sneered. "Strong appeals were made on your behalf. I would not have obliged, if I were the governor."

"Who made those appeals?" she asked. "I do not want to abide by them."

"If you must know, appeals included Governor John Winthrop, Junior of Connecticut, Governor Temple of Acadia and Nova Scotia, as well as your son, William," Captain Oliver said. "There were several other protesters whom I cannot recall."

"But those men would have stated their cases days ago. Why did the reprieve not come until I was on the gallows?"

"I am not at liberty to explain," Captain Oliver said. "I am only acting in obedience to the order of the court."

"May I see the reprieve?"

Captain Oliver reached into his pocket, took out the note given to him by the rider, and began to read. "Mary Dyer shall have her liberty within 48 hours after this day to depart from this jurisdiction with her son or other family member to take her home. If she returns to the Massachusetts Bay Colony the execution will be consummated."

Mary scanned the crowded and settled on her sister and son. She greeted them with a warm smiled accompanied with a touch of anger in her eyes.

Martha silently returned her greeting as she breathed a sigh of relief. *It is hard for me to understand how such a normal person as my sister could put her service to God over her love and care of her family. Why would God require so much from her? I am amazed how she can carry it out with so much grace and tranquility.*

When the Marshal took Mary's arm to lead her back to the prison, Mary slumped to the ground in a state of shock. The marshal picked her up and carried her back to her cell with Martha and William Junior following close behind. Much to Martha's surprise, the guards let her and William Junior accompany Mary to her cell.

As soon as the cell door clanged shut behind them, Mary revived and looked sternly at her son. "Will, why did thee come? Do thou not understand what I must do?"

Will took his mother's hand. "Yes, I understand. I have recently been convinced that the Quaker ways are God's ways. Father wanted to come and plead thy case, but he was certain he would be put in jail as well and there would be no one to care for the younger children."

Mary turned to her sister. "Thou will never know how much I appreciate thee supporting me and caring for my children while I am doing what God had called me to do. Even though thou are not completely convinced in the Quaker ways, thou has demonstrated the true meaning of love of family and faith in God."

Tears ran down Martha's cheeks as she hugged her Mary. "I only wish I had the faith to follow God's direction that you have."

Mary pulled back from their embrace. "Martha, I hope thou understand that I cannot accept this reprieve. Tonight I will ask the jailer to bring me a quill and ink so I can write to the Massachusetts General Court."

"What could you say to the General Court to make any difference?" Martha asked.

Mary shook her head. "I don't know if the court will listen, but God will. I will tell them 'my life not availeth me in comparison to the liberty of the truth'."

Outside noise began to echo through the small window in Mary's cell. As they peered through the bars, they could see crowds gathering in the streets around the prison. Captain Oliver was trying to suppress the demonstrations, but to no avail. The crowd kept shouting, "Let Mary go...Let Mary go."

Suddenly the jailer appeared at the cell door. "All visitors must leave. We will release Mary in the morning under the guard of four horsemen who will escort her out of town for fifteen miles. From there she is on her own and must never return to Boston."

Chapter Twenty-Seven
Seeking

Shelter Island, 1659-1660

William Dyer once again welcomed his beloved wife home with open arms after another ill-advised trip to Boston. For Martha, life resumed a sense of normalcy in her little home in Newport. Samuel was now married and lived with Anne Hutchinson's granddaughter in a little house William had helped him build in the pasture beyond the Dyer's home.

One evening while relaxing in her front yard after sunset, Martha began reflecting on the events of the last few years. *I marvel at William's patience and love for Mary, even while it is obvious he does not fully understand what motivates her. Few husbands would be able to cope with their wife's extreme dedication to a cause in which they did not share. However, we all agree with the principle of freedom of religion and speech, which Mary is willing to risk her life.*

As the weeks passed, Martha watched William share with Mary the trials and frustrations he faced in helping administer the city of Newport and the colony of Rhode Island as a whole. William told how some colonists claimed the Natives stole their property and livestock only later to learn the colonists did it themselves and had blamed the Natives. He told Mary about the lack of charity the settlers were showing toward each other as the community grew and its businesses prospered. However, to Martha, it appeared Mary only feigned interest in the local happenings. Her mind seemed miles away.

One evening as winter approached, Mary joined Martha in her small house next door. "Martha," she said as she sat on the bench next to the hearth. "I have been extremely happy since I returned to Newport. William is so kind to me, and it is good to be with the children again, but I am not free...I may be free of not having a guard at the door and no court and executioner is awaiting me. However, I am not free unless I am doing what God calls me to do."

Martha sighed. *This is the restlessness Mary feels when she is contemplating another trip.* She looked at her sister. "What do you think God is calling you to do? Hopefully, it is here in Newport?"

Mary smiled. "After listening to William's frustration with the local government, I am beginning to understand why Anne Hutchinson expressed disbelief in governments and magistrates. God is calling me to something different. He is calling me to Shelter Island to visit the Sylvesters. There I can rest, fellowship with other Quakers, preach the gospel, and search for what God will have me do next."

Martha took a deep breath; a wave of frustration came over her. "I have heard many Quakers have sought refuge from Puritan persecution on Shelter Island to regain their physical and spiritual strength. But can't you search for God's leading in Newport with your family?"

The fire flickered in the fireplace and reflected from Mary's face. Her expression was quiet and pensive. "I went to Boston willing to lay down my life to stand against the anti-Quaker laws, but I failed. I went to New Haven to speak against their treatment of Quakers and failed. I need time to seek God and again find direction for my life. Shelter Island is a good place to pray and reflect without distractions. Would you come with me? However, we must not tell William where we are going. He will search for me and bring me home."

Martha's heart pounded. *I hate to leave the children and William once again, but if I do not go with her, Mary will go by herself and she will be lost to us forever.*

In spite of Martha's apprehensions, two days later she and Mary were sailing across the Long Island Sound to Shelter Island, which lay between the north and south forks of Long Island.

The small boat Martha and Mary were riding slowly approached an inlet on Shelter Island. They wrapped their shawls tighter around themselves to protect against the cold December wind. From the distance, Martha could see a large house on the hill looming above them surrounded by cabins on the side and back. While the captain moored the boat on the bank, a man and a woman hurried from the house toward the ship in spite of the cold December wind. Martha and Mary stepped onto the rocky beach, trying to regain their balance for the rough waters.

"Welcome," Gissel Sylvester greeted. "You must be Mary Dyer whom I've heard so much about. We learned you were heading this way."

"I am," Mary said meekly and motioned to her sister. "This is my sister, Martha Clarke. We would like to take refuge on thy island until the Lord shows us further direction."

"By all means," Gissel said as she took Mary's arm. "We would be honored. We have several guest houses behind our home where travelers may rest for as long as they need."

The crisp wind whipped their skirts as Martha and Mary followed the Sylvesters to their home. "Please, come in and have a warm meal before we take you to your room."

"We wouldn't want to be a burden on you," Martha mildly protested. "We still have food with us."

Gissel turned and gave Mary and Martha a warm, smile. "After a cold, brutal trip coming across the bay, you need to have a hot meal. It is no burden at all; we have special kitchen helpers to prepare our meals."

After touring the Sylvesters' large home which they referred to as 'Woodstock', the Sylvesters, Martha, and Mary gathered around the long kitchen table while the Black kitchen help served them warm bread, stew, and apple pie. When they were had finished the meal Nathaniel said, "Tomorrow is Sunday. We have four workers who paddle us the six miles to Southold, Long Island to attend church. Would you care to come with us?"

Mary and Martha exchanged confused looks. "I thank thee for the kind offer," Mary replied sweetly, "but we are extremely weary and will need several days to rest."

Through an open door to the kitchen, Martha watched the Black help go about their routine tasks. *I thought the Sylvesters were Quakers. Did not George Fox send a warning to the colonies that 'every captured creature under the whole Heaven deserves liberty and freedom'? That should include all Black and Indian slaves.*

Martha sat back and listened to the others exchange news from Newport and other Quaker community while the embers burned low in the fireplace. She admired the trimmings of affluence around her. Nothing further was mentioned as to the church they attended on Long Island, nor the Sylvesters' Black help.

When the sisters began to tire, their hosts lit two candles and led them to their guesthouse. "We again thank you for your kindness," Martha said as the Sylvesters turned to leave. "I do not know how we can ever repay you."

"Knowing your work of hosting weary travelers in Rhode Island is payment enough," Nathaniel said. "Consider this your temporary home. Good night."

As soon as the door closed behind them, Mary and Martha stretched out on the rope beds on the far side of the room. The candle flickered dimly on the table beside them. Finally, Martha whispered, "Mary, I do not understand the Sylvesters. I thought they were Quakers, but if they attend church in Southold and do not practice Quaker ways they must be Puritans."

Mary nodded and kept her voice low. "They have an interesting background. The Sylvesters have never become Quakers, but they have been extremely sympathetic and hospitable to the Quakers. As I understand it, they met George Fox before they left England. Since the Quaker ideals are opposed to slavery, it created a conflict for them. Nathaniel is a sugar merchant in Barbados which uses an unknown number of slaves."

In the silence of the night, Martha and Mary heard sobbing coming from the next room. Instinctively they hurried to the door of the adjoining room and rapped on the door. Within seconds, a woman with red puffy eyes opened it. "May I help thee?" she said as she wiped away a tear rolling down her cheek.

"We heard your cries from next door, and wondered if there was anything we could do to help?" Martha said. "I am Martha Clarke and this is my sister, Mary Dyer."

The woman's eyes widened and she studied Mary's weathered face. "Are you THE Mary Dyer—the champion for the Quaker cause?"

Mary nodded. "Yes. I try to follow God's leading. What is thy name?"

Fresh tears gathered in the woman's eyes. "I am Cassandra Southwick. My husband, Lawrence is lying here near death. I have been by his side for nearly three days, but can do nothing to help."

"May we come in?" Martha asked.

Cassandra hesitated and then motioned them to enter. She gave a desperate glance at her husband. "He has suffered a great deal."

Martha knelt beside the bed and studied the still body. His face was ashen and gaunt and his face bruised. His arms had black and blue welts on them. "What happened to him? He looks as if he has been severely beaten."

"Yes, he was beaten several times," Cassandra said. "Now he is dying from a broken heart."

Mary wrapped her arm around Cassandra. "Was he beaten because he was a Quaker? Tell us what happened."

Cassandra sunk onto the chair beside the bed, buried her head in her hands, and sobbed. When she calmed she said, "Lawrence, our two children, and I were beaten in the Salem jail. Lawrence received the most lashes."

"What were the charges?" Mary asked. Nothing would have warranted this kind of treatment."

"We were not able to pay the rent for our house," Cassandra said. "The Boston magistrates ordered us beaten and our children sent as slaves to Barbados. We were banished from Massachusetts and do not know where our children are. Lawrence has never recovered. If we had not been Quakers someone would have helped us, instead we were treated worse than criminals."

Mary bowed her head and remained silent for a few moments before she said, "We will do everything we can to help you. Because of treatment thy family and other godly people receive is the reason God is calling me to challenge the anti-Quaker laws. Martha and I will watch over thy husband until morning. Please lie down, and get some much needed rest."

The next day, Lawrence Southwick died. Mary and Martha helped Cassandra wash and dress his body and wrap him in a sheet. The Sylvester's workers dug a grave near the path leading to the woods.

Later in the day, Mary, Martha, Nathaniel and Gisell Sylvester, joined Cassandra at the gravesite to mourn the death. Martha was amazed at the comforting words her sister spoke and the depth of the prayer she prayed. *If anyone hears directly from God, it is my sister,* she thought as she watched an angelic expression spread across her sister's face.

Every morning, Martha watched Mary walk the shores of Shelter Island in deep contemplation. Sometimes she would join her, but when she sensed Mary needed to be alone, she sat on the lawn of the guesthouse and enjoyed the view of the bay. One blustery morning while they were walking the shore together, three Indians approached. "I hope one of them speaks English," Martha whispered.

"The Sylvesters have encouraged their workers as well as the Natives who live on the island to learn English," Mary whispered back and then turned her attention to the Natives. "Hello."

"Are you Mary Dyer?" the leader asked.

"Yes."

"Will you teach us about God?"

Martha gasped. *How did Mary's reputation as a Quaker missionary spread to the Natives while a few Quakers consider her only an eccentric.*

"Most certainly." Mary gave a welcoming smile to each of the Natives and pointed to a trail into the woods. "I know a clearing in the woods where we could sit."

With trepidations, Martha bravely followed her sister into the woods with three strange Natives close behind. A few yards into the forest, they came to a clearing with a gigantic white oak tree in the center. Underneath the tree, twenty Natives and Blacks had already gathered to hear Mary speak.

Martha marveled at the beauty of the simplistic words Mary used to explain the love of God. Even if their English language skills were limited, the Natives and the Blacks related to Mary's warmth and understanding with cheers and enthusiasm. Martha was overcome by their spirituality in spite of the dramatic dissimilarities of backgrounds.

When the shadows lengthen and the evening insects began to chirp, Martha watched the last of the Natives disappear into the woods and the last Black returned to the cabins behind the big house. "Having them come to you and ask you to teach them about God must have been extremely satisfying. It gave me a better understanding of the Inner Light that motivates you."

Mary took her sister's hand. "Yes, it was uplifting, especially since it was completely spontaneous and led by God. Preaching to the Natives on Shelter Island is so different from Massachusetts and Rhode Island. The preachers in Massachusetts are trying to remold the Natives into Englishmen. Roger Williams has devoted his efforts to helping Englishmen understand the Natives, but he is often met with resistance. I understand why Roger is disappointed the Natives in Rhode Island did not adopt the one true God. Because of their love for Roger Williams, they merely added "his God" to their assortment of deities instead of accepting the one and only true God."

Their pace increased as Mary and Martha continued down the trail toward the 'Woodstock'. The smell of cooking vegetables and meat filled the air. When they reached the back of the Sylvesters' house, Martha said, "Your preaching is much easier for Natives to understand than the dictatorial methods of the Puritans and the condescending ways of Roger Williams. No wonder they respond to your message."

During the remainder of their stay on Shelter Island, the number of Natives and Blacks who came to hear Mary preach under the giant white oak tree continued to grow. Their enthusiasm, in spite their limited vocabulary rejuvenated everyone.

While Mary continued to search for God's direction, another traveling Quaker came to Shelter Island to rest. He carried with him a copy of A Declaration of the General Court of Massachusetts that had been sent to England explaining and justifying the use of severe actions against the Quakers taken by Governor Endicott, the magistrates, and the ministers.

Mary's hands trembled as she read the document. "This is full of lies," she fumed. "It is a deceit to the entire world. I cannot live my life as a lie. I must go back to Boston and protest this injustice."

Martha's face blanched. "Are you sure there is no other way?"

"No," Mary stated firmly. "God is calling me back to Boston, but first I must go to Providence and say good-bye to Catherine Scott. I must encourage her family to continue the struggle against the anti-Quaker laws."

Tears filled Martha's eyes. *But what about Mary's family?* She took a deep breath and said, "You know what might happen if you return to Boston." After a long, tension-filled silence, Martha continued. "But if you feel you must, bidding farewell to Anne Hutchinson's sister would be most fitting."

Chapter Twenty-Eight
She Hangs Like a Flag

Boston, May 1660

Noon, May 21, 1660, Mary Dyer and Martha Clarke rode into Boston on a grey mare provided by Catherine Scott. Martha's hands trembled and her heart race. She looked with suspicion at each passerby. *Will they be the one to turn Mary in to the authorities?*

Soon a small group began to follow them, shouting words of encouragement and directions. "Go back. They will kill you." "They let you go before, but now they will surely kill you."

Mary set her jaw. "I must do what God commands. The bloody laws against the Quakers must be challenged."

Suddenly three horsemen appeared around the bend in the street. "Are you Mary Dyer?"

"I am."

"It is my duty to arrest you," said the leader. The other two officers dismounted, and pulled Mary from the mare. They bound her hands and feet and pushed her like a bag of meal across the back of the officer's horse. "You were told never to return to Boston on pain of death. You must appear before the court."

Mary relaxed while she lay face down across the horse. "My body is in thy hands, but my soul is with the Lord."

The officer used his horse's leather switch across Mary's back and snarled. "Quiet. If I hear another sound from you I will take you first to the whipping post before going to jail."

Seeing Mary's treatment from the officers, the crowd faded into the background fearing the officers would associate them as active supporters of Mary Dyer and they world receive the same punishment.

Standing alone, Martha watched in horror while the officers rode away with her sister. She went to a familiar tree stump at the edge of town and dismounted. She sat on the stump sobbing for over an hour. *How did different viewpoints on religion deteriorate to this? Is it necessary for innocent Quakers to die, just to get a law changed?*

When Martha calmed herself, she headed straight to the Boston jail. After crawling along the ground checking the cell windows, Martha located her sister in the third cell. "Mary...Mary, are you all right?"

"Yes," Mary replied softly. "They are furious with my return and an officer left immediately to notify Governor Endicott."

"Is there anything I can do?" Martha asked. "Can I bring you food or water?"

Mary shook her head. "Would thou try to bring my travel bag from the horse? Please pray I will be strong and convince them they must change their bloody laws." She paused and listened a moment, and then whispered. "Thou must go now. A guard is coming."

Martha sadly left the jail and strolled the streets of Boston, unsure what to do. She stopped at local inns and mercantiles to hear the reactions of the people as word of Mary Dyers return to Boston spread. Much to her surprise, nearly every man, woman, and child in Boston seemed to be aware of her sister's case. Emotions ran high and there seemed to be no end of opinions."

"I should have pulled away the ladder from under her the moment I heard someone shout 'reprieve'," she heard someone say.

The crowd jeered and pushed the naysayer aside. "It is Endicott who should be hanged," another shouted.

While arguments about the return of Mary Dyer seemed to be erupting on every street corner, Martha returned to Catherine Scott's mare she had left tethered to a tree at the edge of town. She took Mary's bag containing her Bible, quill, ink, and paper, along with three apples and two carrots and made her way to the grove of trees across the street from the jail. She waited until dark before moving quietly to the familiar windows at the back of the Boston prison.

"Mary...Mary," Martha whispered through the bars in the cell. Through the shadows, she watched her sister move toward the window. Her once young vibrant sister was now forty-nine and greying. The happy bounce in her step was now slow and methodical. "I brought your things from the horse."

Mary reached through the bars. "I thank thee. I especially need the quill, ink, and paper. I want to write a letter to the General Court once again. I must convince them of the errors of their ways and beg them not to fight against God. They must repeal these laws and let the servants of the Lords have free passage among them."

Martha peered into the shadows for movement behind the jail. Seeing none, she turned back to her sister. "Mary, the people are starting to protest in the streets on your behalf. The officers are all over town looking for trouble. I may not be able to come to this window again, but I will do my best to be at your trial. I want you to know how much I love you and how proud I am of you taking the stand you are. Even if I am unable to come to your side, I will always keep you in my thoughts and prayers."

Mary reached through the bars and took Martha's hand. "I understand, do not fret for me, God is with me, even in a dank, dirty jail cell. I am glad thou understand what I must do. Please tell my family I love each one of them dearly. It burdens me greatly William and the children may never realize the depths of my love for them, nor understand why I must follow God instead of my human love. Their lack of understanding is the most grievous pain I bear."

Ten days after her return to Boston, Mary Dyer was again brought before Governor Endicott and the magistrates. When Martha entered the courtroom, an old man with a young boy beside him were sitting by the prisoner's table. She found an unobtrusive seat nearby and waited silently. Her heart pounded and she tried not to clench her fists. When the marshals brought Mary into the courtroom, the magistrates had not yet arrived. The sisters exchanged knowing glances, when Martha looked back; she noticed the man beside the boy was gone. *That is strange to leave a child by himself; I wonder where the man went.*

The marshals offered Mary a seat, but she declined. After a few moments of silence, the boy stepped to her side and whispered. "I know what they will ask, because I heard the magistrates talking."

Mary looked quizzically at the boy, and then exchanged puzzled looks with Martha.

The boy seemed excited to finish his memorized tale. "Another Mary Dyer recently arrived from England who has exactly the same name as yours. If you will say you are that Mary Dyer, you could be released without penalty."

She put her hand on the boy's shoulder. "Did the magistrates send thee here to tell me that?"

The boy's eyes grew wide. His voice trembled. "Yes...How did you know?"

Martha rolled her eyes and exchanged glances with her sister. *I cannot believe the mental torture technique they are using on Mary. They are trying everything so that they do not have Mary's blood on their hands.*

Gradually the courtroom filled with spectators, and the old man returned and took his seat beside the boy. Mary remained standing with her back to the crowd, facing the magistrate's table. A side door opened, and everyone rose while Governor Endicott entered, followed by six magistrates.

Mary stood silently while Governor Endicott and the spectators were seated. After giving introductory remarks to the crowd, the governor turned his attention to the prisoner. "Are you the *same* Mary Dyer who was here at the last General Court? Another Mary Dyer has recently arrived from London and I need to be certain we do not condemn the wrong person."

Martha sensed a note of pleading in his voice as if he were saying, "Mary, this is your way of escape. Please save us all from a tragic situation by claiming to be the other Mary Dyer."

Mary stiffened her back and took a deep breath. In a clear fearless voice, she said, "Yes. I am the same Mary Dyer who was here at the last General Court."

The governor's face reddened and his voice took on an authoritarian tone. "Will you admit to being a Quaker?"

"Yes, I am proud to be a Quaker," Mary answered. "I came to Boston in obedience to the will of God, requesting thee to repeal thy unrighteous laws of banishment on pain of death. I speak only the words the Lord gives me."

Governor Endicott pounded the table. "Do you claim to be a prophetess?"

Mary paused, waiting for the governor's anger to subside. The courtroom became silent, while people seemingly held their breath with anticipation. "I speak what the Inner Light tells me. Does that make me a prophetess?"

"It makes you a heretic," Governor Endicott shouted. "The sentence is passed upon you by the General Court and me. You must return to the prison where you will remain until tomorrow at nine o'clock; from there you will go to the gallows and be hanged until you are dead."

Mary did not flinch. "This is no more than what thou said the last time I was before this court."

Anger flashed in Governor Endicott's eyes. "Away with her!" he shouted. "Away with her!"

At dawn June 1, 1660, Martha Clarke took a position partially hidden in the grove of trees across from the Boston prison. She watched while the military guard began to assemble. Never had she seen as many as gathered that morning. While she waited and the sun rose higher in the sky, the streets became lined with spectators. Emotions ran high when defenders and accusers stood side by side.

Promptly at nine o'clock Mary appeared in the doorway of the prison. The band of soldiers surrounded her as they started the mile-long march to the gallows in the Boston Commons. To cut off communication between the prisoner and her followers the lead drummers played a constant rat-a-tat-tat, followed by a persistent rat-a-tat-tat from behind. Some of her followers were able to defy the drummers and militant marchers by moving close to Mary and pleading, "Mary Dyer, don't die. Go back to Rhode Island where you might save your life. We beg of you, go back? Go back and live!"

Mary wore an angelic smile. "Thou do not understand. I cannot turn back. It is in obedience to the will of the Lord God I came, and I must remain faithful to His will and plan."

When they reached the great elm tree near the Frog Pond in the Boston Commons, drums silenced and Captain John Webb turned to the agitated crowd. "Mary Dyer has been here before and at the last minute had the sentence of banishment upon pain of death suspended. However, she has again broken the law by returning to this town. Therefore, it is *she* who is guilty of taking an innocent life."

"No," Mary Dyer said. "I came to keep blood guiltiness *from* you. I came imploring you to repeal the unrighteous and unjust laws of banishment upon pain of death made against the innocent servants of the Lord. My life does not avail me, in comparison to the liberty of the truth."

Again, Martha watched their former Puritan pastor, the Reverend John Wilson, step forward. He clenched his fist and waved a Bible in her face. "Mary Dyer, repent. Do not be deluded and be carried away by the deceit of the devil."

Mary looked directly at Reverend Wilson and said decisively, "No. I will not repent. The bloody laws of Boston are an abomination to God."

"Then at least permit the church elders to pray for your soul," the minister said sarcastically.

"I do not know of any elder her," Mary replied. "I request the prayers of all the people of God."

Martha was almost grateful when Reverend Wilson took out his large handkerchief, to place over Mary's head. She knew she could not bear watching her beautiful sister's expression of rapture being twisted into distortion.

Mary bravely went forward and climbed the ladder. Edward Wanton secured the noose around her neck and knocked the ladder from under her. Martha could hear her sister's neck snap and then watched Mary's lifeless body dangle in the wind, her dress billowing with the breeze. A weeping bystander shouted, "She hangs there as a flag for others to take example by."

Martha could take no more. She ran to the nearby Frog Pond and wept. She did not know how long she had been there when she heard a man vomiting into the pond. She waited until he was silent before she looked up. *Is that the hangman? The very man who took my beloved sister's* innocent *life.*

"We have been murdering the Lord's people," he shouted while he looked upward toward the western sky. He tore off his sword and threw it into the pond.

A sense of pity flooded through Martha. "Are you not the hangman?"

"Yes, I am the hangman. My name is Edward Wanton and I will never be a hangman again," he said. "Seeing the calm serenity and courageous sacrifice Mary Dyer exhibited, I am now convinced Quakers do communicate with God. Quaker ways are God's ways. I will no longer bear arms against my fellowman, even under penalty of death

First Amendment and 'Wall of Separation of Church and State'

The sacrifice of Mary Dyer's life in 1660 had a direct bearing on the Rhode Island Charter of 1663, which legally granted liberty of conscience, and eventually on the First Amendment to the United States Constitution and the Bill of Rights, ratified in 1791.

The hanging of Mary Dyer on the Boston gallows in 1660 marked the beginning of the end of the Puritan theocracy and New England independence from English rule.

The Rhode Island Charter,

Granted by King Charles II, July 8, 1663.

"....but that all and every person and persons may, from time to time, and at all times hereafter, freely and fully have and enjoy his and their own judgments and consciences, in matters of religious concernments, throughout the tract of land hereafter mentioned, they behaving themselves peaceably and quietly, and not using this liberty to licentiousness and profaneness, nor to the civil injury or outward disturbance of others, any law, statute, or clause therein contained, or to be contained, usage or custom of this realm, to the contrary hereof, in any wise notwithstanding....."

<u>**First Amendment to the Constitution**</u>

Congress shall make no law respecting an establishment of religion, or prohibiting the free exercise thereof; or abridging the freedom of speech, or of the press; or the right of the people peaceably to assemble, and to petition the Government for a redress of grievances.

The Establishment Clause is immediately followed by the Free Exercise Clause, which states, "or prohibiting the free exercise thereof." These two clauses make up what are called the "Religion Clauses" of the First Amendment.

The Establishment Clause has generally been interpreted to prohibit the establishment of a national religion by Congress.

The Free Exercise Clause prohibits Congress from preferring one religion over another, but does NOT prohibit the government's entry into religious domain to make accommodations in order to achieve the purposes of freedom to express religion.

Thomas Jefferson claimed the First Amendment erected a "wall of separation between church and state."

Boston Anti-Quaker Laws

The Boston General Court passed four laws specifically directed at Quakers that Mary Dyer and three other Quakers paid the ultimate price to protest.

October 14, 1656

Being a Quaker, or possessing Quaker writings, became a crime, punishable by fines, whipping, imprisonment, and banishment from the colony. Ship captains or others convicted of transporting Quakers into the colony were also severely punished.

October 14, 1657

Providing shelter or comfort to a Quaker became a crime, punishable by fines and imprisonment. The crime of being a Quaker became also punishable by cutting off ears of male Quakers and boring tongues of male or female Quakers, in addition to previously decreed punishments.

May 19, 1658

Holding Quaker meetings, or either speaking or writing about Quaker beliefs, became a crime punishable by fines, whipping, imprisonment, mutilation, or banishment.

October 19, 1658

The death penalty became a punishment for recalcitrant Quakers who continue to propound their testimonies.

September 9, 1661

More than a year after Mary Dyer's execution King Charles II, issued a mandate to the colonists to send any Quakers already condemned to suffer death or other corporeal punishment back to England along with their respective crimes or offenses charged against them.

Timeline of Mary Dyer

July 1591 - Anne Marbury Hutchinson born.

1611 - Mary Barrett Dyer born.

1630 - Boston, Massachusetts founded by Puritans led by John Winthrop.

October 27, 1633 - Mary Barrett Dyer and William Dyer marry.

Spring 1633 - Reverend John Cotton immigrates to the Boston.

1634 - Mary and William Dyer and Anne and William Hutchinson immigrate to Boston.

October 1635 - Reverend Roger Williams banished from the Massachusetts Bay Colony.

October 11, 1637 - Mary Dyer gives birth to deformed stillborn child.

November 2, 1637 - John Wheelwright banished from the Massachusetts Bay Colony.

November 7, 1637 - Anne Hutchinson's civil trial. She is placed under house arrest.

March 7, 1638 - Portsmouth Compact signed, establishing the town of Portsmouth, Rhode Island.

March 15, 1638 - Anne Hutchinson's church trial.

April 1638 - Followers of Anne Hutchinson banished from the Massachusetts Bay Colony and settle in Portsmouth, Rhode Island.

May 1638 - Anne Hutchinson's last pregnancy which ends in a non-formed mass of tissue.

Late 1639 - The Dyers and forty others establish Newport, Rhode Island.

June 1641 - William Hutchinson dies.

Summer 1642 - Anne Hutchinson and family move to Long Island, New Amsterdam.

August 1643 - Anne Hutchinson, along with sixteen family members, scalped by Indians.

November 1651 - Doctor John Clarke, Reverend Roger Williams, and William Dyer go to England to protest William Coddington's patent for an island government. Mary Dyer sails either with them or on an earlier ship.

February 1653 - William Dyer returns to Rhode Island with the news of the return of the colony to the Williams' Patent of 1643. Mary Dyer stays in England.

January 1657 - Mary Dyer and Anne Burden return to Boston and sent promptly to prison.

August 3, 1657 - The ship *Woodhouse* arrives in Rhode Island carrying Quakers from England.

March 1658 - Mary Dyer expelled from New Haven, Connecticut for preaching about the Inner Light and the notion that women and men are equal.

October 27, 1659 - Marmaduke Stephenson and William Robinson hanged on the Boston Commons while Mary Dyer given a reprieve after the noose is already around her neck.

May 1660 - Mary Dyer returns to Boston.

June 1, 1660 - Mary Dyer hanged on the Boston Commons.

March 14, 1661 - William Leddra of Barbados hanged on the Boston Commons.

1661 - King Charles II explicitly forbids Massachusetts from executing anyone for professing Quakerism.

1664 - England revokes the Massachusetts charter.

1686 - England sends a royal governor to Massachusetts to enforce English laws.

1689 - Broad Toleration Act passed in Massachusetts.

Questions to Ponder and Discuss

1) Does Mary Dyer's civil disobedience compare to the civil disobedience of Martin Luther King and Rosa Parks? If so, how?

2) What other path could Mary Dyer have chosen and still remained true to her convictions?

3) What factors do you think contributed to the Puritan's distrust of the Quakers?

4) Can you identify with Martha? If so, in what way?

5) Why do you think William Dyer remained true to his wife when he did not completely share her cause as a Quaker?

6) What impact do you think Mary Dyer's actions had on her children?

7) What circumstances might lead you to separate from a church group?

8) What circumstances might embolden you to fight for a particular cause?

9) Do you think God speaks directly to people today? If so, how?

10) If the Puritans used scripture only to guide them to God and the Quakers looked to the Inner Light of God to speak to them, could, or should, reason and tradition made a difference in the discussion?

Suggested Readings

Bacon, Margaret Hope. *Mothers of Feminism: The Story of Quaker Women in American*. Philadelphia, PA: Friends General Conference, 1986.

Baltzell, E. Digby. *Puritan Boston and Quaker Philadelphia*. Boston, MA: Beacon Press, 1979.

Boorstin, Daniel J. *The Americans: The Colonial Experience*. New York, NY: Vintage Books/Random House, 1958.

Brown, Elisabeth Potts, and Susan Mosher Stuard, eds. *Witnesses for Change: Quaker Women over Three Centuries*. New Brunswick, NJ: Rutgers University Press, 1989.

Burgess, Robert S. *To Try the Bloody Law: The Story of Mary Dyer*. Burnsville, NC: Celo Valley Books, 2000.

Found! Edward Wanton Testimonial 1680. Last modified 2013. Accessed September 20, 2013. http://www.newporthistorical.org/index.php/found-edward-wanton-testimonial-1680/.

Frost, J. William. *The Quaker Family in Colonial America: A Portrait of the Society of Friends*. New York, NY: St. Martin's Press, 1973.

LaPlante, Eve. *American Jezebel: The Uncommon Life of Anne Hutchinson, the Woman Who Defied the Puritans*. New York, NY: HarperCollins, 2003.

Larson, Rebecca. *Daughters of Light: Quaker Women Preaching and Prophesying in the Colonies and Abroad 1700-1775*. Chapel Hill, NC: University of North Carolina Press, 1999.

Levy, Barry. *Quakers and the American Family*. New York, NY: Oxford University Press, 1988.

Mack, Phyllis. *Visionary Women: Ecstatic Prophecy in Seventeenth-Century England.* Berkeley, CA: University of California Press, 1992.

Mary Dyer: A Colonial Execution. Last modified April 2013. Accessed September 20, 2013. http://www.awesomestories.com/biographies/mary-dyer.

Plimpton, Ruth. *Mary Dyer: Biography of a Rebel Quaker.* Boston, MA: Brandon, 1994.

Rogers, Horatio. *Mary Dyer of Rhode Island: The Quaker Martyr that was Hanged on Boston Common, June 1, 1660.* Providence, RI: Preston and Rounds, 1898.

Taylor, Dale. *The Writer's Guide to Everyday Life in Colonial America.* Cincinnati, OH: Writer's Digest Books, 1997.

Ulrich, Laurel Thatcher. *Good Wives: Image and REality in the Lives of Women in Northern New England 1650 - 1750.* New York, NY: Vintage Books/Random House, n.d.

Winship, Michael P. *The Times and Trials of Anne Hutchinson : Puritans Divided.* Lawrence, KS: University Press of Kansas, 2005.

Yount, David. *How the Quakers Invented America.* Lanham, MD: Rowman & Littlefield, 2007.
11)